Pr

MEANWHILE, BACK ~~AT THE RANCH~~ IN DEADWOOD

Dear Reader,

Last year, I wrote a book in the midst of packing, selling, buying, and moving over a thousand miles. What did I do for an encore with this newest Deadwood book? My family took two—not one, but two!!—three-week road trips while I was finishing, editing, and publishing. It's official now; I'm one twist short of a Slinky.

The first trip was to Deadwood, South Dakota for some fun with fans and friends; the other was to Ohio to see my family and visit some local libraries. Instead of asking me "Are we there yet?" my kids kept asking, "Are you done yet?" I can't tell you how happy I was when I could finally tell them, "Yes!"

Some of the coolest things I've experienced since writing the Deadwood Mystery series are the opportunities I've been given in the pursuit of research. For example, while researching for MEANWHILE, BACK IN DEADWOOD, I was able to go on a ghost tour up in the old brothels in Deadwood's notorious Badlands section. Our wonderful hostess, Ericka Newman, led us from one room to the next in the dark, our flashlights making the evening even eerier. For decades, I'd dreamed of being able to walk through those rooms, experiencing the sights, smells, and sounds. Exploring the brothels was an incredible experience that I'll always treasure.

We also enjoyed a tour of the old Fairmont Hotel, led from floor to floor of this old haunted building by Ron Russo, the current owner. If you ever go to Deadwood, I recommend taking this tour. Even if you don't believe in ghosts, it's fun to see the bones of the Fairmont Hotel.

I hope you get some chuckles and chills out of this latest chapter of Violet Parker's ongoing story. As old man Harvey often says, "Never drop your gun to hug a grizzly."

Ann Charles

www.anncharles.com

MEANWHILE, BACK

~~AT THE RANCH~~
IN DEADWOOD

ANN CHARLES

ILLUSTRATED BY C.S. KUNKLE

Cover Art by C.S. Kunkle (www.charlesskunkle.com)
Cover Design by Sharon Benton (www.q42designs.com)
Editing by the Grammar Chick (www.grammarchick.com)
Formatting by Biddles ebooks (www.biddlesebooks.com)

E-book ISBN-13: 978-1-940364-24-7
Print ISBN-:13: 978-1-940364-25-4

To Marguerite

You take care of me like there is no "in-law" behind the word daughter.

Thank you for your help bringing yet another book together. You edit for me, make sure I'm well-fed, take care of my kids, listen to my woes, and keep coming back for more. On top of all that, you shared your wonderful son with me who follows in your footsteps.

I don't know how you remain so sane after having raised five children while teaching high school English all of those years.

You're crazy awesome!

Love you.

Also by Ann Charles

Deadwood Mystery Series
Nearly Departed in Deadwood (Book 1)
Optical Delusions in Deadwood (Book 2)
Dead Case in Deadwood (Book 3)
Better Off Dead in Deadwood (Book 4)
An Ex to Grind in Deadwood (Book 5)

Short Stories from the Deadwood Mystery Series
Deadwood Shorts: Seeing Trouble
Deadwood Shorts: Boot Points

Jackrabbit Junction Mystery Series
Dance of the Winnebagos (Book 1)
Jackrabbit Junction Jitters (Book 2)
The Great Jackalope Stampede (Book 3)

Goldwash Mystery Series (a future series)
The Old Man's Back in Town (Short Story)

Dig Site Mystery Series
Look What the Wind Blew In (Book 1)
(Starring Quint Parker, the brother of Violet Parker from the Deadwood
Mystery Series)

Coming Next from Ann Charles

Jackrabbit Junction Mystery Series
The Rowdy Coyote Rumble (Book 4)

Acknowledgments

Here's another attempt at me keeping it short and sweet on the Acknowledgments page.

Thank you to my husband. You brainstorm, edit, format, and so much more. I'm one hell of a lucky woman!

I also want to thank the following awesome people:

My kick-butt team of first and second-draft readers, my A+ editor, and my fast and furious beta readers. You all have helped make this book a wild and wonderful adventure for other readers.

My kids for keeping me motivated to get the book done so we could go have some fun.

Mimi "The Grammar Chick" (my editor), and Marguerite Phipps (assistant editor), who both make my words sparkle.

My brother, Charles (C.S.) Kunkle (cover artist and illustrator) for drawing the creepy stuff, and his wife, Stephanie, for knowing what scenes would be cool to have illustrated.

Sharon Benton (cover graphic artist) for keeping in touch and helping even while in Poland.

My publicists and promoters—my mom and brother (Margo Taylor and Dave Taylor), my aunt (Judy Routt), and my sister (Laura Rensberger). Without your help, I'd still be in the corner talking to myself with weird voices.

Wendy Gildersleeve for talking me off ledges, making sure I keep readers posted on what's going on, and enjoying sunny Arizona mornings with me.

Diane Garland for her love of spreadsheets and timelines.

Crazy-eyed Jack Elam (from *Rio Lobo*) for inspiring me to include a sawed-off, double-barreled shotgun in this book.

Jacquie Rogers, Amber Scott, Gerri Russell, and Joleen James for being there to pick me up and dust me off every time I fall.

My family, previous coworkers, and Facebook and Twitter friends. You guys always put a smile on my face!

My brother, Clint Taylor, for saying the craziest stuff online about his affection for the female gender. You keep me laughing.

MEANWHILE, BACK ~~AT THE RANCH~~ IN DEADWOOD

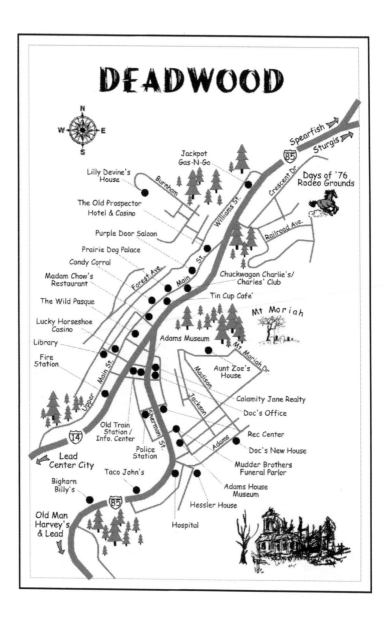

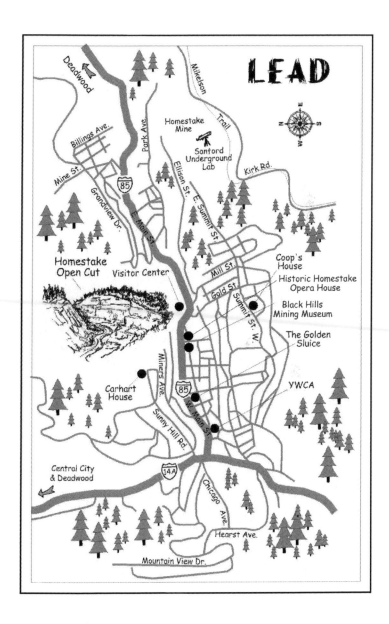

Cast

Violet Lynn Parker (1,2,3,4,5,6)—Main heroine of the series, Doc's girlfriend, Aunt Zoe's niece

Willis "old man" Harvey (1,2,3,4,5,6)—Violet's sidekick and so-called body guard

Dane R. "Doc" Nyce (1,2,3,4,5,6)—Main hero of the series, Violet's boyfriend

Detective "Coop" Cooper (1,2,3,4,5,6)—Deadwood and Lead's only detective

Zoe Parker (1,2,3,4,5,6)—Violet's aunt and mentor in life. Violet lives in Aunt Zoe's house

Layne Parker (1,2,3,4,5,6)—Violet's nine-year-old son

Adelynn Parker (1,2,3,4,5,6)—Violet's nine-year-old daughter

Natalie Beals (1,2,3,4,5,6)—Violet's best friend since childhood

Jerry Russo (4,5,6)—Violet's boss, owner of Calamity Jane Realty

Mona Hollister (1,2,3,4,5,6)—Violet's coworker and mentor in realty

Ray Underhill (1,2,3,4,5,6)—Violet's coworker and nemesis at work

Benjamin Underhill (1,2,3,4,5,6)—Violet's coworker and previous secret admirer

Cornelius Curion (3,4,5,6)—Violet's client; so-called ghost-whisperer

Jeff Wymonds (1,2,3,4,5,6)—Violet's client; father of Adelynn's best friend

Prudence (2,3,4,5,6)—Ghost who resides at the Carhart house

Beatrice Geary (1,2,3,4,5,6)—Violet and Aunt Zoe's neighbor across the street

Reid Martin (2,3,4,5,6)—Captain of the fire department, Aunt Zoe's ex-lover

Tiffany Sugarbell (1,2,3,4,5,6)—Violet's rival Realtor; Doc's ex-girlfriend

Susan Parker (1,2,3,4,5,6)—Violet's evil sister; aka "the Bitch from Hell"

Quint Parker (1,2,3,4,5)—Violet's supportive brother; Layne's hero; giver of her famous purple boots

Freesia Tender (5,6)—Owner of the Galena House

Stone Hawke (5,6)—Cooper's ex-partner; detective called in to help solve cases

Rex Conner (3,4,5,6)—The biological father of Violet's children

Dickie Dowdin (5,6)—Host of TV series called "Paranormal Realty"

Honey (5,6)—Dickie's assistant

Rad (6)—Reality series camera man

Rosy (6)—Reality series camera woman

Eddie Mudder (3,6)—Owner of Mudder Brothers Funeral Parlor

Zeke and Zelda Britton (2,4,5,6)—Soon-to-be owners of the Carhart house in Lead

Chapter One

Sunday, October 21st
Deadwood, South Dakota

Meanwhile, back at the ranch …

My lily white ass was not tough enough to handle the Wild, Wild West, especially if it were chockfull of pissed-off ghosts and relentless ghouls.

Take the century old ranch house that currently filled the windshield of old man Harvey's pickup as he braked to a dusty stop in the driveway.

No, seriously, somebody take it.

Anybody.

As Harvey's real estate agent, it was my job to sell his place. Unfortunately, when I had signed on to represent the ornery cuss, both of us had been unaware his ranch came not only with a ghost or two but with various severed body parts—some dried up, some still juicy.

Harvey killed the engine and looked over at me. "What's goin' on with your face there, Sparky? It's all puckered up like you swaller'd your chew."

"Can it with the *Sparky* crap." I reached across the bench seat and snapped one of his rainbow suspenders. "It's 'Violet,' remember? What'd I tell you about using nicknames right now?"

I had the whole of Deadwood's fire and police departments calling me unflattering nicknames these days. I didn't need my self-appointed bodyguard doing his part to remind me of my flame-filled past, particularly in the presence of the all-seeing reality television crew my boss had lured to town with promises of haunted locations and ectoplasmic costars.

Harvey harrumphed. "But I'm partial to *Sparky Parker.*"

"He's right," piped up my best friend, Natalie Beals, from the backseat of the pickup. "It rolls right off the tongue, just like Pickle-faced Parker always did."

"And Boob-headed Beals," I threw back, pointing my knock-it-off finger at her. The same one I often aimed at my almost-ten-year-old twins. "Now zip those fat lips of yours, or I'll sic Harvey's good-for-nothing dog on you."

"What? And have old Red slobber me to death?" Natalie tugged on the ear of the yellow lab snoring next to her. The sleeping dog grunted but kept his eyes closed. "Harvey, I think your dog's in a coma."

"He's just sufferin' from Cupid's cramps after a night of playin' Don Juan to a saucy poodle two doors down."

"I thought his puppy-making days were over," Natalie said.

"They are, but Red still likes to give 'er the bone whenever he sniffs out an opportunity."

I shoved open my door. "Sounds like he's been hanging around his owner too long."

Natalie joined me out in the crisp October air, shivering in her blue jeans and corduroy coat. I was glad I'd settled on my soft wool slacks and chenille sweater today instead of that bohemian skirt and tunic. We frowned up at the dark clouds gathering in the west. Things were about to get colder here in the hills.

"At least someone's getting lucky these days," Natalie said as we waited for Harvey to grab his empty Army duffle from the back seat.

Damned straight. Too bad it wasn't me. But my luck was about to change. We just needed to get Harvey moved off of my boyfriend's couch and into his nephew's spare bedroom, which was partly why I'd agreed to ride out here today instead of holding down my desk back at Calamity Jane Realty.

Natalie's lack of wild monkey love had to do with her long history of choosing smoking hot jerks as bed fellows and the vow she had taken to quit males cold turkey for a year. "Weren't you the one telling me last night that this sabbatical from men has been good for your self-esteem?"

"Yeah, but it's been killer on my libido. Just because I'm not allowing myself to have sex doesn't mean I don't think about digging in my spurs when a sexy stud rides across my horizon."

"What kind of spurs are we talkin' here?" Harvey asked, hefting his empty bag over his shoulder. "The ones with smooth rosebud rowels or those sharp pointy babies that really sting, like rock-grinders?"

Why did I have a feeling he was inquiring based on experience?

"Never mind, you dirty bird." I led the way to his front porch, pausing with one purple boot on the bottom step. "This place gives me the heebie jeebies."

"Quit bein' such a girl." Harvey grabbed my arm and hauled me up the steps after him. "I swear you're afraid of your own face in the mirror these days."

"You'd be afraid of my face, too, if you saw me first thing in the morning." It was one of the main reasons I hesitated every time my boyfriend asked me to spend the night. The other had to do with how humiliating my stretch marks looked in the harsh morning light.

"There's nothing here that's gonna bite ya." Harvey snickered. "At least not 'til the sun goes down."

Natalie brought up the rear. "Don't let the ghosts and the ghouls disturb you, love," she quoted from the 1959 version of *House on Haunted Hill*, adding an ominous Vincent Price-sounding laugh.

I grimaced over at the police tape marking off a section of the porch in front of the hanging bench swing. Almost two weeks ago we'd caught Red chewing on a decrepit antique boot that still had some of the previous owner's foot left inside. Just the memory of the dried chunks of skin and bones made me take a couple of sidesteps away from the Caution tape fluttering in the late-morning breeze.

"You two smartasses are not making me feel all warm and happy inside."

"Warm and happy is Doc's job." Harvey fished in his back pocket. "Where is your stallion roamin' about today, anyway?"

"He had a client from down in Rapid call this morning with an emergency. Something to do with late taxes and a list of needed financial papers. He said he'd meet us for lunch if you still want to grab some food later."

"Darn tootin', I do. You haven't bought me my weekly meal, and we have a signed contract sayin' you're supposed to keep me well-fed until you sell my place."

At the rate of success I was having thanks to all of the body parts showing up, I'd be keeping Harvey fat and happy until one of us keeled over from old age.

"Late taxes, huh?" Harvey pulled a couple of long wood screws and a screwdriver from his back pocket. "I thought Doc was a financial planner, not a bean counter."

The more I got to know Mr. Dane "Doc" Nyce, the more I came to realize he was a jack of all trades, master of much—things like managing money, fixing anything mechanical, sniffing out ghosts, and sexing the clothes right off of me.

But not a master of wanting to get hitched. Definitely not that. Not with how fast he'd left his last girlfriend after she'd mentioned shopping for wedding bands. My two kids weren't helping on that front either, both acting out their fears about a new man coming into their world by being rebellious snots.

But them acting out didn't matter now, because truth be told, when Doc found out how dark and gruesome my family history was, I doubted he'd want me sneaking around his back door anymore.

What man in his right mind would want to spend the night next to a woman who came from a long line of killers? Hell, with some of the bad dreams I'd been having the last few months, Doc could be one nightmare away from my smothering him with his own pillow … or ripping his tongue out with my bare hand.

I cringed at that all-too-real memory.

Harvey patted his other pocket, shrugged, and then held up the screwdriver. "This'll do in a pinch."

I glanced at the tool. "What're you gonna do with that?"

"Open the door."

"Why don't you just use the key?"

"I left it clear back in the pickup." He said that as if we'd hiked for miles to reach the porch.

"Move over," I pushed him aside. "Let me punch in the

lockbox code. The spare is in there."

"Look, you guys, there's no need for a key." Natalie reached around me. "It's not fully shut."

She pushed on the door. It swung inward silently, the hinges well-oiled in prep for showing it to potential buyers.

I frowned at Harvey. "You left the door unlocked again?"

After we'd found the foot-filled boot on his porch, Harvey had been staying down in Deadwood day and night. He was supposed to be locking everything down tight, as in the house, the barn, even his tool shed, by order of Deadwood's only detective, aka Harvey's bossy nephew.

"I did lock it." His bushy eyebrows morphed together into a hairy caterpillar. "Deadbolted it even."

"Maybe we should call Detective Cooper," Natalie whispered, peeking over my shoulder into the shadowy house.

"And tell him what? We found an unlocked door?" I'd pissed off the detective enough times to know better than to bug him unless I was face-to-face with a dead body. Even then I'd hesitate to call him and risk another slicing from that jagged razor he called a mouth.

"That's a bad idea." Harvey eased into the house with Natalie and me tiptoeing in tandem behind him like a pair of cartoon scaredy cats. "Coop's been runnin' with wolves and rattlesnakes since his ex-partner got called in by the chief to help solve some of the murders Miss Crazy-curls Parker here keeps findin'."

"Leave my hair out of it." I tucked in some unruly blonde curls the wind had freed from my French knot. "The bodies are not my fault. I just seem to be having a run of bad luck lately."

Harvey snorted. "Bad luck is losing a couple hundred at the poker table. You keep stumblin' knee deep into manure with no shovel to be found. That takes a real special skill."

"You're his uncle," Natalie said, still fighting her case. "Cooper might want to know somebody left your door unlocked so he can chew them a new ass."

Ass chewing was one of the things Cooper did best, but I scoffed at her naivety. "You think Detective Cooper is going to drop everything he's doing to race out here to make sure the house is safe for us to pack up Harvey's skivvies and long johns?

You're forgetting how much that man would like to string me up like a piñata and knock the sweet stuff right out of me."

"Violet does have a way of makin' Coop's tail twitch."

"And that muscle in his jaw," I reminded Harvey.

We peeked through the rest of Harvey's house and came up empty-handed much to my relief. While Harvey went back to his bedroom to pack clothes and whatnot to take to Cooper's place, Natalie and I held court in the kitchen.

Natalie leaned against the kitchen bar. "Fine, we won't call Cooper, but what about his ex-partner? Do you have Detective Hawke's number?"

I gaped at her. "Did you hit your head on the back window when Harvey bounced through that pothole down the road?"

"What? It's an idea. You're the one who wants me to get in tight with this new detective, find out what goods he has on you to support his theory, right?"

Cooper's ex-partner turned current partner, Detective Hawke, had recently had an epiphany. Rather more like an incredibly asinine theory that involved me, a flying broomstick, and a big green nose with warts on it.

"I said to talk to Detective Hawke on the sly and find out why he thinks I'm a witch. Not invite him out here for a barn dance so you can ply him for details while you two salamander left and do-si-do."

"It's *Allemande Left*, you knucklehead." Natalie crossed her arms over her chest. "Where did you learn how to square dance? From one of those Sally Struthers' Correspondence School classes?"

"You get my point, mouth. You have to be careful when you're playing Mata Hari."

"I will be, but you're going to have to set me up on a date with Hawke or something, because I can't find out what he's got on you unless I can get in for a close-up."

"I'll figure something out." I poured myself a glass of water. "What's taking Harvey so long?" While our search of the house had turned up nothing, the sooner we headed back to town, the sooner my blood pressure would return to normal.

Natalie joined me at the sink, staring out the window.

"You smell like old Red," I told her.

"Better than smelling like you." She snatched my glass of water from me and took a drink. "Before you know it, we'll be wading through snow. I need to prep my place for ..." She trailed off, leaning closer to the window. "Look at Harvey's barn."

I followed her gaze, staring at the old, ramshackle building. "What about it?"

Besides it needing a fresh coat of paint, it seemed in good enough shape. My fingers were crossed that by next spring, the sheriff would have figured out what was going on out here with all of the body parts so we could see about at least renting the place as a vacation getaway. While selling it might be a bit of a bust due to disclosure rules, tourists wanting to experience some Black Hills country living would love this place.

She pointed out the window. "Look at the doors."

I stole the glass of water back, sipping from it as I watched the doors sway in the breeze, opening slightly and then closing. "That's the wind moving them, you know, not some ghost."

"No duh, meteorologist Vi." She poked me in the shoulder. "But where's the chain and padlock he put on when we were here last week?"

She was right. Both were gone.

The doors swayed open slightly again as we pressed our noses against the window pane.

"Harvey," I called without looking away. "Did Cooper say anything to you about removing your padlock and chain when he was out here investigating earlier this week?"

I heard some shuffling coming toward us from the hallway.

"We may need to call Coop," Harvey said, his voice hesitant.

"About the padlock and chain?" There was no need to go that far, was there?

"What padlock and chain?" He came up behind me.

"The ones missing from your barn doors." I turned to find him holding a dried washrag that was covered with brown stains. "What's that?"

"Dried blood."

That got Natalie's attention. "How can you be sure?"

"You can smell it." He held it out for us to do just that.

I recoiled. "I'll take your word for it. Where did you find it?"

"In my bathroom wastebasket. That wasn't the only mess left behind. Come take a gander under my sink."

I followed him into his bathroom and squatted in front of the open cupboard doors. There were bottles tipped over, bandage wrappers strewn about, blood smears on the inside of the cupboard doors, a disarray of wadded towels, and more brown stained rags left behind.

"What do you think?" I asked Harvey and Natalie. "Maybe somebody was hurt and broke in here to fix themselves up."

"That's one notion." Harvey stroked his beard. "We should probably call Coop and have him weigh in on it."

"I agree," Natalie said from where she leaned against the door jamb, wringing her hands together. "And then you can suggest he bring Detective Hawke along so I can start working my magic on loosening his lips."

I'd rather she worked her magic on sealing them shut.

"Like I told you before, Nat, you're going to have to be subtle. This guy is a detective, albeit a shitty egotistical butthead, but he'll know when he's being set up."

"And if subtlety doesn't wind his crank," Harvey said with a wide grin that showed off his two gold teeth, "you could flash him your hooters. That'll loosen his lips and then some. Trust me, a sweet set of hooters is as good as any truth serum the Army ever came up with."

"That's your answer to everything," I told Harvey.

"You can look down your nose at me, girl, but it works. Just ask the widows down at the senior center."

"I'd rather not." I stood and brushed my hands off on my slacks. "While you were packing, did you notice anything missing in your bedroom? Anything of value?"

He shook his head. "Not yet anyway."

I pulled out my cellphone and took a few pictures of the bloody rag and the mess under the sink. "There, we'll show these to Cooper when we move you into his place tonight. He can come out tomorrow and see them for himself."

Back in his bedroom, Harvey grabbed an armful of socks

from his dresser and stuffed them into his duffel bag. "What were you bellyachin' about out there in the kitchen?"

"Your barn doors," Natalie answered. "The padlock and chain are gone."

His eyes narrowed. "My doors were still sportin' my padlock the other day when I was here with Coop."

Something didn't feel right about this—the unlocked front door, the dried blood, the missing padlock and chain. I palmed my phone, debating on making that call.

"Let me finish packing," Harvey said, "and we'll swing by the barn on the way out of here. I need to let Red out to water the bushes before we head back to town anyway."

Natalie and I stood there swapping worried frowns while Harvey stuffed more clothes into his bag.

"Let's skedaddle." He grunted as he hoisted it.

I helped him adjust the heavy pack on his back. "Criminy, you could use a mule to carry this thing. How many clothes do you need?"

"Depends on how many women I'm gonna be wooing this winter. The fresher the duds, the fresher the women."

Natalie chuckled and led the way out. Harvey made sure the door was locked behind us.

At the pickup, Red was waiting for us with his head sticking out the window, sniffing the wind.

Harvey let him out the driver's side. "Get down outta there, boy. Go lift a leg before we head back to town."

The lab hopped out of the pickup like he was still a pup, turned his nose up again, and then dashed toward the barn.

I watched him, my mouth catching air. Who was that dog? "I've never seen Red move that fast before."

Harvey tossed his full pack in the back of his truck, securing it with some bungee cords. "When he needs to lift a leg, he doesn't stop to smell the posies."

Natalie nudged me, pointing at the doors. "Look."

We watched as Red sniffed around the doors. Then he nosed them open and slipped inside.

"Red just went in the barn," Natalie told Harvey.

"Why'd he go in there?"

I wasn't sure I wanted to know why.

Harvey started toward the barn, calling back over his shoulder. "Violet, grab old Bessie from under the seat, would ya?"

"Why do we need your shotgun?"

"In case he's sniffed out a mountain lion or some other critter that's holed up inside my barn."

"I'll get it," Natalie said.

He pulled the doors open. "Red! Here, boy."

Red whimpered in the shadows off to the right, giving me goosebumps. "Why's he making that sound?"

Natalie cocked Harvey's shotgun like she was Rooster Cogburn readying for a passel of bad guys. "Something has him spooked."

"Point that thing at the ground, would ya?"

"What? I've been shooting since Gramps taught me how back before I even needed a bra."

"Give Bessie to me." Harvey took the shotgun from Natalie. "Red's probably whimperin' because he hurt himself jumpin' out of the truck like he did. He keeps forgettin' he's not a young pup anymore. You two wait here." With a hitch of his pants, he and his shotgun headed off in the shadow-filled direction of Red's whimpering.

Happy to obey, I stood in the shaft of sunlight coming through the doors. I was getting really tired of finding pieces of people and animals out here in the boonies. "Maybe we should call Cooper."

Nat jammed her hands on her hips. "Now you start with this shit?"

Red's whimpering turned to a growl, then a bark.

"Well, I'll be a twice-baked potato," I heard Harvey say. "What'd ya sniff out there, ol' boy?"

Something creaked, like metal on metal. What had Harvey and Red found? The Tin Man?

"Harvey?" I took several steps into the shadows beyond the shaft of light. "Is everything okay?"

"Jesus H. Christ!" Harvey's voice sounded higher, surprised.

Red let out a volley of barks.

"What'd they find?" I whispered.

"Let's go see." Natalie caught my wrist and tugged me deeper into the barn.

We found Harvey standing in a wood-walled grain bin. Dust floated in the light of his flashlight beam. The place smelled like straw and stale grain, slightly fermented, almost rotten. Harvey was holding Red by the collar with one hand and a flashlight with the other, his shotgun pointing at the ceiling while tucked under his armpit. In front of him was an ancient-looking bank safe. Dust covered the dark metal.

Harvey's forehead was zigzagged with lines when we joined him in front of the safe. "I think you need to call Coop now," he told me.

"Not me. Detective Cooper hates receiving phone calls from me."

"I reckon he's gonna want to eyeball this sooner rather than later, and I don't think snappin' a picture of it with that phone of yours will cut it. Here, help me put Bessie down." I took his shotgun and carefully leaned it against the wall.

"Why do you keep an old bank safe in your barn?"

"It was too darn heavy to carry into the basement."

I didn't doubt it. The thing was almost as deep as it was wide.

"Did somebody break into your safe and take something?" Natalie asked.

"Nope. They broke in and left somethin'." Harvey reached out with the toe of his boot and pulled open the door. It creaked all the way. Aha, so this was the Tin Man.

"Left what?" I took the flashlight he held out to me.

"See for yerself."

I did.

Then I let out a small scream, more of a squeal really, and stumbled backward into Natalie.

"Oh, my God! What is that?" Natalie held me by the shoulders, using me as a shield.

"Is that a man in there?" I asked and then gulped.

Harvey tightened his grip on Red, who was straining to investigate further with his long snout. "It sure looks like one, from what I can tell." He reached inside the safe with his free hand.

I grabbed the back of his suspenders, pulling him away from the safe. "What are you doing?"

"Gettin' what's mine." He tugged free of my grip and reached inside again, extracting a sawed-off shotgun. "This here shotgun belonged to my grandpappy. It was his favorite. See the way the triggers are wired back?" He held it up so we could see the copper wire. "Grandpappy kept it that way because the triggers got busted, but she still shoots true. There ain't no way I'm lettin' Coop and his boys lock it away in that evidence cage for the rest of eternity."

I looked at the tangled pretzel-like mess of arms and legs stuffed in Harvey's safe. "How long you think it's been in there?"

Natalie sniffed from where she was hiding at the back of my neck. "Eww. It's just starting to smell."

Yeah, I'd noticed and didn't want to think about it too much.

Harvey poked the body with the double barrels of his grandpappy's gun. "This one's still juicy. The flies are just beginnin' to show up for the party."

I gagged. I couldn't help it.

Harvey closed the safe door, stepping back. "Who's making the call this time?"

"Natalie," I volunteered, shoving my cellphone at her.

"Why me?" She pushed my phone away.

Because I'd recently figured out that Detective Cooper had an Achilles heel—he was smitten by one Miss Natalie Beals. The thing was, Natalie didn't know about this attraction yet and with the positive effects of her sabbatical on her self-esteem, I didn't want to mess with her head by letting the cat out of the bag. Or in Cooper's case, the sabre-toothed tiger out of the cage.

I grabbed her hand and slapped my phone into her palm. "Because you lost the coin toss."

"That was for riding in the back seat on the way out here." She tried to make me take back my phone, but I danced out of her reach.

"Give me that." Harvey grabbed the phone. "If you want somethin' done right, you have to do it yerself." He tapped on the screen, pulling up my contact list. "Where's Coop's name—

ah, here we go." He held the phone up to his ear, eyeing both of us in turn.

"Hey, Coop." He paused, listening. "Yeah, it's me." Another pause. "I know, I'm borrowing her phone." Pause. "Well, we're out here at the ranch gettin' my stuff and Natalie went and sniffed out some trouble in my barn."

"What?! Harvey! It wasn't me." Natalie tried to back away, but I caught her arm and planted my heels.

"Sure. I'll let you hear it straight from the horse's mouth." He held the phone out to Natalie, a ghost of a grin on his lips. "Coop wants to talk to you."

Sputtering, Natalie took the phone. "Uh, hi, Detective."

Harvey snickered, hip bumping me. "That's how you drive a skittish heifer up a chute."

After baring her teeth at Harvey, Natalie returned to Cooper. "Yeah, we sort of found another body." She winced, holding the phone away from her ear until the ranting from Cooper's end quieted. "Well, it's hard to tell who it is." She winced again through his reply, and then hit me with a furrowed brow. "Because it's missing a face."

Chapter Two

Meanwhile, back in Deadwood …

By the time we made it back to town several hours later, the parking lot at Bighorn Billy's Diner was empty except for two trucks and Doc's black 1969 Camaro SS.

We piled out of Harvey's pickup, leaving Red snoring in the back seat. His hunting adventure for the day had apparently worn him out. It had worn me out, too, but as much as I would have liked to join Red's snore-fest, I had two things I wanted more: food and Doc, preferably together.

Conway Twitty was soloing on the golden oldies country station inside the restaurant, crooning about something being only make believe. Too bad Conway was full of crap. As much as I wished what we'd discovered this morning had been another nightmare, that dead body stuffed into Harvey's safe was as real as my file at the Deadwood Police Station. The very file that was going to grow even fatter after all of the writing Detective Hawke had been doing in his stupid little notebook during his onsite interrogation.

The other two vehicles must have belonged to the cook and the waitress, because the diner was empty except for Doc, who rose from the corner booth as we weaved through vacant tables toward him. Dressed in black pants and a dark brown button up shirt that matched his eyes, he looked better than a bacon-wrapped filet.

My stomach growled in disagreement. It thought the filet would be sexier.

The frown on Doc's face matched my mood. After enjoying another session of Detective Cooper and Hawke's rubber glove therapy, I felt snarly and bushy tailed.

"You okay?" Doc asked me while helping me slip out of my coat. His fingers lingered on my shoulders.

"Sure, aside from Cooper's teeth marks on my ass."

Harvey snorted from where he had settled in next to Natalie. "Doc can rub some healin' ointment on your hindquarters later. For now, plant your keister on that there seat. I'm hungry enough to swallow a steak and the cast-iron skillet it was fried in."

Doc waited for me to slide in first and then joined me, his palm warming my thigh through my wool pants. "Cooper bared his fangs at you again today, huh?"

"Only once or twice."

Actually, the detective had appeared relatively cool on the surface while looking at the dead body and soaking up the crime scene. But I'd been around him while he was in a pissed off state enough to know that the ticking muscle in his jaw worked like a pressure cooker valve. It was only a matter of time before his head blew right off, and I needed to stay clear of the blast zone.

"It was Detective Hawke who went all lock-jawed onto Violet's ass like a honey badger," Natalie clarified. "It's a good thing she doesn't have testicles for him to latch onto."

Doc chuckled. "I for one am thrilled she's testicle-free."

"I swear," Harvey turned the coffee cup in front of him right-side up. "That fool Hawke has as many brain cells as a turtle has feathers."

"Sounds like a good time was had by one and all." Doc squeezed my leg. "I wish I could have been there with you." His words were light, but his forehead was weighed down with worry.

Me, too.

"It was a regular ol' knee-slappin' barn dance, let me tell ya." Harvey waved the waitress over.

After we'd placed our drink order and the waitress had left, Doc turned to me. "What did you mean in your text message about there being no face?"

"From what we could tell, the killer had sliced clear around it," I drew a circle around my own face with my finger, "and then peeled it off."

Natalie shuddered visibly, as she had several times while we waited at the ranch for Cooper to tell us we were free to go. This wasn't her first time hanging out with a corpse. Considering how quiet she'd been since leaving the ranch, I wondered if she were having flashbacks to one dark and freaky night months ago at Mudder Brothers Funeral Parlor when she'd been locked up in the freezer with another dead guy.

"There were no fingertips either," Harvey added. "Whoever skinned his mug also sliced off the ends of each of his fingers. I told Coop they looked gnawed off to me. He's gonna have a hell of a time identifying this one."

"Christ." Doc rubbed the back of his neck. "You two keep tumbling deeper into the Twilight Zone, don't you?"

"Us three," I said, nodding at Natalie. "She was there, too, don't forget."

"I'm not sure I want to join your musketeer club." Natalie blew out a shaky breath. "Unless we get to slam back shots at the weekly meetings."

The waitress returned with our drinks, shutting us up on the subject of mutilated bodies for the time being and shifting the focus to food.

Harvey and I both craved meat—him a T-bone, me a ribeye, both medium rare.

Natalie gaped at us. "How in the hell can you two eat red meat after this morning?"

"What happened this morning, sugar?" the waitress asked Harvey.

I aimed a zip-it glare at Natalie.

"We hit a deer out on 385," Harvey explained. "Guts flew from here to Nebraska. A real humdinger of a mess."

The waitress took it in stride. "It's that time of year."

Natalie looked green around the gills when the waitress aimed her order pad in her direction. "Just a small house salad for me, please."

Doc brought up the rear with his order of thick-sliced bacon and eggs, including extra bacon on the side. As soon as the waitress was out of earshot, he bumped shoulders with me. "The extra bacon is for you, if you want it."

He ordered extra bacon just for me? Oh, boy. Could he see the little hearts floating all around my head?

Natalie leaned forward. "Who would've done something as diabolical as that?"

I was still enjoying the warmth of Doc's bacon love. "What? Order extra bacon?"

"No, you dork." She reached across the table and pinched my arm. "You know what I'm talking about."

"Ow!" I wrinkled my nose at Harvey. "Did you teach her that?" The old bugger was prone to pinching me when he wanted my attention.

He didn't answer, just flashed his two gold teeth at me.

"I'm going to be afraid to close my eyes tonight," Natalie continued. "You might need to make room at your Aunt Zoe's place for me."

Harvey and I exchanged knowing glances. We'd both seen our fair share of weird, macabre shit surfacing lately up here in the hills.

"Okay, but I draw the line at my bed," I said, trying to lighten her mood. "Your snores could wake the dead in Mount Moriah." Deadwood's star-studded cemetery sat right up the hill behind my aunt's place.

She stuck her tongue out at me. "Only when I sleep on my back."

"You can come share my bed at Cooper's place," Harvey offered. At my narrowed gaze, he held up his hands. "What? I wasn't even thinkin' about hanky panky. I snore, too. We'd serenade each other in dreamland."

Natalie pointed her spoon at me. "You're not exactly the quietest sleeper, you know."

"I don't snore."

"No, but you moan a lot. It's kind of creepy in the middle of the night."

I looked over at Doc. "I moan?"

He shrugged. "I find it sexy, myself."

I wondered how long that had been going on. Nobody had ever mentioned me moaning in my sleep, at least not before I started having chronic nightmares about dead killers and melting demons stalking me.

Natalie leaned back in her seat, sliding her fingers through her brown tresses. "I can't believe we found a dead guy. This morning seemed like any other, and then 'Bam!' my life took a sharp left."

Welcome to my world. She should try starting her day down in the Mudder Brothers' basement autopsy room attempting to identify a decapitated body. Better yet, how about discovering a shrunken skull next to a wadded up tangle of arms and legs in a spooky apartment?

"At least it still had a head attached," I said, sugaring my coffee. After the rigmarole this morning, I was going to need to pop coffee beans like Tic Tacs to stay awake when I returned to work after lunch.

"Yep." Harvey smirked. "But Coop sure didn't appreciate you pointing that out to him."

Cooper's growl had rivaled Red's at the time.

"So who actually found the body?" Doc asked.

"Red sniffed it out," Natalie said.

"Good old Red, the crime finding canine," I added with a quick grin at Harvey. He and I had gotten the giggles in the midst of Detective Hawke's twenty questions game when I'd told him if he didn't like my answers he should interrogate Red and have him bark once for *No* and twice for *Yes*.

"You know what I don't get?" I aimed my question at Harvey. "Your grandpappy's double-barrel shotgun."

"I already told ya; he wired the triggers back because they were busted."

"Not that. I don't get why it was in the safe with the dead guy."

"What do you mean?" Natalie asked. "Isn't that where you store it?"

"Nope." I beat Harvey to the answer. I'd been around the old goat long enough to know that all shotguns were stored within grabbing distance at all times.

"I keep 'er in the hall closet, loaded and ready to shoot troublemakers."

"What did Cooper have to say about the gun being in the safe with the body?" Doc asked.

Harvey, Natalie, and I all squirmed as his gaze traveled

around the table.

"Nothing," I spoke first.

"Nothing as in this is more top-secret police business kind of 'nothing'? Or he was just plain stumped?"

"Nothing because we didn't tell him about it."

"Why not?"

"Well, Harvey sort of extracted the shotgun from the safe before the cops arrived and stashed it under the seat in his pickup."

Doc's focus volleyed between Harvey and me. "You guys removed evidence from the crime scene again?"

"Not me." I pointed across the table. "It was all Harvey's doing this time."

Harvey just shrugged off my accusation. "It's a family heirloom. Coop's boys would've taken my grandpappy's gun and never given it back."

"That's probably true." Doc sipped his coffee. "Was it still loaded?"

"There was one spent cartridge in the chamber. The other one was unfired."

"Slugs or buckshot?"

"Rock salt. With those broken triggers, you have to hold them hammers back with your thumb and then let 'er rip to shoot. Rock salt was safer in case my thumb got tired when I got to swingin' those sawed-off double barrels around." He toyed with his spoon.

"So somebody got off one shot," I said.

"If the victim was waving around your grandpa's big old shotgun, who in their right mind would play target practice with him?" Natalie asked.

"Who says it was the dead guy who fired it?" Harvey tapped his spoon against his mug. "It mighta been the killer who used it, and then stuffed it in the safe with the body."

Natalie thought on that. "Is there any way to tell?"

"Normally, Coop would dust it for prints. But since the fingertips are missing' on the one body that stayed behind after the murderin' hoedown, that won't do much good."

"Did either of the detectives find any other clues while you guys were there?" Doc asked us. "Anything in the house or barn besides the bloody rag and the mess under the bathroom sink Violet told me about?"

"Nothing they felt like playing show and tell with," I spoke for all of us.

"Did you three notice any signs of fighting in Harvey's house? Any evidence that the gun was fired inside?"

I glanced at the others. We all shook our heads. "No, the place looked as clean as usual besides the bathroom."

Surprisingly, Harvey was a bit of a neat bug. Even more shocking, his skills at interior decorating and house staging would give Martha Stewart a run for her money.

"Makes you wonder," Doc put his arm over the back of the seat, his fingers stroking my chenille covered shoulder.

"If someone was dallyin' in my underwear drawer?"

Doc chuckled, but shook his head. "Who went in the house? Did the victim break in, patch himself back up, find your grandfather's shotgun, and then go out to face off with his killer?"

"Or was it the killer who cleaned himself up after doing the deed?" I finished for Doc.

"Exactly." His fingers strummed down my arm. "I'd love to hear Detective Cooper's thoughts on the victim. Was he hiding in the safe initially or was he stuffed in there after death?"

"What difference would that make?" Natalie asked.

Doc glanced from Natalie to me. "It would tell us more about what kind of killer we're dealing with here."

"You mean what kind of killer Detective Cooper is dealing with." I thought about how hair-raising it was that somebody had taken the time to cut off the dead guy's face … or had it been cut off when the guy was still alive? That thought gave me a whole new rash of chills. "I don't want to be anywhere near this one if Cooper digs deep enough to make the killer start to sweat."

"I see what you mean about Detective Hawke," Natalie said to me. "His ego was at flood stage today."

"Nope. That was normal level." Which was why I'd threatened to crush his balls under my boot heel a few weeks ago upon our first meeting. Ever since then, he had been out to prove I had a violent streak, including this stupid Wicked Witch from the East notion.

"Ahhh," Natalie shot me a knowing grin. "Now I see why you are dumping him off on me."

"Your reservoir of tolerance for assholes is way deeper than mine."

"True. Yours is more of a mud puddle at best. At least we're done with him and Cooper on today's mess."

"Oh, we're far from done, trust me. Harvey and I have danced this police jig a few times. Both detectives will be back with their clicking pens and stupid notebooks, asking the same questions over and over. It's their legal form of torture."

"This wound is just startin' to fester." Harvey glanced toward the restaurant's kitchen. "Company's a-comin'."

The waitress was on the way with a tray of steaming food. "Here we go." She set the tray on the table next to us and started doling out plates.

My stomach took control of my brain and all thoughts of faceless bodies and twisted killers took a back seat to red meat and bacon.

A half hour later, we all headed out to the parking lot.

Doc caught my arm as we neared Harvey's pickup. "You going home or to the office?"

"The office. I need to spend a couple of hours at my desk taking care of paperwork for the Carhart house sale."

A sale about which I had mixed feelings. On one hand, the commission would be nice, as well as a third sale under my belt since starting at Calamity Jane Realty last spring. On the other hand, there was a very demanding ghost named Prudence who had been hovering in that house since the late 1800s and who kept finding new ways to freak the crap out of me through creatively delivered eerie messages from beyond. I liked the couple buying the place, though, and they were still determined to make it their home away from home even after my full disclosure of multiple murders and hauntings. Now if I could just get Prudence the ghost to quit messing with me.

"I'll take Violet to work," Doc said over my head to my partners in crime-witnessing. "I'm heading that way."

I'd rather spend a couple of hours in his office next door to Calamity Jane Realty, hiding away from Cooper, Hawke, and all of my other troubles, but I doubted my boss would appreciate me not being within hollering distance.

"I'll see you two later." I followed Doc to his Camaro.

He held open the door for me. While he zipped around back, I flipped down the visor mirror and applied a coat of the new lip gloss I'd bought with Doc in mind.

He slid in behind the wheel. "Are you really okay after that mess out at Harvey's place?"

I thought about my answer. "Wouldn't it figure with my luck these days that instead of finding money in a safe, I found another dead body?"

He started the car and shifted into gear. "You do have a way of stumbling onto macabre leftovers."

Leftovers summed up that body. "It was pretty horrific, but I've seen worse."

"Yes, unfortunately you have." He pulled out onto the road and headed toward downtown Deadwood. "Do you have a few minutes before you have to be at work? I have something I want to show you in my back room."

I'd seen a lot of things while in Doc's back room. Let me correct that—I'd seen a lot of Doc sans clothing, his and mine, while in his back room. A smile crept onto my lips. "Will it involve clothing being removed again?"

He did a double take, his gaze lingering on my mouth the second time around, and then sliding south over the front of my sweater. "Would you like it to involve clothing being removed?"

"What a silly question."

His hand wandered over to my thigh, his fingers trailing upward along my inseam. "You are very soft today. I had trouble keeping my hands off of you at lunch."

"It's all of your extra bacon softening me up." I was serious. If I kept eating like I had been for the last couple of weeks, I was going to have to break down and start exercising. I'd sooner battle orange-eyed demons and hissing albinos than spend one second on a treadmill.

He rolled into the parking lot behind our offices, pulling into his usual spot. "Tell me something, Boots." He used the nickname he reserved for when he was feeling frisky. He shut off the car and turned my way, ogling me like I was a cooler showcasing tasty pies and cakes at a dessert buffet. "Are your underwear as soft as your pants and sweater?"

"They're fur-lined, baby," I lied, feeling frisky myself in spite of my recent troubles with a faceless body along with a handful of prickly cops.

He sucked his breath in through his teeth. "Damn. You're like one of those hot cave-chicks from the Flintstones." He opened his door. "Come on, Pebbles Parker. You need to see what I found."

I met him at the trunk, shivering in the cool fall air. We crossed the parking lot to his back door, which he locked behind me. Without a word, he grabbed my hand and pulled me into his back room, shutting the door behind us. The place smelled like old varnish and a hint of Doc's woodsy cologne.

"Are you keeping somebody out?" I asked as he moved over to the rows of bookshelves lining the walls and pulled a book out. "Or making sure I don't leave?"

He chuckled as he flipped through the book. "I have better ways of making sure you don't leave."

"If you're even considering trying handcuffs, don't."

Detective Cooper had ruined the sexiness of them when he had slapped them on me and hauled me off to jail earlier this month.

"I take it you're still pissed about Cooper making an example of you."

"I'll hold my grudges against that butthead until the day I die."

"There's the tiger I know and fantasize about while in the shower. Maybe we should get you a tiger striped negligée to go with your fur-lined panties."

"Okay, but only if I get to hold the chair and whip."

He hit me with one raised eyebrow. "I think your and my tiger fantasies are very different."

"You mean yours doesn't include elephants spinning on beach balls and monkeys riding tiny bicycles under a Big Top tent?"

He laughed, lowering the book and strolling over to me. "No elephants in mine, but I might be able to incorporate the monkeys."

"Trust me, you won't regret it."

Lifting my chin, he leaned over and kissed me thoroughly, leaving me weak kneed and breathless with a hankering for more. Holy heart breaker! His kisses were as addictive as crack.

"I've wanted to do that since you walked into Bighorn Billy's."

"Next time don't wait so long."

"You taste like peaches today."

"I bought a new flavor of lip gloss."

When I leaned in for another round of show-don't-tell, he held the book up between us. "You need to look at this before I forget why I brought you in here and give you a hands-on demonstration of what I like about your lips, that sweater, and ripe peaches."

"Fine, party pooper." I took the book from him, staring down at a grainy black and white picture.

"Come here. You need more light." He turned on a lamp sitting on a stack of milk crates.

I followed, holding the book under the light.

From what I could tell, it was an early 1900s picture of the inside of a general store, every nook and cranny overflowing with products. There were shelves filled with canned and dry goods along with what looked like jars of candy. The side walls held shovels and pickaxes, rugs, and clocks. Against the back wall of the shop, I could make out racks of clothing and a sign advertising shoes and hats.

The woman behind the counter looked typical of many women of the early twentieth century who had lived a hard life out West. Her hair was pulled back in a bun, her face makeup free. The harsh lighting made the angles on her face more pronounced, her eyes dark. The high-collared dress elongated her neck.

"What am I looking for here?" I asked.

Doc pointed at one of the shelves on the right wall.

I held the book closer. The dark glass bottles looked very familiar. "Are those what I think they are?"

"If you look closer with a magnifying glass, there's a price for mead by the bottle next to the cash register."

I gaped at him. "Those bottles look exactly like the one I borrowed from that crate in Mudder Brothers' side room back in August."

"*Borrowed*, you say?"

"Leave the hair splitting to Detective Cooper." My focus returned to the photo. "Do you think there's a connection somehow?"

"I'm not sure, but there's something else in this photo that I wanted you to see besides the mead." He pointed at the woman behind the counter. "That's Ms. Wolff."

Ms. Wolff? This time my lower jaw bounced off my toes. The same Ms. Wolff who had called me almost a month ago out of the blue and told me she had to talk to me immediately because she'd be dead soon … and then followed through with that dearly departed prediction right before I arrived at her apartment with Harvey in tow?

I frowned at the picture caption. "It says here it's a Miss Hundt."

"Hundt means *hound* in German. Wolff is wolf. Suspiciously similar, don't you think?"

"So you think she's one and the same?"

"I don't think, I know."

"How can you be so certain?"

"Didn't Prudence the ghost call the timekeeper 'Ms. Hundt' when she spoke to you through me last time we paid her a visit?" At my grimace and nod, he continued. "And you and I both realized that when Prudence was asking you to bring her the timekeeper, she meant the keeper of time, aka clocks, aka all of those Black Forest clocks on Ms. Wolff's wall."

"Right, the creepy, nightmare-spurring wall."

"But what makes me even more certain this is Ms. Wolff is the fact that I saw her up close. I know her face."

"You mean from when we had the séance in Ms. Wolff's apartment and you joined with the ghost of Big Jake Tender?"

Doc nodded.

Big Jake had been in Ms. Wolff's company when he had died almost a century ago. During one of Doc's adventures as a ghost medium in the boarding house Big Jake had built, Doc had witnessed this scene and more through the dead man's eyes. I shivered just remembering that séance and how close we'd come to losing Doc in the past for good.

"You're positive this is her?"

He nodded again.

"How can you be so sure?"

"If you saw an old black and white picture of John Wayne, would you know it's the Duke?"

"Of course. But I've seen the Duke hundreds of times on TV."

"Ms. Wolff was hovering over Big Jake while he died. Her face is sort of stuck in my mind, the stricken look of pain over losing him still fresh."

I stared at the photo again, searching the background with this new information in mind. That back wall with the clothing and sign about hats struck a chord. "That's it!"

"What?"

"The different sized clothing and shoes in her closet, and all of those hat boxes full of fancy hats. They were from when she ran this store." There'd been dresses and shoes from various time periods. I'd thought maybe they were clothes from the costume room of the Homestake Opera House up in Lead. Turned out they were just leftover stock.

"That makes sense." Doc took the book back from me, rubbing his jaw as he scrutinized the photo. "I was able to go back through some of the history books at the library and figure out which building this store operated out of and what's there now."

"The building is still intact?"

"Yes, it houses the Candy Corral."

"The one owned by Ms. Wolff's buddy, Zuckerman?"

"One and the same. We need to pay her a visit." He took the book from me. "You in the mood for some chocolate?"

"Only every time I take a breath." I'd thought about visiting

Zuckerman to ask her a few questions a week or so ago but then had gotten distracted with enjoying a regular life. It was time to follow through on that idea and find some more answers about the whole Ms. Wolff fiasco and why she'd had my son's picture stuck in the frame of her bedroom dresser mirror.

My cellphone rang in my purse. I pulled it out. It was Mona, my favorite coworker and real estate idol. Had she heard me through the wall? Maybe I had another new client next door waiting for me. "I need to take this."

Doc nodded and stepped back, giving me space.

"Hi, Mona. What's going on?"

"I have an urgent message for you."

"From Layne?" My son tended to call with false emergencies involving the need for supplies for his latest chemistry experiment or archaeological dig in Aunt Zoe's backyard.

"No. Eddie Mudder."

"Eddie Mudder?" I repeated, snagging Doc's attention. "What did he want?"

Why would the remaining owner of the local funeral parlor want to talk to me all of a sudden? We hadn't spoken since that horrible night back in August.

"He said he needs to talk to you about something extremely urgent."

Was I unknowingly on the verge of death and he wanted to get a jump on planning my funeral? "Okay, I'll swing by the funeral parlor after I finish up the Carhart house paperwork today."

Doc shook his head at me, showing his feelings on that plan of action.

"Eddie explicitly stated he does *not* want you to come to the funeral parlor. He made that very clear and left a phone number for you to call tonight at ten."

"That seems a little odd."

"Well, Eddie wouldn't really fit in with Beaver Cleaver's family."

True, but he'd be a shoo in for the Addams Family with his resemblance to Lurch. "Thanks for letting me know, Mona. I'll be over there shortly. I'm just looking at something next door at

Doc's."

"I hope it's something that makes you smile."

There was something in her tone that made me think she said that for a reason other than wanting me to be a happy camper. "Why do you say that?"

"Jerry phoned in earlier from the conference down in Rapid. He's calling an emergency huddle for tomorrow morning. We all need to be at Bighorn Billy's at nine sharp."

"Super-duper," I said without smiling. My boss's huddles usually revolved around new marketing ideas, such as the catastrophic one that landed me on a huge-ass billboard off Interstate 90 coated in bright red lipstick and wrapped in a pink silk suit—his version of a sexy Realtor. I was of the opinion I looked like a vampire-poodle dipped in Pepto-Bismol. "I'll be over there shortly."

"Tell Doc 'hello' for me."

"Will do." I hung up and proceeded to spew everything that Mona had just told me in one long breath, including her 'hello.'

"Wow," he said when I had finished. "You were starting to turn blue there at the end."

"Why does Eddie want to talk to me all of a sudden? Do you think it's about George and what happened? Does he know about the bottle of mead I stole? Does he think I had a hand in messing up his family business?"

"I don't know, but I'm going to be there tonight when you call."

That flipped my frown upside down. "You're coming over after we get Harvey all settled in at Cooper's?"

"If that's okay with you and your aunt."

"Of course. We can talk about this some more." I tapped the book he still held. "And if you're a good boy, maybe I'll let you take a peek at my fur-lined underwear."

He laced his fingers through mine and lifted my hand to his lips. "Yabba dabba do, Boots."

Chapter Three

Monday, October 22nd

Meanwhile, back at Bighorn Billy's …

Ray Underhill planted his stupid ass across the table from me at Bighorn Billy's. The fake-tanned cretin stared at me with nothing but contempt. And here I'd thought spending yesterday morning with a faceless corpse and two prickly detectives had sucked.

I sneered at him.

He sneered back.

Where was Harvey's heirloom wired-trigger shotgun when I needed it?

Jerry Russo, the owner of Calamity Jane Realty, dropped into the seat between Ray and me, breaking up our Mexican standoff. With his hair still damp and his cologne overpowering the smells of breakfast happiness that wafted out from the kitchen, I guessed Jerry had come straight from the Deadwood Rec Center.

While I preferred to start my day slamming the sleep button and then hitting the coffee pot, Jerry preferred his slamming and hitting done on the basketball court. In his younger years, he had played ball professionally until he'd hurt his shoulder. That was when he had married into the real estate business. His marriage had ended long ago, but his love of real estate sales had stayed true. Unfortunately, so had his lust for marketing.

Jerry waved our waiter over. "Have you guys ordered yet?"

Mona, looking stunning in her pink mohair sweater, peered at him over her rhinestone-rimmed reading glasses. "Only coffee."

"And some vitamin C," said Ben Underhill, holding up his glass of orange juice.

Poor Ben had the horrible lifelong affliction of being Ray's nephew. I liked Ben even though our friendship had gotten off to a rocky start thanks to a creepy blind date and his uncle doing his damnedest to get me fired. Ray had been dead set on Ben taking my place at Calamity Jane's, and for a while I'd been sweating daily about losing my job to him. In the end, Jerry had decided to keep me on board and hire Ben, too, creating what he called his "five-man realty dream team."

Luckily for Ben, he came packaged with testicles and a love of basketball. He and Jerry had hit it off from the start thanks to Jerry's matching package. My package, on the other hand, did not include balls of any sort, period. While Doc might be happy about that fact, when it came to fitting in at work, a pair surely would have come in handy.

The five of us took turns placing our orders, starting with me. While I waited for everyone else to finish, I tapped my foot along with Johnny Cash, who was singing through the overhead speakers about walking the line. The Man in Black's words fit my life at the moment, considering the monumental efforts I was making lately to keep my job, protect my kids from their sperm-donor of a father, and not end up in jail again.

Oh, and to avoid my Aunt Zoe.

I loved my aunt dearly, but she insisted on trying to tell me more about how I had come from a long line of killers and what that meant for my future. Thankfully Aunt Zoe was leaving today for an important glass art conference she went to every year down in Denver and not returning home until next weekend. That gave me a week of reprieve from dodging her and her warnings about the destiny that was waiting for me. As far as I was concerned, the destiny she was referring to could take a number and go to the back of the line … or just go away. I had no problem being destiny-less. Getting my kids to adulthood in one piece would be enough of a challenge.

Jerry clapped his big, basketball-sized hands together, jerking me out of my reverie. "Okay, let's get this ball into play. Ben, we'll start with you. Share with the team what's in your playbook today."

Jerry spoke in Sport-uguese. Luckily for me, I'd played ball back in high school eons ago, so I could translate with only a few fouls.

Ben dug in, telling about the one pending sale he had and the various pipeline possibilities. Ray followed with more of a long-winded gloat than a status report. Mona came next, her pendings still plentiful even in the cooling market. I brought up the rear, fast forwarding over my lack of any potential buyers for Jeff Wymonds' house and Cooper's place, skipping Harvey's ranch and the dead guy mess entirely, and wrapping up with the final paperwork to be signed yet for the Carhart deal.

"What about the rental for Rex Conner?" Jerry asked.

The sound of that sonuvabitch's name was all it took to make a red haze coat my vision and a wildfire race through my lungs. I closed my lips, swallowing down the ball of fire that threatened to spew forth and sizzle the blond eyebrows right off Jerry's rock-hewn face.

"Have you found a rental that comes close to fitting his needs?" Jerry dumped a sugar into his coffee, unaware that I was sitting there struggling not to morph into Tolkien's Smaug.

Sure, I'd found the perfect rental for Rex the-piece-of-shit Connor. It was an ice hut on a lovely frozen lake in Siberia. No wait! Russia's frozen tundra was not far enough away for the man who had fathered my twins and then left before they were even the size of jelly beans. Maybe one of Saturn's moons would do.

"Not yet," I answered.

"Surely there has to be something out there that would make him happy."

Surely there was, but I refused to give it to the dickhead. Rex wanted me to pretend to be his wife. He'd even tried to blackmail me into the role earlier this month. He wanted my kids to play along as well, creating the instant family he needed to get the highfalutin job promotion he was trying to land up in Lead at the old Homestake Mine turned scientific research lab.

The biological father of my children was one big bowl of rat bastard stew, and I kicked myself daily for ever letting him seduce me into bed way back when. However, I loved the two children for whom he had donated his sperm during a two-for-one special deal—the same two children who had no idea that Rex was their father. Nor did they know that their dad was back in town trying to mess with my world in order to get some stupid promotion.

To make this Rex matter even stickier, my boss and coworkers had no clue of Rex's role in my life. Mona knew I had some issues with him, but none of them had an inkling that he was my twins' real father, and it needed to stay that way for the kids' protection.

I swallowed the coconut-sized lump made up of fury and disgust pulsing in my throat and somehow managed to put a smile on my lips and aim it at Jerry. "Mr. Connor is very picky. I'm still looking for that perfect rental he can call home for as long as he needs it."

Or until I killed him.

Maybe I could still broker real estate deals from prison? Now that might make for a fun-filled reality TV show.

"Let me know if you need help with taking care of that client," Ben offered, his smile kind yet knowing. He and Mona had walked in right after a rather tense physical moment between Doc, Rex, and me. They'd both agreed to zip their lips about witnessing anything and had stayed true to their word so far.

"That's some great teamwork, Ben," Jerry said. "You all are doing a bang-up job on the sales boards."

Thank you, I mouthed to Ben as the waiter appeared. He nodded back, and took the plate of food the waiter handed him.

Jerry dug in along with the rest of us, talking to us in between bites. "The reason I called this huddle today is to fill you in on how things are going to play out with the Paranormal Realty camera crew."

My gut clenched. Ever since Jerry's not-so-genius marketing idea to have a reality television crew come to town and do several Paranormal Realty shows on the haunted locations throughout Deadwood and Lead, I'd been walking around feeling like a thunder cloud of doom was waiting to downpour all over my head.

"Mona is going to play dispatcher back at the office while the filming is being done." He wiped his mouth with a napkin and focused on Mona. "Red, you're going to need to be my assistant coach, covering incoming calls for whoever is working with the camera crew each day, as well as offering help from home base with any issues that may pop up while they're on location."

She agreed but with a small frown. What was with that frown? Did she know something the rest of us didn't?

My esophagus tightened, putting a squeeze on the bacon I'd just sent down the pipe. I sipped from my glass of water, sending down reinforcements to push everything along.

"Ben and Violet," Jerry's gaze swung back and forth between us. "You two will be our point guards. You'll be representing Calamity Jane Realty on camera, making us look good. You'll take turns being with the camera crew every other day during filming."

I looked over at Ben, who was nodding with a smile. He seemed genuinely pleased that he was going to be on televisions throughout South Dakota and beyond, showing supposedly haunted houses. Had someone spiked his orange juice? If so, I wanted some spiked juice, too.

I gulped down a cry of alarm. The idea of speaking in front of a camera every other day made my hives break out in a sweat.

Jerry moved on, oblivious to my outward signs of discomfort as usual. Mona had me locked in her sights, though, and judging from her worried expression, she could read me like a radiation hazard sign.

"My man, Ray, here is going to run our defense." When I just stared at Jerry while the warning alarms blared inside of my skull, he added, "In other words, he'll be going with Ben and Violet during the days they are going to be on camera, making sure all goes smoothly."

There it was—the mushroom cloud of doom.

"Why?" was all I could get out.

"Because I realize that by having this TV crew here and cameras rolling, there is the potential for us to not be at the top of our game. None of us at this table want Calamity Jane Realty to become a laughingstock on national television. Ray's job will be to make sure you two look good in front of the camera at all times."

I'd rather be drawn and quartered than spend full days with Ray while a camera followed us around. I chanced a glance at Ray and ran into his molar-grinding smirk.

"Violet and Ray," Jerry seemed to pick up on the spiky vibes flowing back and forth between us, "I know that you two have some compatibility issues you need to work through."

Compatibility issues? Had Jerry been taking Human Resources classes on the side? Did my wanting to sock Ray in the nose every time I saw his fat orangutan face fit under the column of Compatibility Issues?

"I expect you to be able to put your differences aside and show good sportsmanship in front of the camera crew. We don't need this to turn into some reality TV soap opera. Can I count on you to do your best for the team on this?"

"Of course," Ray answered Johnny-on-the-spot. I was surprised he'd heard Jerry's question what with his head jammed so far up our boss's ass.

Jerry turned to me. "How about you, Violet?"

"I won't let you down," I said and meant it. I'd try my best. And if Ray ended up buried alive in a grave down in South America, I'd try my best to have an ironclad alibi.

The rest of the meeting slogged past while I forced food down the hatch. Jerry focused on some new regulations for Realtors that were being considered by the state ruling committee and what the Deadwood Historic Preservation Committee had been up to lately when it came to selling historic buildings.

The rest of the day moved along in fast motion around me while I stared unseeingly at my computer and chewed on my knuckles about Ray, TV cameras, haunted houses, and everything that could go wrong when adding me to that mix. The list of possibilities was amazingly long when I wrote them all down on paper as a means of therapeutic release. They wadded up incredibly easily, though.

At some point during the afternoon, Doc called and we discussed his coming to dinner tonight. Before he hung up, he asked if I'd tried to reach Eddie Mudder again. Eddie von Lurch, as I'd renamed him, had not answered last night when I called at ten o'clock precisely. Nor had he answered at ten-thirty, ten-forty-five, or eleven. I'd given up then and forgotten all about calling back today thanks to Jerry's bomb about Ray's new reign of terror.

When I pulled into Aunt Zoe's drive, I was surprised to see her truck still sitting there. I looked at the time on my cellphone—half past five. Wasn't she supposed to have left earlier this afternoon for Denver? Hadn't she planned to drive down there with a friend?

Harvey's pickup was there, too, which I'd expected since I'd asked him to get the kids from school and watch them until I made it home from work.

I shivered all of the way up the sidewalk to the front porch. The nights were below freezing regularly now up here in the hills, most days only warming up enough to melt the frost for a few hours. The smell of wood smoke mixed with the pine trees made me want to cozy up in front of the fire tonight with Doc. It was a romantic fantasy, probably spurred from something I'd seen on an erection pill-popping commercial. Reality would undoubtedly be much different thanks to my two kids and the misadventures that came with them.

The house smelled like baking pork when I walked through the door. By the time I reached my Aunt Zoe's kitchen, I was salivating like the big bad wolf. My two little piglets were pounding around overhead, their homework spread out on the table.

Harvey stood in front of the stove, wearing one of Aunt Zoe's Betty Boop aprons while stirring something in a saucepan. He looked over at me, his gaze homing in on my face. "Somethin' go sour on the cob at work?"

"What makes you ask that?"

"You look mad enough to argue with a fence post."

That pretty much summed it up, but I didn't feel like whining to Harvey about the can of worms Jerry had dumped over my head today. "Is Aunt Zoe still here?" I deflected, hanging my purse on the back of a kitchen chair.

He pointed the wooden spoon he was using at the ceiling. "She's fillin' up her saddle bags for her big shindig."

I leaned over the saucepan, breathing in a fruity smell. I'd expected BBQ sauce, not something orange colored and sweet. I reached out to stick my finger in it and see what it tasted like.

Harvey smacked away my hand. "Don't even think about it,

girl."

"What is it?"

"My momma's famous apricot sauce."

I licked my lips. "It smells delicious. I just want a taste."

"It's for the pork chops, not yer finger." He hip-bumped me away from the stove. "Go wash up for supper."

Okay, but first I wanted to change into something that had no waistband. At the top of the stairs, I slipped off my right shoe, kicking it through my open bedroom door. It almost hit Aunt Zoe, who was sitting on my bed with her luggage at her feet. I limped into my room wondering what was going on.

She looked beautiful in the soft lamp light radiating from my nightstand with her long, silver-streaked hair tied back. Her sapphire sweater and a scarlet bohemian skirt matched her personality—vibrant and a little wild.

"What are you still doing home?" I asked, leaning against my dresser. "I thought you were leaving this afternoon."

"My co-traveler had an emergency and needed to hold off leaving for a few hours. He should be here soon."

"If you leave now, you won't make it into Denver until the middle of the night."

"That's fine. We'd planned on spending the first night at his condo anyway. We'll check into the hotel tomorrow."

"You're staying at *his* condo?" I put my hands on my hips. "Is this the guy you went on a couple of dates with last month?"

"One and the same."

"The guy who looks a little like George Clooney."

She nodded.

"The one who you didn't want to get involved with because he's in the process of getting a divorce?"

"Yes, dear. That's him. Would you like me to draw you a picture?"

If he looked like Clooney, I'd rather she took a photo of him. But I hadn't made my point yet. "And now you're going down to Denver with him AND spending the night at his condo."

"It's a two-bedroom."

"Are you sharing a hotel room with him, too?"

She shrugged. "It's cheaper that way. Those rooms are a

couple hundred a night, and we'll be staying there through Saturday."

"Is there one bed or two?"

Aunt Zoe chuckled. "You're my niece, not my mother."

"This is a bad idea. You could get hurt again."

That wiped the smile from her lips. "Not possible. I have my heart all tucked away safe and sound. I'm done with letting it rule me."

I didn't completely believe that. I'd seen how fiery she got when a certain fire captain came knocking. There were no old flames being doused when the two of them circled and growled, and a lot of smoldering going on when they were apart.

"If it makes you feel better, the room has two queen beds. Besides, it's strictly platonic and he knows it."

"I still don't like it." I knew Aunt Zoe was a big girl, but I was really partial to that certain fire captain, and I sort of had this 'happily-ever-after' fantasy for Aunt Zoe and him that I didn't want some glass maker with a condo in Denver to screw up.

"You're one to talk about risky heart ventures, Violet Lynn Parker."

Boy, oh boy. She had me there.

Aunt Zoe patted the bed next to her. "Now quit lecturing me and sit." After I joined her on the bed, she squeezed my hand. "Your eyes are bloodshot and your makeup is smudged in some spots and completely wiped off in others. What happened at work today?"

My aunt knew me way too well. I flopped back onto the bed, staring up at the ceiling. "The television people are coming a week earlier than planned."

"Why?"

"Because they're anxious to get rolling and Jerry has them all primed for Ben and me to take them around to some of the local haunted houses."

Aunt Zoe snorted. "Your boss is a horse's patooty."

She'd had her dander up about Jerry since that first week when he'd walked into the office and declared that I needed a makeover. Her bra-burning feelers had gotten bent out of shape about the gobs of makeup, fake eyelashes, and new clothes he'd invested in on my account. The huge billboard out on Interstate 90 showcasing me as a floozy version of June Cleaver had stirred up the bees in her bonnet only more.

"But that's not the worst of it," I continued. "Jerry has decided that Ray has to go along with whoever the camera crew is working with each day to supervise and make sure Calamity Jane isn't shown in a bad light."

She scoffed. "What part of being on one of those reality television shows is putting Jerry's business in a good light? They're going to want some drama, and drama equals negative publicity."

"Jerry is a firm believer that there's no such thing as negative publicity."

Coming from the world of professional basketball had skewed his view of publicity in my opinion. He had a THINK BIGGER sign on his desk. At six foot eight with shoulders that barely fit through doorways, he'd really taken that saying to heart. What he didn't understand was that some of us liked being smaller, wanted to make a decent living and that was it, not reach world-wide fame.

"Yeah, well he's an idiot when it comes to you." Aunt Zoe leaned over and tucked some of my curls behind my ear like she had when I'd come to her crying as a kid. "I don't appreciate one iota how he's using my darling niece in his over-the-top marketing schemes."

"Thank you." I caught her hand, holding it against my cheek. "You always know what to say to make me feel better."

Her smile made her look even prettier. "Have you tried that apricot sauce Harvey's got on the stove? That should make you feel absolutely wonderful."

"Not yet." I sat upright. "He sent me away to get cleaned up for supper first."

She looked me over. "You look pretty clean to me, kiddo." Then she leaned over and dropped a quick kiss on my temple. "When I get home from Denver, you and I need to talk about you know what."

I groaned. "Can't we just put it in a capsule and bury it in the backyard to dig up some time far off in the future?"

"You can't skirt your responsibilities, Violet." Her voice was soft but firm. "You know that's true deep down in here." She poked my chest above my heart.

"I have plenty of responsibilities already wrapped up in those two kids who are yelling at each other as we speak."

Apparently Addy was hogging the bathroom again and Layne needed to pee. As I listened, the hollering and pounding grew louder. "Crap. I need to go play referee before they break down your bathroom door."

"There's a saying, 'You cannot find peace by avoiding life.'"

"Yeah, well here's an old Polish proverb that Nat likes to quote, 'Not my circus. Not my monkeys.' Coming from a long line of killers is *not* my circus."

"I'M TELLING MOM YOU'RE USING HER PERFUME TO MAKE ELVIS SMELL BETTER, YOU BIG BUTTHOLE!" Layne screamed at the top of his lungs.

Dammit, that perfume was not cheap.

I pushed to my feet, frowning down at Aunt Zoe. "However, those two primates out there screeching at each other are my monkeys."

"You better go before they start flinging poo at each other." She pushed my butt, shoving me toward the door.

"Layne," I hollered down to where he stood pounding non-stop on the bathroom door, "use the one downstairs, for heaven's sake."

He hit the door one last time before stomping toward the stairs behind me. He glowered up at me as he neared. "But my science experiment is in there."

Oh, hell. What was the mad scientist up to now? I shook my head. I didn't really want to know.

As he passed by me, I noticed a red mark on his cheek. "Hold up, buster." I caught his arm and swung him around, taking hold of his chin. "What's this?" I gently touched the angry looking scratch that appeared to be bruising around the edges. "Did your sister do this to you?"

My kids sometimes played rough with each other. Other times they just hauled off and started hitting, especially when I wasn't there to string them up by their tennis shoes.

"No." He pulled out of my grip, looking down. "I fell."

"Did you scrape up your hands, too?"

He stepped back. "I'm fine, Mom. Don't cry about it. I fell down, that's all." He turned his back on me and raced down the stairs.

I stood grimacing after him. Ever since I'd announced that Doc was my official boyfriend, my kids had been giving me the cold shoulder. Addy had wanted me to marry and have babies with her best friend's almost-divorced father, Jeff Wymonds. Layne had liked being the only man of the house and now was certain I was going to kick him out onto the street. No matter how much I tried to explain to both kids the illogical directions of their thinking, neither were budging.

The doorbell rang.

"Layne, get the door," I called down the stairs.

"I'm in the bathroom," he yelled back and slammed the bathroom door.

"My what wonderful, loving children I have," I grumbled, heading downstairs to get the door myself. "The Von Trapps would be so envious."

"That's probably my ride," Aunt Zoe said from behind me at the top of the stairs. "I'll go grab my purse."

When I opened the door, it wasn't a Clooney look alike. Instead he looked more like Sam Elliott.

"Reid!" I stepped back in surprise.

"Hey, Sparky." Reid Martin, Deadwood's fire captain and Aunt Zoe's red-hot ex, stood on the front porch. He'd started using the 'Sparky' nickname for me after my Bronco had been lit on fire and died a hot and smoky death. "Can I come in? I need to talk to your aunt."

I nodded, opening the screen door for him.

"Her shotgun isn't within reach, is it?" he asked, shutting out the cold behind him.

Before I could answer, I heard Aunt Zoe's footfalls clomping down the stairs behind me. I turned with a wince. "Look, Aunt Zoe. Reid stopped by to see you off."

Her cheeks darkened with each step down, her glare searing our visitor. It was a good thing Reid was used to working around heat. He should've brought his firefighter suit to be safe.

"What are you doing here?" she bit out when she joined us in front of the door, dropping her luggage and purse at her feet.

"It's like Sparky said," he eyed Aunt Zoe from top to bottom. "I came to say goodbye. I like that color on you."

"Who told you I was going anywhere?" She shot a squint in my direction.

"Not me." I held up my hands. "I swear."

"Sparky's innocent. Although Coop would probably disagree." The wink he sent me made me wonder if Detective Cooper had told him about the body in the safe. "Zo, it's no secret that you've been attending this conference in late October for years."

"True, but how did you know that I was leaving for it tonight?"

That was a good question considering she was supposed to have been out the door hours ago.

"That's not important." He jammed his hands into his tan coat pockets, shuffling his boot heels on the wooden floor. "I hear you're not going down alone this year."

She crossed her arms in response.

"You should have told me. I'd have taken time off work and driven you down."

"Humph!" She lifted her chin. "I'd sooner hitchhike."

"Liar." He glanced at me out of the corner of his eye and then looked toward the kitchen.

That was my hint to give them a moment alone.

Aunt Zoe must have caught his signal, too, because she latched onto my arm. "You stay right here."

Not this again. I'd had to witness Reid's heart getting stomped on by her a few weeks ago when he had set up a romantic evening for them out in the forest, and she had dragged me along. This time I didn't have a glass of wine to hide behind.

"So who's riding down with you?" Reid asked.

"It's not your business."

"Humor me, Zo."

Aunt Zoe shrugged. "A good friend. He owns a couple of local art galleries."

"Are you only riding down with him or is there more?"

"We're rooming together."

Reid's jaw tightened. He looked toward the door, nodding. I doubted that he agreed with her choice, though.

"I don't like it," he said, confirming my suspicion.

"It's not up to you to like."

His focus snapped back to her face, his gaze piercing. "Maybe not, but that doesn't stop me from feeling it."

The doorbell rang.

Uh oh. Was that her ride? How would Reid react to him face-to-face? Would there be some kind of brawl? I took a step back, pulling free of Aunt Zoe's grip.

She bumped Reid aside and opened the door.

"Hey, Zoe," Doc's voice came through the screen. "I thought you were on your way to Denver."

"I will be shortly. Come on in."

I barely gave Doc time to make it over the threshold. Grabbing him by the hand, I towed him up the stairs. "Come with me, I need to show you something in my bedroom."

"Your bedroom?"

At the top of the stairs, I nudged him toward my room.

He pulled me inside with him and stole a kiss. Well, considering how easily I gave it to him, there wasn't much thievery involved.

When Doc pulled back, his dark gaze searched my face, a frown building on his brow. "You seemed off when I called you earlier, and now that I've gotten a good look at you, I'd guess you had a bad day. What happened?"

"I'll fill you in later," I whispered and then held my index finger to my lips. Slipping out of his arms, I tiptoed back into the hallway.

As I approached the top of the stairs, I heard Aunt Zoe say, "You need to leave. My ride will be here soon."

Then I heard the front door open and peeked around the corner. Aunt Zoe was holding the door wide.

Reid took a step toward her. "If you get into a bind, call me. I'll drive straight down and get you."

"You don't need to rescue me. I can handle men."

"Really, Zo?" he grabbed Aunt Zoe by the shoulders. "Then handle this." He kissed her, slow and cautious, like he was stepping into a flame-filled building. I could feel the heat from it clear up at the top of the steps. When she grabbed onto the lapels of his coat and pressed against him, my jaw unhinged.

A scuffling sound made me step back from the peep show. I looked around. Doc was leaning against my door jamb, watching me with one raised eyebrow.

"Now I see why Coop has such a problem with your nose," he said quietly, grinning.

I wrinkled said facial feature at him.

I heard the screen door creak and then slam down below. When I peeked around the wall again, Aunt Zoe stood alone, staring out into the twilight.

No sooner had the rumble of Reid's diesel truck faded when I heard the crunch of gravel in the drive.

Aunt Zoe lifted her purse and luggage. "Violet." She turned, looking up at where I stood on the top step.

I searched her face for any sadness or anger, but her straight face left me clueless. "Are you leaving now?"

"Yes. I'll call you when I get up tomorrow morning."

"You doing okay?" I probed, which could be translated as: Did Reid's kiss spark some old flames back to life?

"I'm fine. But in case anyone is wondering if anything has changed, it hasn't."

Hmmm. That lip lock a few moments ago hinted at a different ending.

After blowing me a kiss, she shouldered her way out through the screen door and left.

Harvey came from the kitchen and closed the door behind her. He smiled up at me. "Methinks the shrew doth protest too much," he said, jumbling his Shakespeare.

"Reid is certainly not giving up without a fight," Doc said, joining me on the stairs.

"You think he still believes he has a chance?"

"I know so. He told me as much the other night during poker at Cooper's place."

A series of strangled-sounding clucks followed by a loud

squawk came from behind us.

"What in the hell was that?" I asked Doc.

He pointed his thumb over his shoulder. "It came from your bedroom."

I followed him back into the room. We stood there next to my bed, listening. A thump came from my closet.

"It's in there," I whispered.

Doc eased across the room. I followed on his heels, leaning into him as he reached for the door and slid it open.

An even louder squawk made me jump back.

Elvis, my daughter's chicken, flapped around in the bottom of my closet, working herself into a feather-flying frenzy. Then she half-flew out of my closet and ran out the door and down the hallway.

I watched her go, struck silent by it all.

"That was unexpected," Doc said, plucking a feather from my hair.

I looked in my closet, taking in all of the feathers—covering my shoes, sticking to my clothes, floating around us. "Criminy! How long had she been in there?"

Doc bent down and withdrew something from the inside of one of my suede ankle boots. "Apparently, long enough to leave you a little present." He dropped his find in my palm.

I glared down at the warm egg. "I'm gonna kill that damned chicken."

I heard the bathroom door open down the hall. Addy!

"Adelynn Renee, freeze!" Shoving the egg back at Doc, I stormed into the hall. "That's it! Elvis is leaving the building … for good!"

Chapter Four

Tuesday, October 23rd

Meanwhile, back in Elvis's Graceland …

The next morning dawned silent and rippling with tension. The verdict was in—I was officially the worst mother of the year. Neither of my darling children would speak to me at the breakfast table, directing all of their answers to my questions through Natalie, who'd crashed overnight in Aunt Zoe's room. She couldn't quite shake her skittishness from finding the dead guy out at Harvey's place.

I pointed my coffee cup at my stone-faced daughter. "Did you put Elvis in the basement like I told you to after she took her morning constitution outside?"

Addy turned to Natalie. "Tell my mean mom that *my* chicken is locked up in her prison cell downstairs."

Natalie couldn't hold in her grin when she looked at me. "Miss Adelynn would like to relay to the *Hard-Headed Woman* at the table that Elvis is doing the *Jailhouse Rock* today."

Addy tapped Natalie's arm. "And let her know that Elvis loves her, and that's why she laid an egg in her boot."

"Miss Adelynn would like to add that you should not get *All Shook Up* about one egg because Elvis is really *Stuck on You*."

"And tell her," Addy said through a mouth full of cereal, "that I am not taking Elvis back to that horrible place where I got her no matter how much my mean mom yells at me."

"Miss Adelynn wants me to tell you that she will not *Surrender* Elvis back to the *Heartbreak Hotel*."

"Elvis is my best pet ever. If she goes, I go."

Natalie's eyes positively twinkled as she picked up her coffee mug. "Miss Adelynn feels that her chicken is *A Big Hunk 'O Love*, and declares *Don't Be Cruel* to Elvis or they'll both leave."

I cocked my head at Natalie. "Are you done, knucklehead?"

She looked at Addy. "Are we done, Miss Adelynn?"

"Whatever." Addy pushed back from the table, her lips locked up tight as she placed her dish in the sink and then stomped out of the kitchen.

Back to the silent treatment. That was fine with me.

"My overall interpretation is that your daughter still feels you're the *Devil in Disguise.*"

I tossed my spoon into my cereal bowl. "You're a real Groucho Marx this morning."

"You know Harpo's my favorite. I love that curly hair. He reminds me of you."

"Was Elvis serenading you in your dreams again or what?"

"I was really on a roll there, wasn't I?"

"Oh, you're definitely on something this morning." I stared across the table at Layne, who was slurping the last of the milk in his bowl. The bruise on his cheek had turned dark blueish purple. I worried my lower lip. "Layne, did your teacher see that bruise on your cheek yesterday?"

He shrugged.

"Did she ask you about it?"

He shrugged again.

My pool of patience evaporated like a mud puddle in Death Valley. "Darn it, Layne. Stop shrugging and—"

Aunt Zoe's phone rang, interrupting my rant.

According to the Betty Boop clock over the kitchen sink, we had fifteen minutes until it was time to head to school. Whoever was calling had better make it quick.

Layne popped up from the table and got the phone. "Hello?" He listened, then held the phone out to me but looked at Natalie. "Tell *Violet* it's one of her boyfriends."

I shoved my chair back, snatching the phone from him. "Get your shoes on right now," I spoke in a harsh whisper.

"Whatever!" he echoed his sister and ran from the room.

I was really beginning to hate that word. I covered the mouthpiece and yelled after him, "Whatever me again, young man, and I'll ground you 'til Christmas."

"They were such a happy, peaceful family." Natalie sounded as if she were narrating a *Twilight Zone* episode.

I pointed the phone at her. "Keep it up and I'll sic Coop on you." I lifted the phone to my ear. "Hello?"

"That's Detective Cooper to you, Parker." The sound of Cooper's voice on the line made me cringe.

"Iya ... um ... oops?"

"On whom are you going to sic me?"

"Uhhhh ..." my wide-eyed gaze hit Natalie. I pointed at the phone and then pushed up on the end of my nose so it looked like a pig's snout.

"What?" She lowered her cup, squinting at me. "I don't see anything in your nose."

And here a moment ago she'd been so brilliant with Elvis's hit songs.

"Natalie." I came clean with Cooper.

"What about Ms. Beals?"

The topic of discussion made a pig snout face back at me before sipping her coffee.

"She's here and that's who I'm going to sic you on."

Natalie froze with her cup to her lips, her big doe eyes staring right into my bright headlights.

There was silence at the other end of the line for a few ticks of the clock. I heard the creak of his chair and some shuffling sounds. "Good. That's good."

Natalie snapped back to life, aiming some rude hand gestures at me.

I pointed at her, puckered my lips in a fake kiss, and then pointed at my butt before focusing back on Cooper's words. "What do you mean *good*, Detective? Good that I'm going to sic you on her? Or good that she's here?"

"It's too early for this shit, Parker." His tone was downright snarly all of a sudden.

The silly man had forgotten to whom he was speaking. I got all bristly back. "Hey, you're the one who called me, so don't get your Fruit of the Looms in a wad."

He growled.

After the morning I'd had, I growled right back. "Is there a reason you called me, Detective? Or did you just wake up from your bed of nails and think, 'I should call Violet and see how fast I can piss her off?'"

He sighed. It sounded more weary than frustrated. "Listen, Parker, when you and Ms. Beals finish painting flowers on each other's toenails, I need you both to come down to the station."

"You know I won't step one flower-covered toe in that building unless you have a warrant."

"I don't have the time or patience for games today, Parker." I heard the tiredness again.

"What's wrong? Is your uncle keeping you up partying into the wee hours?" Harvey had been sleeping in Cooper's spare bedroom for two nights now.

"He likes to watch movies late at night. I only got four hours of sleep the last couple of nights."

"Yeah, he does like the classics." I missed watching old westerns with the buzzard. He knew all of the actors by name and the juiciest gossip about their personal lives.

"And then he gets up early and makes a huge spread."

I frowned at my soggy cereal that tasted like sugar-coated pieces of cardboard. "Harvey has trouble sleeping sometimes."

Cooper yawned. "I've already downed a pot of coffee trying to stay awake this morning."

"Some days after your uncle spends the night, I eat a handful of coffee beans to get the caffeine into my system faster." I blinked, suddenly realizing I was having an almost pleasant conversation with Cooper. "Wait a second. Are you being civil to me in order to woo me down to your office?"

"Is it working?"

"No."

"Damn it, Parker. I need to talk to you and your other two stooges about Sunday … in private."

I reminded myself that Cooper's job was on the line, and while the detective made me want to beat him with a rubber chicken most days, I didn't want him to end up writing parking tickets instead of hunting down killers. Besides, the jerk would probably ticket the crap out of me every chance he got as payback.

"Fine." I checked the time again, doing some quick calculating. "Meet us at your house at nine."

"Why *my* house?"

"Because your uncle is probably still there and I can pretend this is work-related. I don't want my boss finding out about the dead guy at Harvey's ranch yet." I was afraid Jerry would want to incorporate it into the Paranormal Realty camera crew's agenda.

"You mean you actually listened to my orders for once and kept your big, fat mouth shut? Is there a Texas-sized asteroid heading toward Earth and nobody warned me?"

"You know on second thought, Detective, you can stuff those coffee beans where the sun doesn't shine. I've heard coffee enemas reduce colon toxicity. Maybe you would actually be a tolerable asshole after ten or twenty flushes."

I waited, poised and ready for him to volley another insult into my court.

Instead he chuckled. "That was a good one, Parker. I'll give you that. Don't be late or I'll get that damned warrant." Without further ado, he hung up on me.

I hissed at the phone and tossed it into the wastebasket. "Trash talk from there, bossy-butt."

Natalie pushed up from her chair, fishing the phone out on her way to the sink. "How was Deadwood's dastardly detective this morning?" she asked, wiping off the back of the receiver.

"More like bastardly." I crossed my arms over my chest with a huff or two, leaning back against the counter. "He wants to talk to the three of us about the body."

She set the phone on its base. "Why?"

"To walk through the events of Sunday morning again."

"When?"

"After I drop off the kids at school."

"You said this would happen." She leaned against the counter next to me. "So why are you so ticked off at him?"

"He's such a relentless hardass."

"That's what makes him so good at his job."

"Would it hurt him to use velvet now and then instead of steel wool when he talks to me?"

"I think Cooper has only two modes when it comes to

dealing with women—hard and harder." She stroked her neck. "Makes me wonder what he'd be like in the sack."

"Oh, I'd like to put him in a sack all right." I sneaked a glance at her, wondering if she'd picked up on the heated glances Cooper had kept shooting her way Sunday morning at Harvey's ranch when she'd been working her magic on Detective Hawke. "And then I'd dump him and his abrasive personality into Pactola Lake."

That snapped her out of whatever Cooper fantasy was playing in her head. She shoulder bumped me. "If you need help with rolling him over the edge and into the drink, I'm your girl."

I eyed her. "You're not smitten with him like half of the Deadwood and Lead female population, huh?"

"Smitten? Nah. He's nice to look at but only from a distance. Trust me, I learned my lesson that one night. I'm still extracting the burrs from brushing too close to him."

Years back, Cooper had rejected Natalie's attempts to lure him home with her, claiming he didn't like to get involved with the local population. Rejection was not something Natalie was used to from a male, at least not until after she'd had sex with him a few times and the fun of the chase was over for the jerk.

"Besides, you know I'm on sabbatical from men."

Which I thought was exactly what she needed for a while. Cooper had picked a bad time to change his rule about local girls. "I don't think you've gone this long without a boyfriend of some sort since junior high when you had to wear that retainer."

"I know. It's incredibly freeing not to worry about how I look or care what I say around guys. Who knows, I may stick with this sabbatical for more than just a year."

Good! I was tired of watching my best friend's heart get ripped into pieces, only to be duct taped back up and then torn apart again. I didn't trust Cooper to be any different from the scumbags in her past when it came to treating Natalie with the care she deserved. "The increase in your self-confidence is amazing, especially around men."

"Really? You can tell?" At my nod, she gave me a sideways hug. "It's all thanks to you and Doc."

"Oh, jeez." I grimaced, feeling like a wad of gum stuck to the bottom of her shoe. "You know I'm really sorry about that mess."

Natalie had confused lust for love when we'd first met Doc this last summer. I, on the other hand, had mixed both together and blown the roof off my life. In spite of knowing how my best friend felt about Doc, I'd ended up in his bed, in his back office, against the wall in his house, and wherever else we could find time alone.

"Stop it, Vi."

"You should make a sash for me that says 'World's Shittiest Best Friend.' You could throw in a pair of devil horns for a headpiece along with a bouquet of bullthistles."

She pinched me. "I said stop it. I meant what I said as a good thing. You've taught me what a loving relationship should be like with a man."

Moi? The queen of relationship disasters? Had she spiked her coffee this morning with tequila? Hell, the Hindenburg had crashed and burned slower than most of my love affairs. The only reason Doc and I had lasted so long was because …

Actually, I had no idea why we'd lasted this long. Doc must be a sadomasochist. It was just a matter of time before he wised up, probably after I filled him in on the ol' Parker family history rife with executions of all sorts, including one or two by my own hand. If he were smart, he'd at least ask for his house key back so I didn't sneak over in the night and accidentally snuff him out, too.

"Is Hawke going to be there with Cooper this morning?" Natalie's question pulled me from the whirlpool where I'd been swirling faster and faster.

"He didn't say." Knowing Cooper's rocky history with his partner, I doubted Detective Hawke would get an invite to our little tea party unless the Chief of Police insisted upon it.

"Then there's no need for me to sort through your closet for a low-cut shirt."

I had a feeling Cooper might beg to differ. "T-shirt and jeans it is," I confirmed.

She pushed off the counter. "I'll go get ready."

T-minus two kids later, I parked the Picklemobile in front of

Detective Cooper's house up in Lead. The old green pickup sputtered when I pulled out the key, coughing a few times before the engine finally gave up the ghost and the exhaust boomed its final sayonara.

"There's no sneaking around in this thing, is there?"

I patted the Picklemobile's dash. "She's no Stealth fighter plane, but she gets me from A to B."

"It's more like one of those old German tanks." Natalie shoved open the passenger side door. "Hey, your For Sale sign is hanging crooked. It looks like one of the chain links broke. I'll fix it before we leave."

"Thanks. We've had some good wind gusts the last few nights." I climbed down from the pickup, picking up the smell of wood smoke in the crisp mountain air. The slam of my driver's side door echoed down the hill toward the huge hole in the ground otherwise known as Homestake Mine's Open Cut.

I took a few steps until I was standing at the end of Cooper's front walk, and then turned, staring down at that big pit. Half shrouded in the cool fog left over from a rainy night, it looked cavernous—a gaping toothless mouth. I could almost see one of my sale-pending properties, the Carhart house, that overlooked the mine.

Prudence-the-ghost, who'd spent the last century haunting the Carhart house, once had used the house's previous owner as a microphone in front of me. During her ventriloquist act, Prudence had told me in a roundabout way that something most likely non-human periodically came out of one of the drift tunnels down at the mine's bottom to collect bodies that were left there. Only whatever this mysterious beast was hadn't come out of the drift to cart off the body of my previous boss when she was left there.

Or rather the pieces of my boss.

Damn it! I hated it when my brain turned into a butthead and brought up ugly shards of the past when I wasn't prepared. I closed my eyes and tried to see Jane as I wanted to remember her, alive and vibrant, writing her to-do lists on the whiteboard at work.

Instead, my thoughts turned to Jane's killer, the spikey-haired psychotic bitch I'd gone head-to-head with in the bowels of the Homestake Opera House last month. Detective Cooper had yet to locate the pointy psycho, but I had a feeling she'd be back for Round Two someday. She didn't seem the type who could turn the other cheek and resist the lure of revenge.

While part of me shivered at the thought of facing off with Jane's killer again, another bared its teeth and pawed the ground. After what she'd done to Jane and Helen Taragon, I had some revenge of my own to work out of my system.

"Come on, *Daydream Believer*." Natalie spun me around and pushed me up the walk in front of her. "Dirty Harry is waiting for us."

Sure enough, Detective Cooper stood in the doorway, looking tight-faced and squinty-eyed with a curled upper lip. He must have been practicing his Clint Eastwood face in the mirror this morning. All he needed was a poncho, a pistol, and a hand-rolled cigarette.

"*Hola*, Blondie," I said to him with a Spanish accent, the iconic soundtrack from *The Good, the Bad, and the Ugly* whistling in my head. I paused at the bottom porch step, waiting to see if he'd draw on me.

The usual muscle in his cheek twitched. "You're late, Parker."

"I reckon so," I shot back in my best Josey Wales voice.

"You do realize you're mixing Eastwood's characters."

I squinted back at him. "Everybody's got a right to be a sucker once."

Natalie clapped at my encore performance. When I bowed, she nudged me aside. "Honey, we're home," she sang to Cooper, climbing the steps.

"Morning, Ms. Beals." His voice had warmed about fifty degrees compared to the arctic gusts he kept blasting at me today.

"Knock off the formalities, Coop," Natalie patted his shoulder. "You've seen me almost naked. I think that puts us on a first name basis."

What?!! Since when had Cooper almost seen Natalie in her birthday suit? This was news to me. Why hadn't Natalie mentioned it before now? Was seeing her almost naked what had spurred Cooper's change of heart about her? Wait, did Cooper even have a heart?

Natalie patted him on the chest as she slipped by him and stepped over the threshold, completely missing that his gaze followed her inside.

But I didn't. Nor did I miss the warning that sharpened his steely gray eyes when he caught me catching him.

"Move it, Parker." There was no love left over for me, only snarls. "I have to be somewhere for lunch."

"So do I." That was kind of a lie. I'd mentioned to Doc last night before he left that I might stop by his office at lunch if nothing came up, but Cooper brought out the need in me to have a pissing match. I indicated for him to lead the way inside. "Let's get this cavity search over with."

Inside his house it smelled like bacon and cheese. My knees almost gave out from the heavenly aroma alone. Damn, I missed Harvey.

Speaking of the ornery bird ... Harvey stepped out of the kitchen as Natalie and I made ourselves comfortable on Cooper's black leather couch. I took one look at Harvey's skull and crossbones covered suspenders and smirked. "You've been living with your nephew too long."

"I've only been here two days."

I heard an indistinguishable grumble come from Cooper, and then he settled into the chair opposite us. He pulled out his notebook and clicked his pen a couple of times, raising both blond eyebrows at me. "Does that bother?"

"You tell me after I cram it up your nose."

Harvey stepped between us, blocking my view. "Why's your stinger already half out this mornin', girlie?"

"Blame your nephew." My stomach growled at the smell of bacon grease coming off Harvey's clothes. "You have any bacon left over?"

"Nope. Coop finished it off when he came back home to wait for you two."

Thwarted again by the damned detective.

"Scooch your cheeks over." Harvey wedged his bony ass between Natalie and me. "All righty, Coop, we're all here coolin' our saddles. Let 'er rip."

Cooper pointed his pen at Natalie. "Tell me again what happened Sunday morning, starting from the time you arrived outside of Uncle Willis' house."

Natalie leaned her elbows on her knees and dug in. When she got to the part about the unlocked front door, Cooper stopped her with, "How did you know the door was open? According to the pictures Detective Hawke took, there were no indications the jamb of the door was forced or tampered with."

That was a suspicious question. "Why would you ask that?" I butted in. "Surely, you don't think Nat had something to do with this whole mess."

"Ms. Beals was also the one who noticed the barn doors were no longer chained together, which is what led you three to find the dead body." Cooper scribbled something on his notepad. "It's my job to determine a coincidental discovery versus a manipulative redirection."

"In other words," Natalie said, "did we really just stumble upon a faceless dead man, or did I sneak out there the day before, kill the guy, and then pretend to accidentally discover him along with Vi and your uncle the next day? Is that about right, Coop?"

"There are several possibilities to consider." Cooper avoided her stare.

I jutted out my chin. "Nat's no killer and you know it."

"I have fantasized about cutting off pieces of one or two of my ex-boyfriends, but never the face. That's just twisted."

Harvey grunted. "And choppin' off a man's twig and berries isn't?"

She shrugged. "That depends on how much tequila I've downed before picking up the machete."

I shot Natalie a shut-it glare and then nudged my head toward Cooper, who was busy writing a novel on his notepad.

"She could've aided and abetted," Harvey pointed out.

The bucket mouth let out an 'oof' when my elbow connected with his ribs. "Whose side are you on here?"

"How did you know the front door was open?" Cooper returned to his original question, his pen poised above the paper.

Natalie shrugged. "There was a crack showing."

"Thank you." Cooper jotted down a few words in his notebook. "Please continue where you left off with Sunday morning's events."

Natalie cleared her throat and walked him through what had happened in the house and then out in the barn. All the while, Cooper kept his head down, taking notes.

When Natalie finished, I spoke up, "You know what I wonder?"

"This isn't your interview, Parker."

"What do you wonder?" Natalie asked, peeking around the back of Harvey's head. "Besides who was the better archenemy of Bugs Bunny: Elmer Fudd or Yosemite Sam?"

"I told you Yosemite Sam was the bigger badass, hands down. His huge hats prove it."

"Plus his arsenal of cannons," Harvey agreed.

"I don't know," Natalie argued. "I still say those big hats hinted at insecurities due to a short-man complex. Elmer had more self-confidence."

"Jesus, you three." Cooper squeezed his forehead. "Can we get back to Sunday's events?"

"Fine, Detective Party Pooper." I clasped my hands together. "What I wonder is why there was no blood on the floor in the barn. Shouldn't there be lots of blood if you cut off a face?"

"There was the dried blood on the rag," Natalie reminded me.

"Yeah, but that wasn't necessarily the dead guy's blood."

"You think the killer might have cut himself while slicing off the face?"

"Maybe, as ironic as that would be." I looked at Cooper, who was watching me with unhappy eyebrows. "Did you find any drops or smears of blood in the barn?"

His lips tightened. "That's police business."

I didn't let that stop me. I leaned forward, addressing my couch mates. "Did either of you notice dried blood on the dead guy's clothes or in the safe?"

Both shook their heads.

I turned back to Cooper. "When you cut the face off

someone who is already dead, there'd be no heartbeat to pump out blood, right?"

"I'm here to ask the questions, not you."

"Why my barn?" Harvey tugged on his suspenders. "Why my safe?"

Why his grandpappy's gun? I chewed my lower lip, wondering how one thing led to the next.

"Did you find blood anywhere else on Harvey's property?" I asked Cooper, not expecting an answer.

He didn't disappoint. "That's none of your business, Parker." He shook his pen at me. "And don't you go out there sniffing around either."

"Or what? Let me guess, you'll arrest me."

"If you're lucky." Cooper aimed his pen at his uncle. "Your turn. Make sure you include anything that seemed off to you on Sunday morning."

"Ol' Red was off his feed at breakfast."

"I meant anything having to do with the body at the ranch."

"That does have to do with the body. Ol' Red is the one who found it in the barn. I'm guessin' he sniffed out the raw meat lickety split because he hates that dog food you picked up for him. Can't say I blame him, either." Harvey snorted. "It's full of too much healthy shit."

"If Red's going to live in my house and do his business on my yard, he needs to eat dog food, not table scraps."

"Red fancies people food."

"He ate one of my motorcycle boots."

"That's 'cause he likes ya."

Harvey echoed my daughter's reasoning for a chicken egg winding up in my boot. Personally, I didn't think Red had a preference when it came to boots. The last one I'd seen him chewing had belonged to someone long dead who'd left part of his foot behind.

"Red needs to be deputized if you ask me," I said, poking at Cooper since he kept throwing that police business hogwash at us. "He could team up with you and really make headlines. I can already see the tagline for your billboard out on Interstate 90." I looked up, pretending I was reading a billboard. "The Deadwood

Duo: Digging Up Crime One Crook at a Time."

That lip curl was back. "Nobody asked you, Parker."

Natalie joined in the fun. "Oh, oh, I got one. How about: Deadwood Duo is the name, sniffing out felons is their game."

When Cooper's glare shifted to her, Natalie thumbed in my direction. "She started it."

Cooper returned to his uncle. "There were some scratches on one of the barn doors, bigger than the last time. Did you forget to clean the bait out of your illegal traps again?"

Harvey looked up, pretending to inspect the ceiling. "Hmmm, looks like ya popped a nail in yer drywall there."

"Don't mess with me old man. Besides the rag with blood and the disorder of contents under your bathroom sink, did you notice if there were any other differences at all?"

Harvey stroked his beard for a handful of seconds. "Nah, nothing that caught my eye."

"When was the last time you'd been in your bedroom?"

"When you and I stopped by the house a few days ago."

Cooper nodded, making a note of something. "Why was your safe unlocked?"

"I told you before; I leave it unlocked because I can't remember the combination."

"But the locking mechanism still works?"

"As far as I know. I haven't locked it in a few years."

I pondered what Cooper was getting at for a head scratch or two, and then it clicked. "You're trying to figure out why the killer didn't lock the safe, aren't you?"

"You think he was planning on coming back?" Natalie picked up on my line of thought.

"Maybe," he said.

The fact that Cooper answered with something other than his usual "police business" mantra added to my concern about this possibility. My worried brow probably matched Harvey's. "If that's the case, how is he going to feel when the body is gone?"

"Mighty perturbed, I'm guessin'."

"Was there evidence of foul play?" I asked Cooper.

"Isn't a missing face foul enough?" Natalie grimaced.

"I mean like stab marks or a dent in his skull."

"Or gunplay," Harvey prompted.

I shot him a what-the-hell glance. I thought we were keeping our lips buttoned about guns of any kind.

"What makes you think there might have been gunplay?" Of course Cooper latched onto that like a badger.

"How did he die?" I threw at Cooper, trying to shift the focus off any thoughts about the shotgun now stuffed under the front seat of Harvey's pickup.

"That's also police business."

"What was the time of death? Can you at least tell us that?"

"Are you worried about your alibi, Parker?"

I wrinkled my lip at the boneheaded detective in reply.

"Did he have any tattoos?" Natalie asked.

"I'm not at liberty to disclose that at this time."

Did that mean *Yes*? If so, did the dead guy happen to have a tattoo of a goat head turning into a pig? Like the one on the nut job demon lover who'd tried to kill me? The same tattoo Doc had "seen" on some tooth-pulling, burlap bag-wearing murderers while he was playing medium with Prudence the ghost?

Thinking about Prudence and her killers made me curious about something else. "Did he have all of his teeth?"

Cooper's squint reappeared. "Why would you ask that?"

I skirted the truth. "I was curious if the killer had removed the ability to identify the victim based on dental records." What I really wondered was if the guy still had all four canine teeth, and I had a feeling Cooper knew that.

"Right. Next you're going to try to convince me that the tooth fairy is real."

Well, I wouldn't call Prudence a fairy—more of a tooth trophy hunter.

Before I could reply, he switched gears. "Your turn, Parker. Go through Sunday's events, starting with pulling into my uncle's drive."

I grimaced. Here came the rubber glove treatment. I just hoped he'd use lubricant this time.

Without preamble, I started through my version of the story again, skipping the shotgun part the same as Natalie and Harvey had done. I ended with when Cooper and Hawke had pulled up and started bossing everyone around.

"We didn't boss you around. Giving orders at a crime scene is our job. Top priority is securing the area and evidence."

"You were a little bossy," Natalie seconded.

"You were barkin' orders like your Aunt Gertrude at the Thanksgivin' table."

Cooper glared at us in turn, his frown lines deepening into ravines and then canyons.

Harvey looked away, scratching his neck.

Natalie cracked her knuckles one at a time.

I twiddled my thumbs, glancing at the clock on Cooper's dining room wall, wondering what Doc was up to right at that moment.

All was quiet on the front line as we waited for a yell of "Incoming!"

Cooper snapped his notebook closed. "There's only one problem I see with all three of your stories about that morning." He paused, probably for effect. Oh man, did they teach him that in Interrogation 101? I tried not to roll my eyes as he tucked the little book into his coat pocket, building up to his interview summation.

"Spit it out, boy. The longer you chew on it, the worse it tastes."

Cooper clicked his stupid pen. "Nobody's talking about how my great grandfather's sawed-off shotgun played into Sunday's events."

My heart leapt from my chest and raced out the front door. It was all I could do to hold a straight face and not turn to gape at Harvey and Natalie.

Damn Harvey for taking the shotgun from the scene of the crime. I highly doubted Cooper was going to buy that I had nothing to do with removing evidence this time.

"That ol' gun?" Harvey asked. "What does that have to do with this mess?"

"We found the tin tag on the floor inside the safe with the dead man."

The what? What was a tin tag? Was that some part on an old gun?

"But we can't find the shotgun anywhere."

"You sure 'bout that?" Harvey's face gave away nothing. I needed him to show me how he did that in the face of the terror of being locked up in that urine-stinking jail cell.

"I searched your usual hiding spots." Cooper clicked the pen again.

"That sounds like a bit of a pickle," I said, wanting to save Harvey from having to outright lie to his nephew or worse, admit the truth. Tampering with evidence was going to look bad on my ever-growing record.

"It's a pickle all right." Cooper threw his pen, like a gauntlet, onto the coffee table between us. "Especially since we found evidence of rock salt in a wall of the barn."

Chapter Five

Meanwhile, back in the land of the non-living …

After announcing that detail about the rock salt in the barn wall, Cooper nailed each of us in turn with those steely eyes of his, settling finally on me.

We were dead meat.

Detective Cooper had his teeth sunk in, and I highly doubted he'd let go until one of us whimpered.

Harvey's stupid family shotgun was going to land us in a chain gang cleaning up litter in the median of Interstate 90.

I felt a wheeze of fear trying to crawl its way up from my lungs. I opened my mouth, searching for something to say that would send the detective back into his dog house where his usual chew toys waited for him.

Before I could get a word out, Natalie let out a hair-raising screech.

I nearly jumped into Harvey's lap in surprise.

All three of us gaped at her.

She pointed at the floor. "Spider."

Spider? I looked down at her feet, then hit her with a wrinkly brow. First of all, there was no eight-legged beastie to be seen. Second, I'd known Natalie almost my whole life and had never seen even a peep of arachnophobia from her before, not even when she'd found a nest of Daddy-longlegs in the basement of my parents' house during a sleepover back in seventh grade. Hell, she'd practically petted the creepy crawlies that night.

I was about to ask her what in hell was wrong with her when she narrowed her eyes at me.

Oh! She was saving our bacon. Her distraction now had Cooper searching the floor around her feet for the phantom spider. Thanks to Natalie's quick thinking, Cooper's interrogation was momentarily knocked off track. I needed to make my escape before he could get it back on the rails.

I shot to my feet. "If we're done here, Detective, I need to get to work. I have paperwork and a boss waiting."

Cooper glared up at me. "We're not done, Parker."

"Great! I'll look forward to hearing from you again as this case gets more exciting." Or not. Besides, what could be more exciting than a skinless face?

On second thought, maybe I shouldn't have asked that question since I really didn't want to find out the answer.

Without giving Cooper the opportunity to bid me further adieu, or to block my path with some police "Red-Rover" maneuver, I bee-lined for the door.

Natalie raced out after me. "Wait for me, crazy!"

I keyed the pickup to life as Natalie was climbing into the cab and barely gave the old truck a chance to catch its breath before stomping on the gas. I wanted to get the hell out of Dodge before Cooper decided to throw us in the think-tank on some trumped up charges based on his suspicions alone.

A glance in the rearview mirror as we sped away found Cooper standing on the front porch watching us leave, his arms crossed. I lowered my head a fraction, half-expecting him to whip out his gun and shoot out the back window of our getaway truck.

"We're up shit creek," Natalie said after we made it to the bottom of the hill and turned right toward Deadwood. "It's only a matter of time before one of us cracks."

I thought of that piss-reeking, pubic-hair sprinkled urinal in the jail cell down at the Deadwood Police Station and grimaced. "It's not going to be me."

"Ha!" Her tone was full of disbelief.

"What do you mean by that?"

"You almost spilled your guts back there. If I hadn't played Little Miss Muffet to distract him, you'd have upchucked the truth."

"No way."

"Yes way. Your eyes got all big and round like they do when you're freaking out."

"No, they didn't."

"Oh, they definitely did. You've never been very good at keeping secrets what with your twitchy nose and scaredy-cat eyes." She looked at her hands. "Well, except for that doozy about Doc, but I was too blind with a stupid crush to notice your usual cues then."

My cheeks warmed. I wished I could crawl down by the gas pedal until this awkward moment blew out the window. I thought about blurting out that Cooper had the hots for her to make her feel better about the whole Doc and me affair, but it would only feed that insecure part of her psyche that this sabbatical from men was supposed to starve to death.

I slowed as we entered the Deadwood city limits. "Cooper is not going to make me crack."

"Right."

I ignored her sarcasm. "He and I have done this circle and snarl dance several times." I could count on only one hand the number of times the detective had actually been nice to me. "I know when to lunge and when to tuck tail."

"I'd advise tucking tail as much as possible on this one. That man is positively stressed to the max."

That made two of us. "Yeah, well you'd better focus on prepping for your next go around, because knowing the detective as well as I do, I can assure you that he'll be back again. Next time, he'll bring a bigger trap."

"Please, we both know that I have a titanium lock on my lips when it comes to secrets. Remember back in ninth grade when you dragged Bobby Razinski into the boys' locker room while he was waiting for his bitchy girlfriend to finish cheerleading practice and slipped him the tongue?"

"That wasn't me, dodo. That was you. I was just there with you."

"Oh, that's right. But you were the one who bet I didn't have the guts to do it."

I wrinkled my nose. "I still can't believe you stuck your tongue in his mouth. Bobby always had food in his braces and dragon's breath."

"It wasn't the most pleasant of kisses, but I've had far worse since."

"Now that's just sad," I said.

"I know. Beer makes you do dumb things. Anyway, my point is that I kept it a secret that you'd dared me to do it even when Bobby's bitchy girlfriend came at me in the parking lot a couple days later."

"Come on, you and I both know you'd been wanting to knock her off her pedestal ever since she stole Bobby's older brother from you."

"It's just wrong to dump one brother while seducing the other. That girl needed a dose of her own medicine."

I pulled up in front of Aunt Zoe's place. "You coming over again tonight, oh Keeper of Great Secrets?"

"I'm not sure. I need to go out and check on my parents and then head down to Rapid to check on my Aunt Deborah's place, make sure nobody has tried to break in or messed with anything. She's decided to spend the winter down in Arizona."

"You're kidding. Claire's mom is going to live in an RV Park all winter?" I had grown up in the house next to Deborah Morgan and her wild and crazy daughters, who also happened to be Natalie's cousins. It was through the Morgan sisters that Natalie and I first had met back when playing hide and seek had been our favorite pastime. "Isn't that a step down on the social ladder for your aunt?"

"According to Claire, Deborah has found herself a new man down there, and she's going to shack up with him for the winter."

"So the wild pigs have started to fly in Arizona?"

She opened her door. "They aren't pigs. They're javelinas."

"Know it all."

"Who'd have thought there was a man out there nutty enough to risk getting naked anywhere near my aunt?" She hopped down from the Picklemobile. "I'll call you later."

I waited until she'd stepped up into her pickup and started it before heading down to work.

My cellphone rang just as the Picklemobile was backfiring to a stop.

"Hello?" I said, dropping the keys in my purse.

"I NEED TO SPEAK WITH VIOLET PARKER!" bellowed a voice I hadn't heard for almost a week.

I jerked the phone away, my ear drum ringing in complaint. "Cornelius," I growled and switched the phone to my other ear. "I told you before to stop yelling at me when I answer the phone."

While I appreciated that Cornelius Curion had bought a haunted hotel through me recently, and I was still jumping for joy about my portion of the money he had paid for said hotel (which was currently fattening my previously anorexic bank account), his eccentric phone etiquette often made me want to throw my phone at a tree ... again.

Now that Cornelius and I were done partnering in the Realtor-client game, he wanted me to hook up with him on a new gig—playing a real-life version of *Ghostbusters*.

"Is this Violet?" Cornelius whispered, his volume level swinging to the opposite end of the scale.

"Of course it's me." I kept my voice normal. "You called my phone."

"What's the code word?"

What code word? Had we established a code word at some point, and I'd spaced it? Hold up. Why would we have a freaking code word?

It was probably best not to ask. I tried to think of something that a man who looked and dressed like Abe Lincoln, who swore he could converse with ghosts on a daily basis, and who demanded protein drinks for breakfast each morning, would pick for a code word.

"Paranormal?" I asked.

"Have you put much thought into that?"

"About five seconds' worth."

"It sounds like only three. How about I come up with a code word instead?"

How about what? "I thought you wanted me to give you the code word to receive whatever information it is you're calling to tell me."

Cornelius laughed. "Oh, Violet. In spite of your silliness, I remain firm in my belief that you'll make an incredible slayer."

My breath caught. How did he know about my killer family history? "What do you mean?"

"What do you mean what do I mean?"

"Why did you call me that?"

"Violet? I was under the impression it was your name. Would you prefer another flower name? We can do anything but Freesia. It would get too confusing if there were two of you."

The Freesia he was referring to was Freesia Tender, the great-great niece of Big Jake Tender who'd built the Galena House, a beautiful old boarding house turned apartment building. Freesia now owned said building and wanted to sell it with my help. The upside of Freesia's property was that it was well-built, and we were almost ready to put it on the market. The downside was that we were waiting for Detective Cooper to remove the police tape from the door of one of the apartments, which happened to be the site of multiple murders over the years.

Oh, and then there was that lovely little "Haunted" line in the disclaimer, too. But every other building and home in Deadwood and Lead were supposedly haunted, so I strived to remain optimistic about its sale potential.

"I'm perfectly fine with my name, Cornelius."

"You sure? I've always been fond of the chlamydia flower."

I nearly choked on my spit. "Chlamydia is not a flower," I said when I could speak without coughing. "I think you mean clematis."

"No. I once knew a girl named Chlamydia. She was an amazing medium, especially when it came to calling up Viking ghosts."

"No shit?" Maybe that was where he had gotten his one-horned Viking hat he liked to wear during séances.

"Truly. I remember her well. She was sweet and very pretty, like a young Shirley MacLaine. I met her in college when she was modeling for a fine arts class."

"Let me guess, she was naked at the time."

"Impressive. Your channeling abilities are growing stronger by the day, Violet."

"Here's another guess—you asked her out after class."

"I'm not sure I like it when you're reading my mind. What

am I thinking now?"

"Never mind that. Are you sure she didn't say, 'I have chlamydia,' when you asked her out, but you were so enamored by her amazing nakedness that you heard, 'I am Chlamydia,' instead?"

"She did have an extremely perky set of—"

"No!" We were not going to go there. That was out of bounds for our level of friendship.

"Eyebrows," he continued.

"She had perky eyebrows?"

"Yes. They were very round-shaped, just like both of her very round—"

"You know what? Let's just stop this train before it crashes into the station."

"Nostrils," he finished, ignoring my interruption.

I needed to get out of this quicksand and back onto solid ground. "You said I'd make an incredible slayer. Why did you call me a slayer?"

"I didn't. I said you'd make an incredible *sayer*. As in soothsayer. You know, with your ability to open channels and see the future."

"I think you called the wrong number, sir."

"Is that another foretelling?"

"No, it's a forewarning."

"Ah, because your phone will be in the hands of someone from the past. I got it."

Good, because I didn't. In fact, I couldn't even remember who had called whom at this point. Then it all came tumbling back like a dead cow caught in the surf. "Why did you call me, Cornelius?"

"I need you to arrange a verbal exchange with your associate."

"Freesia?"

"No, the other one. The tall one who can meld with beings from the past."

"You mean my boyfriend, Doc?"

"Yes, that one. Bring him to my suite. I need him to listen to something."

Cornelius was living temporarily in one of the suites on the third floor of his hotel.

"If you're going to propose another séance, I'm not sure he'll be interested."

"It's not me that I want him to hear."

He shushed someone in the background.

"Is someone there with you?" I didn't want him to be mentioning Doc's or my name in relation to the paranormal world in front of anyone else.

"No."

"Then who were you shushing?"

"That is the exact reason why I need to talk to your tall associate. He needs to come to my suite and help me."

"Help you with what?"

"With speaking to the people surrounding me."

"I thought you said nobody was there."

"I'm talking about the people in my walls, Violet." He made a shushing sound again. "The dead ones."

"Say what now?"

The phone went silent.

"Hello?"

Nothing.

"Cornelius?"

Still nothing.

The nincompoop had hung up on me.

Bahhh! I thought about banging my phone on the steering wheel, but since Doc bought it for me after my last one had ended up in a toilet in the Homestake Opera House, I settled for burying it in my purse.

Doc's Camaro was not in the parking lot. He'd mentioned something last night about a trip over to Spearfish to meet a new client. He must still be busy impressing them with his big, money-savvy brain.

He and I were supposed to put our heads together soon to discuss what I could do with the money I had made off the hotel sale to Cornelius so that it wouldn't burn a hole in my account and float away. Make that whatever money would be left after I bought myself a used set of wheels and could give Harvey back his aromatic Picklemobile.

I crossed the parking lot. Ben was the only one in the office. As I neared my desk, he smiled up from a book he was reading. Reading on the job? That was new. Usually Ben had his nose to the real estate grindstone while I surfed the Internet and daydreamed about the fancy dancing I'd do when I sold more houses in a month than Ray.

"Wow, Violet. You look very bohemian today."

"Thanks, Ben." I was tired of looking at the same boring clothes in my closet, so I'd raided Aunt Zoe's.

"That top looks nice on you. What color is it?"

"Periwinkle." I shoved my purse in my drawer. "Where is everyone?"

"Mona and Ray are both out with clients, and Jerry had to run down to Rapid to see about a business property someone wants him to sell personally."

"What's with the book?"

"Jerry wanted me to read it. You have one, too. Check your chair."

I pulled out my chair and stared down at the book sitting on it. A Post-it note was stuck to the front. I picked up the book and read Jerry's scrawl on the note: *Violet, this will help you warm up for the camera.*

I tore off Jerry's note and read the title aloud. "*Giving Good TV—How to Knock 'Em Dead on Camera.*" I dropped the book on my desk and then fell into my chair. "Is this crap for real?"

Ben shrugged. "It's not that bad of a read. I've only fallen asleep twice since I started it."

"How far in are you?"

"I just started the second chapter."

I laughed in spite of the absurdity of our situation.

We eased into a companionable silence. Ben read while I finished up some paperwork on Freesia's Galena House and worked on an ad I wanted to place for Cooper's and Jeff Wymonds' places on a vacation homes website.

Midway through the afternoon, I stepped out to grab a quick sandwich. When I returned, Doc's car was still missing from the parking lot. I called his cellphone and got his voicemail, so I left a message filled with some heavy breathing, a few sexy moans, and a sultry "Call me, hot stuff," request. That should give him a chuckle.

Everyone but Jerry cycled through during the rest of the afternoon. After sharing a few dirty looks with Ray, exchanging some jokes about starting a book club with Ben, and getting a few tips from Mona about the website ad, it was time to head home. Ray and Ben wasted no time hitting the road. Mona followed in their wake. Harvey had called earlier to tell me he'd picked up my kids from school. He'd agreed to hang out with them until six, but then he needed to go home and get Cooper's dinner prepared, the lucky detective, so I took my time shutting down and packing up.

I was checking my cellphone one last time for any messages when someone knocked on the front window. I looked up to find Doc waving at me on the other side of the glass.

I smiled at him. It felt big and silly, very loose on my cheeks, but I couldn't help it. Doc had a way of turning me into a loose woman all around.

He pointed at the door.

His wish was my command.

A breeze blew in with him, carrying a couple of leaves with it from the courthouse's Silver Maple trees across the street. I locked the door behind him.

He took his time inspecting my outfit, his gaze darkening when he saw my choice in footwear. "I got your message, Boots." He caught my hand, drawing me closer. "I like this uninhibited, gypsy look. It makes me want to do wicked things to you. Especially since you're wearing my favorite cowboy boots."

Doc smelled like the outdoors, all fresh and woodsy and cool. But his lips were hot, and his kiss was positively steaming.

"What kind of wicked things?" I asked when he took a break from making me burn from the inside out.

"The kind that make you moan and pant, like you did on my voicemail."

I grinned. "I thought you might get a grin out of that."

"I'm going to make it your ringtone on my phone."

"Don't you dare."

"Then again, I have enough trouble not thinking about you naked whenever you call."

He kissed me again, slow and enticing, tantalizing me with his tongue and magic hands.

As tempting as it was to get all breathy and moan-filled for real in my empty office, I had kids waiting at home. Plus, those damned plate-glass windows offered a first rate peep show to anyone passing by. Public exhibitionism made my skin turn red. The one show Doc and I had performed for a pack of bikers needed no encore.

I pulled away from his heat. "Feel like walking me out to the Picklemobile?"

"Sure." He followed me over to my desk. "What's this?" He picked up the book Jerry had given to me and read the title. Disbelief creased his forehead when he finished. "No way."

"Yes way. I have homework. Jerry gave a copy to both Ben and me." I took the book from him and shoved it into my purse. "You want to come over for supper and a movie tonight?"

"What about your homework?"

"Here's an idea: After the kids go to bed, you could read it to me while I give you a relaxing rubdown."

"That sounds more like a bribe."

"They say studying with a partner is more fun."

He frowned at the book sticking halfway out of my purse. "How fun and relaxing are we talking?"

"Very, very fun and super relaxing."

His focus locked onto my lips. "Like that time in my shower with the chocolate and peanut butter flavored soap?"

I trailed my fingernails down along the buttons of his dark green shirt. "You'll have to come over and find out, hot stuff."

"Deal." He caught my fingers, which were now toying with his belt buckle, and lifted them to his lips. "But this time, how about keeping your claws retracted."

"Why? Did I hurt you last time?"

"Only in a good way." He kissed my knuckles. "But your kids will be within hearing distance this time."

True. We'd have to keep things PG tonight, darn it. "What if I promise to be gentle?"

"Where's the fun in that?"

"Come read to me and I'll show you."

He hesitated.

If he opted out of tonight, it was probably just as well. Earlier, while skimming the first chapter of Jerry's book, I'd been considering broaching the subject with Doc of how I was carrying the DNA of a line of killers. I'd played the "what-if" game with several different endings to our conversations, none of them happily-ever-afters.

"You got yourself a deal, Boots." He let go of my hand. "But first I need to take care of a few things in my office."

On second thought, maybe I'd stick to erotic massage and leave the truth-telling for another day.

I hoisted my purse strap over my shoulder. "How did the meeting with your new client go?"

"She liked what I had to offer, had already checked with my references, and wanted to start right away, so I followed her back to her office and we got busy."

"She?" Gotten busy doing what?

"A widow."

"A widow as in a twenty-five-year-old stripper who married a rich, old dying oil tycoon, and now that he's pushing up daisies she has tons of cash and is on the hunt for a hot and sexy boy toy?"

He chuckled. "More like a sixty-six-year-old successful entrepreneur who is ready to retire but afraid to stop working since her husband is gone."

Okay, so my version was a little heavy on the Hollywood drama. "You could still be her boy toy."

"Your name is already written on the bottom of my foot."

Ah, hell. When he said stuff like that, I felt like leaping into his arms and licking his whole face. Rather than slobber all over him, I decided to switch subjects to something less heart palpitating.

"Cornelius called me today." I headed over to the light switches by the front door.

"How is your favorite paranormal investigator enjoying his new digs?"

"Well, that's sort of why he called." I shut off all of the overhead fluorescents but one.

"What did he say?"

I didn't waste Doc's time with the insanity that had passed between me and Abe Jr. "He wants to talk to you."

"Me? Why?"

I paused in front of him for emphasis. "According to him, there are dead people talking in his walls, and he needs your help shutting them up."

Doc searched my face.

"No joke." I waited for him to start laughing.

Instead he nodded. "Okay." He started toward the back door.

I caught his arm, stopping him. "What do you mean okay?"

"In the English language, that's another word for *sure*."

"Smartass." I poked him in the ribs, making him grunt. "You mean you're willing to go up to Cornelius's suite and talk about dead people?"

"Yes."

"Why?"

He put his hand on my lower back and urged me down the hall. "Let's just say that after the last two séances with your orangutan pal from the Planet of the Apes, I'm curious what his abilities are in the paranormal realm."

"I think this is a bad idea." I glanced into Jerry's dark office as we passed by, making sure everything was shut off. "Cornelius could expose you in a way that's detrimental to your business reputation."

I realized as I got within reach of the back door that Doc's hand was no longer pushing me along. I looked over my shoulder and skidded to a stop at the sight of him standing opposite Jerry's office, staring into the dark doorway, his body rigid.

"What's wrong?" I walked back and peered into the shadows with him. "What is it?"

He sniffed like he used to when we were house hunting together. "There's something in there."

I gripped his arm. "Please tell me you're smelling Jerry's gym shoes."

"It reminds me of …" he trailed off and took a step back.

"The stinky, mean ghost?"

Doc had had trouble since the first time he'd walked through the front door months ago with an angry ghost that haunted my office. Most of the time, he went out of his way to avoid it. So, what was with him hanging around to shoot-the-shit with it tonight?

"No, something is different."

"Different how?"

"With the scent. Hold on." He grabbed me and pushed me behind him, blocking me. "Here it comes."

I wrapped my arms around his waist, pressed my cheek against his back, and closed my eyes. His muscles tensed and his breath caught, his heart picking up speed for a ten-count. Then he relaxed again.

"Is it gone?" I whispered.

He didn't answer.

I opened my eyes. "Are you okay, Doc? Do you need to sit down?"

"Let's clear out of here." He took me by the elbow and practically dragged me down the hall and out the back door. Without saying a word, he waited while I locked up. As soon as my key left the lock, he grabbed my arm and tugged me across the mostly empty parking lot toward the Picklemobile.

I pulled free after we reached the old truck and crossed my arms over my chest. "Dane R. Nyce, you tell me what happened in there right now."

He glanced back at the door, as if to make sure nothing was following us. "There's a new presence in your office."

Splendid. As if one pissed off freaky entity wasn't enough. "Is it as nasty as the other one?"

"I'm not sure."

"Why not? Did it pass through you too fast to pick up any details?"

Being that I was a total dud when it came to seeing, hearing, or smelling ghosts, I had only a very sketchy idea how this sixth-sense stuff worked. Usually, the ghost moved through Doc, and he saw a glimpse of how the person had died. Then it went on its merry way and Doc spent a day or two figuring out whom he'd shared a moment with in history.

"No." He scrubbed his hand down his face. "I picked up a few hints."

"So what's the problem then?"

"Violet ..."

"Don't play cryptic medium with me. Just lay it out there and let it wiggle."

He gripped my shoulder, his eyes shadowed as he stared down at me. "Jane's back."

"Jane?" My brain made a loud beeping sound, like it was performing an emergency broadcast system test. I shook my head to clear it. "You mean Jane Grimes, my boss?"

"Yes, that Jane."

My knees weakened, but Doc held me upright. "What? How? Why would ... ?" I licked my lips and breathed in a steadying breath. "Are you sure?"

"Positive."

I shivered in the cool evening breeze. "What is Jane doing back?" I whispered, as if her ghost might hear me across the parking lot.

"I don't know." He tucked me into his chest, wrapping his arms around me. "But from the intensity in Jerry's office and what I picked up," he said over my head, "she's pissed as hell about something."

Chapter Six

Meanwhile, back in the land of the living …

Later that evening, I sat on the edge of my bed while the kids argued in the bathroom over teeth brushing etiquette.
Jane was back.

That was some mind-numbing, ectoplasmic shit.

I buried my face in my hands, trying to come to terms with what Jane's return from who-knew-where meant to those of us still breathing oxygen.

Did I tell Mona? Jerry? Ray?

No, definitely not Ray. That would just be more ammunition in the war raging between us.

It was probably a bad idea to mention it to Jerry, too. If he didn't fire me on the spot for temporary insanity, he'd find a way to use Jane's presence to boost ratings on that blasted TV show.

That left Mona, who once had told me she believed in ghosts. But would she believe that it was Jane? Would she wonder how I had figured out Jane was paying us a visit? I couldn't let Doc's secret out, not even to Mona. It was his business to tell, not mine.

I could tell Harvey about it, though.

Aunt Zoe, too. I hadn't mentioned it earlier when she'd called home after settling into her room at the conference hotel. She'd sounded tired. For Reid's sake, I hoped it wasn't from staying up all night horsing around under the covers with her traveling buddy. I'd been too chicken shit to dig for details about her love life and had kept it to chatter about the kids and work, asking only about the convention and how her pieces had faired on the trip down.

What about Cooper?

Cooper … Hmmm. Doc and I had told our secret about playing patty-cake with other worldly beings to the detective a couple of weeks ago, but Cooper hadn't said a peep to me about that conversation since he'd walked away that night. How would he react if I told him Jane was back? Would he laugh? Or would he understand what her return could mean in figuring out how and why she'd ended up in the bottom of Homestake Mine's Open Cut?

I needed to let that one sit on the back of my tongue for a while and see if it started tasting bitter.

"I think they're coming to blows in there," Doc's voice interrupted my internal debate.

Feeling numb inside, I lowered my hands to peek at him over the top of my fingertips. The yelling and slamming of drawers had intensified. It was no wonder Doc had heard it downstairs while he cleaned up after supper.

Dear Lord, what must he be thinking, especially after the way Addy and Layne had misbehaved during supper when they hadn't been giving us the silent treatment. I wouldn't have been surprised midway through our grilled cheese sandwiches and tomato soup if Doc had grabbed his keys and disappeared in a puff of exhaust.

He leaned against the door jamb, a dish towel draped over his shoulder. "Are you up to refereeing the rematch of Hulk Hogan versus 'Macho Man' Randy Savage going on in there? Or would you like me to give it a shot?"

My hands slid the rest of the way down my face in surprise. He wanted to help? "You're willing to risk life and limb by entering that room?"

"I've faced off with scarier beings."

"Yeah, but they weren't rabid."

That made him chuckle.

I stood, hesitant. I didn't want him to feel like I was pushing him into a daddy role, but on the other hand I was curious how he would handle this situation.

"Are you sure you want to do this?" I asked.

It felt like we were taking a big step here in our relationship. As much as I wanted to turn it into a full-on leap, I was afraid that he might realize I was wanting it to be a leap and instead stumble back a few feet.

Frickety-frack, this boyfriend-girlfriend crap was tough. Some days, playing cat and mouse with albino-like killers seemed so much simpler.

Doc's gaze searched mine. "Are we still talking about me breaking up a fight?"

His question told me plenty. I crumpled up the does-he-love-me-enough-to-help-raise-my-hellions daisy I'd been playing with in my head and nodded a little too hard. "Yeah, I just don't want you to feel like I'm asking you to be something you're not … well, something that you don't want to be … I mean, maybe you do want to be it, but not necessarily right now, here, with me … at least not at this very moment … in time."

He raised one eyebrow, his lips quivering on the edge of a smile. "Are you done tiptoeing through that minefield?"

I grabbed my pillow and threw it at him. "Shut up and go deal with my kids."

He bowed and then grabbed my pillow and tossed it back at me. "I'd be happy to, my lady."

Right then Addy let out an ear-clanging scream, sounding like Linda Blair while a priest branded a cross onto her forehead.

Doc glanced down the hall. "I think so, anyway." Concern creased his face when he looked back at me. "Should I take some holy water with me?"

I nodded. "Grab a priest while you're at it."

"Will do." He pushed off the door frame and disappeared from view.

Meanwhile there I sat, wincing, wondering how fast this was going to go south.

I heard the bathroom door close.

Silence followed.

Twisting my hands together, I waited for my two banshees to start shrieking at Doc. For him to come back and ask me to return the key to his house.

All was still.

What did that mean?

I eased out of my bedroom and stole down the hall. Maybe I

should press my ear to the bathroom door to make sure all were still alive inside. Halfway there, the house phone rang downstairs. The extension in Aunt Zoe's bedroom trilled a split second later. I sped past the bathroom door and detoured into her room.

"Hello?" I flicked on the lamp next to her bed, comforted by the exotic fragrance of her favorite perfume lingering in the room.

"Violet Parker?" said a deep, deep voice I didn't quite recognize. The guttural way he said my name made goosebumps pop up on my arms.

"Yeah?" My reply was heavy with trepidation. Maybe being Violet Parker right then was a bad idea.

"There's a viewing Thursday evening for the late Ebenezer Haskell."

"Another Haskell died?" Sheesh, that family had been prolific in death lately. They needed to start a punch card. After ten stiffs they'd receive a free casket.

"Be at Mudder Brothers for the viewing."

"Who is this?" Had somebody given my phone number to a local obituary hotline?

"Do not park in the parking lot."

There was no way this was a legit phone call. "Cornelius, are you messing with me?"

"Dress in disguise."

This definitely had to be Cornelius. Only he would find it amusing to play Trick-or-Treat at a funeral parlor. "Like with a fake moustache and a clown wig?"

"Make sure to hide your hair and face."

My hair? Cornelius rarely commented on my hair, except for that time he had confused me with a poodle wearing sunglasses advertised on the side of a bus. Maybe it was Cooper. The detective had some weird fixation with my hair and not in a good way like Wolfgang. Wait, Wolfgang's obsession with my hair had been pretty twisted, even if he'd told me repeatedly how beautiful it was.

"What do you have against my hair?"

"Do not talk to anyone at the viewing."

This was beginning to sound a lot more like Cooper by the

second, all bossy and emotionally detached. "Can I bring a friend?"

"That would be a bad idea."

"Even if it's Natalie?" I tested, figuring I'd get some reaction to her name if it were Cooper.

"You must come alone."

No hesitation or change in tone. Hmm. "Who is this?"

"You will receive further instructions tomorrow night."

Maybe it was Detective Hawke. He'd found a new way to get me alone so he could badger me with more silly questions while he clicked his stupid-ass pen.

"Listen, I'm not going to that funeral parlor unless you tell me who you are."

"Someone who's concerned about your welfare."

The voice was deeper than Hawke's, though. Maybe he was using one of those voice changers. "That sounds like a corny line from a movie. Try again."

"Someone who fears for your son's life."

I almost swallowed my tongue along with his reply. "That isn't funny."

"I'm not joking."

The line went dead.

"Hello?" I tried anyway.

Game over.

Holy crap!

I raced back to my bedroom, phone still in my hand, passing my two kids in the hall on the way. "Get to bed, Addy."

"I am, Mother," she said to my back. "And don't worry; Elvis is all locked up like a prisoner in the basement."

"Don't talk back, Adelynn Renee." I grabbed Layne by the shoulder and stared down at his face, making sure all freckles were still where they belonged. "What happened to your ear?" It had a scab on it, fresh from the looks of it.

"Nothing."

"It doesn't look like nothing." I tried to turn him so I could see it better.

He tugged free of my grip. "Quit babying me, Mom."

Don't mind me, I thought, watching his stiff shoulders

disappear into his bedroom. I was just trying to keep him alive and breathing.

Where was Doc? I checked the bathroom on the way to my bedroom, finding it empty. He probably went back downstairs. I needed to tell him about that phone call, but before I let panic take the reins, I wanted to check on something.

I tossed the house phone on my bed and grabbed my cellphone from the dresser, dialing Cornelius's number. Amazingly, he answered on the first ring. "I said I wanted a wake-up call at nine-oh-three a.m., not p.m."

"Cornelius, this is Violet."

"Violet who?"

"You know which damned Violet."

"Ah, yes, the one with a temper."

Detective Hawke must have been whispering in his ear. "Did you just call me?"

"Should I have?"

"Just answer the question," I bit out.

"Have you taken your pills tonight, Violet?"

"Cornelius, did you call me a moment ago or not?"

"Not."

"Okay, thanks."

"Did you speak with your tall—"

I hung up on him, not in the mood to chit chat about loud, dead neighbors.

I punched up Cooper's number.

"This better not be about another dead body, Parker."

It sort of was, being that I'd just been ordered to attend another Haskell funeral, but I didn't want to get into that with the detective until he'd answered my question.

I heard the low rumble of conversation in the background, along with the clinking of glasses. It sounded like he was at a bar. "Did you just call me?"

He scoffed. "Contrary to what you think, this world does not revolve around you."

"Whatever. Did you call me or not?"

"Although with that hair of yours, I wouldn't be surprised if it rivaled the moon in gravitational pull."

If only I could reach through the phone and hit him upside the head with a beer bottle. "Just answer the fucking question."

"No."

"Who is that?" I heard a female ask.

Was that Natalie? It didn't sound like her voice. It was smokier and more sexpot-ish like Doc's psycho ex-girlfriend, Tiffany Sugarbell. Tiffany also happened to be a rival agent with a realty company out of Spearfish, and I wouldn't put it past that bloodthirsty bitch to try to steal Cooper and his house away from me as payback for my winning Doc's affection.

"A pain in my ass," Cooper answered whoever it was. "What makes you think I called?" he asked me.

"None of your business." I hung up on him. Damn, that had felt good!

That left Detective Hawke. I hesitated, my finger hovering over his number still located in the received calls queue from the last time he'd called and harassed me with questions. Screw it, I had to know.

"Hawke speaking," he answered almost instantly.

"This is Violet Parker. Did you just call me?"

"No, but I've been wanting to talk to you about—"

I hung up on him, too. Striding over to my window and back, I chewed on my knuckles. Then I saw the other phone next to my pillow. I grabbed it and hit the automatic callback button. It rang and rang and rang.

"Come on," I whispered, back to pacing.

"Yeah?" Someone finally answered.

"Who is this?"

"Jim."

"Jim who?"

"Jim, the sucker who's blowing his savings on a goddamned slot machine that won't pay out. Who's this?"

I could hear the bells and dings of a casino in between Jim's huffs. Whoever had called me must have used a payphone. "This is gambler's anonymous, Jim. What casino are you in?"

"I don't know. The one with Gold in the name. Why? Did my wife call you?"

Crap, it wasn't Cornelius's hotel. Who in the hell had called me? "No, your banker did. Go home to your wife, Jim, and take her some flowers while you're at it." I hung up the phone and tossed it back on my bed.

Now what?

I knew the answer to that—I was going to have to don my funeral attire Thursday night, including a hat and veil this time. Just the thought of that wall of one-way mirrors in Mudder Brothers made me shiver. Who would be watching me from the other side?

"Your kids are in bed waiting for you to say goodnight," Doc said from the hall. When I looked over at him, his expression sobered. He stepped into my room. "What's wrong?"

"Someone called me while you were with the kids."

"Who?"

"I don't know." I gave him a quick replay, doing my best imitation of a deep, scary voice.

"Violet, you're not going to Mudder Brothers alone."

"I can't take Nat or Harvey. People in town know who they are." Not to mention I'd been there before with them. I dropped onto my bed, my legs feeling wobbly now that I'd accepted my fate.

"True." He sat down next to me, taking my clammy hand in his, warming it. "But I doubt anyone will know who I am."

"Doc, it's a funeral parlor." The potential for ghosts aplenty was huge.

"I know."

"A waypoint for the dead. Possibly lots of them."

He squeezed my hand. "Right now, I'm more concerned about the living."

* * *

Wednesday, October 24th

The next morning, I woke to the sound of my phone ringing. Cooper's name showed on the screen. I groaned and sent it to voicemail, in no mood to do any mental jousting before I'd downed some caffeine.

Sitting up, I rubbed the sleep from my eyes. The pillow next to me was empty except for an indent. Doc had been lying on the bed next to me reading that damned book of Jerry's last night when I'd fallen asleep. Where was he now?

I climbed out of bed, heading for the window. His Camaro was still parked in the drive.

Out in the hallway, I could hear the sound of Doc's low voice echoing up the stairwell. The smell of coffee brewing floated along with it. I followed both down to the kitchen and found him leaning against the counter, talking on his cellphone.

He held his finger to his lips when I entered the room and then pointed at his phone. *Cooper*, he mouthed.

"Sure, I'll let Violet know as soon as I talk to her. She's going to want to know why, though."

He listened, his face giving away nothing, so I went over and poured myself a cup of coffee.

"Are you double-checking stories or do you think you missed something last time?"

Nice try, Doc, but I doubted the pissy detective would say anything other than his usual mantra about "police business."

"Really?" Doc replied. "Sounds like a good idea to me."

What!? I set my mug down and crossed my arms, glaring at Doc's phone. No fair. I was the one who saw the dead guy, not Doc. How come Cooper wouldn't share with me?

"Oh, it's definitely still on for tonight," he told Cooper. "It's Reid's turn to bring the beer, right?"

I wrinkled my nose at his phone. I still didn't like how chummy the detective was getting with my boyfriend. I knew Doc was an ace at keeping secrets, but I didn't trust Cooper as far as I could kick him. One slip of the tongue from any of us about that damned shotgun and the detective would be chasing me around Aunt Zoe's front yard with handcuffs at the ready.

"Sure," Doc said, "we can move the game to my place."

So, there'd be no Doc reading me a bedtime story about smiling big for the TV camera tonight. I wondered if Harvey was joining the poker game, too. I wouldn't mind sharing some John Wayne and popcorn with the old buzzard.

"You wish. Plan to be schooled at the poker table, as usual."

I sweetened up my coffee as he signed off with Cooper.

"Morning, Tiger." Doc came up behind me, looping his arms around my middle. "You smell like peaches and cream." He brushed my hair aside and nuzzled my neck. "Cooper wants you to call him as soon as you can."

"Oh, yeah?" With Doc's mouth on me, I had trouble holding onto my urge to hiss at anyone at the moment, even Cooper. "What has him all fired up this morning?"

"He wants to go back out to Harvey's place."

I leaned back into Doc, breathing him in. His aftershave was fresh, his jaw smooth. He must have packed his shaving kit in his overnight bag. "If he's calling for my permission, he has it."

"He wants to take company with him."

"He can take a bus full of tourists for all I care." Especially while Doc's hands were busy stroking my libido awake. "Where did you sleep last night?" I had no memory of him there after the sandman had paid me a visit.

"The couch."

"Why?"

"Just in case the kids woke up in the night." He kissed the nape of my neck, his tongue teasing me.

That was probably smart, since I had trouble not touching him when he was in bed next to me. While my kids knew Doc was my boyfriend now, they hadn't seen us having a slumber party under the sheets yet. I figured it was best to wait on that for a while yet, at least until they stopped freaking out about Doc and me running away into the sunset without them.

"Cooper said to tell you he'd swing by your office at nine-thirty to pick you up."

Talk about a bucket of ice being dumped down my pajama pants. "What?" I turned in Doc's arms, frowning up at him. "Why me?"

"He'll have Harvey with him, too." He snagged my coffee from the counter and took a sip. "Hey, that didn't turn out so bad. It's the first time I've used your aunt's coffeemaker." He held it out for me to try.

I sipped it, liking the taste but not his news. "What if I'm too busy at work to go play Clue with him? Had he thought of that?"

"I doubt it. Cooper has a one-track mind, especially with all of the murders happening around Deadwood and Lead lately. He's even been talking about work during poker."

"Speaking of poker, be careful around that law dog." I explained to Doc about yesterday morning's interrogation at Cooper's house before adding, "I wouldn't be surprised if he tries to ply you for information about that shotgun."

"What shotgun?"

"Harvey's grandpappy's," I said. Hadn't he been listening to me just now?

Oh. Duh. He was playing dumb. I took another sip of coffee. "I need more coffee before my brain is conscious enough to keep up with yours."

"Who wants your brain right now? I'm more interested in what's underneath this." He opened my robe, his gaze soaking up my worn Elvis T-shirt. "I'm jealous of Mr. Presley." His fingers explored the curves of my breasts. "No bra yet, nice."

A thud resounded from overhead.

Doc's hands froze. "What was that?"

"It sounded like a halo hitting the floor."

I heard Addy start yelling something about it being her turn in the bathroom.

"Yep, one of the angels is awake."

"Damn." Doc pulled his hands away, tying my robe shut.

"I'M BRUSHING MY TEETH!" I heard Layne yell and then a door slammed.

"Make that two angels. Hey, that reminds me, what kind of voodoo did you use on them last night to stop their fighting and get them into bed without complaining?"

He winked. "I can't give away my secrets."

"I guess I'll have to seduce it out of you."

"You should definitely try."

I pulled his mouth down to mine, enjoying a quick kiss before Addy and Layne joined us and the shouting began. "Thanks for staying the night."

"You owe me a massage, Boots."

"MOM!!!" Addy hollered down the stairwell. "Layne is hogging the bathroom, and I need to wash my hair today!"

"I'll deliver when we finish the book." I patted Doc's chest. "You should run while you can."

"And miss out on all of the excitement? I don't think so." He pushed me in the direction of the dining room. "I'll get some grub ready. You go round up the herd."

The rest of the morning went off as usual—filled with accusations, dirty looks, and a lot of teeth grinding. Geez-oh-pete, it were as if my two munchkins were trying to win the award for the worst behaved children on the planet. Doc probably wouldn't last the year at this rate. I could only imagine what he thought of my parenting skills up to this point in their lives.

After saying goodbye to Doc, who was heading back down to Spearfish today, I dropped Addy and Layne off at school. Everyone was in the office but Ray when I walked in. I dropped my purse on the floor next to my desk, scanning the room, wondering if Jane were there, too.

"Violet?" Jerry called from his office. "Can you come here for a moment?"

I hesitated in his doorway, not sure if he wanted me to step inside, not sure if I wanted to. Maybe it was just my imagination, but I could swear I picked up a hint of the floral and vanilla bouquet of Jane's perfume along with Jerry's usual cologne.

"I got a call from Detective Cooper this morning."

I pressed my lips tight. Cooper had been quite a little busybody lately. He must have eaten two bowls of Wheaties for breakfast, the overachiever. "Really?"

"He was looking for you. Said he has some spare time this morning and would like you to show him some houses outside of town. What's your schedule look like today?"

If Cooper had gone so far as to try to clear a path with my boss, I'd better go along with his plan. "It's open."

"Great." He leaned back in his chair. "Did you get a chance to read the book I left you?"

"Yes," I sort of lied. I'd listened to some of it, anyway.

"Good! I really want Ben and you to knock the viewing public off their feet."

"I'm going to give it my best," I assured him.

At his nod, I turned to leave. "Oh, one more thing, Violet." His voice stopped me. I looked back. "Did you happen to notice anything odd before you locked up last night?"

Besides his dead ex-wife floating here and there? Officially, I hadn't noticed her; Doc had. "No, why?"

He pointed at the corner of his office. "When I came in this morning, the stack of papers I had sitting on that file cabinet were strewn all over the place. It was like a mini-tornado had come through."

Or a pissed off ghost. Why had Jane messed with the papers? "Hmmm. That's odd. Maybe a breeze came through the back door when one of us was leaving. Your lights were off when I left, so I didn't really look in here."

"Could be." He rubbed his square jaw. "All right. Good luck this morning with Detective Cooper. Let me know if there is anything I can do to help."

I left him frowning at the file cabinet, his rock-hewn face sporting an almost funny befuddled look.

Welcome to the club, Jerry.

A half hour later, Cooper waited for me out back in a Deadwood police SUV. "So much for being inconspicuous, Detective," I muttered and climbed into the back seat. "It smells like bacon in here."

Harvey let out a howl of laughter. Cooper shot me with a glare. "Keep it up, Parker, and I'll keep driving south and drop you off at the Nebraska state line."

"I'm serious." I leaned forward and sniffed. "Did you make bacon for breakfast, Harvey?"

"Sure as shootin', I did." Harvey half-turned in his seat, both of his gold teeth showing in his grin. "Who put that rosy color in your cheeks already today?"

Doc, of course, but I wasn't going to let that cat out of the bag after Doc had pretended not to be standing next to me when Cooper had called earlier. "It's called blush."

"If you say so." He checked out my long indigo skirt and dark red velvet tunic. "But you look a lot more like you do now than you did when you was you a while ago."

As hard as I tried, I couldn't make a lick of sense of that.

"What does that even mean, Harvey?"

"He's complimenting you," Cooper interpreted and then pulled out onto the main drag. "Where were you this morning, Parker?"

"In the shower." I didn't even try to deny that I knew he'd called. "I figured you'd hunt me down eventually."

Harvey snorted in agreement. "Cooper could track a bumblebee while blindfolded in a blizzard."

It sounded as if both men had doubled up on their Wheaties. "How much coffee have you had this morning, Harvey?"

"He woke up this way," Cooper said. "Like a ray of sunshine," he added, not sounding too happy about it.

"Sleepin' at Coop's is good for me." Harvey reached over and tweaked his nephew's ear, which earned him a scowl. "I'm feelin' happy as a pig in a peach orchard now that I'm retired."

Cooper slipped me a frown in the rearview mirror.

Harvey may be kicking up his heels now, but a blind mouse could sense that Cooper was wanting to kick something else. That was even more incentive for me to keep a safe distance from the detective.

As Cooper was starting up Strawberry Hill, I realized that we were missing someone. "Do you want me to call Natalie and have her meet us at Harvey's?"

"No!" Cooper's response was quick and sharp.

"Your fangs startin' to itch, boy?"

"Sorry," he said to me in the mirror, "but I don't need Ms. Beals with us today. You two will be enough trouble."

Harvey kept us entertained while we rode out to his ranch, telling us about some adventures he'd had years back over in Idaho's Owyhee County with a rancher's daughter who liked to ride bareback, "… if you two know what I mean." Wink, wink.

Cooper and I groaned in unison.

Not soon enough, we pulled into Harvey's driveway. All was quiet on the creepy front, nothing moving about but the wind.

Cooper led us into the house first, walking us through one room after the next. He asked about the shotgun, that morning's events upon arrival, what we'd been wearing, what we'd had for breakfast, the last time we'd visited Harvey's place, how long we'd stood in each room, and on and on. It was his own hellish version of Twenty Questions.

When we finished in the house, we moved out to the barn and started the game all over again.

Several times Cooper asked us about the shotgun, each time in a slightly different manner. Every time Harvey and I tiptoed carefully around the truth with our answers.

The old safe was empty this time, of course, but I still cringed when Cooper opened it. He reached into his pants pocket and pulled out something that he held out for Harvey to see.

"This tin tag look familiar?" he asked his uncle.

Harvey leaned in close, his bushy eyebrows sewing together. "Sure does." He poked at the small, rectangular shaped piece of metal. "Must've fallen off grandpappy's gun somehow or t'other."

"And it just happened to land in this old bank safe way out here in the barn?"

"If that's where you found it, I'm guessin' so."

Cooper glared at Harvey, then me. "You two must think I'm an idiot."

"Can't say I've ever used that particular noun when referring to you," I answered honestly. "Detective Hawke is a whole other case, though."

Cooper's nostrils flared. He led us over to the barn wall, pointing out some indents in the wood. "Rock salt," he said to his uncle in particular.

Harvey did a great job of twiddling with his beard, playing dumb. "Yup, sure looks like it."

"Fresh, too. We pulled the crystals out before they dissolved due to the weather."

"Well, this sure is one big, head-scratchin' pickle you got here, Coop."

"I'd like to remind you this is *your* ranch, Uncle Willis," he said, and then he started to drill me on the indents.

I raised my hands, giving up before he got his teeth sunk in. "I don't know anything about rock salt. I've only ever shot slugs and pellets."

Back outside under the clear, brisk October sky, Cooper led us around the side of the barn.

"We found the chain and padlock," he told us as we followed him back to where a couple of smaller buildings stood. "They were in the tall weeds by the corner of the barn."

"Did somebody take bolt cutters to the lock?" I asked.

"No, it was ripped apart."

"The lock?"

"Two of the links. The chain was busted into two pieces. The padlock was still intact."

What kind of tool could rip chain links apart? Weren't those usually welded tight?

"Why in tarnation are ya draggin' us back here for, Coop?"

"Since you two nosey nellies are always showing up at my crime scenes, you're going to help me for once." Cooper looked from one building to the next. "We'll start with searching the outhouse for anything suspect."

The outhouse proved fruitless, thankfully. I kept my distance while Harvey and Cooper checked it out.

"How about you come stick your hand down the hole, Parker," Cooper suggested, sharing a smirk with his uncle. "See if you can find anything fresh for the evidence room."

I crossed my arms over my chest. "How about I shove my boot up where you have that stick jammed, Detective?"

Harvey hooted at that one. "You gotta watch Violet, boy. She's got some real snap in her garters."

Next to the outhouse was the old chicken coop where Harvey told us his mom had kept her prized egg-laying hens. He led the way inside.

Cooper brought up the rear ... as in my rear. "Get your ass inside, Parker. I'd like to get back down to Deadwood before lunch."

If I'd been a mule, I'd have planted both back hooves in the detective's bread basket right then.

Inside, the smell of fermenting chicken feed still lingered in the dust-filled air.

"Could you actually take a few steps inside?" Cooper pushed me further into the old building.

"I'm wearing suede boots, Detective. They are not appropriate footwear for wading through chicken poop."

"Quit being such a girl." He pointed at the stack of nesting boxes against the far wall. "You two search those," he ordered, forgetting we weren't on his payroll. "See if someone left anything behind."

Butthead! "I'll send you the cleaning bill." I waded in on my tiptoes, stepping between the ancient leftovers. The closer I got, the more I knew there was no way I was shoving my arm into those boxes, not while wearing one of Aunt Zoe's favorite velvet shirts.

Luckily for me, Harvey had no qualms about getting his clothes dirty. He began checking in the hens' nesting boxes one at a time.

Cooper nudged me aside. "Move aside, killer."

I frowned after him. "What did you call me?"

"Killer." He tapped on floorboards, listening in between taps. "Uncle Willis, didn't there used to be a few loose boards somewhere around here?"

"Why would you call me that?"

Tap, tap. "Because you like to beat up people."

Oh, whew, just that. I jammed my hands on my hips. "Dear Lord, are we back to you whining about your broken nose?"

"Not just my nose. What about your boyfriend's face?"

"Doc likes it when she's rough." Harvey said, reaching into another one of the boxes. "You should've seen the scratches on that boy's back a couple of weeks ago."

My jaw fell open, my face instantly overheating. "I did not … where did you see … how do you know those are from me?"

Harvey snickered. "It doesn't take a detective's badge to figure out who marked him. Your bite bruises were what had me hornswoggled. What do you think you are? Part vampire?"

"I did not leave any teeth marks."

"Ha! Gotcha."

Cooper grinned at his uncle. "Real slick. I should have you interrogate her for me after her next crime."

I brushed away chicken feathers that were trying to stick to my velvet shirt, pretending I wasn't sweating in humiliation. "If you two are done having a laugh at my expense, I'm going back outside."

"Hold your horses, Sparky." Harvey grunted and reached up to his shoulder in one of the hen boxes. "Look what I found."

He pulled out a black bottle, similar to the one I'd seen in the old picture Doc had shown me recently.

"Hey," I stepped through the chicken poop. "That looks like the bottles I saw in that crate at Mudder Brothers."

Cooper took the bottle from Harvey, holding it up to the light coming through the cobweb-encrusted window. "It's full."

I took it from Cooper, sniffing at the cork, smelling nothing but chicken dust. I'd probably be sneezing downy feathers for days. "You think it's full of mead, too?"

The detective didn't answer. When I looked up at him, his

gray eyes were all squinty with suspicion.

"How do you know what was in those bottles in the crate, Parker? If memory serves me right, you used one as a weapon but never actually popped the cork."

Hells bells!

I'd been so set on keeping the shotgun a secret that I'd forgotten to lock the door on all of my other closeted skeletons.

I shoved the bottle back at Cooper. "Lucky guess."

"Bullshit."

"I was just using the same trick on you that Harvey used on me a moment ago."

"Bullshit."

"You already said that, and technically, we are standing in chicken shit."

"Parker," he took a step closer, gunning down that crooked nose at me. "How do you know the bottles from Mudder Brothers contained mead?"

The door to the chicken coop slammed open.

I screeched and flew behind Harvey, feathers flying in my wake.

Detective Stone Hawke's broad shoulders filled the doorway. "What in the hell is going on in here?"

"Fuck," Cooper growled under his breath, tucking the bottle behind his back.

"You're late for the hen party," Harvey said, thumbs in his suspenders, fat grin filling his cheeks. "Now get to strippin', boy. Me and Sparky here got plenty of ones burnin' holes in our pockets."

Chapter Seven

Meanwhile, back at the ranch …

A fox had gotten into the hen house and his name was Detective Stone Hawke.

Before I had a chance to squeeze out through one of the small chicken-sized doors in Harvey's old shack and scramble down the rooster ramp, Cooper hauled me out from behind Harvey and shoved me toward our intruder.

"Hawke, don't you have some questions for Parker?"

I glared at Cooper, who still had that bottle of mead tucked behind his back. "Really?"

The no-good son of a bitch was throwing me to the wolves … or rather the fox, in this case. Actually, Detective Hawke was more like his namesake, with that darting gaze and regal nose. Whatever he was, there were now too many animals of prey crammed into this coop for my tail feathers not to get ruffled. I snorted, partly because I had tufts of chicken feathers up my nose, but mostly out of frustration with both brutes.

Detective Hawke bristled with suspicion, his thick black unibrow getting all squiggly. "Yes, I do, but first, what are you doing out here at your uncle's ranch with these two suspects?"

"They aren't suspects." Cooper's words were clipped.

Hawke jutted his square jaw, his pork chop sideburns framing his perturbed expression. "Did you clear it with the Chief first?"

Ah ha! Not only was Cooper hiding the bottle we found from his partner, he'd also not shared that he was dragging Harvey and me out here to investigate the crime scene further. It didn't take a relationship counselor to deduce that these re-partnered ex-partners were experiencing some serious communication problems. Their reconciliation was no longer all smiley faces and happy skipping.

Before Cooper had a chance to answer Hawke's questions, Natalie's head poked around the doorway. Her smile split wide at the sight of all of us. "Hey! What's going on in here?"

Harvey rocked back on his heels. "It's a hen party."

"Count me in." Natalie rolled right along with him. "Who's stripping first?"

"We're about to flip for it. Heads for Coop, tails for Hawke. What's your call?"

"Heads, definitely." Her focus shifted to Cooper. "Vi and I made a bet about your nephew, and I bet my favorite hooker heels that I'm right."

No, she wasn't. But now was not the time to prove her wrong. I had an opportunity to escape from Detective Hawke's talons, and it had everything to do with Natalie's ability to wrap macho jerks with inflated egos, like the blockhead standing in front of me, around her pinkie finger.

"I think I'm going to be sick." I waved my hand under my nose, acting out a swoon. "Get me out of here." I grabbed Detective Hawke by the arm of his tan corduroy blazer and dragged him outside with me.

I cast Natalie a come-hither look as we stepped down next to her.

She nodded, linking her arm in mine. "How about the three of us take a little walkabout and get you some fresh air." She waved at Hawke to follow.

He frowned back at the chicken coop, where Harvey stood in the doorway, thumbs in his suspenders, and then jogged to catch up to us.

"Let's get out of this wind." I continued around the side of the barn and out of sight of the chicken shed.

Cooper was going to owe me, damn it. For whatever reason, he did not want his partner to know what we'd been up to and what we'd found. While I doubted he was hiding something from Hawke to save my ass, it might have something to do with Harvey. Cooper's reply about us not being suspects had cemented my decision to help the bossy detective. But I deserved at least one get-out-of-jail-free in exchange for my part.

In the driveway, Natalie's truck was parked behind Cooper's police SUV, while Hawke's sedan cozied up beside them both on the grass.

"That's far enough." Hawke dropped anchor, bringing Natalie and me to a stop in front of the barn doors Cooper had left open.

The detective glanced at the barn and then back at me, stepping closer so that he was practically bumping toes with me. I'd managed to avoid the butthead for long enough that I'd forgotten about his lack of respect for personal space.

"What are you three doing out here, Ms. Parker? This place is off limits, especially to you."

Please, as if I were going to roll over and show him my belly that easily. I held my ground. "A better question is what are you two doing out here?"

Natalie pointed at Hawke. "He called me last night, saying he needed me to answer some questions about what happened here Sunday, and you were unavailable."

"That's because your friend here hung up on me again." Hawke explained to Natalie.

"I was a little preoccupied last night when we spoke." I had a creepy caller to track down, darn it. "I didn't have time for your questions, Detective."

"You never seem to have time." He crossed his arms over his chest, still standing so close that he almost whopped me in the boob with his elbow. "Maybe if I hauled you into the station, Ms. Parker, you'd find a moment or two."

"Bad idea." I lifted my chin, wanting to step back and put some space between me and that minty-stinking cologne of his, but I figured he'd take that as a sign of weakness. "Unless you have a warrant for my arrest, I'd advise against it."

"Anyway," Natalie wedged herself between us, which was a feat in itself. "Detective Hawke asked me to meet him here since it was halfway between the station and my parents' place and I agreed."

I eased back a couple of steps. Was it only yesterday that she'd called requesting a raincheck on supper, saying she wanted to help her dad winterize the house before the weather took a turn? Where had the time gone between spine-chilling phone calls and searches for clues about a dead man?

I glanced toward the side of the barn—still no sign of Cooper and Harvey. I needed to keep Hawke busy a little longer. "Fine, let's get this over with, Detective. Where's that damned pen and notebook of yours?"

Hawke took his sweet ass time with the paper, watching me warily as he clicked his pen. "Why did you have Detective Cooper haul you out here?"

Why did I have ... What made Hawke think I was the instigator for this visit? Oh, right—his witch theory. The dear, confused bozo. Did he actually think I'd cast some spell over the mighty Detective Cooper and coerced him out here to do my wicked bidding? As if there were anything short of a noose along with its accompanying lynch mob that could drag Cooper somewhere he didn't want to go.

I thought about blowing on my knuckles and telling Hawke it was all in a day's work for a witch as powerful as the nefarious Violet Parker, but Cooper's warning about not taking Hawke's witch suspicions lightly made me hold my tongue. While I was pretty sure playing it up wouldn't end with me barbecuing on a stake, Hawke could do his darnedest to make my day-to-day travels very bumpy, and I had enough washboard-filled roads in my life as it was.

I focused on Natalie. "Didn't you tell Detective Hawke about me yet?"

Her face lit up like the prairie grass at sunrise. "I didn't think he could handle it straight up," she shot back.

"Handle what?" he asked.

"The truth," she answered.

I moved closer to her, speaking out of the side of my mouth. "Maybe this isn't such a good idea, Nat. It might really freak him out."

She put her arm around my shoulder and led me a short hop away. "I think Detective Hawke can handle this." She kept her voice loud enough for him to eavesdrop. "I mean, look at him." We both turned and measured him for a few beats. Hawke lowered the notepad, shuffling his loafers. "He's so big and strong and manly," she flirted, wiggling her fingers at him.

He frowned back.

"Vi, surely a rugged detective like him has seen some real kooky stuff in his line of work."

I had to turn my face away from Hawke so he couldn't see while I wrestled my grin back into submission.

Natalie nudged me with her elbow.

"I know, I know," I said under my breath and pretended to cough. Schooling my expression, I faced Hawke again. "But can we trust him?"

Hawke grabbed his belt with both hands. He took on that wide-legged stance I suspected he'd learned at the academy in: How To Look Like A Cop 101. "Ladies, I'm a detective. Classified is my middle name. Now spill."

Natalie led us back over. "Okay, Detective Hawke, but you have to swear not to tell a soul—not even your partner."

"You have my oath of silence."

Natalie and I looked at each other. I waited for her to come up with something hilariously brilliant.

"Tell him, Vi." She passed me the baton, damn her.

I hesitated. What could I say? That I was a vampire? Wasn't that what Harvey had accused me of back in the chicken coop? No, that was too over the top. Although, after Hawke's silly witch theory, maybe a vampire wasn't such a stretch. On second thought, the dumbass might just try to jam a stake in my chest.

What then? I had to think quickly, time was ticking, and Hawke was eyeing me with plenty of disbelief.

Natalie implored me with raised brows. "It's okay, he gave us his oath."

I resisted the urge to flick her nose. She was supposed to help me on this.

All right, what was something totally wacky that Hawke might believe with enough decent acting on my part? Something that even I might believe if it were acted out in front of me?

Then it hit me.

Prudence.

Lord only knew I'd had my fair share of witnessing her

peculiarities up close and personal.

I crooked my finger at Hawke. He and Natalie leaned in close, their heads almost touching.

"I can talk to ghosts," I deadpanned.

Natalie curled her lips in tight. I suspected they were damming a flood of laughter, judging from the sparkle in her eyes.

"You're pulling my leg, Ms. Parker." He tucked his notepad and pen back into his pocket.

"I wish I was, Detective. Trust me, this ability is no gift." I channeled Doc from months ago when he fessed up about his sixth sense. "I've tried everything, from large quantities of hard liquor to a handful of recreational drugs, but I can't stop the voices."

Hawke wore his skepticism like a mask. He wouldn't be an easy sell on this, I could tell. It was going to take some time and finesse, both of which I lacked most days.

"So," he pushed out his chest, impersonating a wall of disbelief, "am I to believe that the reason you have been involved one way or another in all of these murder cases around here is because you talk to the dead?"

"Exactly," Natalie jumped in. "You can't imagine how hard it has been for Vi—for both of us—to keep this hidden from everyone."

"Come on." Hawke smirked at us in turn. "You really think I'm that big of an idiot? That I would buy this load of phony baloney?"

"I told you this was a mistake," I said to Natalie.

"There are no such things as ghosts," Hawke added.

Yeah, I used to drink that flavor of Kool-Aid, too, but then I met Doc ... and Prudence.

Natalie gave me a sideways hug. "It's okay, sweetie. You were honest. We both know in our hearts that someday the truth will set you free."

I thought about dredging up some tears, but I didn't have it in me at the moment to crank on the waterworks.

"If you are truly hearing voices, Ms. Parker, it's probably because you are either delusional or borderline schizophrenic. As

I was just telling Detective Cooper last week, both mental conditions should be noted in your file as a possibility."

His snide tone made me want to flip a personality switch and go Lizzie Borden on him. Delusional or schizophrenic? Name calling was the game he wanted to play, huh? And here I was just going to have a little fun with this ghost talking act, but after facing off for a few huffs with his condescending gaze, I had a change of heart.

I stepped closer to Hawke, invading his space as he so often did mine. Lowering my chin, I stared up at him through my eyebrows like I'd seen done in many creepy films over the years. "Tell me, Detective, have you ever looked in a mirror and chanted, 'Bloody Mary' three times?"

He smirked. "Why would I do that?"

Natalie knew the answer from one of our favorite Halloween childhood tricks. "It's a well-known fact," she told him in a spooky voice, "that if you chant 'Bloody Mary' in a mirror three times in a candlelit room, her bloody corpse will appear behind you."

"Depending on her mood," I continued, faking a shoulder twitch, "she'll either try to scratch your eyes out, strangle you, or steal your soul."

"That sounds like an old wives' tale," he said, but his smirk was gone.

I reached out and scraped my fingernails down his blazer. The corduroy made for a nice sound effect. "Are you sure, Detective?" I twitched again, throwing in a little hitching laugh. "How about you join me some moonless night in a haunted house and we test it out?"

"There is no such thing as a ... haunted house." His mouth said one thing, but he hesitated.

He should pay a visit to Prudence up in Lead. "If you say so, Detective." I grabbed one of the big brown buttons on his blazer and yanked on it, tearing it off.

He jerked away in surprise. "Hey!"

I held the button in front of my eyes, peering at him through the tiny thread holes. "I like to keep souvenirs," I said in a creepy little girl voice and followed it with a squeaky, high-pitched giggle.

"Parker!" Cooper hollered, rounding the front of the barn, interrupting my ghost story. He strode our way, his eyes narrowing as he took in our trio huddled together. "What's going on here?"

I looked at Hawke. "Shhhh. He doesn't know."

"What don't I know?" Cooper stopped next to his partner. He must have his bat-hearing cranked up today.

"About Violet's fear of the dark," Natalie said.

"She has nyctophobia," Hawke went along with us, staring down at my fist that still clasped his button.

Cooper glared at his partner's profile. "Parker is not afraid of the dark."

"I am, too." At least I was now that there were things in it that I couldn't rationally explain away.

"What in the hell are you playing at?" Cooper asked me.

Uh oh. I didn't think I had the acting skills to pull this off in front of Cooper, too.

I turned to Natalie. "Would you be so kind as to allow me a moment with Cooper?"

Natalie wrapped her hand around Hawke's bicep, patting it like he was straight from Muscle Beach. "Detective, didn't you have some questions you wanted to ask me?" She tugged him away from Cooper and me, leading him toward the house. "How about we take a walk around the ranch while we talk in private?"

She led him off as easy as the Pied Piper. Cooper and I watched them go, me with a sigh of relief, him with a growl in his throat.

"What in the hell is that about?"

I shrugged. "He called her last night and arranged a meeting here today, wanted to ask her a few questions about Sunday."

Cooper growled again.

"You seem to be stuck on repeater mode today. Where's your uncle?"

"Going through the tool shed, looking for more bottles. We found four stashed in those hen boxes after you left."

"I didn't leave, Detective. You sacrificed me for your own gain."

"If you're gonna play with the big boys, you need to get thicker skin."

"Well, if you're gonna play with the big girls, you need to grow a set of ..." *darn, he already had balls,* "claws."

The lines on his face softened. "Can we not talk about your sex life anymore, Parker? I don't want to spoil my lunch."

I started to hit him back with something about at least having a sex life, but I wasn't feeling that rabid at the moment, especially while Cooper was watching Natalie fawn over Hawke as they disappeared behind the house. Although, from the sound of the woman's voice coming through my phone last night, he might have one, too. Just not with Natalie.

"When you're done sputtering over there," he continued, "care to explain to me off the record how you knew there was mead in those bottles at Mudder Brothers?"

Instead of answering, I lobbed a question back at him. "Why did you hide the bottle Harvey found in the hen box from your partner?"

"That's not your concern."

"You tell me your secret, I'll tell you mine."

"Hey," Harvey called from the front corner of the barn. He waved us over. "You two are gonna wanna come see what I just found."

Cooper took off toward his uncle at full stride. I hustled after him, my stomach fluttery at the pinched look on Harvey's face.

"Did you find more bottles?" I asked as I fell in step next to Harvey, who led us toward the one building I hadn't been in before.

"Nope. I found somethin' a bit hairier."

"Like what?"

He held the door for us and then walked over to a section of the wooden floor that was missing some boards. A crowbar and several planks had been tossed next to the gaping hole.

I let Cooper go first, happy to play second fiddle.

"Is it a body?" I asked, wincing my way closer.

There was something furry at the bottom of a pit.

Several things furry, actually.

Cooper pulled his pen from his pocket. "I don't think so."

He leaned partway into the hole and poked one of the hairy tufts.

It didn't roll over and bite him, thank the heavens.

Harvey held out a hay-baling hook. "This here'd make a good fishin' hook."

Cooper took it.

What he pulled up made me recoil. "What in the hell is that thing?"

"I'm not one hundred percent sure," Cooper spun the hook this way and that, "but it looks like a mask."

It was the kind of mask worn completely over the head with a neck attached to it and all.

"That reminds me of something Lon Chaney Jr. would have worn during the filming of *The Wolf Man*," I whispered, stepping closer, trying to make sense of it along with Cooper. "Do either of you two remember any reports of Sasquatch sightings in the Black Hills?"

"No." Cooper sat back on his heels, holding the mask out toward his uncle. "Well, what do you think?"

"That's not mine." Harvey leaned over the hole, pointing into it. "Neither are all t'others down there."

Chapter Eight

Thursday, October 25th

Meanwhile, back in Deadwood …

I spent the night running from the wolf man. Only it was Detective Hawke instead of Lon Chaney Jr. chasing me, and the mask looked more like what Cooper had pulled up from the floor cache in Harvey's shed than the furry faced old movie version. The sideburns were Hawke's, though, along with the unibrow and the obnoxious personality.

After dragging my tired ass to the shower, I scrubbed off my nightmare sweat. If only I could wash away the qualms I had about all of those masks as easily.

Cooper had found eight in all, each a little too realistic for my comfort. Harvey had sniffed and inspected each mask, much to my gasps and screeches of disgust, declaring one after the other had real human hair. After the third mask and my third mention of lice and fleas and Lord knew what else might be living on those masks, Cooper demoted me to watchdog and made me go stand in the doorway.

We'd managed to hide the masks back in the cache and return to the front of the barn before Hawke and Natalie returned from their walkabout. I sneaked a thumbs up at Natalie when Hawke wasn't looking. She returned a thumbs down and then pointed at me and mocked strangling me to death.

If that was how she felt after a half hour in Hawke's company, she was going to love going out on a date with him and prying his lips open with alcohol and whatever else it took (otherwise known as Plan B).

That had been the end of our adventures at the ranch for one day. Compared to all of that heart palpitating fun, sitting at my desk back at the office had been a real sleep inducer. With Doc down in Spearfish all day and then having the guys over for poker that night, I was reduced to texting a few words about the masks and the bottles of mead, telling him to call when the poker game ended and I'd fill him in with the details.

By the next morning, he still hadn't called. I'd decided not to read anything into his silence other than the guys had been there late, and he was being considerate of my ongoing need for beauty sleep.

The quiet lasted through breakfast, what with the kids still not speaking to me. After my night of full moon hunts and terrorizing howls, I was happy to let my eyes glaze over while I looked out the kitchen window at Aunt Zoe's glass workshop.

Ah, sweet, soothing silence. No fighting, no yelling, no guilt trips for ruining anyone's life by letting a kind, helpful, handsome man come into our world. I could get used to living in this foreign land brimming with peace and tranquility.

After I dropped off my muted kids, I made a detour on the way to work and stopped at the Tin Cup Café. I needed an excuse to call Doc and find out how poker went with Cooper and his hundreds of questions—a way to butt into Doc's evening's events so I didn't sound like the nosy girlfriend that I was. I paused outside the coffee joint's front door, soaking up a ray of warm sunshine on this chilly morning, and pulled up Doc's number.

Three rings in, he answered. "Morning, Violet." Doc used my name instead of one of my nicknames. How odd.

I double checked that I'd called the right guy, and then stayed my original course "I'm grabbing some coffee, you want one?"

"Definitely. The game ran late last night. Make it a double, please."

That confirmed my suspicions regarding the lack of a phone call. I heard a male voice say something inaudible in the background, and then the sound of a door closing. "You still at the gym?"

"I skipped it this morning."

If he wasn't at the gym, what was with that voice and the door? Maybe I self-prophesized my future and really could hear ghosts now.

"Are you at home still?"

"Yep."

"Is somebody there with you?"

"Cooper just left."

"You mean Detective Cooper?"

"That's the one."

"Did you win a breakfast from him in last night's game?"

"Hey, there's an idea for a wager." I heard some shuffling sounds through the line. "He spent the night."

"So, are you two romantically involved now or was it a slumber poker party?" Both ideas made me giggle.

"You must've downed a cup of smartass for breakfast, sweetheart." He waited until I'd quieted to explain. "Cooper didn't want to drive home, so he crashed on my couch."

"Hold on." I closed my eyes and leaned back against the brick wall fronting the building. "I'm picturing you and Cooper having a pillow fight in your pajamas."

Actually, in my fantasy Doc was beating the crap out of a fully uniformed Cooper with a couch pillow and then handcuffing the detective and kicking him outside. I added the slamming of the front door for an encore.

"How about picturing you sans pajamas having a slumber party with me? If you want to wear one of those silky camisoles I peeled off you last time you spent the night, I have no problem with that, either."

"What? No pillow fighting with me?"

"Naked pillow fights are completely acceptable. You'll inspire me to invest heavily in the goose down market."

"Naked? You have a one track mind, Mr. Nyce."

"When it comes to your skin, Boots, I'm a real train wreck."

"Will I need a reservation to bunk at La Casa de Doc now?"

"There's always room in my bed for you."

But was there room in his life for a killer and her two offspring plus one annoying chicken?

"I'm on my way out the door." I heard the slam of a door as soon as his words were out. "I need to head down to Spearfish after I grab something from my office. How about I meet you in the parking lot in a few?"

"Sure. I'll be the one carrying two coffees."

"Great. I'll be the one drooling over the hot blonde carrying two coffees."

When he said stuff like that, it made me want to bite and scratch him all over again.

Doc was leaning against the trunk of his Camaro when I pulled into the parking lot behind Calamity Jane Realty. He looked stark raving handsome in his black pants and leather jacket over a cream button-up shirt. He opened my door, taking the drink carrier from me and setting it on top of the old pickup.

My boots had barely touched the ground when he pulled me close.

"Morning." He kissed off the lip gloss I'd just applied on the way between the Tin Cup Café and work. "Mmmm, cherry-flavored Violet lips. My favorite."

I stepped aside so he could close the pickup's door and grab his coffee from the carrier. "Let's go into your office, and I'll give you another one of your favorites."

He blew out a breath. "Damn, Boots. You're not playing fair today. I'm running late already."

Sipping my coffee, I gave him a sly wink. "All work and no play makes Doc a randy boy."

That made him chuckle. "I was thinking last night about that massage you owe me."

"Oh, were you?"

"And this morning," Doc added.

"While you were eating breakfast with Cooper?"

"No. I was too busy dodging his questions about you and that bottle of mead then."

I grimaced. "Sorry about that."

"He told me about your find in the chicken coop out at Harvey's place."

"Did he tell you that he hid the bottle from Detective Hawke, along with those masks?"

"He mentioned the masks but nothing about his partner."

"I think he's keeping stuff from Hawke now."

"Why would he do that?"

"You tell me. You're the one who spent the night with him."

"Yeah, but he doesn't talk much in his sleep."

"Are the rumors true? Does Cooper's teddy bear sleep with a loaded pistol, too?"

"No, it's a 12-gauge." Doc leaned down and teased me with his mouth for a few breathless beats. "Gotta go, Tiger. I'll be at your place in time for dinner. Then we can head to Mudder Brothers and find out who's stalking my girlfriend this time."

"Happy number adding."

He waved as he backed out of his parking spot and then rumbled away.

I whistled "Dixie" all of the way to Calamity Jane's door.

"Violet." Jerry didn't even let me make it past his office. "Will you tell the others we need to huddle up. I'll be out there in two shakes."

Huddling for Jerry meant that all of us sat at our circled desks while he held court in the center like a head coach who'd called a timeout to direct us on our next play.

I nodded and joined my three coworkers out front, delivering his message while I tucked my purse in my desk. I settled into my chair, coffee in one hand, pen and paper in the other, and waited to get my huddle on.

Was that even a saying?

Jerry didn't disappoint. "Okay, team. I just got off the phone with Honey, Dickie's assistant."

We all knew who Honey was. Unlike her golden sounding name, she had straight black hair, resembling Cher more than Goldie Hawn. Honey was nice enough but not super sweet like her namesake, and she pretty much ran the show while Dickie acted as the front man. I hadn't figured out yet if she ran his personal life as well as his professional life, but Dickie did tend to spend more time than normal admiring her long hair and even longer legs.

"Honey said they would be arriving tomorrow with their crew. They'll spend the weekend prepping for the show and plan to start filming on Monday."

Eek, Monday. That would be here before I knew it. I took a big drink of coffee, wishing I'd spiked it with some Baileys this morning.

Jerry pointed at me. "Violet, you'll run the first play."

"What exactly does that entail?"

While I was getting better at deciphering Jerry's sports metaphors, not having seen the play board, I didn't know if that meant taking something to "the hole" or passing whatever off to Ben, Ray, or Mona.

"Leading Dickie and his film crew around The Prospector Hotel."

Hold the phone! Did he just say ... "Come again?"

"You know. Your most recently sold property," Jerry added. "You're still on good terms with Mr. Curion, right?"

"We still keep in touch." And some days I felt like reaching through the phone and strangling Cornelius.

"I need you to pay him a visit, tell him about the upcoming Paranormal Realty filming, and see if he'd like some free publicity for his new acquisition."

"But that hotel is not on the list of places we came up with for Dickie's crew to film." I knew that for a fact because I'd purposely left it out, knowing how eccentric its owner was ninety-nine percent of the time.

"I added it to the list," Ray spoke up.

That earned him a glare. "Without consulting me first?"

"You're the talent, Blon—Violet. Your job is to make Calamity Jane Realty look good on camera." He tried to hide his sneer behind his tooth-whitened smile. "My job is to make the location look even better. The Old Prospector Hotel is a well-known haunt in the Black Hills. It's the perfect location to get the ball off the sidelines and score out of the gate with a three pointer."

The horse's ass knew how off the bell curve Cornelius was. Hell, he had even gone so far as to try to woo Cornelius away from me after Ray's attempt to secure a different buyer ended in a catastrophic fail.

I looked at Jerry, whose hair was freshly buzzed since I'd seen him last. "Doesn't a basketball game start with a jump ball?"

"Quit being smart," Ray snipped. "You know what I meant."

"Violet," Jerry's gaze bounced between Ray and me, his

blond brows wrinkled. "Do you foresee a problem with filming at Mr. Curion's historic hotel?"

I could think of plenty of potential disasters involving my ghost-talking friend and his little buddy, a life-sized Safari Skipper who had trouble not bubbling over about the cool tricks I had done at the séances we'd attended together.

"Define problem?"

"Something that would make Calamity Jane Realty, you, or the hotel look bad in the public eye?"

Since it was Jerry asking me this, I ignored my gut reaction to the idea and gave it some thought. Cornelius had big dreams of opening a world renowned haunted hotel that brought visitors to Deadwood from around the globe. The TV show would bring him some free publicity, good or bad. Any of the ghost fans who watched the show might then flock to Deadwood to see the haunted hotel and drop money all over town, helping other business owners. Some of the diehard, ghost-loving buffs might even want to buy a house … from me.

Well, when I thought about it that way, "Nope, there are no problems."

I'd just have to figure out a way to keep Cornelius in check so that he looked mildly eccentric, not ludicrously idiotic. For starters, no dressing like Abe Lincoln on camera and talking to walls.

"Excellent. You need to contact the owner after we finish with our huddle and have him sign the release papers Honey faxed to me yesterday."

"Will do."

"I'll also need you to get a release for that supposedly haunted house up in Lead that overlooks the Open Cut Pit."

"The Carhart house?" I shot Ray another blast of burning hatred. Prudence and her past were also not supposed to be on that list.

"That's the one." Ray's gloat made me want to grab my stapler and commit a technical foul on his head.

Maybe I'd sic Prudence on his ass when we were there. That was if Zeke and Zelda Britton, the soon-to-be new owners of the Carhart place, were game to have their house on television. "Do I need the almost owners or the seller to sign off on the paperwork?" I asked Jerry, not even bothering with an attempt to convince him that taking a TV crew into Prudence's lair was a splitting-atoms level of a bad idea.

"When will the sale close?"

"Early November if we have no delays."

"Maybe we should get both to be safe," Mona suggested, giving me a supportive smile.

Someone should get Prudence's okay, too, but that wasn't going to be me. That ghost had freaked the shit out of me too many times to count. I might have to call in sick if we ended up filming in her lair.

"Okay," Jerry clapped his hands, a signal that the huddle was almost over and we'd be sent back onto the court to play ball again soon. "We're on our way to tying up all loose ends. Violet and Ben, I'd like to huddle with you two this afternoon to discuss clothing and makeup choices and to toss some scripted lines around."

Ben and I both nodded like matching bobble-heads.

After a final "Go team!" Jerry headed back to his office.

I pulled up Cornelius's phone number. He didn't answer, so I left a detailed message and hung up.

Downing my coffee in one long gulp, I stared out the plate glass windows and watched traffic roll by as usual.

Doomsday was a weekend away.

I fought the urge to climb under my desk and wait for the mushroom cloud.

* * *

Harvey's pickup was parked out front when I pulled into Aunt Zoe's drive after escaping from Jerry's day-long seminar on how to walk, talk, and dress for the camera. He seemed to have forgotten I'd read the book—sort of.

I shut down the Picklemobile and sat there for a few sighs, switching modes from upcoming television starlet to wickedly cruel mother.

Finally Jerry's years of being a pro-basketball player hounded by the paparazzi, wanting to talk about his wins and losses both on and off the court, were paying off. Back then, he'd learned from his fellow veteran teammates how to shine for the cameras even when his reputation was tarnished. Now he was teaching Ben and me the tricks of his glamorous trade.

It was too bad Jane hadn't hired Tiffany Sugarbell instead of me back in April. The redheaded siren would have loved being in the spotlight, showing off her wares and talents in front of the cameras.

Me? I just prayed I made it through each day of filming without falling flat on my face or ass, or both. My smoldering reputation as Spooky Parker, the ghost Realtor, was about to get a squirt of lighter fluid.

If only I had Aunt Zoe's creative talent and could do something with my hands other than wrangle children and kill white-haired freaks who weren't quite human. Neither of which I was doing that well currently.

Maybe Doc would consider paying me to be his sex slave if this whole thing went south. I'd be content to work for room and board for three minus one chicken.

Inside the house the aroma of cooking meat blocked all further worries from surfacing. My nose led me straight to the kitchen, not even giving me time to shed my coat and kick off my boots. Harvey stood next to the sink mixing something in a bowl.

"What is that?"

"My momma's famous 'slaw recipe."

"No, that smell." I inhaled.

"Meatloaf."

I peeked into the oven, licking my chops. "It's heavenly."

"It's just baked meat and some spices."

Just baked meat … "My dear, wonderful, amazing Chef Harvey." I smiled for the first time since saying goodbye to Doc this morning. "How about you and I tie the knot and then you can cook for me and my kids every night."

He hooted, leaning back on his heels. "No way in hell, girl. You're too big of a nut to crack for this ol' boy. Besides, I'm savin' my pennies for one of them there catalogue women."

"What's a catalogue woman?"

"Mail-order bride."

"Oh, yeah? What do those run these days?"

He looked me up and down like I was on the auction block. "A helluva lot less than a dame with two foals."

"What about Miss Geary?"

Harvey and Aunt Zoe's neighbor across the street had enjoyed each other's company both night and morning-after for quite some time until she'd kicked him to the curb a while ago.

"She's a daisy, but she's into the younger studs now from what I hear."

As in Rex, my ex, who'd used Miss Geary so that he could spy on me and my kids from close range. "I haven't seen Rex's car parked in her drive for weeks."

"That's because she found a new beau over in Sturgis. He has a chromed out Harley with one of those 'bitch' seats on the back." He pushed me toward the dining room. "Now go get dressed for Ebenezer's funeral while I round up the kids for supper."

Right, the funeral. Joy.

Luckily for me it was Halloween time, because they didn't sell funeral hats with veils at any of the regular department stores down in Rapid. However, in one of those stores that pops up in time for the spook-filled holiday selling costumes, animated yard decorations, and zombie pieces, I'd found just what I needed to disguise myself for the evening. I debated on adding a fake bloody stump for an arm, but I was supposed to blend in, not make people scream. Besides, it was a funeral after all, so I needed to remain respectful of the dead while trying not to end up as one of the non-living myself.

By the time I'd tucked up all of my hair in a nest of bobby pins and gotten all duded up minus the dress, hat, and veil, Doc had rolled into the drive. I greeted him at the door in my bathrobe.

He stood under the porch light dressed in the same slacks and jacket, but the cream shirt had been switched with a black one.

"Come in, Johnny Cash. Did you have fun stuck over in Folsom Prison today?"

"Not at all." Doc stepped inside and shucked his coat. "How about you put those lovely lips next to my ear and blow my blues away."

I closed the door behind him, noticing the tiredness in his eyes. "Next to your ear, huh?"

"For starters." He pointed at my robe. "What's under there?"

"A weapons arsenal that will make your knees wobble."

"Nearly naked and deadly, I like that in a woman."

I went up on my toes and hit him with a kiss. "Your lips are cold. Stick around after the funeral and I'll warm them up for you."

Grabbing his arm, I tugged him to the kitchen. Harvey was setting sliced pieces of meatloaf on the table.

"Where are the kids?" I asked Harvey.

"They already ate. Addy's down in the basement playin' with her chicken, and your boy's up in his room. He was fillin' my ears with stories from some book Doc gave him."

I looked at Doc. "Another ghosts of Deadwood collection?"

"Something like that." He held out my chair, waiting for me to sit before joining Harvey and me at the table.

For the next fifteen minutes, I forgot all about the chaos going on in my world and frolicked around in meatloaf land while Harvey and Doc talked about things I couldn't remember moments later.

"Damn, this is good meatloaf," I told Harvey as I plowed through my second piece.

"Get that googly look out of yer eyes, girl. My answer is still 'no.'"

"Answer to what?" Doc asked.

My face warmed. I mimed zipping my lips at Harvey. Talking about the M word in front of Doc always made my armpits sweaty.

"She offered to get hitched, but I don't want her. She comes with too many horns and rattles for this old man."

Doc lowered his fork, a smile rounding the corners of his mouth. "You asked Willis to marry you?"

I opened my mouth and then closed it, worried I'd somehow jam my slipper in it.

"Yes sirree." Harvey beat me to the answer. "But she only wants me for my cookin'." He faked wiping tears from his eyes with his napkin.

Doc chuckled. "Can't say I blame her. You do have a way with tongs and an oven mitt."

"That's what some of them feisty old mares down at the senior center whisper about me, too."

I pushed my chair back, taking this opportunity to flee. "I need to get dressed." I carried my pretty much licked-clean plate to the sink. "Harvey, I'll do the dishes when we get back from Mudder Brothers."

"Don't worry, the young'uns can help me clean up. It's good for 'em."

I patted him on the shoulder. "Thanks, heartbreaker." I shot Doc a glance, not quite meeting his eyes. "Give me ten minutes."

I shot out of the room like the starter pistol had fired.

True to my word, ten minutes later I kissed my grumbling kids on the head, snapped Harvey's suspenders, and followed Doc out the door.

Doc didn't mention my marriage proposal on the way down to Mudder Brothers, thankfully. It was probably in part because I filled the ride with inane chatter about my day, determined to keep things light and breezy between us.

He parked behind his office. When I started to climb out of his car, he caught my hand.

"Promise me you won't sneak down into the basement tonight. I'd like to keep from repeating any parts of our last adventure in the bowels of Mudder Brothers."

Bowels was the spot-on word for all the crazy crap that went down that night.

I crossed my heart. "Trust me, I don't want to go inside that funeral parlor with all of its spooky rooms any more than you."

He released me. "Let's go see what this is all about."

While I waited for him at the bumper, I secured my black hat and veil, completing my disguise. "What do you think? Am I sufficiently camouflaged?"

"I think I like your Morticia Addams look much more."

"How about if I speak French to you? Would that make it

better?"

"I don't know." He tucked my arm in his and led me across the parking lot. Mudder Brothers night lights acted as a beacon up ahead in the darkness. "Give it a whirl."

My French was pretty limited. "*Bon appétit.*"

"Not bad, especially after that meal by the old guy who jilted you. Try some more."

I wasn't going to touch that jilted remark with a ten foot pole. "*Déjà vu.*"

"Yes, I do feel a bit like we've done this before. Although last time started out a bit more alarming."

"*Oh là là.*"

"I like that a lot. Makes me want to watch your mouth when you say it. Let's try that one again later when I have you in my bed."

We were reaching Mudder Brothers' crematorium-slash-garage. I swung wide, wanting to avoid it now that I knew more about what was inside.

As we drew close to the front door, I threw out one more. "*Voilà.*"

"Appropriately chosen, *ma belle Violet.*" He lifted the veil, searching my face. "Oh, Tish. Look at you, so pale and mysterious. Nobody will be looking at the corpse in there."

That made me snort. "Okay, Gomez."

He winked and dropped my veil. "Please be careful tonight, *cara mia.*"

"*Oui oui.*" I wasn't sure if he was still in character with that endearment he'd thrown out or not, but it warmed the cockles of my cockles nonetheless. I squeezed his hand. "Good show, old man. Come on."

"Hey, that's my line."

I entered Mudder Brothers first, pausing for a moment in the foyer to remove my smile from behind my veil and slip into a somber act.

Nothing had changed on the inside since the last time I'd been there. Well, other than the removal of George Mudder's name from the license in the frame on the wall next to the ladies restroom.

Doc had said he'd wait about ten minutes before coming inside, so I made a quick pit stop in the ladies room to make sure my disguise was fully in place and no blonde curls were escaping. I stared through the veil into the mirror. Only my chin was visible. Had I gone too far? Would my mysterious caller even recognize me?

It was time to go see. With one last tuck of my hair, I stepped out and ran right into Rex Conner, the non-support-paying rat bastard. He appeared to be on his way to the men's room, which was one door down.

"Sorry about that," he said after I'd extracted my face from his chest. "Are you okay?"

He wore a black suit and a dark red tie, his blond hair perfectly coiffed, his jaw stubble free. Perfect as always on the outside while undoubtedly still rotten to the core on the inside. What in the hell was he doing here?

I kept my chin down so he couldn't see my face through the veil and lowered my voice. "I'm fine."

Pulling away before he had the chance to study me further, I made a beeline for the parlor, grabbing a program from the visitor sign-in table on the way. Inside, fifty or so mourners were congregated to pay their respects to Ebenezer, who lay front and center in his silver casket.

I slid into one of the rows near the middle of the room that had three empty seats by the wall lined with a one-way mirrored glass. I purposely took the seat against the wall, wanting to make sure if there were somebody watching from behind the glass, they'd see me. Drawing a handkerchief from my small black purse, I pretended to dab my eyes as I searched the room, on the lookout for my mysterious caller.

Up front Eddie Mudder lurked near the casket, adjusting flowers and toying with the temperature gauges. His infamous organ music that usually creeped me out was missing tonight. Maybe the Haskells had requested a silent viewing.

A dark-blonde, wavy-haired woman in a navy blue suit handled those coming up to pay their respects. She was new at Mudder Brothers, at least new since I'd been there last. Where had Eddie picked her up? Maybe she was a Haskell family member who'd stepped up to keep people moving past the casket. Whoever she was, the mourners seemed at ease with her, taking comfort in her touch.

Now that I had settled in for the show and had nothing to do but wait for my caller to reach out to me, I pondered Rex's presence here while I scanned the program made up for Ebenezer.

Had someone called him, instructing him to show up tonight, too? Someone who knew Layne was his blood offspring? Or was this all tied to Rex somehow? Had Rex gotten himself into some stupid mess that was going to rain problems down not just on him, but me and mine by association?

Lord, how I'd like to throttle the son of a bitch's neck and dump him down an old mine shaft. Maybe it was time to get that restraining order that I'd blown off before because he'd moved states away and shown absolutely no interest in the kids.

I glanced over my shoulder and saw Doc slip into a seat a couple of rows back on the other side of the room.

He held my gaze for a second or two, and then opened the program telling all about Ebenezer, his life's work, and his remaining family.

The churning in my guts slowed, a calm washing over me from knowing Doc had my back.

Through the hazy veil, I searched the room again. Starting with the casket at the front of the room, I looked at each of the other mourners. There were twice as many people at this funeral than had been at the previous two Haskell funerals I'd attended with Natalie and Harvey. Ebenezer must have been popular.

Or had more money to will.

My eyes traveled over the sea of gray, white, brown, and blond heads. The red-headed population had no representatives present tonight. Tiffany should have come. She'd have loved standing out in the crowd.

Okay, that was kind of catty, and I should probably grow up and stop poking fun at the broad just because she'd tried to steal two of my clients away with her hot body and good looks. Not to mention that she'd had sex with my boyfriend. So what if Doc hadn't been seeing me at the time; that was splitting hairs.

A mature woman would try to be nice to the ultra-competitive bitch and try *not* to fantasize about rubbing gum in her flaming red hair or hanging weights off her perky breasts until they sagged or jamming a …

Wait. I was sliding backwards down a slippery slope. I needed to step back and get a clear perspective on reality.

I had Doc. *For now, at least.*

Cooper might want to shoot me, but he didn't want to change real estate agents.

Cornelius wanted to keep me around because he'd decided I was his own personal ghost channeling genie.

So, there. Tiffany's threats were all in her head. I needed to work harder not to let them get into mine.

Someone took the seat next to me.

I scooted over a little to make more room and held the handkerchief up to my face again.

"Nice try, Violet, but I can smell that it's you under all of that black." The sound of Rex's voice made me grind my teeth all over again.

"Go away, Rex."

"If you're going to disguise yourself, use a different perfume. Not many women share your scent. Trust me, I know. I've been with a few and haven't found one yet."

Was that supposed to be romantic? Him sniffing women, looking for a scent match? Ewww. "What are you doing here?"

"I'd think it was obvious." He pointed at the casket.

"So you didn't get a phone call?"

"Was I supposed to? Is that how they are inviting mourners to funerals these days? I'd prefer a text, if so."

I couldn't decide if he were playing with me or serious.

"Listen, Rex." I realized I was whispering a little too loud and stopped, shielding my mouth before continuing. "I don't appreciate this game you're playing."

"It's no game, not when I've spelled out exactly what I want from you. I don't know how to make it clearer."

"So you threaten my son."

"What are you talking about?"

"That call."

"What call?"

I lifted my veil, glaring flat out. "Don't mess with me, Rex. I will hurt you."

"Right, you'll sell my kidneys on the black market. I remember your threat."

"Excuse me," Doc's voice cut in. He towered over Rex. "How about we go visit the late Mr. Haskell?"

I dropped my veil. Doc and I weren't supposed to know each other, had he forgotten? "Do you mean me, sir?" I asked, staring straight forward.

"No. I'm talking to your seatmate." He hooked Rex under the arm and lifted him out of his chair, hanging his arm around my ex's shoulders like they were old pals. "Let's go pay our respects, Rex."

Without giving Rex a chance to disagree, Doc propelled him out to the aisle. He nudged the bastard toward the casket and then stood shoulder-to-shoulder with him over the body, speaking in Rex's ear. I'd have loved to be a fly on the inside of that casket.

Hold up, I take that back. I didn't want to be a fly anywhere near a dead person.

"Excuse me, Miss," the pretty blonde in the navy suit handed me a program. Her brown eyes sort of reminded me of Doc's, so dark it was hard to see the pupil. "I think you dropped this."

I checked my purse. "No, mine's right here."

"No, it's not." Her smile tightened, like it was freezing onto her face. "This one is yours, trust me." She took my hand and shoved the program into it.

"Okay then," I said, like I was calming a crazed escapee from the nuthouse. "You're right, this one is mine." I folded it and tucked it into my purse. "Thank you for returning it to me."

Those dark brown eyes rolled ever so slightly. "No problem. Enjoy the rest of the show."

I frowned after her and her long wavy tresses. She walked toward the front of the room, consoling an older woman on the way while offering her a tissue.

Who was that? I needed to ask Natalie about her. She'd probably know. She knew everyone in Deadwood and most in

Lead.

I stared into the one-way glass next to me, wishing I could see through it into the storage room on the other side. The very room where I'd found the bottle of mead Cooper was so curious about stashed in a huge crate. Was there anyone back there tonight? Somebody who was busy watching me, waiting to get me alone? Did he have white hair, bulbous eyes, and want to remove my spine for killing his twin?

Shivering, I looked back to the front in time to watch Doc lead Rex down the center aisle. Both men avoided making eye contact with me, or rather veil contact.

I sneaked a sly look behind me to see if Doc was removing Rex from the premises.

He turned Rex into the last row, shoving him forward toward the seats in the back corner. Nope. It looked more like he'd made a new pal for the night to anyone who might be watching.

Doc took the seat next to Rex, crossing his arms, staring straight ahead. Rex on the other hand was busy pouting, blotchy cheeks and all. When he looked over at me and wrinkled his nose, Doc planted a quick jab into Rex's ribs.

A few people turned at the sound of Rex's moan. Doc handed him a tissue and patted him on the back, murmuring to the lady in front of him something that had her nodding and dabbing at her eyes, too.

We sat there through the end of the viewing. I waited for most of the other mourners to leave, expecting someone else to take the seat Doc had made Rex vacate, but nobody joined me. I even walked up front and paid Mr. Haskell a visit for a few minutes, but I was alone in my goodbye to the man I didn't know from Adam.

Doc cleared his throat, catching my attention. He nodded toward the door. I took the hint and left, waiting outside in the thick shadows at the side of the building for him to follow.

He stepped out, sans Rex, a couple of minutes later. "Where's your pal?" I asked after he'd joined me in the dark, and we'd started back toward his car.

"He whined about needing to go to the little boys' room

after I accidentally clipped him in the lip with my elbow."

"Accidentally, huh?" I took my hat off and scratched around some of the bobby pins that had been tickling my scalp for the last half hour.

"Yeah. It was sort of a reflex reaction, inspired by his parting comment about my girlfriend."

I bumped him with my shoulder. "You're my hero."

"I took a page from your book." Doc put his arm around me. "He's lucky I didn't give him one of those love pinches you like to bestow on me."

I chuckled. "You're such a baby."

"Payback, Boots. You just wait." He reached down and pinched my butt, making me giggle some more. "So, did you talk to anyone while I was up front with your ex paying my respects to Mr. Haskell?"

"Besides Rex and the lady in the navy suit who might be working for Eddie now, I didn't talk to anyone tonight." I shivered in the cool night breeze, slipping my arm under his coat and around his warm back. "Maybe it was Rex who called me, although he seemed oblivious about it when I asked."

"I don't think it was him. He told me that he came because Haskell was on the board of directors for the science lab." We'd reached Doc's car, where he held the door for me. "He claimed it was a career move for him, that was it."

I waited for Doc to crawl behind the wheel. "So if it wasn't Rex, who was it?"

"Maybe Rex sitting next to you messed up the plan."

I frowned out the window at Mudder Brothers as we pulled out of the parking lot. "Maybe."

We drove the short distance to Aunt Zoe's in silence, except for a couple of yawns from Doc. He walked me to the door but then paused on the porch.

"Are you coming in?"

"I'm whipped. I'm going to go home and crash. Unless you want to have that slumber party tonight."

"I wish. It's a school night and Aunt Zoe's not home until Sunday."

"Okay, but before I go …" He pulled out a few bobby pins.

Tendrils of curls cascaded down along my cheek. "There, that's better." He kissed me goodnight until my hands clutched his jacket. "Come see me before work."

"Are you heading back down to Spearfish?"

"I don't think so." He took my hand and dropped the bobby pins in it. "Night, Tish."

"Bonsoir."

That earned me one last quick kiss.

I watched until he'd backed out of the driveway and then slipped inside. Harvey was snoring on the couch, with Addy and Layne sacked out in sleeping bags on the floor below him. The credits to *Raiders of the Lost Ark* were scrolling up the TV screen.

Kicking off my heels, I limped into the kitchen and tossed my purse on the table. My lip gloss and wallet spilled out, along with the two programs.

After pouring myself a glass of water, I walked over to the table and picked up the two brochures, unfolding the one the crazy woman had insisted I take. So Mr. Haskell was a muckety-muck up at the lab, huh? Someone high enough up the chain of command that Rex had felt attending his funeral would up his chances for a promotion.

I opened the program to read about good old Ebenezer again and froze at the sight of some words scrawled along the edge.

Turning the paper sideways, I read: *We were being watched tonight. I'll be in contact again soon.*

I fell into one of the kitchen chairs.

Who in the hell was behind this? The blonde in the blue suit who'd insisted I'd dropped my program? If not her, she was at least in on it. And who had been watching us? Had my albino nemesis's twin brother been hiding behind that one-way glass like I'd wondered?

I read the writing again and shivered, getting up to make sure the back door was locked and then doing the same with the front door.

Sliding to the floor, I wrapped my arms around my knees. My heart was busy holding a drum competition in my chest.

After the night I'd had, I could think of only one thing to do—wait for the next damned phone call.

Chapter Nine

Friday, October 26th

Meanwhile, back at a haunted hotel …

I woke up feeling low down and dirty, like armpit lice. I'd spent the night going through the parlor room at Mudder Brothers Funeral Parlor, replaying the scene in slow motion over and over while questions pinballed around in my head.

Who was my secret messenger? Who'd been the "watcher" that had mucked up the meeting? Was Rex really there for career purposes? What had Doc been saying to Rex up at the casket? Who was the blonde in the navy suit? Why wasn't Eddie playing his funkadelic organ music like normal? Had there been anyone hiding behind the one-way mirrored glass, and if so, had he recognized me through my disguise?

No answers came from all the hours of lost sleep. By dawn's early light, I'd come to the same conclusion as last night. This was going to be a waiting game.

"Mom?"

I looked over at Layne, who stood in the doorway rubbing his stomach. "Morning, sweetie. What's going on?"

"I don't feel so good."

"Are you sick?"

"I think I might throw up."

That made me leap out of bed. Superheroes had nothing on a parent whose kid was about to spew all over the floor.

"Into the bathroom, Mr. Parker." I guided him there, making sure he had a damp washcloth and towel within reach, and closed the door to give him the privacy he preferred in such cases. "I'll check back with you soon."

"Okay, Mom."

"What's wrong with him?" Addy asked from her bedroom doorway.

"He's not feeling well."

"And you believe him?"

My jaw unhinged. "Of course I believe him. Just like I'd believe you if you told me you were sick."

"Hmmm." She looked at the bathroom door with narrowed eyes and then backed into her room, shutting the door behind her.

What the hell? No compassion for her sick sibling? Maybe Addy was possessed. I should ask Doc if he'd ever come across a possessed person in his travels, and if grounding the victim for a week would bore the entity running the puppet strings so much that it would die all over again.

I grabbed my cellphone on the way downstairs and dialed up Harvey.

"Ya miss me already, girl?" He'd left last night after I'd put the kids to bed to head home, aka Cooper's place.

"Something like that."

"First ya wanna get hitched, and now yer pesterin' me before I've had my mornin' prune juice. I can see I'm gonna have to draw some boundary lines in the sand here."

"Sure, leave me all jilted, tease me with remarks about you and prunes, and then pour salt in my wounds with this talk about boundaries." Oh, the irony. After all of the way too personal comments he'd made to me about sex and his past love life, it should have been me dragging the stick through the sand.

"If it's any consolation, you ain't the first woman whose heart I've cracked in two."

I snorted at his cock of the walk tone. "Anyway, Mr. Heartbreaker, I called because I'm wondering if you can help me out today. Layne's sick to his stomach, and I have to be at work this morning to meet with the television people and go over the schedule."

"I'll be there shortly."

"If you need to finish making Cooper's breakfast, don't rush." I'd rather not have a hungry law dog biting at my buns for screwing up his breakfast.

"Coop ain't here."

"Wow, he leaves early."

"He never made it home last night."

"Really?" The poker game was the night before, so where had Cooper gone last night? Somewhere with Tiffany? Then again, I hadn't heard from Natalie last night.

"I think he was plannin' on meetin' somebody at the bar, so he musta rode that filly home." He snickered. "If ya know what I mean."

"Ewww." I made a gagging sound. "Come on, you know the rule—no sex talk before breakfast."

"Girl, some days you are one big ol' fun-sucker."

"Yeah, yeah, yeah. I'm going to get dressed. You have a key, so let yourself in when you get here."

"Be there in two shakes."

True to his word, by the time I'd gotten ready for work, Layne was resting on the couch with some dry toast and a puke bowl by his side, Harvey was in the kitchen frying eggs and bacon, and Addy was sitting at the table chatting away about being a chicken farmer when she grew up. Life was back to normal minus Aunt Zoe, whose clothes I was wearing again today because I loved her collection of beaded velvet skirts.

I was upstairs making sure the lights were off in the kids' rooms when Cornelius called.

"This is Violet!" I said, loud and clear.

"Why are you yelling at me?" he asked.

I couldn't win with the oddball. "Because I didn't want you to think I was a ghost."

"That's just silly, Violet. Why would I think you of all people are a ghost?"

"I don't know. Because you keep saying you're hearing them in the walls."

"Oh, I am hearing them, but I would never confuse you for the dead."

He should probably wait to make that judgment until he'd seen me first thing in the morning after a night of running from the Wolf Man. "That's good."

"Especially not after what I've heard about you."

What had he heard? From whom? Was it Ray? Tiffany? Detective Hawke? Cooper maybe? Surely not Freesia. She and I were hitting it off well. I started to ask him what he'd heard but then decided I should have more caffeine first.

"Why did you call me this morning, Cornelius?"

"I got your message from yesterday."

Oh, right. The release form. "Are you willing to let the television film crew go through your hotel?"

"Of course."

"They'll want to interview you as well."

"Even better."

I didn't feel nearly as enthusiastic about it as he did. "I'll need you to sign a release form from them."

"Fine, bring it tonight along with a bottle of wine."

"What's tonight?"

"When you and your tall friend come over and listen to some interesting sound bites I've collected over the last two days on my EVP recorder. Be here at seven-thirty-seven, and whatever you do, don't bring a Merlot wine. They never like Merlot."

I didn't even bother asking about the precise time or the wine. Previous experience had taught me it was best to let some stuff blow on by me when it came to Cornelius. "Remind me what an EVP recorder does so I know we're on the same page."

"It records sounds that humans don't normally pick up on their own, such as ghost chatter."

"So you actually can hear ghosts talking on this thing?"

"Yes, but only a word or a short phrase usually."

"Why do you want Doc and me to come over and listen?"

Eavesdropping on ghosts was not high on my list of preferences for a Friday night date. If I was going to have to get a babysitter for tonight, I'd prefer to have him sign the release, to discuss things that should not be said on camera, and then to enjoy some one-on-one time with Doc for the first time in way too long.

"Because I need your tall friend to figure out why the amount of chatter has increased."

"Okay."

"Also, I think one of the ghosts wants to talk to you."

"Me?" I lowered myself onto the bed. "Why? What's it saying?"

That was when I realized the grand-stander had hung up on me.

I hit the redial button and it went straight to his voicemail. "You silly nincompoop!" I left as my parting comment to his abrupt ending before shoving my phone in my purse. I headed downstairs to stuff some bacon and eggs in my mouth while I chewed on my problems.

After I dropped Addy off at school, I went straight to work. Because my mind was still festering about Cornelius's call, I forgot to swing by Doc's office like he'd mentioned last night until I received a text from him an hour later.

How'd you sleep, Tiger?

Crap, I needed to talk to him face-to-face, but according to Mona, Jerry was due to arrive with Honey and Dickie any minute now.

I texted back, *Can you meet me outside the back door now?*

As soon as his *Yes* hit my phone, I pushed back my chair. "I'll be right back," I told whoever was listening. "I need to grab something from the pickup." I took my purse with me for some 'show and tell' business with Doc.

I hurried down the hall and out the door.

Doc was waiting.

"Follow me," I told him and led the way toward the Picklemobile.

When we got there, I pulled the program from last night out of my purse and handed it to him.

"What's this?"

"The blonde in the blue suit at Mudder Brothers gave it to me."

"You mean the one helping Eddie Mudder run the show last night?"

I nodded. "While you were up at the casket with Rex, she insisted I'd dropped it and pretty much shoved it into my hand and wrapped my fingers around it."

He turned it sideways and read the scrawled message. "You've got to be kidding me."

"I wish I was."

"When did you see the note on this?" He held up the program.

"After I got home."

"And you didn't call me?"

"You were exhausted."

"Violet, I'm never too tired to help you. Next time something like this happens," he handed the program back to me. "Call me, day or night."

"Even if there's nothing you can do about it?"

"Even then."

"You're like one of those old time 'docs' who made house calls." I gave him a quick once-over, admiring the way his jeans and black thermal shirt hung on his frame. "You do have a pleasant bedside manner."

One of his eyebrows lifted. "Just *pleasant*, huh?"

I shrugged and inspected my nails, faking boredom and nonchalance. "I suppose with some practice, it could improve."

"How do you propose I go about working on that?"

"Maybe after Aunt Zoe gets home on Sunday, I can come over and we can play doctor."

A grin leaked out, spilling onto his lips. "So you think a hands-on approach is the best solution?"

"When it comes to your hands, definitely."

"Should I administer wine therapy during the session, or will it be peanut butter fudge ice cream in the recovery room again?"

Wine ... something was trying to surface from my memory. Oh, tonight with Cornelius and his wispy chatterbugs! "That reminds me, Cornelius called."

"Practicing my bedside manner reminds you of Cornelius Curion?"

"Well, you are both tall and like to play with ghosts," I joked and then continued with the other reason I'd needed to meet Doc in the parking lot. "Anyway, Cornelius wants us to come over to listen to his ghost buddies. He taped their voices on his fancy EV-something doohickey."

"Why am I not at all surprised that he has an Electronic Voice Phenomena recorder?"

I decided to skip Cornelius's cryptic message about one of the ghosts wanting to talk to me. Knowing Cornelius, he was just dangling a lure to make sure I showed up tonight.

"So," I caught Doc's hand, lacing his fingers with mine. "What are you doing tonight, Mr. Nyce?"

"That depends."

"On what?"

"What my girlfriend is doing tonight."

"She's going to listen to some spooky recordings ..." I switched to my Rod Serling voice, "in the Twilight Zone."

"Then the Twilight Zone is where I'll be."

"Thanks." I kissed the back of his hand. "I'll make up for it later."

"You still owe me a massage." His gaze raked down over me. "I like this outfit. You have sort of a velvety gypsy look going. You raided your aunt's closet again, didn't you?"

"She's got the coolest clothes."

Jerry's Hummer pulled into the lot. I could see Dickie sitting in the front seat next to him.

"Crud." I let go of his hand. "There's Jerry. I gotta go."

"Who's with him?"

"The people from the television show."

Doc tipped my chin up, inspecting one side of my face and then the other. "Gorgeous. Go get 'em, superstar."

"Thanks. I'll call you later."

I made it to the door just as Jerry and the others were exiting his Hummer. I was back at my desk with a busy look on my face by the time they all strolled inside.

Dickie and Honey had brought a friend this time. He was in charge of the film crew. After introductions, which included much hoopla and fanfare, Jerry and the TV people headed to his office. Ben and I would be called into the game later and were instructed to get warmed up, per Coach Jerry.

"Oh, Violet, one more thing." Jerry waved the others inside his office and came back to my desk.

"You want me to go get coffee and doughnuts?"

"No. You're not my secretary." He leaned closer. "Ray mentioned that the Galena House was rumored to be haunted.

That's one of your properties, right?"

I nodded, not liking the way the wind was blowing on this already.

"We're going to need a release from the owner if we're going to film there."

I was already working on three releases, what was a fourth? However, there was a small snag with the Galena House. "You do realize that the police still have that one apartment blocked off with crime scene tape, right?"

As in the late Ms. Wolff's place, where Harvey and I had found her shriveled head lying next to her shriveled body.

"That will make it even more interesting for viewers because of the potential for danger."

I sighed at the way his brain always found the marketing angle in all situations, good or bad. "Okay, I'll run over this morning and see if I can get Ms. Tender to sign the release."

"Great teamwork, Violet." He clapped me on the back, probably leaving a bruise.

Mona handed me a copy of the release form as I headed out the door a half hour later, sending me off with a bitter sounding, "Good luck, Vi."

The frown on her lips said plenty about her feelings on all of this.

When I parked in front of the Galena House, two things gave me pause. One was Freesia, who was standing on the porch while cloaked in a long black wool coat that looked a lot like the one Cornelius sported when he was playing Abe Lincoln Jr.

She waved at me after the Picklemobile announced our presence with its usual backfire. Freesia's smile warmed me up even though the day was still in the mid-forties.

The other bit that had me scratching my head was the man who was standing next to her, his notepad and pen at the ready.

What was Detective Cooper doing here? And what had I done to earn that squinty eyed stare he aimed at me?

There was only one way to find out. I made my way up the sidewalk to the front porch, noting that my Calamity Jane Realty FOR SALE sign had a kink in one of the chain links thanks to last night's gusts. The sign at Cooper's had been kinked, too.

Danged chains. I'd have to straighten it before I left.

"Everything okay?" I asked, focusing on Freesia.

"No, Parker," Cooper butted in. "It's not, and the fact that you're here makes it even more interesting."

"What did I do now?"

"I'm missing some clocks."

"So you automatically assume I'm some kind of time bandit? I haven't even been to your house in a week."

"Not *my* clocks, Ace." He stuffed his notebook in his coat pocket. "Ms. Wolff's clocks."

"What makes you think I have anything to do with it?"

"Because only three people in this town have a master key to get into any of the apartments in the Galena House." He pointed at Freesia. "She's been here all along, so there's no need for her to remove the clocks. I know for a fact that I haven't touched them. So that leaves the last key holder—you."

* * *

"I have no idea where those damned clocks are," I told Doc when he showed up at Aunt Zoe's door after work carrying two large pizzas.

Doc frowned through the screen door. "What clocks?"

"The ones in Ms. Wolff's apartment. Didn't Cooper call you? Ask you to verify that you were my alibi last night?"

"No. Should he have?"

I growled. "It was all hot air and threats then; I should have figured."

"That's probably Cooper's version of smoke and mirrors." Doc held up the boxes. "I'll trade you two pizzas for a ticket inside."

"Oh, sorry." I held the screen door open for him, taking the boxes from him. The cardboard alone smelled good enough to gnaw on. "Thanks for bringing supper. This will go over much better than the gruel I'd planned on serving."

"Dang. I love your gruel."

I left him to close the door behind him, grumbling under my breath all of the way to the kitchen about Detective Cooper and his stupid threats about search warrants and orange jumpsuits.

Fortunately for me, Dickie and Honey had kept me pretty distracted for much of my day. Or maybe it was more fortunate for Cooper, since I'd searched the internet during what little down time I had to find out how to make an authentic voodoo doll. If memory served me right, Cornelius had a good grasp of that particular religion.

I set the pizza on the table while Doc got out plates. "Tell me what happened," he said as he pulled glasses from the cupboard.

I told him about how Cooper had stopped by to look around the crime scene again at Ms. Wolff's place and had found several clocks missing from the living and dining room walls. How Freesia claimed she hadn't seen hide nor hair of anyone around the place. How Coop had said I was the only other one with a master key, then had made disparaging remarks about my "wild hairs" and threatened to throw me in jail if I were lying about the clocks like I had about the bottle of mead.

I huffed, grinding my molars all over again. I should have known that damned slip of the tongue about the mead would snowball into an avalanche of trouble.

Doc gave me a hug, stroking my hair. "Coop's just upset. Things at work have been getting a lot more intense lately, and he's under the gun for answers that he doesn't have."

I leaned my forehead against his chest. "How do you know about this?"

"He mentioned it during the poker game when Reid asked how things were going at work."

The doorbell rang.

"That's probably Natalie." I headed out of the kitchen, yelling up stairs for the kids to come get some pizza before opening the front door.

"Mmmm, pizza," Natalie said as she slipped off her coat. "Where's Harvey's pickup?"

"He had to leave as soon as I got home from work. Something about a hot date and having to stop by the place he's sharing with his bunghole of a nephew to grab his love potion."

She grinned. "Bunghole of a nephew?"

"The low-down, dirty rotten …"

"Sheepherder," she finished for me. "Did you and Detective Cooper have words today, Vi?"

"He spit words at me while I tried to defend myself."

"Spill it."

"Pizza first." I led her to the kitchen.

Layne chowed down three slices in no time, which made me wonder if Addy had been on to something this morning when questioning his stomach ache claim.

Addy finished two pieces minus the crust.

"May I be excused so I can feed my crust to Elvis?" She kept her focus on her plate, her expression stony, poised for battle. She knew my feelings on feeding that chicken table scraps.

Not in the mood to clash swords tonight after the day I'd had, I caved. "Sure."

She raced down the basement steps while Layne trudged back up to his room. Both kids had been polite to Doc throughout the meal, thankfully, but their continued silence toward me said plenty.

While Doc put away the remaining pizza and cleaned up, I told Natalie the whole story about Cooper and the missing clocks. Venting cooled my head a little, and Nat's firm agreement that Cooper was indeed being a thick-headed baboon made me feel even better.

Her ease at toasting to my snarling opinions about the damned detective had me pretty certain Cooper hadn't been serenading Natalie last night when he was supposed to be home in bed with AK-47s dancing in his head. That left me wondering even more if it had been Tiffany's voice I'd heard in the background when I'd called earlier this week.

"I'll be right back, Violet," Doc said, tossing the towel on the counter. "I need to go home and grab something." He gave me a quick kiss before heading out the door.

Natalie shooed me up the stairs to change out of Aunt Zoe's skirt before I ruined it. She knew me and my clumsiness all too well. I'd ripped or stained many, many pieces of her clothing over the years.

Doc returned shortly.

"Thanks for watching them," I told Natalie. "I'll text you after we leave the hotel."

Natalie knew where we were going tonight, but I'd skimmed on the *why* part, keeping it to a matter of getting a release form signed. "You better! In the meantime, I'll spoil your little blessings rotten."

"They're already spoiled."

"Then I'll make them even rottener." She waved at us from the porch. "Watch out for her, Doc. Cornelius has a history of adding to her nightmares."

She didn't know the half of it, mostly because I hadn't told her anything yet about the paranormal world in which I'd stuck my toe. Or more like jumped in up to my waist.

Doc saluted her as he held the car door for me.

Several minutes and a few blocks later, we parked in the public garage located behind The Old Prospector Hotel.

Doc turned to me. "I brought you something." He took my hand and dropped a couple of tiny white packages sealed at both ends into it.

I held one up, trying to read it in the orange light from the parking garage. "Crush once. Use and discard." I looked at Doc. "What are these?"

"Smelling salts. I'd like to make it through tonight without another black eye, if possible."

I laughed and crammed the two packages into my pocket. "I thought you liked it when I played rough."

"Well, I do like it when you kiss the bruises better." He opened his car door. "Let's go hear what has Cornelius's ghosts all excited."

Alarms rang as soon as we stepped inside the lobby. Not the hotel alarms, but the ones in my head.

Sitting in front of a row of Triple Cherry slot machines near old Socrates, the long-dead, bald-nosed stuffed mule, sat two people with whom I'd spent the afternoon in Jerry's office: Honey and the camera guy.

I stepped back onto Doc's foot. Good thing I was wearing tennis shoes and not my cowboy boots. "Sorry." I dragged him off to the side out of Honey's line of sight.

"What's wrong?"

"Two people from the television show are in here gaming." I peeked around a slot machine, double-checking that they hadn't moved. Nope, still there. "I don't want them to see me here."

Especially since I didn't know how this would all end.

"Isn't there a side door by the stairwell?"

"Yeah." Unfortunately, Honey was between us and it.

I had a gut clenching thought. "You don't think they're staying here, do you?"

"It's possible."

"I wouldn't think this place is posh enough for Dickie's sort." I peeked again. Honey sat in the same place, but the camera guy had moved a slot machine down.

Doc pulled me back. "You sneak outside through the lobby doors and go around to the side; I'll slip by them and make sure it's not locked."

As far as I could remember, Honey had no idea who Doc was, so that should work. "Okay. See you shortly."

Doc's plan worked like a charm.

We stole up the same back stairwell where Doc had first come across a young prostitute ghost almost a month ago. But there were no spooks lingering around to freak me out tonight. No talk of Doc's aversion to marriage, either, which was another misadventure we'd shared in the stairwell.

Cornelius's suite was located on the third floor. For the first time, Doc had no qualms, no queasiness, nothing on the way up to it, not even in the hallway outside the suite's door.

"Last time you were here," I whispered, "thirteen ghosts came at you all at once. Where are they now?"

"I don't think I want to know."

We reached Cornelius's door. I gave the signal knock as instructed by his text this afternoon. Three loud knocks, two quiet ones, and then three more loud ones.

"Is there a secret password, too?" Doc asked.

"I hope not or we'll be out here all night."

The door creaked open, but nobody peeked through the crack. I pushed it further open. The foyer was empty. Doc and I stepped inside, letting the door click closed behind us.

The suite was semi-dark, lit by computer screens. An old black and white version of *The Thing* played on the television screen, adding a flickering effect to the walls. If I hadn't had Doc's hand on my lower back propelling me forward, I might have turned and fled back out the door.

"Cornelius?" I whispered loudly, afraid someone or something else might reply in his place. Something black and covered in pustules with glowing orange eyes.

"Violet," he popped up from a chair behind the row of computer screens, making me squawk in surprise.

Doc chuckled, squeezing my shoulder. "You've been hanging around Addy's chicken too long."

"Did you bring the wine?" Cornelius asked, waving us to join him behind the monitors.

The whole setup looked like a command center. I wondered if he could watch the space shuttle land from this setup.

I held out the wine bottle. "It's not a Merlot."

He took it. "This is white?"

"You didn't say it had to be red."

"I know. I was making sure it was white."

"It's a Riesling."

"Perfect." He put it on the round table in the dining area. "They're going to love it."

"The ghosts?"

"No, my collection of Venus flytraps."

I let that one roll off and caught Doc's hand, pulling him closer. "I also brought my tall friend along."

Cornelius looked up at him. "Hello, Medium."

"Good evening, Ghost Whisperer," Doc shot back without hesitation, sliding me a glance.

I swallowed a chuckle.

"I'm glad you could join us." Cornelius gave Doc one of those crooked smiles of his that tended to make me think the world was tipping sideways. "Violet tells me you have a romantic interest in her."

Even more so when he followed with something as odd and embarrassing as that. I coughed out a gasp, glad for the shadows that hid my red cheeks.

"Did she now?" Doc winked at me. "Violet tells me you're having trouble with some talkative ghosts."

"They're incessant."

"How long has this been going on?"

"Since the last séance when Violet channeled Big Lips Lolly."

Oh, dear Lord, I'd forgotten about my award-winning acting that night when I'd pretended to get in contact with the long-dead prostitute Doc had run into in the stairwell.

Doc smirked. "I remember that night very well." He touched his cheek where I'd elbowed him hard enough to knock him off his chair and leave him with a helluva shiner.

I wrinkled my nose at him.

Cornelius indicated the table. "Pull up those chairs, and I'll let you both hear the clamor going on in my walls."

We each took a spot on either side of Cornelius. He unplugged a pair of headphones from what looked like a very expensive stereo with all sorts of lights and knobs and then turned up the volume.

"Now listen closely." He hit the Play button.

A bunch of hissing and static followed.

I looked at Doc. He held up a "wait" finger.

What sounded like whispering started, mixing in with the white noise.

"Are those …" I started, leaning closer to the speaker.

"Voices," Cornelius finished.

A rash of chills covered me from head to toe. "Turn it up a little more."

"You're going to get a kick out of this part coming up."

"Why?"

He turned the volume up. "Just listen."

I did, my palms sweaty.

Hissss … tea party … hisssssss … fire … hisssssss … my Wolfgang … hiss.

The voice sounded high-pitched and young, like Addy's.

Cornelius hit the Stop button.

I clenched my hands together. "Did I just hear the word 'Wolfgang'?"

Doc nodded, his dark gaze solemn, his brow pinched.

"That is correct," Cornelius answered, as if I'd given the right question to an answer on *Jeopardy*. "It's the same name you spoke the first time you visited my suite."

"No, I didn't," I lied, not wanting it to be true.

"You denied it then, too, Violet, but I was recording that night, remember? You were in a trance-like state at the time."

Fine. Maybe I had. "So the name *Wolfgang* on your EV-thingamajobbie is what you wanted us to hear tonight?"

"There's more." Cornelius hit Play again. "Keep listening."

I didn't want to, but I leaned in again anyway.

Hisssss ... onlyyouIlove ... onlyyouIlove ... onlyyouIlove ... onlyyouIlove ... onlyyouIlove ... hissss.

My breath log-jammed in my throat. My finger was trembling when I reached out and pressed the Stop button.

"Those were the words he said to me that night," I whispered in the sudden quiet.

"While you were in the room with the others?" Doc asked.

"Yes." The *others*. As in the three decomposing little girls the bastard had murdered.

"Who are we talking about?" Cornelius's gaze ping-ponged between Doc and me.

I covered my mouth with both hands feeling like I needed to bar the door, or something—a scream or my supper or both—would come rushing up my esophagus and out through my lips.

"You okay, Violet?" Doc asked. I shook my head but motioned for them to continue. He turned to our host. "Is there anything else from this particular ghost?"

"One more thing." With his finger paused over the Play button, Cornelius frowned at me. "It's why I wanted you to listen to it in person."

He hit Play.

I stared at the speaker, afraid to breathe.

Hissssssss ... my beautiful ... hisssssssssss ... Violet ... hissss.

I stood up so fast my chair fell over backward. "Holy shit!"

Doc and Cornelius both stared at me while the static kept playing.

I was huffing as if I'd just returned from a sprint up Main Street and back. "Wilda's still here."

Chapter Ten

Meanwhile, back in the Purple Door Saloon …

One shot of tequila wasn't going to cut it tonight. Not after hearing Wilda say my name.

"Three shots of tequila for starters," I ordered from the blonde-hating bartender at the Purple Door Saloon.

He must have seen on my face that I was in no mood for any snarls or attitude from him tonight, because he agreed to have them delivered to me in the corner booth without a single hint of gruff.

I crossed the room without really seeing the faces of the other patrons. Settling into the booth, I waited for Doc, whom I'd left behind in Cornelius's suite.

There was no way I could sit there in that room, not with the thought of the ghost Wilda standing there next to me, watching me, whispering things in my ear that I couldn't hear. That would fuel the kind of nightmares that would wake me up screaming at the top of my lungs. No thanks. So I'd told Doc he could find me at The Purple Door when he and Cornelius were done listening to the other ghosts and raced out of the hotel like it was crashing down around me.

A purple-haired waitress brought my shots over. I thanked her, giving her a nice tip, wondering if she'd colored her hair to match the bar's name in order to make her boss happy.

Criminy, the things we did for money. I slammed back a shot, coughing into my hand as it burned its way down.

That was the whole reason I'd agreed to sell the Hessler house. I had been desperate for a sale, worried I'd lose my job, afraid I'd no longer be able to pay my bills and end up moving back in with my parents.

Well, that and the fact that Wolfgang had been so charming. I picked up the second shot glass, staring through the tequila at the blur of lights and shapes beyond. God, what a sucker I'd been.

All of those fucking clowns. I shuddered, remembering Mrs. Hessler's obsession with painted faces, overly happy eyes, and ghastly smiles.

The second shot of tequila went down easier than the first, my eyes watering only a little. I licked my lips and set the empty shot glass next to the other one.

My thoughts flitted through mouth-drying memories from that night in Wolfgang's house. The wallpaper covered with violets. The taste of tannins from the drugged wine. The stench of decaying flesh. The creepy clown candle in the center of the cake. The sinus-burning odor of lighter fluid. The crackling of the fire. The burning heat.

His words echoed in my head …

"She won't leave me alone. She screams at me nonstop, blaming me, threatening to destroy all of the good in my life."

"Is she screaming now?"

His gaze focused over my head. *"No."*

I peeked over my shoulder and saw nothing but the bedroom door. *"What is she doing?"*

"Just watching. Making sure I follow through."

I picked up the third shot and swallowed it down in one big gulp. Ahhh, no trouble at all with that one. The shot glass fell in line with the other two. The fear that had me all lathered up at the sound of Wilda's voice quieted, no longer kicking at the stall door to break free and gallop screaming into the night. I signaled the waitress to bring me two more shots. Those should make me forget the Hessler chapter in my life for a while.

Wolfgang.

His face swam before me with his quick smile and rakish blond hair. Those deep blue eyes had warmed my blood at first, and then had scared the holy hell out of me that night when he told me what his dead sister Wilda wanted.

"She refuses to leave me alone unless I kill the one I love … She's the eye-for-an-eye type."

He'd believed that if I died, Wilda would go, too. Only then would he be free of the little ghost girl who haunted him day and night.

But he'd died, not me.

Was that why Wilda was still hanging around? Waiting for me to keel over? Or was it because I'd burned her house down and had a hand in killing her brother? Was this a revenge haunt? Was she determined to finish what her brother had started?

Memories blurred my vision, or maybe it was the shots of tequila catching up with me. At some point two more tequila-filled shot glasses appeared in front of me. My hand was reaching for the first one when someone slid into the booth opposite me and stole them both away.

I frowned, blinking up into the face of Detective Cooper. "Give those back."

He shook his head. "This is a bad idea, Parker."

"This," I pointed at the shot glasses in his hand and then back at me, "is out of your jurisdiction, Detective."

"Are you driving home?"

I shook my head.

"Are you here with Ms. Beals or Nyce?"

"Doc drove."

"Where is he?"

"Listening to ghosts."

Cooper's eyes narrowed. "How drunk are you?"

"Not nearly enough yet. Give me back my shots."

"Seriously, where's Nyce? It's not like him to leave you to get soused on your own."

"I told you he's listening to ghosts." I crossed my arms, resting my elbows on the table. "Maybe you should get your stupid notebook and pen out and write that down so you don't have to ask again."

His face crinkled, apparently unhappy about me insulting his accessories. "Listening to ghosts where?"

"At The Old Prospector Hotel with my buddy Cornelius." I lunged forward to grab my shot glasses from him, but he held them out of reach. "Why do you always have to be such a fucking asshole, Cooper?"

When he hit me with a full-on gunslinger glare, I realized what I'd said. "Oops." I sat back in my seat. "That was the tequila talking, not me."

"I doubt that. Why are you here slamming back shots while your boyfriend is in a haunted hotel supposedly talking to ghosts?"

"I said he's listening, not talking."

"Jesus, Parker. Just answer the goddamned question."

I gave him a glare of my own. "You won't believe my answer."

"Try me."

"Fine. I'm drinking because I heard something tonight that scared the hell out of me."

"What? A ghost?" I could hear his sarcasm crystal clear.

"You know what, Cooper? Fuck you." I pointed both index fingers at him. "And fuck your bullying day-in and day-out. I'm not in the mood to deal with your bullshit tonight, so go ruin someone else's life."

I slid out of the booth, stumbling to my feet. They served shots at the bar, too, which was where I was going to plant my butt. I smoothed my shirt down over my waist and took a step in the bar's direction. And if that blonde-hating bartender so much as looked at me funny, I was going to grab a pool cue from the back room and jam it up his …

Cooper grabbed my arm. "Get back here, Parker."

He propelled me back into the booth. My landing was lacking in grace, arms and legs flailing. The toe of my shoe flew up as I hit the seat cushion and connected with the bossy detective's shin.

He grunted and grimaced. "Damn it, Parker!"

I righted myself and tucked my legs under the table. "That's what you get for manhandling me, bully."

"What's going on here?" Doc's voice cut through the tequila haze now starting to cloud my brain.

"Parker's trying to drown in tequila," Cooper told on me. He stepped back to make room so Doc could slide into the booth seat next to me.

Doc cupped my chin, searching my eyes. "You okay, Tiger?"

I shook my head. I wasn't going to be okay with Wilda's freaky message for a long time. "But I'd be more okay if Cooper would let me drink those other two shots."

Doc looked at the table. "You've already had three."

"I know. I'd like two more to grow on, please." I pinched the back of my hand. "I'm not numb enough yet."

"Oh, sweetheart. Come here." He wrapped his arm around my shoulders, pulling me close.

Cooper dropped into the seat across from me again, still rubbing his shin. "What's wrong with her?" he asked Doc.

"I tried to tell you, but you made fun of me." I turned to Doc. "She's coming to get me, isn't she?"

Doc shook his head. "We don't know that for sure."

"Who's coming to get her?"

"She wants revenge," I told Doc. "I killed her brother." I thought of Aunt Zoe and her account of our family history. "She's right. I'm just like all of the others."

Cooper leaned over the table. "Did you say kill?"

Doc grabbed one of the shot glasses Cooper had taken away and placed it in front of me. "One more, but that's it." When I lifted it to my lips, he ordered, "Sip it."

While I sipped, he looked at Cooper. "Violet is not a killer."

"Yes, I am." My Aunt Zoe had told me so, and she never lied about stuff like protection charms and executioners.

"She's drunk," Doc explained, squeezing my thigh warningly under the table. "She had a nasty scare tonight and needs to go home after this drink and sleep it off."

I guffawed. "I doubt I'll do much sleeping tonight unless I get to drink this shot *and* that one."

"What happened?" Cooper asked, watching me sip, his face all angles and creases.

"You know, Detective," I pulled my face out of my tequila and informed him, "you should smile more. It makes you less hateable."

Doc lifted the hand I was using to hold the shot glass toward my mouth. "Sip, Violet."

I obliged.

"It's tough to explain," Doc told Cooper.

"Try me."

"Okay." Doc blew out a breath before digging in. "You remember Wolfgang Hessler?"

"Of course."

"He had an older sister who died when he was young."

"Yes. Wilda Hessler. She was a year or two ahead of me in elementary school."

"Right." Doc looked down at me, his eyebrows raised as if he were asking for my permission to continue.

I shrugged and took another sip of tequila. The sharp edges of fear from tonight were now worn off, leaving me with a what-the-hell attitude.

"The night the Hessler house burned down," Doc continued, "Wolfgang told Violet that his sister's ghost was in the house with them."

"In the room," I corrected. "Standing there watching him dump lighter fluid over those poor little girls."

Cooper stared at me, no smartass comments, no insults, no glares. Just his steely gray eyes watching me.

Was he assessing my sanity? My state of drunkenness?

"Violet told me a couple of days later," Doc continued, "that she suspected Wolfgang was hearing voices in his head, not the actual ghost of his sister."

"I thought Wolfgang was only deranged."

"She figured that he suffered from something like a Dissociative Identity Disorder."

Cooper nodded. "She'd mentioned something about that when I took her official statement."

"She was wrong," Doc said.

"She was?"

I patted Doc's arm. "And he was right."

"About what?" Cooper asked.

"I had told her that Wilda was in that room with Violet and the little girls," Doc said.

"As a ghost?" His skepticism was loud and clear.

"Yes, as a fucking ghost, Detective," I snapped. He was lucky right then that I couldn't breathe fire.

"Your girlfriend is a mean drunk," Cooper told Doc.

"Not usually. She's had a rough week."

"Ha!" I laughed without humor and finished the shot.

"So, when Parker said you were right, she meant—"

"Doc knew Wilda was a ghost," I explained, "and that she was haunting the Hessler house."

"Because of your medium abilities?"

"Bingo." I tried to touch my finger to my nose and ended up poking my cheek hard enough to make me wince.

"So what happened tonight that has Parker sloppy drunk?"

I looked at Doc. "Can you somehow tell Wilda that Cooper made me do it?"

Doc winked at me. "Violet and I were over at The Old Prospector Hotel listening to some chatter that Mr. Curion picked up on his EVP."

"He has an EVP?" Cooper asked, apparently already aware of what the acronym stood for.

"It's one of his many expensive ghost hunting toys."

"Why does that not surprise me?" Cooper downed my last shot of tequila, damn him. "So, what did you two hear on the ghost airwaves?"

"Wilda," I answered.

"And what did Hessler's sister have to say?"

"She repeated things her brother said to me."

"And you don't think this is some kind of trick of Curion's?"

I shook my head.

"How can you be sure?"

"Because there were three dead girls, Wolfgang, and me in the room that night." I took a breath. "And Wilda's ghost, apparently. I've never told anyone the exact words Wolfgang said to me that night."

"Why did you withhold them?" Cooper asked.

"Because I felt sorry for Wolfgang."

"He was a mass murderer."

"He was a lonely boy who was hated by his mother for most of his life. On top of that, his sister murdered his father."

"So on this EVP recording you heard the same words Hessler said to you while you were alone in that room on the night of the fire?"

"Yes, but on the recording, they were spoken by a young girl."

"Wilda Hessler?"

I nodded. "She was there with us in the bedroom that night, just like Wolfgang said." I patted Doc's chest. "Doc was right about her."

"How did you know she was there?" he asked Doc.

"I didn't know if she was in the room with Violet until tonight," he clarified, "but I knew Wilda was staying in the house after I experienced her death."

"See, now that's where I get hung up." Cooper flagged down the waitress, ordering two more shots.

"I'm driving tonight," Doc told him after the waitress left. "Not drinking."

"Those are for me." He shook his head. "I need something to help me swallow this ghost business."

"Take it slow. It's easy to choke on if you gulp."

"Okay," Cooper said, looking from me to Doc. "Nyce, you said you experienced Wilda's death."

"Yes."

"First hand?"

"Through her eyes."

"I don't get it."

Doc waited until the waitress had delivered the two shots and left before explaining how it all worked to Cooper. By the time he finished, Cooper had emptied both shot glasses.

"And tonight Parker heard from Wilda via Curion's ghost talk radio." At Doc's nod, Cooper looked at me. "You haven't heard from her before now?"

"Not directly."

"Explain."

"Cornelius told me a few weeks ago that a girl ghost who lived in his walls wanted to have a tea party with me. At the time, I thought he was a little off his rocker." Officially that was still my verdict but not when it came to the paranormal world.

"And now you believe him?"

"Yes."

"And that scared you."

"No. Knowing Cornelius is legit doesn't really scare me, it just makes me think the world is nuttier than I realized. What scared me is learning that Wilda wants to talk to me."

"But if she's a ghost, she can't really hurt you can she?"

I shot Doc a smirk. "We should introduce him to Prudence."

"Prudence?" Cooper rubbed his forehead. "Where have I heard that name?"

Doc shook his head at me, so I didn't remind Cooper that Wanda Carhart had mentioned Prudence to him after Millie and her lover had tried to kill me.

"What are *you* doing here tonight, Cooper?" Doc asked, changing the subject.

"My uncle has a date."

Oh, yeah. That's why Natalie instead of Harvey was watching my kids tonight. "So you don't want to sit home alone?"

"No, I don't want to be home period. He invited her over for dinner and is planning on making her breakfast, too." He grimaced. "My walls are paper thin."

I grimaced along with him.

"Where are you going to sleep?" Doc asked.

"There's a couch down at the station in one of the offices." Cooper glanced toward the bar. "Or I could probably sleep at her place."

I looked to see who he was talking about and groaned at the sight of Tiffany Sugarbell weaving her way toward our booth.

"That's a bad idea," Doc said.

"Says who?" Cooper hit him with a raised brow.

"The voice of experience."

I tried to slide under the table to escape the red-headed siren and the sure-to-come reminders that my boyfriend used to frequent her bed. After listening to Wilda's sweet nothings tonight, I had no energy to fight the jealousy ogre sure to start clubbing away at my heart as soon as Tiffany opened her fat pouty lips.

Doc caught me under the arm and hauled me back topside as the Jessica Rabbit clone sashayed up to our table.

"Hello, boys." Tiffany didn't acknowledge me. "Is there room for one more at your table?"

"No," I blurted.

"That's up to Cooper." Doc tugged me his way. "Violet and I were just leaving."

"Wait, Doc." Tiffany ran her finger down Doc's chest as soon as he stood up. "You sure you don't want to call her a taxi and stay for a game of pool? It's been a while since I've schooled you."

"Oh, puhhhleezzz." I blew a tequila-scented raspberry at her once I'd landed on my feet, making her recoil. "Don't you think it's time you got it through that pretty red hair of yours that Doc is done fiddling with your perky boobs and tight ass?"

"Violet," Doc warned.

I waved him away. I was so tired of this she-bitch playing seductress with the man I was doing my best to woo into a tree, K-I-S-S-I-N-G him senseless until he decided he couldn't live without me.

"He's got me now." I thumbed my chest.

Tiffany gave me a once over. Judging by her expression, she found me lower than a bag of dog poop. "What makes you think he won't get bored with you, too, Violet? Even curls and curves get boring for a guy with Doc's appetites."

As if I hadn't already spent hours and hours stewing about that very thing. Sheesh, she had nothing on my own demons. "You know what your problem is, Tiffany?"

"I'm too smart for my own good?" She lifted her nose so she could look down it at me. "What do you propose? I dye my hair blonde, get a spiral perm, and start throwing myself at the boys like you do so I can get laid?"

Cooper sucked a breath through his teeth. "I wouldn't make fun of Parker's hair if I were you."

I crossed my arms over my chest, my chin leading the way into the center of the ring. "Not everything in a relationship revolves around sex, you ginger-headed bimbo."

Tiffany closed the distance between us, her pushup bra bumping into my forearms. "That's where you're wrong," she said, sounding superior. Her gaze moved over my shoulder, openly flirting with my boyfriend. "Especially when it comes to Doc and his insatiable needs."

I cast a glance at Cooper. "You should probably start reading me my rights, Detective, because I'm about to assault and batter the hell out of this skinny bitch."

"Hey, Nyce." A grin hovered on Cooper's lips. "Maybe you should—"

"Right. We're leaving now." Doc looped his arm around my waist and dragged me back to my corner. "You need a ride home, Cooper?"

I struggled in Doc's arms, not getting anywhere but winded and dizzy.

"I'll be fine. Get Parker out of here before she starts breaking pens and frothing at the mouth again."

"You really need to keep her on a leash," Tiffany told Doc, all sugary sweet now that she'd retracted her fangs.

I lunged, claws extended, but Doc's arm was like an iron bar around my stomach.

"Tiffany," Doc hauled me back another couple of steps. "I believe it's in our best interest if you seek financial counseling from someone else in the future. I'll send an official letter next week."

Two bright red spots appeared on Tiffany's cheeks. "You can't drop me, Doc."

"I can and I am." He lifted me clear off the floor and aimed me toward the door. "Time to get you home, Tiger." He set me on my feet and nudged me along in front of him out into the night.

I shivered in the cold air, sobering under the weight of reality. After walking along in silence beside him for several beats, I glanced sideways at him. His mouth was set, his dark hair ruffled over his brow. What was he thinking? Was he upset with me for making him lose a client? For not sitting there like a good little girl and allowing Tiffany to feel him up and down? Or was he still back in that hotel suite with Cornelius, listening to the whispers from the walls?

"I really don't like your ex," I told him, breaking the silence, swaying slightly from the tequila.

"Yeah." Doc put his arm around me, pulling me close. "I feel the same about yours."

Chapter Eleven

Saturday, October 27th

Meanwhile, back in Aunt Zoe's kitchen …

The next morning, I made my way downstairs into the kitchen one step at a time.

"Rough night, party animal?" Natalie asked from the kitchen table where she sat reading the Black Hills Trailblazer.

"I'm not sure." My memory was glitchy after that third—or was it fourth—shot of tequila. "Where are my sunglasses?"

"It's raining."

"I know." I stood with my hand on the refrigerator door, hesitating. "But I need some cream for my coffee and the fridge light is too bright."

"That's just sad." She came over and nudged me aside. "Go sit and tell me what happened last night."

"You tell me." I retreated to the table, falling into a chair. "I don't remember much after I left the bar."

"Doc brought you home and carried you from the car to your bed. You were completely passed out and sporting some noxious tequila breath." She placed the milk on the table in front of me.

I tested the smell of my breath in my palm and grimaced. "That must be why my mouth tastes so bad."

"No." She set a cup of coffee down next to the carton. "You threw up after Doc left and then refused to brush your teeth before passing out again."

"Oh, bleck!" I took a sip to remove the weird tasting tang from the back of my tongue.

"Yeah, when I hauled you back to bed, I almost keeled over from your sewer breath."

Thank God Doc had left me in Natalie's hands and gone home for the night. "I really appreciate you staying the night, Nat."

"You were more entertaining than my empty house." She lowered herself into the chair across from me.

"Want to spend another night? This time hanging out with me and my kids?"

"Sure, but what about Doc?"

"He could probably use a break from me." Fall down drunk girlfriends weren't so funny when they were in their mid-thirties.

"I doubt that. If your lover boy decides he wants to join us, he's more than welcome."

I squeezed her hand. "So what's on tap for today?"

"I'm going to lunch with Detective Hawke."

"What?" I felt like I'd missed the last episode of my life thanks to my silly tequila-fest.

"He called here last night looking for you. I took the opportunity to arrange a lunch date with him. I'm going to cement it in his head that you can indeed talk to ghosts." She tipped her head back and let out a fake, evil laugh. "That was a genius idea you came up with, by the way. Much better than pretending to be a witch."

Sipping my coffee, I considered telling Natalie about Wilda Hessler's message from beyond, but a streak of pain flashed through my head. I focused on pouring more liquid down my throat.

Good thing going into work today was optional. I could take care of rounding up those signed release forms without having to show my face at Calamity Jane's, where the television crew had planned to hang out with Jerry for another day of planning and script building.

The phone rang, making me cringe. "Whoever it is, tell them that I'm dead and have gone to a better place."

"Where's that? I hear Tahiti is nice this time of year." Natalie moved way faster than I could, reaching the phone by the second ring. "Hello? Hi, Zoe. How's Denver?" She listened for a few moments. "That sounds marvelous. How's your roommate?" After a moment, Natalie chuckled. "Lucky you."

I frowned, not liking the implication that came with that. Poor Reid.

"Yeah, she's right here."

Natalie brought the phone over to me.

"Hi," I said. My head felt like a watermelon on a popsicle stick, so I rested it on the table and looked at the world sideways. "How's the conference?"

"Exhausting. I was ready to come home two days ago. How are you doing?"

I thought about telling her I'd come to accept that she was right about my being a killer, but Natalie knew nothing about that, so I kept it simple. "I have a terrible hangover."

"What happened?"

"Something I heard last night sort of shook my world, so I decided to drink my way through the aftershocks."

"You know my sure-fire fix for a hangover, right?"

I wrinkled my nose remembering the last time Aunt Zoe had blended up her usual cure: a banana, some ginger root shavings, a tablespoon of honey, a cup of lemon juice, and a pinch of cayenne pepper. "Yes, but I'd rather writhe and moan all day."

"Suit yourself. Are you going to be okay?"

"This hangover too shall pass."

"I mean about what you heard."

"Probably."

"What was it?"

"Uh …"

"Is Natalie sitting there?"

"Yep."

"Have you told her about the ghosts and albinos yet?"

"Nope."

"You're going to need to let her inside soon."

"Sure."

"Okay, I'll wait until tomorrow to hear what spurred you to hide inside a bottle of tequila."

"How'd you know it was tequila?"

"Violet, how long have I known you?"

"All my life?"

"Exactly. Take it easy tonight and I'll be home tomorrow to

help you work through whatever is worrying you."

"I miss you, Aunt Zoe." I ran my finger around the rim of my coffee cup. "Drive safe!"

"Miss you, too, baby girl." I still loved it when she called me that. "Give the kids a kiss for me." She hung up.

Natalie leaned down and tipped her head sideways like mine. "You need to tell me what drove you to drink last night."

"Can we wait until the construction workers hammering in my head go home for the day?"

"Sure. Are you going to be okay while I go take a shower and get all gussied up for my lunch date?"

I gave her a thumbs up.

By the time Natalie returned, showered and beautified, I'd found my sunglasses and was busy steaming my face and the dark lenses over some honey lemon tea.

"You look good," I told her. "Is that my skirt?"

"Yep. It's your sweater, too."

"And my boots."

She crossed the kitchen, acting like she was on the catwalk. "Today Ms. Beals is wearing a Violet Parker exclusive. Notice how the knit tiered skirt swishes around the leather boots while the white cashmere sweater makes her chest look bigger." She twirled at the end of the kitchen and strolled back toward me. "Ms. Beals is sure to discombobulate the great Detective Hawke with this sexy ensemble all while convincing the big dolt that her best friend can hold hands and sing *Kumbayah* with the coolest ghosts in town."

In spite of my aching head, I chuckled. "With that push-up bra, you're more likely to discom-boob-ulate the buttinski."

"My goal is to have Detective Hawke jumping at shadows before the week is out. He'll be convinced that not only is Deadwood full of ghosts, but that you have the power to make them your minions."

The Who started playing from the direction of Natalie's coat, which was draped over one of the kitchen chairs.

"My phone." Natalie dug it out of her coat pocket, checking the screen. "It's Kate."

"Kate who?"

"Kate Morgan, my cousin, ya numbskull." She answered the phone. "What's going on, Porn Star?" She walked over to the table and collected her empty coffee cup. "When?" She carried the cup to the sink. "Tomorrow? You're shitting me." Setting the cup on the counter, she turned toward me with a smile that lit up her face. "You're on. What time do you think you'll pull in?" She nodded to her cousin, even though I was the one watching her. "Sweet. I'll see you then. Be safe." She hung up, still grinning.

"What's going on with Kate?" I sipped my tea.

"She and Claire are driving up to get a trailer load of Kate and Aunt Deborah's stuff. They'll be in Rapid some time tomorrow morning."

"Are you going to go help them load up?"

"Yeah, wanna come?"

I hadn't seen Claire or Kate in a long time. "Yes, but I can't. Aunt Zoe's coming home and Addy has a school project due on Monday."

"Weekend homework sucks."

Especially for Addy who hated most everything school related. "While you're down there next door to the bitch from hell," who happened to be my little sister, "could you three gang up on her Mob style and physically convince her to pack her bags and move to Cape Horn?"

Natalie laughed. "For you, I'd personally fly her down there and drop-kick her ass out of the plane."

"You're the best, Nat."

"I know and don't forget it." She collected her coat from the chair and stuffed her phone back in the pocket. "I'm off to lunch. Wish me the patience to stomach Detective Hawke and all of his macho sexist talk."

"Or you could just stick a fork in his forehead."

"Don't be giving me any ideas." After a bow, she left me alone with my hangover.

While I worked my way through another cup of honey lemon tea, the kids came and went during commercials from their Saturday morning cartoon lineup, foraging in the pantry as they passed through the kitchen. The cloak of silence had been lifted slightly, but they were still holding a grudge. So was my headache, so the extra quiet today was okay with me.

After some more time with my head in my hands, I finally felt like dragging my body upstairs to find my cellphone and address book. I had a few calls to make before I could crawl back under the covers and curl up while the kids wreaked havoc around me. Thankfully, Cornelius had signed the form I'd left behind in his suite last night when I had raced out of The Old Prospector Hotel and had sent it along with Doc to give to me. That left three other property owners to contact.

The first call was to the owner of the house in which Lily Devine was supposedly killed by one of her clients long ago. The owner was wary at first. Then I gave him the spiel Jerry had told me to use about how this show could increase the interest in the property, especially if we emphasized how kind and generous Lily had been. By the time I'd finished, the owner not only had agreed to sign the form, but had also offered to dig up some old photos he had of Lily at the house, too.

One down, two to go. Next up, the Carhart house in Lead. Since Prudence the ghost didn't have a direct line, I called Wanda Carhart. The house was almost out of her hands, but not quite. She answered right away, probably thinking I was calling to tell her the place was officially sold.

"Hello, Violet." She sounded happy and relaxed now, where before she had been a skittish mess. Moving away from that house and all of its grisly memories was changing her for the better.

"Good morning, Wanda. I'm calling with an odd request."

"You want me to get ahold of Prudence for you?" Wanda had had a direct line to the busybody ghost when she'd lived in the house, which had given me the heebie-jeebies almost every time I'd been there to visit.

"Gosh, no." I'd sooner break dance across red-hot coals. I explained to her about the need for a release form.

"Will this cause any potential problems with the sale going through?"

"Not if the new owners also are on board. I'll be calling them next."

She thought about it for a few seconds. "What about

Prudence?"

I'd asked myself that very question ever since Ray put the Carhart house on the docket. "How do you think Prudence will feel about this, Wanda?"

If anyone had a clue of what could go wrong when I walked into that place with the film crew, it was Wanda.

"I don't know," she answered. "She's not overly fond of strangers. There were a few times back when you first had the place for sale when other Realtors stopped by to look around and see if it was something their clients would like. None of them stayed very long, especially if they visited the upstairs bedrooms."

I wasn't surprised. Upstairs was where Doc had run into Prudence both times he'd gone into the house. It was also where Honey had been possessed when I was ordered by Jerry to take Dickie and her there for a preliminary viewing.

"It would be wise," Wanda continued, "if you stopped by ahead of time and asked Prudence yourself, Violet."

"Uhh …" Or I could not ask Prudence and just call in sick the day the film crew decided to visit the Carhart house. "Yeah, I could, I guess."

"Well, if Prudence and the new owners are okay with a television crew there, then I'd be happy to sign your form."

I hung up feeling anything but skippy-dippy. Based on my experience, I had a feeling taking television cameras into that house was not going to end well.

I called the new owners next, the Brittons, and Zelda was thrilled to have her new dwelling be on TV. She wanted to confirm with Zeke first but gave a preliminary approval.

That left one more—Harvey's ranch. I already knew Harvey was on board, but he'd told me that with all the findings going on out there, Cooper would have to give his blessing or all they could film was the outside of the buildings.

I called Cooper, wincing with each ring.

Five winces in, he answered. "What do you want now, Parker?" He sounded deflated, not pissed and biting as I'd expected.

"My boss would like me to take the Paranormal Realty TV crew out to your uncle's ranch and film inside the house," I paused to clear my throat and build up the nerve to tack on, "and the barn."

Dead silence came through the line.

"Listen, Detective, I don't really want this to happen, so if you're hesitating on telling me 'no' for any reason, don't."

He still didn't speak.

"Besides," I added, "it was Ray Underhill's idea, and between you and me, I think he's doing it just to get under my skin."

Cooper knew all about Ray and my lovey-dovey hatred. He'd taken both of our statements after the Mudder Brothers incident and knew full well to keep Ray and me separated at all times. Unlike Jerry, Cooper didn't care if we played nice or not; he just wanted answers about the missing albino juggernaut that neither of us had.

"Well, Parker," Cooper finally spoke up. "I'd love to be the one to smack your hands and tell you 'no fucking way.' But as of yesterday afternoon, I'm no longer assigned to that particular case."

It was my turn to be quiet, mostly because his announcement knocked the wind out of me, or at least the breath I needed to say anything other than, "Hunnuhwa?"

"Was that even English, Parker?"

I plugged my lips back into my brain. "What happened?"

"That's police business."

Of course it was. "We're back to that again are we?"

"Sounds like it."

"Is there someone else I can contact to get the official veto on the TV crew filming at the crime scene?"

"You can start with the man now in charge of the case."

"Who's that? Your chief?"

"Detective Hawke," he said his partner's name as if it tasted rotten on his tongue.

"You've got to be kidding me."

"I wish I was."

A thought struck me. "Is that why you were hanging out at the Purple Door last night?" Had he been there drowning in his drink just like me?

"Mind your own business."

"Jeez! Do you drink acid every morning for breakfast, Cooper? Or does your body just over-produce it naturally?"

"Are we done here, Parker?"

"Sure. I need to hurry up and call Natalie now anyway," I said without thinking, planning to add to her undercover to-do list for her lunch with Detective Hawke.

"What does this have to do with Ms. Beals?"

Crud. Of course he wouldn't let my slip of the tongue slide by him. "Nothing. Never mind."

"If you think you can undermine the police by getting Ms. Beals to somehow skirt the law on your behalf—"

"Quit your squealing, Wilbur." I cut him off mid-rant.

"Who's Wilbur?"

Oh, yeah. He didn't have kids. "The pig from *Charlotte's Web*. You know, the well-known children's book." When he didn't reply, I added, "It's hard to make fun of you when you don't understand my insults."

"Don't drag Ms. Beals into your fuckups, Parker."

"Sheesh! You need to take a vacation or something, mellow out, and have someone extract that rod of iron rebar from your anal cavity while you're at it."

"Me? Who was the one slamming shots of tequila last night, all wound up about a little girlie ghost?"

"I'm not ashamed of being a big scaredy cat." His mention of last night's disaster reminded me of something. "So, uh, did you go home with Tiffany after we left?"

"Where I sleep is none of your concern."

"Whatever. I'm going to hang up now, Detective, and cross my fingers that I don't have to hear your voice for at least a week."

He sighed. "With that kind of attitude toward your clients, it's a wonder you make any sales."

"Client? Oh, right. That."

"Yes, that. Instead of moving outside of the city limits this winter, I have my uncle and his harem of women shacking up with me."

"I'm trying, Cooper, but I can't control the market."

"I know."

"In the meantime, I know a wonderful ranch house in the country you could move into temporarily. It comes with four bedrooms, two baths, and various body parts scattered around the property."

"Real funny, Parker. Now leave me alone so I can do my damned job."

He hung up on me.

I was in no mood for that today. I hit the redial button.

"What now, Parker?"

"Just this!" I hung up on him.

Then I turned off my ringer. After sending Natalie a quick heads-up text, telling her that Hawke was now in charge of the ranch investigation, I stuffed my phone in my underwear drawer and went to wash away the bitterness left behind after talking to Cooper via a long, hot shower.

The rest of the day passed quickly. While I made my way back from hangover hell via liquids and sleep, the kids entertained themselves by arguing over movies, toys, and bathroom visitation rights. Doc texted a few times, making sure I was alive and well. He was working down in Hill City for the day, and didn't figure on being home until later tonight. I told him about Natalie hanging out with me and extended an invitation but didn't figure he'd show. I couldn't blame him after last night's disaster.

Not to mention that whole thing about my coming from a family of killers business. He hadn't taken me seriously when I'd told Cooper and him that I was a killer. That was too bad, because I'd rather have the truth out in the open than still be sitting on it, waiting for it to crack wide and swallow me whole.

Natalie showed up at the house around suppertime, bringing her mom's famous taco casserole. Her parents had been like a backup set to mine. They still tried to take care of me whenever they could, and I loved them dearly for it.

Her lunch with Detective Hawke had gone swimmingly, as in she'd spent an hour swimming in his bullshit while getting nowhere on any front that helped with our many problems. He'd boasted about being the lead on Harvey's ranch situation to her, and when she'd tried to find out if there was anything new with that, he digressed into his history of being the lead in many cases, going on and on in mundane detail about each until stabbing a fork in her own forehead seemed like the best plan of escape.

After the kids went to bed, we settled onto the couch with two spoons and a tub of peanut butter fudge ice cream between us. I texted Doc but didn't hear back, so I called and left a message. Maybe he was still down in Hill City, working from a hotel room. It wouldn't be the first time he hadn't gone home while on a job.

It was after eleven when Aunt Zoe's phone rang. I practically vaulted off the couch in my haste to get it before the kids woke up.

"Hello?"

"Violet Parker?" It was a woman's voice. The number on the phone had a weird area code. Oh, please don't be the highway patrol from another state with bad news about Aunt Zoe.

I gripped the phone tighter. "Yes?"

"You need to come to Mudder Brothers right now."

All of the spit in my mouth dried up. "Why?"

"Someone has a very important message for you."

"What message?"

"I have no idea."

If this truly was the highway patrol, someone needed to school them on how to deliver this kind of news. "Is it a bad message?"

"Lady, I just said I don't know."

"Well, don't you think that if you call me this late at night with an important message you should have an idea what the message entails?"

"Listen, I was told to call and tell you to go to the garage ASAP. The door will be unlocked. My work here is done."

The garage? That was where they kept the bodies on ice. "Who is this?"

The line went dead.

I hit redial and got some wasted woman who couldn't remember the name of the bar where the payphone I'd called was located and proceeded to tell me about her lousy ex-boyfriend.

"Who called?" Natalie asked from the kitchen doorway.

"My mysterious caller from the other night had one of his lackeys contact me."

"So what did this lackey want?"

"I'm supposed to go over to Mudder Brothers garage, sneak inside, and wait."

"The morgue? When?"

"Tonight."

"Nope. That isn't going to happen."

I worried my lower lip with my teeth.

"Please tell me you're mangling your lip because it itches, not because you're seriously considering going."

"You could watch the kids for me."

"Bad idea."

"What if I call Doc and have him meet me there?"

"Better idea."

I tried Doc. It rang and rang until I got a message that his voicemail was full, so I hung up. "He's not answering."

"Try your other bodyguard then."

I did. Harvey's phone sent me straight to voicemail, which usually meant he was busy with a lady friend. "No luck there, either."

"Shit." She wrapped her arms around her midriff, hunching her shoulders. "I don't think you should go, Vi. Not alone."

"If I don't go, I won't find out who or what is threatening Layne's life."

"If you do go, you could lose yours."

"I don't get that feel from this guy."

"Are you some kind of seer of the future now?"

I wouldn't exactly put me in that category, but my gut said I needed to go. "Maybe."

"What about Detective Cooper? You could have him meet you there."

"Have you been smoking crack? Absolutely not."

"Why not? Because he took your tequila shots away?" She pointed at me. "You still haven't told me why you were drinking last night."

I waved her off. "If Cooper catches wind of me at Mudder Brothers, he'll have me arrested."

"I'd rather have you in jail than dead. There has to be someone else you can take. What about Detective Hawke?"

"Now you're just being a silly nilly."

"Try Doc again."

I tried. Still no answer, only the message about his voicemail being full.

Why was his voicemail full? That seemed odd.

"This is a really bad idea, Vi. Like the queen of bad ideas."

"What's the king?"

"When you decided to have sex with Rex a decade ago."

She had a point there. Instead of sleeping with him, I should have just shot him in the nuts and called it good.

Hey, that had given me an idea! "I'll be right back," I told Natalie and raced down the basement stairs. Elvis was sleeping on a pillow bed in her cage. I took a closer look. Was that the pillow missing from my bed? Then I remembered why I was down here and left the pillow investigation for another time.

Aunt Zoe's shotgun shells were stacked high on a shelf in an old cupboard. I grabbed a box and took the stairs two at a time.

"What are you going to do with those?" Natalie asked when I showed them to her.

"Grab Aunt Zoe's shotgun and take both with me."

"Okay, I'm changing my answer. You taking a loaded shotgun into Mudder Brothers' makeshift morgue at midnight is the king of worst ideas ever."

"I'm not going to load it, just have the shells in my pocket if I need them."

"Vi, do you hear yourself? This is the sort of stupid stuff that blonde bimbos in those slasher horror flicks try."

"I'm not a blonde bimbo. I do know how to load and shoot a shotgun, remember?"

"Of course. I've gone shooting with you. But I really don't think you should do this alone, not with the freaky stuff that went down at Mudder Brothers before. You're like a wounded baby wildebeest stumbling into a lion's den."

I wrinkled my nose at her. "You really need to stop watching those nature documentaries with Layne."

She ran her fingers through her hair. "I know, but the

footage is so amazing."

"Here's an idea—how about I take you with me?"

"What about the kids? We can't leave them here alone."

"I mean on my phone."

"Huh?"

"We do that speak-n-see thing where we talk back and forth while looking at each other in real time."

"So you take me in the morgue with you while I sit here at the kitchen table?"

"Exactly. Then I'm not completely alone and you can contact the cops if anything goes wrong."

"Like you ending up as a new resident in the morgue." She shook her head. "I don't know. That still seems risky."

"Who are you and what did you do with the daredevil version of my friend?"

"I'm cool with being a daredevil, but I don't have kids. Maybe I should go."

"He doesn't want to talk to you. He wants me."

"You could just wait until the next call."

"Nat, if someone is out to hurt my son, I want to know who, damn it!"

"Fine! Go do something incredibly stupid. See if I care."

"Fine, I will." I started out of the room.

"But take me with you on your phone!"

"I'd be happy to." And I meant that. I wasn't relishing going into a morgue at midnight on my own, but if I truly carried the DNA of a killer, then I should be able to handle hanging out with dead people.

Five minutes later, I borrowed Natalie's pickup, since it was far more of a stealth vehicle than the Picklemobile, and was on my way. Aunt Zoe's gun was stashed under the seat along with a chef's knife from the kitchen as a backup weapon, a box of shotgun pellet-filled shells was in my pocket, and Natalie's face was on my cellphone reiterating how harebrained this idea was.

I parked behind the Rec center. The rest of the lot was empty, but I took a shadowed spot far from the orange street lights as an extra precaution. I sat there with the engine ticking, gearing up to step inside a building that housed the dead—and not the wispy, chain-rattling kind.

"I don't think you should take the shotgun, Vi."

I stared down at my phone where Natalie sat all warm, safe, and comfy in my aunt's kitchen. "That's easy for you to say, you're staying topside during this mission."

"I offered to go."

"I know, I know."

"I'm afraid you're going to blow your own toes off."

"You know I'm a fine shooter."

"Yeah, but how are you in dark, tight spaces when someone or something is rushing you?"

What would be rushing me in a morgue? The answers my imagination came up with made me gulp. "This may surprise you, Nat, but you're not helping me here."

She made chicken sounds into the phone.

"I'm not a chicken."

"That's not me. Elvis somehow escaped her cage. She just popped out through the flap in the basement door."

"Don't you let that damned bird near my bedroom."

"I'll tell you what. If you leave your aunt's shotgun in the pickup, I'll keep my eye on Elvis."

"Okay, sheesh. I'll leave the gun behind, but I'm taking the chef's knife."

"Good. Now get going already if you're going to do this before you pee your pants just thinking about it."

I stuffed her in my coat pocket and grabbed the knife from under the seat, trying to hide it against the length of my body as I eased through the shadows toward Mudder Brothers garage. I crossed my fingers that Cooper didn't cruise by with a spotlight. I was pretty sure he'd arrest me without bothering to read me my rights for tiptoeing through the shadows in a hoodie while wielding a big ass knife.

Something fluttered off to my left up in the pine trees that covered the hillside. I quickened my steps, too scared to shine the flashlight toward the trees, more afraid of what I might see than getting ambushed from the side. I tried to keep Layne in the forefront of my thoughts as I tiptoed along the back of the garage, his safety my motivation to keep going instead of turning around, running back to Natalie's truck, and locking myself inside.

There were no vehicles in the Mudder Brothers parking lot. I stalled outside the door to the garage, listening, wondering if I were being set up by one of my white-haired, bulbous-eyed enemies. The night felt soupy with silence. A car cruised up the road every so often, the passengers coming and going with no worries about the frozen dead people inside the garage I was about to enter.

A horn honked in the distance, making me jump.

"Are we there yet?" Natalie asked from my coat pocket.

I pulled my phone out. "Shhhhh." I flipped the view to focus on me, holding my flashlight under my chin so she could see my face.

She flinched back from the screen. "Stop that," she scolded. "I'm freaked out enough as it is."

She was freaked out? That was rich. "Keep your lips shut or I'll mute you. I'm going inside now."

"Where's the love?"

"In my pocket, which is where I'm putting you again." I stuffed her away.

I turned the doorknob. It was unlocked, as the caller had said it would be. The door opened with a raspy sounding creak, like someone had used sand instead of oil on the hinges. As soon as I stepped into the room, I picked up the faint odor of formaldehyde. Then again my brain may have been conjuring up the smell for effect. It was often an asshole like that.

"Are you inside yet?" my pocket asked.

I growled at Natalie's lack of shushing.

Swinging the flashlight and the chef's knife around like a ninja princess, I made sure there wasn't a party of zombies waiting for me. The place was empty except for two gurneys against the side wall and several stacks of various-sized boxes. The door that I knew led to the crematorium was shut, as was the one leading to the deep freeze.

"What're you doing now?" My pocket refused to shush.

I moved over to the boxes, shining my flashlight on them. They were all sealed, no words written on the outside.

"Vi? Are you there?"

That was it. Where was that mute button?

I pulled my phone out again, giving her a 360 degree view lit by the flashlight. "I'm waiting for my caller. If you don't be quiet, I'm going to mute you."

"If you mute me, I'm tucking Elvis into your bed and sprinkling chicken feed under your sheets."

"Don't you dare."

"You should go check out the other rooms. The freezer has multiple shelves."

I knew exactly what those shelves were for. "No, I'm not going near those doors. You and I are waiting right here for a few more minutes, and then we're leaving."

"Where's the knife?"

"I stuffed it in the back of my pants." Not really, but it made me sound tough.

"You're going to cut yourself a new butt crack."

In spite of the fear making me tremble, I giggled. "You know what?"

"What?"

"I'm glad I brought you with me, Max Headroom."

Natalie made a static sound and then said in a robotic sounding voice, "M-m-me, t-t-t-too, Violet P-P-Parker."

"That's a rotten imitation of Max."

"Well, it's been like umpteen million years since—"

The door made that raspy creaking sound again.

I killed my light. Muffling the phone's glow against my boob, I held my breath. Natalie must have figured out what was up, because she held her tongue.

The door clicked shut.

I shoved the phone down my shirt into my bra.

Footfalls crossed the concrete floor toward the freezer room. I could see a dark hulk-like form move through the shadows. It had to be a man ... if it was human.

I lifted my flashlight along with the chef's knife, back in my ninja princess stance. God, I hoped he couldn't hear my heart, which was trying to head-butt its way through my ribcage.

"Hold it right there!" I flicked on the light

Nobody was there. *Shit!*

I moved the flashlight beam from the freezer door to the crematorium door to the exit, landing on nobody. I took several steps toward where I'd seen his shadow, knife at the ready.

Where did he go?

Then I heard it.

Breathing.

Right behind me.

Chapter Twelve

Sunday, October 28th (just after midnight)

Meanwhile, back at the morgue …

I screamed. Not the long-winded, window rattling kind, more like a short screech.

Eddie Mudder shouted back in surprise, his tall, Lurch-like form reeling backward. He stumbled into the wall behind him and something hit the wall with a thud.

"Ouch." He rubbed his head.

"Eddie!" I gasped. "You scared the hell out of me."

He shielded his eyes. "What's with the big knife?"

In lieu of answering, I stared at him, still huffing. I'd forgotten how rich and full bodied his voice sounded. Natalie had once told me Eddie should have been hosting his own late night radio show rather than prepping dead bodies for a long dirt nap.

He protected his torso from a strike. "You're not going to turn into Norman Bates on me are you?"

"What?" Oh, the knife. I lowered it. "Of course not."

I pointed the light upward, casting the two of us in an ambient glow. With Eddie's mesmerizing voice, all we needed was a Barry White love song in the background and a crackling fire in the cremator furnace, and we'd be all set for a romantic evening in the morgue. Maybe Eddie still had some of that mead stashed away in a crate somewhere. What had Doc called it? The elixir of love?

"What did you bring the knife for?" he asked, still rubbing the back of his head. "I didn't tell you to bring a knife. That's dangerous."

I snorted. "What part of having a secret meeting in a morgue at midnight doesn't reek of danger? You're lucky I only brought a knife." An Uzi would have been my weapon of choice given the option. I did a skirrrrch in my head. "Wait! You're my secret caller?"

"Yes."

"You disguised your voice."

"I had to in case anyone else was listening in." He stepped closer, towering over me. "I have to be careful. They're watching me now, and after what happened to George," he shook his head, his face contorting in pain for a moment. "I don't want to end up where he is."

Neither did I. "Who called me tonight on your behalf?"

"Grace."

"Who's Grace?"

"My second cousin." He cocked his head to the side. "Or maybe she's my first cousin once removed. I can never remember how that works."

"Plain ol' cousin works for me."

"She's here to help me out until I either sell the business or find someone to share the load with me. This," he waved his arm around the garage, "is too much for one person, especially with all of the bodies you keep finding."

"Those aren't my fault."

"Detective Hawke isn't so sure. He mentions your name every time he talks to me about the deceased I store in here these days."

That big mouthed detective needed to have my boot stuffed down his gullet for talking about me behind my back. On second thought, maybe I'd sic Prudence on him, tell her he wouldn't give me back her precious box of trophy teeth.

"Is Grace the blonde who was working the room at the Haskell funeral?"

He nodded. "She's always been good with people. Just like George was." He sighed, all sad and lonely.

My heart sniffled for him, but I wasn't here to comfort him. "Why do you want to talk to me, Eddie? Is this something to do with what happened that night in the autopsy room? Something about George?"

"Not George. It's something to do with you."

"Me? What about me?"

"Someone stopped by last week. He showed me a picture of a boy with blond hair and hazel eyes holding what looked like a dinosaur egg made of glass. He wanted to know if I had any idea who the kid was."

My vision tunneled. That was Layne's picture, the one that had been tucked into the mirror in Ms. Wolff's dresser until it had disappeared recently. "A man came by asking you about my son?" Why would he come to Eddie? Maybe he figured with Eddie's role in the community, he knew most of the locals.

He nodded. "But it wasn't a man. It was one of them."

"Them?" I had a lot of "thems" in my world, so I wanted to be certain to which *them* he was referring. "What do you mean by 'them'?"

"One of those white-haired ghouls that hung around here when George was still alive."

I knew exactly who he meant. I'd had many nightmares starring that very "ghoul" along with his decapitation-happy twin.

"Let me talk to Eddie." Natalie said from where I'd stuffed her in my bra.

Eddie stared down at my chest. "That's odd. I could swear a voice inside your shirt said it wants to talk to me."

"It does." I dug down inside the neckline of my shirt, pulling out my cellphone. "Actually, it's a she—it's Natalie." When Eddie continued to stare at me without acknowledgement, I added, "Natalie Beals. She's on the phone with me right now."

"You brought her along on your phone? Very clever."

I had my moments, even though they were few and far between. I held up my phone, hitting the button that flipped the focus to the camera on the backside. "Nat, say hi to Eddie."

"Hi, Eddie," she said, all sunshine and blue skies.

Eddie held up the two-finger peace sign back.

"Eddie, did the ghoul say why he wanted to know who Layne was?"

"No. He had other questions, too."

"Like what?" she asked.

"What I knew about his brother's killer."

"What do you know?" I wasn't sure what Cooper had told Eddie after his brother, George, had died.

"Not much, except that you and Natalie were involved somehow. The police have been very closed-lipped about most everything. They ask me questions but never answer any that I ask in return."

"You and me both," I told him.

"Did you give him Violet's name?" Natalie asked.

"Of course not. You and I both know why he's asking questions." He frowned down at me. "You're in danger, Violet. This ghoul, he's stronger than his twin was."

I'd witnessed his brother pick up and throw Doc like he was a rag doll. How much stronger could he be? Like Incredible Hulk strong? "They both looked the same size to me."

"I don't mean physically. This one is smarter. He was always watching and planning. George once told me he was the brains of the two."

So I'd killed the dumb thug and left the mastermind brother behind? Not one of my brighter moves by far.

"When he finished asking me questions," Eddie continued, "he warned me about you."

"What do you mean?"

"He told me to beware, that death would follow you."

That warning seemed oddly familiar, something someone had told me once a while ago. Maybe it was just something from a nightmare. I pointed at my chest. "Death follows me?" The ax swinging juggernaut had been his twin, not mine.

"Then he called you some weird name and left."

"What was the name, Eddie?" Natalie asked.

He scratched his jaw. "It sounded gurgly, ending with a *rickter* sound."

I knew the exact name I'd been called. Someone else had recently called me it, too, and then ended up with a shrunken and shriveled head. "Was it *Scharfrichter*, Eddie?"

"That was it. What does it mean?"

It meant *executioner* in German, but I didn't feel like spreading the English version around town. "It means that I have a new nickname in Deadwood."

And a killer reputation that went with it.

* * *

I waited until the sun had come up before heading over to Doc's place. I drove Natalie's pickup so I wouldn't wake up the whole neighborhood with the Picklemobile's noisy exhaust. Natalie planned to hang out with the kids until Harvey or Aunt Zoe could spell her, since I had to go into the office to spend time catching up on what Jerry and the film crew had planned for me tomorrow.

Last night, I'd tried calling Doc once more after returning from my top-secret Mudder Brothers meeting, but I'd still gotten the message saying his voicemail was full. Natalie had practically shoved me back out the door, insisting that if Doc wasn't answering the phone, I go over and pound on his door. I'd dug in my heels, reminding her that we had a perfectly good shotgun and a few boxes of shells ready and waiting. In the end, my bullheadedness had won the battle. Judging from her red-lined eyes and crazy hair at breakfast, she hadn't slept much better than I had.

I pulled up in front of Doc's house and cut the engine, staring at his door through the shroud of fog that blanketed the hills this morning. Should I tell him about the albino ghoul using my new nickname? About why he was using it? Maybe it was time to get this damned deadly family history of mine out in the open so it could fester in broad daylight.

My mind made up, I palmed his house key and headed up the walkway. The thud of my boot heels on the concrete sounded muffled thanks to the cool mist swirling around me. I pulled my leather coat closed, but it didn't stop my nerves from quaking. Not much would after finding out the juggernaut's twin was sniffing around, searching for me.

I debated on ringing the doorbell or knocking, but then I pictured Doc all wrapped up in his sheets and decided it might be more fun to surprise him awake. The lock clicked with a quiet thunk. I closed the door behind me, turning the deadbolt.

The house had a silence that comes only with early mornings

and a lack of fighting children. For a moment, I thought I smelled coffee, but it was probably just my cravings for caffeine messing with my head. Tiptoeing up the stairs, I winced when one let out a small creak. Then I heard the sound of a door closing followed by the water kicking on in the shower.

Perfect. Even better. Maybe I'd join him.

I'd reached the top of the stairs when something clinked in the kitchen and then the microwave kicked on.

That gave me pause.

Was somebody else here with Doc?

I peeked along the upstairs hallway; all of the doors were closed except for the room at the end that Doc used as an office. Meanwhile down in the kitchen, the faucet turned on and off.

Somebody else was here. Someone who had spent the night and was now in need of a shower. Someone who had made Doc not want to answer his phone when his girlfriend had kept hounding him late last night.

The jealousy ogre woke up with a start. Who was here? Was it a certain red-headed ex? Had she showed up on his doorstep last night wearing nothing but a trench coat and heels? Was this some sort of revenge she was dishing my way for the other night at the Purple Door?

No, no, no. Doc wouldn't do that to me.

Are you sure?

Not entirely, no. A decade ago, I'd walked in on the father of my children and my sister having sex. Besides lighting a fire of anger that still smoldered inside me, seeing Rex and Susan in the thick of passion in my own bed had left thin scar tissue overlying deeply engrained trust issues.

I sat down on the top step, or more like my knees gave out and I fell on my butt. What should I do? Was I up to confronting a cheating boyfriend after a night of hyperventilating off and on about a tall, snake-eyed ghoul chasing me through Deadwood's infamous haunts? Should I slink right back out the way I came in and go home to lick my wounds before painting on a brave face and heading in to practice my lines? Or should I pack up some clothes, grab the kids, head to the airport, buy tickets to somewhere in the southern hemisphere, and run far, far away from this super-cell of a shitstorm?

Before I could make a decision, I heard footfalls coming from the kitchen. Doc came into view at the base of the stairs. His eyes widened at the sight of me sitting there.

"Violet, when did you come in?"

"A few minutes ago." I held my poker cards close to my chest, waiting to see how he was going to play his hand.

He rested his forearm on the square newel at the bottom of the stair rail, his bare foot planted on the first step. Something on my face must have kept him from coming up to join me.

"What's going on?" he asked, his expression cautious. Wise man.

"You tell me, Doc."

"I'm making breakfast."

"Oh yeah? For who?"

His eyes narrowed. "What's going on in that beautiful head of yours, Violet?"

"Just so you know from the start, flattery isn't going to cut it this morning. I tried calling you several times last night around midnight, but got your voicemail every single time."

The sound of the shower kicked off. That was fast. Just a quick rinse maybe to wash the sex off from last night?

Or not. I needed to give Doc the benefit of the doubt before letting that jealous ogre park itself behind the controls.

"Why were you trying to call me?"

"I would have been happy to fill you in last night, had you not been too busy to take my call."

"I'm never too busy for you."

"Then why didn't you answer? Were you afraid I might hear that you had company?"

He pointed up toward the bathroom. "You mean that company?"

"Of course I mean *that* company."

"Actually that company crashed well before midnight."

"So you're admitting that you spent the night with someone?"

He pinched his lips as if choosing his words carefully or trying not to laugh. "Well, sort of."

In the pregnant pause that followed his confession, I heard the shower curtain open. I looked down at where my hands dangled between my knees, wishing he'd played the denial card. My heart felt bruised every time it thumped in my chest.

"Why were you calling me at midnight, Violet?"

"I needed you." That came out sounding more raw than I'd intended. I lifted my chin, determined not to let him see any more signs of weakness. I came from a family of killers, for crissake. It was time to suck it up. "I had a bit of a situation, but you were obviously too preoccupied to be bothered."

On second thought, that option to go home and lick my wounds suddenly seemed like the best choice for me, ASAP. I stood. "I should go. Now is not a good time for this."

Never would be too soon.

"Quit dancing around what's bothering you, Violet. We're beyond that now."

Were we? "Your voicemail is full."

He grimaced. "I wondered if that would happen."

I took a couple of steps toward him. "But you should have been able to see my number on your Recent Calls list." I stopped two steps above him, almost eyelevel. "I'm not buying that you had no idea I called, so don't even try that bullshit on me."

"I'm not." His dark eyes held mine. He seemed so damned calm and rational. Was that a hint of a smile on the corner of his lips?

"Okay," I said, unfamiliar with this style of arguing. Most of my fights involved at least a little bit of yelling or throwing something in frustration. Could it be I'd woken up in another dimension? A world full of unemotional Vulcans? "Listen, I need to go home and start over again. Do you mind stepping aside so I can leave you to enjoy breakfast with your companion?"

"I'm not moving and neither are you." When I hit him with a glare, he raised his brows. "I want you to join us."

I tilted my head. "That's just mean."

"I'll throw in some bacon."

"What in the hell is going on, Doc?"

He snagged my hand, holding tight when I tried to pull it away. "Why were you calling me so late last night, Violet?"

"You should have answered your phone and then you'd know."

"I couldn't. I left it at my client's office."

And the walls came tumbling down. "Ohhh." Of course it was something that simple. But that still didn't answer who was in his bathroom.

"I didn't realize I'd left it until after I got home," he continued. "I decided to wait to contact him until today about getting it back."

"Don't you ever delete your voicemails?"

"Yes, but that's another problem I didn't want to deal with last night." He pulled me down a step, closing the distance between us. "Why were you calling me last night?"

"I got a call."

"From who?"

"My secret pal."

His eyes creased with concern. "What did he want?"

"Actually it was his helper who called. She told me to meet him at midnight in Mudder Brothers' garage."

"Please tell me you didn't go."

I squared my jaw. "Layne's welfare was at stake."

"You took someone with you, though, right?"

"You weren't taking my calls."

"What about Harvey?"

"He was on a date."

"Christ, Violet." Exasperation rippled across his face. "You went to the morgue all alone at midnight to meet someone who has been calling you with threatening messages?"

"They weren't threats, they were warnings." I pulled my hand free from his. "Besides, I wasn't completely alone."

"Let me guess. You had Jiminy Cricket in your pocket?"

"Not Jiminy, Natalie."

He stared at me, clearly not registering.

"I took Natalie on my phone. We used that see-and-talk feature."

He scoffed. "You took Natalie on your phone with you to meet a potential killer?"

"Well, somebody had to stay home with my kids."

He turned and sat down on the step next to my boots, covering his face. "She's going to be the death of me yet," he told his palms. Then he dragged his fingers down his cheeks and asked the front door, "Why didn't she come and get me? I live four blocks away. The one day I forget my cellphone and she goes to meet a killer alone in the dark at a morgue."

"It's more like five blocks, maybe six." I sat down next to him. "And I didn't want to bother you because I thought you weren't taking my calls."

"Why would I not take your calls, Violet?" He bumped my knee with his. "You're my girlfriend, crazy."

"Because you were busy with your company." I pointed up the stairs, reminding him we weren't alone.

"Listen to me, woman, and burn this in your brain." He cupped my jaw. "No matter who I'm with, I am never, ever too busy for you."

"Even if it's another woman?"

"Ever."

"Like a certain redhead who likes sports sex?"

"Ever."

"The same redhead who I'm afraid is in your upstairs bathroom as we speak?"

He let go of my chin. "It's not Tiffany."

"Then who is it?"

Doc glanced over my head. He stood and pulled me up with him. "See for yourself."

I turned slowly.

Cooper stood at the top of the stairs in black jeans and one of his bullet hole T-shirts. His blond hair was spikey and disarrayed, bristly to match his normal temperament.

"Oh, fudge." If I'd have known Cooper would be here, I'd have worn a Kevlar vest under my sweater. "I'd rather it have been Tiffany, I think," I said under my breath.

Doc chuckled.

"Parker, did I hear you tell Nyce you were at the morgue last night?"

I looked back at Doc. "What's Cooper doing here again? Please don't tell me you're dumping me for him." That would be a knockout punch to my self-esteem.

He lifted my hand and kissed the back of my fingers. "I prefer my blondes to come with long curly hair and lots of curves."

"So Cooper was the one in the shower?"

Doc nodded. "He's going to move into my spare room for the winter and give his uncle the place to himself."

I frowned up at Cooper. "Why would you do that?"

"Uncle Willis has been there one week and turned the place into his goddamned love nest already."

But why Cooper? I frowned at Doc. "You realize he's going to threaten to arrest me every time I come over to see you, right?"

The ever-growly detective came down the stairs, his steely eyes piercing me. "You didn't answer my question, Parker. Were you at Mudder Brothers last night?"

"Why?" I stepped closer to Doc, ready to use him as a shield. "I didn't do anything wrong."

"Besides go there without me," Doc mumbled.

I wrinkled my nose at him. "How was I to know you'd forgotten your cellphone and were hanging out here at home having a pillow fight with Detective Cooper?"

Doc grinned at my joke, Cooper didn't. "Next time," Doc said, "stop by and get me."

"Who was in the morgue with you?" Cooper crossed his arms, lording down over me from halfway up the stairs.

I crossed my arms back. "None of your business. Neither of us were breaking and entering or harassing anyone, so there is nothing you can use to threaten me with an arrest this time, Detective."

"That's where you're wrong, Parker." He held up his cellphone. "I got a text from Detective Hawke while I was in the shower. He asked if I knew where you were."

"Why? What's he want from me now?" I doubted it was to find out my recipe for chocolate chip cookies.

"A 911 call came in last night from Eddie Mudder. Something about a prowler outside the morgue. When the cops showed up at the funeral parlor, Eddie's assistant mentioned your name."

"Grace is Eddie's cousin, not assistant."

"And how do you know that detail?"

"That doesn't matter. Is Eddie okay?"

"We don't know."

"Why not?"

"Because Eddie called and then disappeared."

I placed my hand over my chest, remembering Eddie's words about being watched. He'd warned of the danger I was in, but he must have been at risk as much as me. Had someone seen us sneak into the morgue last night? Was it the juggernaut's twin? Did the creepy ghoul know Eddie was trying to help me and now Eddie was paying the price for reaching out to me?

"Do you know something about this, Parker? Because if you do, you need to tell me now. No more fucking around."

"I ... I don't know where Eddie is."

Cooper nodded slowly, his gaze measuring me. "I believe you about Eddie, but what about the body?"

"What body?"

"The faceless one you found in my uncle's safe."

"What about it?"

"Last night, when you were in the morgue *not* breaking and entering or committing any other crime, did you happen to help Eddie move the dead guy anywhere?"

"Eww. No, of course not. Why would you ask that?"

"Because Eddie's not the only missing body. Our faceless friend is gone, too."

Chapter Thirteen

Meanwhile, back in Lemon-ville ...

Why was it when life gave me lemons, it dumped them on my head by the truckload?

First the dead guy in the safe, then Wilda, now the albino's twin and Eddie. There was only so much freaky shit a girl could handle before she took up permanent residence under her bed.

Standing opposite to where I sat bellied up to Doc's kitchen bar, Cooper drilled me about my meeting last night with Eddie. While he chowed down two pieces of toast and gulped coffee, I backtracked to the first phone message Eddie had left with Mona and wrapped it up with my return to Aunt Zoe's after Eddie's face-to-face warning.

Per his usual modus operandi, Cooper made me repeat my story two more times, taking notes in his little notebook with each retelling. Then he gnawed on my ass for another five minutes about how I should have contacted him right after I got the first call and how irresponsible I was being with my safety. After getting another text from Hawke that he refused to share, Cooper left in a huff.

I flipped off his back as he shut the front door. The damned detective was lucky I hadn't had lemons to throw at his head on the way out.

Doc stuck a plate with eggs and bacon under my nose. "Eat up, Superstar. You have a big prep day at the office to get through."

Picking up the fork he had left on the plate, I groaned. "Don't remind me."

He parked on the bar stool next to me with a matching plate of his own. We ate in silence for a few bites.

He took a sip of coffee and then turned to me. "Do you really think I'd let Tiffany spend the night here?"

I froze mid-bite, my neck warming. "Maybe," I answered, shoving a piece of bacon into my big, dumb jealous pie-hole before I made matters worse.

He returned to his eggs, eating a couple more forkfuls. I peeked over at him, worrying about what was going through his head.

"Violet," he took another swallow of coffee before continuing. "What's it going to take to make you trust me?"

Boy, was that a loaded question. I chewed on it for a few more seconds, vetoing anything having to do with a wedding band or the words 'I love you,' since asking him to offer either seemed to dilute the potency of them.

In the end, I settled for the truth. "Time."

He poked at the last couple bites of eggs with his fork. "I'm not Rex."

"I know."

"Yeah, but do you understand that I'd never do anything to hurt you like he did?"

I picked up another piece of bacon, studying it while I gulped back the rush of emotions trying to rise up my throat and leak out my eyes. As I turned the bacon this way and that, blinking back tears, I considered spilling the truth, telling him how gaga I was for him, explaining that my silly jealousy was born from a fear of losing one of the best things that had ever happened to me. But then I thought about my family history and how I should probably come clean with that particular nasty skeleton before I opened my mouth and poured my heart out onto my plate next to my eggs.

"Doc," I set the bacon down and wiped my fingers on the cloth napkin on my lap. "We need to talk about something."

His eyebrows pulled together. "This sounds serious."

My phone rang in my pocket, playing the whistling version of the Harlem Globetrotters' theme song. "Crap, that's Jerry calling."

Doc grinned. "The Harlem Globetrotters?"

"It seemed fitting."

"Very."

"I should probably take this."

He nodded.

I pulled it out of my pocket. "Hi, Jerry."

"Violet, we have a bit of a problem."

"What's wrong?"

"Dickie's camera man is coming down with a cold."

"So you want me to get some medicine for him?"

"No, Honey has taken care of that. The second camera jockey is still healthy, but we need to rearrange the schedule and get as much done as possible in case either of them gets too sick to work for a day or two."

"What does that mean?"

"We're going to start filming today instead of tomorrow."

Ack! "But … but … I'm not ready."

"You're ready enough. If you could come in a little early this morning, we can talk about your script and get you practiced on the mic. Then you'll head over to the Devine house and do a few takes."

"With Ray?"

"And me. I want to watch how things go today, see if any ideas for more ways to make Calamity Jane Realty shine even brighter come to mind."

I thought about suggesting we jam a big spotlight up Ray's ass and see if light comes out through his mouth, but I doubted Jerry would appreciate my sense of humor in the thick of this sudden change of plans.

"I'll be there as soon as I can."

"Thank you, Violet. Don't forget to wear the outfit we discussed."

"Right." I growled in my throat, my loathing surfacing for that pink silk suit. Why did Jerry have such a hard on for pink? There were plenty of other perfectly good colors that didn't leave me looking like I'd been spun around the inside of a cotton candy maker.

"You're not getting sick, too, are you?" he asked.

"No, just clearing my throat. See you shortly." I hung up and wrinkled my lip at the phone.

"Another sunny day in real estate paradise?"

I wiped my hands on my napkin. "Something like that. We're going to start filming today instead of tomorrow." I slid off the bar stool and carried my plate over to the dishwasher. "I have to go home and change into the outfit Jerry wants me to wear, grab my makeup, and try to get the red lines out of my eyes."

Doc followed me to the front door. "What did you want to talk about before Jerry called?"

Oh, jeez, I couldn't just throw out that I was a killer and then run off to work. "It can wait. It's not that big of a deal," I lied. After my jealous reaction this morning, I didn't want to leave him thinking anything was wrong between us.

The crinkles at the edge of his eyes showed his suspicion otherwise. "You sure?"

Nope, but I was going to do my best to remove the doubt from his mind. With all of the shit tornado-ing through in my life right now, I needed Doc to keep holding my hand and not let go.

I walked back to where he leaned against the archway into the dining room. Going up on my tiptoes, I framed his smooth-shaven face with my hands and pulled his mouth down to mine. Starting slow, I flirted with his lips. When he teased back, I warmed things up, my tongue tempting his. He took the bait, his breaths quickening, his body hardening.

"I've missed you," I whispered when I stopped to catch my breath and then dove in for more. He tasted like heaven with a side of happily-ever-after, and I wanted to drag him upstairs and show him how much I needed everything he was willing to give.

I wrapped my arms around his neck, putting my whole heart into the kiss this time, pressing against him while his hands travelled up and down my back.

"God, woman," he said, breaking the kiss. His breath was uneven, matching mine. "You have the most talented mouth."

"You think?" I trailed my lips along his jawline, purring as his hands slid up under my sweater, exploring my curves, lighting the furnace inside me with his fingertips. "How do you like this?" I scraped my teeth along the shell of his ear, spurring a groan from deep in his throat.

"Stay a little longer, Boots."

"I can't."

"I'll make it worth your time." His hands slid down over my skirt, pressing me against his hips.

It had been way too long since we'd last had a moment alone to explore and play. I felt my resolve weakening. "Oh, yeah? How?"

The Harlem Globetrotters whistled from my pocket again. Jerry wasn't done giving me orders. *Damn!*

I pulled away, staring up into dark brown eyes full of wicked promises.

Double damn!

"You'd better answer," Doc said, "before he sends Curly Neal or Meadowlark Lemon to come and bounce-pass you all the way into the office."

I held my phone to my ear. "Hello?"

"Violet, could you bring all three outfits I bought for you? Honey wants to make sure the pink suit doesn't clash with what Dickie's wearing."

I wondered how they'd feel if I showed up looking like Ronald McDonald, red nose, big shoes, and all. "Got it."

"See you shortly." Jerry hung up.

"Thanks for breakfast." I told Doc, shoving my phone back in my skirt pocket.

"Anytime." He helped me slip on my coat. "And I mean that, Boots."

"Thanks." *And I love you, Doc.*

"Don't be going to any more morgues without me." He toyed with my coat collar.

I stole one more kiss from him for the road.

"You're going to be the death of me, you know," he said when I pulled away.

Being the *Scharfrichter* that I was, I hoped to hell his words ended up as the jest he intended and not the prophecy I feared.

I smiled, keeping things easy-breezy. "Not if your new roommate throws me in the slammer first."

"Don't worry." He held the door for me. "Cooper's on your side."

"I hope so, because if you're wrong, I'll be wearing the latest fashion in chain-gang." I winked at him. "They'll make for some kinky conjugal visits, though."

* * *

Later that afternoon, after a morning filled with hair and makeup prepping, script practicing, and microphone testing, I stood in the garishly-striped bedroom where Lily Devine reportedly had taken her last breath in this rough and tumble world.

Across the room, Dickie and Honey stood huddled together, arguing about infinitesimal filming details down to the exact place on the floor where he should stand. Every so often, they'd turn and confer with the getting-sicker-by-the-minute camera guy, who I'd found out went by the name Rad.

I wasn't sure if Rad was his first name or last, and I didn't bother asking. Frankly, after finding out that not only was the albino's much shrewder twin looking for me, but that he'd likely kidnapped or killed Eddie for warning me, I didn't give a crap if the camera guy called himself Don Quixote and attacked windmills. My main concern was that he made sure I didn't look like a laughingstock on television.

"Hey, Realtor lady," called the fourth member of Dickie and Honey's TV crew from the bedroom doorway—a woman I guessed to be in her early forties. Rad had introduced her as Rosy *something*, one of his camera carrying cohorts when I'd arrived at Lily Devine's house. He'd told me her full name while we had been standing there on the front porch waiting for Dickie and Honey, but the last part had zipped in one ear and out the other, because right then I'd seen a police cruiser coming our way. The fear that Detective Hawke was coming to drag me down to the station had almost sent me running into the pine trees behind Lily's house. Much to my relief, it turned out to be some other cop doing a neighborhood drive-by.

Rosy waved me over, setting the camera down on the floor just inside the room. With the way her biceps bulged under her T-shirt whenever she hefted the camera around, she reminded me of Rosy the Riveter. I sort of expected her to flex her muscles for me and cheer, "We can do it!"

When I joined Rosy the Riveter, she led me out into the hallway. "Rad wanted me to do some random filming throughout the house while they get Dickie prepped." She glanced around a little wildly, her eyes wide, and then leaned in closer. "I saw something kind of weird," she whispered.

In this house? I'd been in Lily's old haunt several times and hadn't seen anything. Then again, I was a dud when it came to the wispy crowd, so my lack of ghost spotting meant diddly squat.

Normally I'd be skeptical about her claim, but after some of the spooky stuff I'd witnessed in this town, I was all ears. I glanced down the hallway toward the open doorway at the end that led to one of the other bedrooms. "What did you see?"

"Let me show you." Rosy led the way to the basement doorway and started downstairs. "It's down here."

I hesitated at the top. I didn't like the basement in this house and it was all Doc's fault. The first time I'd been in the place I'd been showing him around and he'd refused to come down the basement stairs after me, ordering me to come back up immediately.

Rosy looked up at me from the bottom step, the fluorescent lights making her brown hair look auburn. "What's wrong?"

"Nothing," I said, shaking off my willies and clomping down to join her. "So what was it?"

She led me around to the underside of the stairs. "I was checking back here to see if there was a trap door or some creepy little storage cubby like I've seen in some other old houses we've filmed, and I noticed these."

I bent down and looked at where Rosy was shining her penlight. High on the wall, mostly hidden from view by the stairwell, were two large, rusty eyebolts sticking out of the wall. "What's weird about those?"

"I saw this movie once where a serial killer was keeping his victims chained to the wall in his basement using these suckers. He had them screwed into the posts so the victims couldn't pull them free." She turned the penlight on me, making me squint. "Do you think Lily Devine's killer kept her chained up down here before he murdered her?"

I stepped back, rubbing my forehead. "I haven't heard that version of the story."

To be honest, before today, I hadn't really heard any details of what happened besides the bit about her supposedly being killed in the bedroom with the striped wallpaper—the very room where Honey and Dickie were probably ready to start filming by now ... I hoped. After reading my lines earlier about the house's grisly history in front of the camera several times, I was ready to wrap it up, go home, and climb into a pair of pajamas.

As if on cue, Honey called down the stairwell for Rosy and her camera. "We're ready to film Dickie's piece."

Had I called that or what? Maybe I should try my hand at soothsaying as a side gig.

I checked my cellphone as Rosy headed up the steps, grimacing at three messages from Detective Hawke in my voicemail. Geez, Louise! That man should change his name to Detective Badger with the way he locked his jaws onto something and refused to let go.

I started to follow Rosy up the stairs but then decided to take a picture of the eyebolts to show Doc. Maybe he knew the details of how Lily's last moments had gone and could confirm or negate Rosy's theory. Bending down, I leaned under the stairs, waiting for my cellphone camera to adjust to the lighting and focus. I took three pictures of the bolts from different angles and then double-checked to make sure they came out okay.

The stairs over my head creaked.

With a gasp, I stood up quickly, banging my head on the bottom of one of the steps. Cursing myself for being such a Nervous Nelly, I stumbled out from under the stairs. The top of my head throbbed thanks to the Fred Flintstone-like lump popping up.

"What are you doing down here, Blondie?"

Ray had found me. Damn!

I'd managed to avoid the cocky asshole back at the office and had driven separately claiming that I needed my own wheels in case my kids had an emergency. But now there wasn't much I could do to dodge him until Dickie and Honey finished filming for the day.

"I'm just checking out something." I straightened my pink silk suit jacket, brushing off some dust I'd picked up from under the stairs.

"Jerry called." Ray told me, frowning at my hair. "He's on his way."

Jerry had been delayed helping Ben and me round up the last of the release forms from a couple of clients. He was going to call the police station one last time and try to get an "okay" for a visit out to Harvey's ranch. I didn't have much faith he'd succeed on that front, especially with the faceless body now missing, but who was I to jump up and down all over his hopes.

"They're almost ready for you again upstairs." Ray reached out toward my hair and I jerked back. "Relax, Blondie. You have a cobweb in your hair."

I held still while he plucked it out, resisting the urge to grab his arm and bite him for crowding my space with his abundance of Stetson cologne. Someone needed to teach the blockhead how to dab not dump.

"Got it," he shook the cobweb off his hand.

"Thanks," I mumbled, trying to mean it. Being civil to the man I dreamed daily about dumping hot coffee on took a lot of willpower. "I'll go touch up my makeup before it's show time again." I tried to walk around him, but he snagged me by the elbow.

"Don't screw this up like you do everything else."

And we were back to our mutual hatred. At least he was doing a bang-up job of hiding it from the TV people.

I shook off his hand. "I know my lines, I've practiced, I'm ready to go." After tossing and turning, worrying about that damned albino twin all night, I wanted to go up there and rattle off the remaining bits Mona had written about Lily Devine, then spend the night avoiding Detective Hawke while catching up with Aunt Zoe about her trip ... and maybe whispering sweet nothings in Doc's ear, given the chance.

I started up the stairs and then remembered Ray's role in the freaky events that had happened the night George Mudder was killed. Did Ray know something about the albino goon's twin that could help me keep Layne safe?

I came back down. "Ray? What do you know about George's killer?"

His cheeks darkened to a deep red, his gaze narrowing. "What the fuck are you digging at, Blondie?" he said under his breath. "You sure you want to dance this dance with me again now that Detective Hawke has you under a microscope?"

Crikey! How many people had Hawke been running his mouth to about me lately? If he kept it up, the detective and I were going to have a fist-to-gut chat about my feelings on police harassment.

I glanced at the top of the stairwell, making sure we didn't have an audience. "Calm down, Ray. I don't want to fight about this. I just need to know what you know about that big white-haired goon who threatened to perform surgery on you with a scalpel and then killed George."

Ray closed the distance between us. "Listen close, Violet, and get this through your pretty little blonde brain. What I was doing with George Mudder prior to you butting in and making a mess of everything is none of your goddamned business."

I held my finger up under his stupid fake-tanned face. "First of all, I didn't butt in. You screwed up somehow and tipped the goon off."

"If you're as smart as everyone thinks you are," Ray continued, all menacing with a muscle in his jaw pulsing, "you'll keep your nose out of it."

He and Cooper really had a fixation with my nose. I raised another finger under his. "Second, I'm not asking what you were doing with George; I'm asking what you know about the white-haired creep who tried to cut you into pieces of sushi."

He rested back on his heels. "Why?"

"Curiosity."

"I don't believe that for a minute."

"Okay, let's just say that ever since that night, I've been thinking."

He snickered. "Blondie, you should skip thinking and stick to doing what you do best."

"What's that, Ray? Saving your imbecilic, chauvinistic ass? Because while you keep telling the cops and others your tall tale about how things went down in that autopsy room, you and I both know the truth—had it not been for me, you'd be dead."

"If it hadn't been for you, I would have never been found out and George would be alive."

"How is your screw up my fault, Ray?"

His mouth opened and closed like a dying fish, no words coming out. He looked away, his face scrunching into something even uglier than normal. "Because you put me off my game with your threats."

I placed my hand over my chest. "Little ol' blonde-haired me messed with your big smart manly head?"

"Fuck off, bitch." He glared at me. "We're done here. Get upstairs and let's finish this shit for today."

I would love to, but I wasn't done with him. "I'm not going up those stairs until you tell me what you know about the white-haired goon's twin brother—and don't pretend you don't know who I'm talking about."

He crossed his arms over his chest, his lips pressed tight like a stubborn child.

"Come on, Ray. I need your help." When he continued to stand there with his lips zipped shut, I grabbed one of his arms and squeezed. "Damn you, Underhill. Listen, Eddie Mudder told me that the albino's twin brother came around looking for my son. I'm afraid of what's going to happen if the brother finds Layne."

When Ray still refused to talk, I threw up my hands. It was that or wrap them around Ray's dumb thick neck and squeeze. "This is bigger than you and me, Ray." I looked around for something to kick besides Ray's shins, but the concrete walls could mean a broken toe and ER visits cost a ton of money, so I snarled through my teeth at the jackass avoiding my glare. "What was I thinking? Like you'd actually try to be something other than the selfish prick you always are and help me keep my child safe."

I started up the steps, done with the horse's ass.

"The other albino goes by the name Mr. Black." Ray's voice made me pause midway up the stairs.

I came back down a few steps. "That's ironic, considering the color of his hair."

Ray shrugged. "That's about all I know. Black stayed in the background, letting his brother—or whatever he was to him—act as the front man."

"You think they might not be brothers?"

"I don't know what they are or were, and I was smart enough not to ask questions. It was George's business; I was just there to find out a few answers for the cops as part of the deal. In the end, I got sloppy because you had me off my game. George tried to protect me from those two goons, as you call them, and was murdered for it."

George was hiding Natalie from the one who was threatening Ray that night, too. "I'm sorry George was killed. He seemed like a kind man."

"Too kind. That's what got him into trouble. He couldn't say no, and those two assholes preyed on that weakness."

We stood there in an awkward silence for a moment. I had no idea what to say to Ray when he wasn't acting like a dickhead toward me. Footsteps crossed overhead.

"Violet?" Jerry's deep voice echoed down the stairwell. "Ray?

Where are you two?"

"Thanks for telling me Mr. Black's name," I said quietly so Jerry couldn't hear us.

"If I were you, Blondie, I wouldn't ask around about him too much."

"Why? You think the cops will come after me for badgering you for information?" I half-jested.

"It's not the cops you should be afraid of now." Something in his expression gave me pause.

"Ray, does Detective Cooper know about Mr. Black's name?"

He shook his head.

"Why not?" I would have thought he'd have spilled all of the details during Cooper's post-murder interrogation.

"Because George warned me about Mr. Black." He looked at his hands, then back at me, his expression haunted. "And George wasn't prone to exaggeration."

I took another step down, my grip on the stair rail tightening. "What did George say?"

"That Mr. Black has a fetish."

"A fetish for what?"

Ray's gaze was flat, serious. "Body parts."

"Oh, Jesus," I whispered, remembering the barbed hook Mr. Black's brother had threatened me with, the same bloody weapon left at the bottom of the Open Cut next to Jane's shredded body. "Here there be monsters."

Chapter Fourteen

Meanwhile, back in the garage-turned-morgue ...

Later that evening, after wolfing down a meal of pork chops, candied yams, and apple dumplings thanks to Harvey's handiwork, Aunt Zoe and the old buzzard sat drinking coffee at the kitchen table while Doc and I washed and put away dinner dishes.

The kids were upstairs in their room serving out their punishment after getting into an argument after dessert. Layne had barely finished swallowing his last bite of dumpling when he declared he didn't feel good and asked if he could stay home from school again tomorrow.

Addy had expressed her skepticism about his illness in her typical sisterly way. "Liar! Mom, he's trying to skip out of school because he's being a big baby."

"I am not!" Layne had emphasized his rebuttal by reaching out and punching her shoulder with so much aggression that I was stunned for a moment.

Addy let out a warrior yell that would have made Chief Crazy Horse's stone-chiseled profile smile. She swung back before I could catch her arm, clocking Layne in the cheek, leaving a nasty red welt that was still there after icing his cheek off and on for the last half hour.

So up in their rooms they sat, grumbling about how neither had been treated fairly during my ten-second mock-trial before I'd delivered their sentences.

I rinsed the soap off the green and blue colored glass serving plate, one of Aunt Zoe's experimental pieces, and carefully handed it to Doc. "Sorry about that fiasco with the kids after supper."

He took the plate and started towel drying it. "Addy has a wicked backhand. She takes after her mother."

His grin became a chuckle when I flicked rinse water at him. He snapped my butt with the towel, making me squawk.

"Violet and Doc," Aunt Zoe interrupted our cavorting, "don't make me send you both to your room, too."

Harvey snorted. "That'd be like shuttin' a bull in a stall with a heifer in heat."

I hit Harvey with a double-barreled squint. "I am not in heat, thank you very much."

He opened the lid of Aunt Zoe's Betty Boop cookie jar, and grabbed an Oreo. "You're sure showin' signs of estrus what with the way you were chompin' at the bit at supper, droppin' silverware and then yer napkin, knockin' over yer water."

"I was having trouble focusing, that's all." He would too if he had an albino with a body part fetish asking around town about him.

He took a bite of the Oreo, getting crumbs in his beard. "Then there's all of your caterwallin' lately, particularly around the kids. Reminds me of the way my heifers would wander around the pasture lookin' for a mate, mooin' night and day until a bull would mount up and put 'em out of their misery."

I heard Doc laughing under his breath and smacked him on the chest, avoiding his all-seeing gaze. It wasn't my fault that there always seemed to be someone or something interfering with us spending any alone time in his bed, or his office, or his garage, or anywhere. A girl had needs, too, especially when the guy was as talented at multitasking in the sack as Doc.

"See," Harvey grabbed another cookie. "Look at you getting all touchy feely." He sniffed the air. "Hell, I can smell your pheromones clear over here." He pointed the cookie at me. "Girl, you're in heat."

I was certainly getting sweatier with humiliation by the moment, damn it. "Harvey, zip it before I come over there and gag you with your suspenders."

He smirked at Aunt Zoe. "I bet she's so fertile Doc could plant a nail in 'er and grow a horseshoe."

I turned to my beloved aunt, who looked like she was doing

her best to keep a smile from falling out through her tucked in lips. "I swear to God, Aunt Zoe, if you encourage him any further I will call a certain fire captain and tell him you're in heat, too."

Reid had phoned me when I was leaving Lily Devine's house, asking if Aunt Zoe had made it home safe and still single. I'd confirmed both, crossing my fingers the latter was true. It would be really easy to hit the redial button and tell Reid to come over and take a look at Zoe for himself.

Her eyes got all squinty. "Don't you dare, Violet Lynn."

Harvey hooted. "Tell Reid we need him to stop by and put out his old flame."

Aunt Zoe leaned over and tried to cram another cookie in Harvey's mouth, making the old cuss snort and chortle even more. He winked at Doc. "I got 'em both all lathered up now, don't I?"

"You're going to need a chair and a whip if you keep this up, old man." Doc tucked Aunt Zoe's serving dish away in the cupboard.

The phone on the kitchen wall rang, breaking up the cookie wrestling match going on at the table. I waved Aunt Zoe back to her corner and answered it. "Hello?"

"Parker." It was a statement from Cooper, not a question.

"Well, if it isn't Little Miss Sunshine." I covered the mouthpiece and told the three eyeballing me, "It's Cooper."

I said, "To what do I owe the pleasure of hearing your melodious voice?"

"Did you have pot brownies for dessert tonight, Parker?"

"Nope. Your uncle made apple dumplings sans marijuana. But if you want to grab some joints from the evidence room for an after dinner toke …" I purposely let that comment trail off, not trusting Cooper to catch the jest in my voice about doing something illegal in his jurisdiction.

"Real funny, Parker. You can practice your stand-up routine some more tomorrow at the morgue."

"I can what?"

"You need to meet Detective Hawke and me at the Mudder Brothers morgue first thing in the morning."

"Why?"

"Because you were the last known witness to go in there the night Eddie and the body disappeared."

"But you already took my statement three times during breakfast at Doc's."

"Detective Hawke has some new questions to ask you."

"Come on, Cooper. Can't you help me with a get-out-of-jail-free card on this one?"

"Nope, and if you don't show up, I can guarantee Detective Hawke will come to your place of work with a warrant. He's picked up your scent now, and there's no shaking him."

"My scent?"

"Yeah, like a hunting dog. Get it, Parker? Or do I need to draw you a picture with stick people?"

I blew a raspberry in the mouthpiece. "Draw a picture of that, Coop."

"Your level of maturity astounds me some days. And it's Detective Cooper to you."

I sighed. "Fine, what time do I have to be there?"

"What time do you start work?"

I didn't have to be in super early since I had been on camera today, but Cooper didn't need to know that. "Eight-thirty." I padded the time so they'd think I had important work to get to right away in the morning and not drag out the interrogation any longer than necessary.

"Be there at seven," Cooper said. The line went dead.

I hung up the phone and then flipped it off for good measure. "Harvey, someone needs to teach your nephew some phone etiquette."

"Give him a break. His mama fed him castor oil for constipation when he was just a babe."

What in the world did that have to do with him being a dick to me on the phone?

"What was that about?" Doc asked, hanging the dish towel on the rack.

I told all three of them about my appointment at the morgue first thing tomorrow. When I finished, Aunt Zoe's frown matched the one lining Doc's face. Harvey scratched at his beard, working Oreo cookie crumbs loose.

Aunt Zoe was the first to speak. "Why can't they ask you these questions at the station?"

"Probably because Cooper knows the only way he's going to get me inside that station is by dragging me in handcuffed and kicking."

"This here sounds like one of Hawke's ideas, not Coop's," Harvey said. "I'd bet my left nut that dandy is trying to show off how big and red his rooster comb is in front of ya."

"He better be careful flashing his comb around," I griped, "or I just might blast a hole through it with ol' Bessie."

"Someone had better warn Cooper that you'll be carrying tomorrow, Tiger." Doc checked his watch. "I need to go. Walk me out?" he asked me.

I nodded, following him into the dining room.

Doc grabbed my sheepskin coat from the wall hanger and held it out for me.

"Is it going to be a long goodbye?" I slipped my arms in the sleeves.

"I need to talk to you alone for a moment." His tone made anxiety flap its wings in my chest.

He held the door, shutting it firmly behind us, and then led me past his car to the sidewalk.

I shivered in the cold night air, buttoning my coat as we strolled along. "The frost is going to be thick in the morning."

He captured my hand, his palm warm. "They're calling for a chance of snow later this week."

Weather talk, great. That was a sure sign that a thundercloud was coming my way.

We walked along in silence for a few steps, the stars sparkling overhead in the cold mountain air. Our breath steamed around us. The scent of wood smoke mixed with pine trees, making me want to go home and snuggle under the covers with Doc beside me. I peeked at him out of the corner of my eye, noting the stiffness in his shoulders and gait that had nothing to do with the temperature.

"Would you like me to go to the morgue with you in the morning?" he asked.

Of course. "Thanks, but no. Cooper didn't invite you, and I'd hate to cause any tension between you now that you're roomies."

"If you change your mind, let me know. I'm happy to tag along and hold your hand so you don't use it to punch Detective Hawke in the nose."

"Ah, how sweet." I hugged his arm. "You know me so well."

The silence between us returned, worry filled on my part. Our footfalls on the sidewalk echoed in the quiet coldness. A car door slammed further down the road.

Two houses away from Aunt Zoe's place, I pulled him to a stop. "What's wrong, Doc?"

He looked up at the stars, and then his dark gaze locked on me. Under the orange streetlights, his eyes looked black. "I have something to show you."

"What?" Anticipation had me fidgeting with my coat buttons. It wasn't like him to be apprehensive when we were alone. That was usually my song and dance.

Pulling out his phone, he tapped the screen a couple of times and then held it out to me.

I took it, frowning down at the glowing screen. Tiffany's name was listed on the screen over and over. He reached out and made the screen scroll down. Tiffany's name continued to fill the screen.

"What's this?" I asked.

"My voicemails."

Then I noticed the timestamp on each call, some spaced every fifteen minutes, others every five minutes. "What the hell?"

"You wondered yesterday why my voicemail was full," he explained. "This is why."

Criminy, the bitch was persistent, I'd give her that. I looked up at him, my gut boiling. "Let me guess? She wants you back and is willing to do anything if you'll kick me to the curb."

"I haven't listened to them."

No way. "Not even one?"

He shook his head.

"Why not?"

"I'm not interested in hearing what she has to say." He

jammed his hands in his coat pockets, leaning back on his heels. "You're welcome to listen to them, though."

My finger hovered over one of the more recent recordings, curiosity overflowing. What would Tiffany offer in exchange for his attention once again? For his touch? For another stay in his bed? I stared at her name until the letters blurred. How desperate was she? Did she offer to fulfill every single one of his sexual fantasies? Did she promise never to bring up marriage again? How pathetic and low would she go for him?

I looked at him, meeting his shadowed gaze. What would I offer if I were in her shoes and Doc were no longer frequenting my doorstep? Would I beg? Would I cry? Or would I have too much self-respect to show any emotion? How strong was my pride when it came to losing the guy I'd fallen head-over-heels for? I hoped never to find out.

Returning to the screen, I tapped the option to select all of the messages and deleted them in one fell swoop. "Here." I handed his phone back.

He glanced down at the screen, then back up at me. "You deleted them."

"That's her business, not mine."

He nodded and stuffed the phone in his jacket.

"But I will say that you have one psycho ex-girlfriend there. You're going to have to deal with her at some point."

"I keep hoping she'll just go away."

"The thing about 'crazy' is that it doesn't ride away into the sunset. It just hides in the closet and keeps jumping out to scare the crap out of you when you least expect it." I smiled without meaning it. "My sister taught me that."

"The bitch from hell?"

"The one and only."

He pulled me close, kissing my forehead and then nuzzling my hair. "You smell like apple dumplings."

"You should see what I taste like."

Tipping my chin, he did just that, his tongue teasing mine. "You taste like apple dumplings, too."

"You should see what I feel like?"

He chuckled low and sexy, his mouth hovering over mine.

"Harvey's right. You're all heated up tonight."

Laughter bubbled up from my chest, ruining the moment. I stepped back, shaking my head. "Harvey is going to pay for embarrassing me in front of you and Aunt Zoe."

He put his arm around my shoulders and started leading me back toward Aunt Zoe's. "Don't be embarrassed. I like it when you're in heat."

I elbowed him playfully.

He kissed my temple, running his palm down over my backside as we strolled along, warming me from the bottom up.

"Doc, do you remember when I showed you Lily Devine's house?"

"Was that the one with the blinding wallpaper in that one bedroom?"

"Yeah. Remember how you didn't like me standing down in the basement there?"

"That's right. There was a bad smell down there."

"But the story goes that Lily was killed in that wallpapered bedroom by her john, not the basement."

"Maybe she was. Maybe what I picked up wasn't Lily."

Hmmm. I hadn't thought of that. "The camerawoman on Dickie's crew found two eyebolts embedded in the wall under the basement stairwell. She has a theory that Lily was chained under the stairs by her killer, possibly tortured before he finished the job."

Doc was quiet for a few steps. "Interesting. Disturbing if true, but interesting."

"You want to go find out?"

"Not tonight. Unlike you, I prefer to visit houses of the dead long before or after the witching hour."

I poked him in the ribs through his coat. "Smart ass."

"Tell you what, let me look into what information I can find on Lily's death first, and then we'll take a field trip."

A cold breeze whipped down the street as we crunched up Aunt Zoe's gravel drive, pelting us with dry leaves from the few deciduous trees on the street.

"Natalie asked us to go with her to the Purple Door Saloon on Wednesday night."

"On Halloween? A costume party?"

"Yes. You interested? It's short notice on a costume, I know."

"You're going?"

"Probably. Nat loves Halloween. It's her favorite holiday, and Aunt Zoe said she'd watch the kids for me."

"If you're going, I'll go. What costume are you wearing?"

I had an idea. Something I thought would be fun. "It's a surprise."

He pulled me to a stop next to his car door, wrapping me in his arms. "I like surprises when it comes to you and what you're wearing ... or not wearing."

"Good. I'll take the kids trick-or-treating first, then I'll come home and change before we head out."

"You want company with the kids?"

My heart swelled at his willingness to tag along. "Sure, if you don't mind putting up with my obnoxious spawn for yet another evening."

"Violet," he tucked some curls behind my ear. "I like your kids. You don't need to keep apologizing for their actions. I don't expect them to love that I'm dating their mom right out of the gate, and I get that I'm a threat to the status quo."

I leaned my forehead against his chest. "I just wish they'd return to being the fun-loving kids they used to be when I first moved in with Aunt Zoe last spring."

"They will. You and I both know that hidden behind their dirty looks and smart attitudes are two scared children. It's going to take time for them to understand that I'm not here to take you away from them."

"Thanks," I unzipped his coat partway and slid my hands inside, seeking out his warmth for more reasons than the cool October night. "But I'm probably going to keep apologizing for what they say or do. Humility comes as part of the parenting package." At least they weren't as bad as Wilda Hessler poisoning local pets and her father. Oh, that reminded me of something I'd been wanting to ask Doc since the night we'd visited Cornelius's suite. "Whatever happened with Cornelius that night when I heard Wilda's voice on the recording and ran out?"

"If that recording is legit, he wasn't kidding. There are a lot of voices constantly all around him."

"What were they saying?"

"Mostly nonsense." He unzipped his coat the rest of the way, wrapping it around me so I was cocooned against him. "It sounded like a dozen different conversations going on at the same time, like a cocktail party minus the music."

"Weird." I rested my cheek against him. "Why do you think they're talking so much? Is it something we caused with those séances?"

"Could be. Or maybe it's something else."

The way he said that made me think he had something particular in mind. "Like what?"

He hesitated, stroking my hair.

"Come on, Doc." I pulled back and smiled up at him. "After all we've been through, you're not going to play shy now are you?" When he frowned down at me, still not speaking, I added, "I've seen you naked."

That made him grin. "What's that have to do with Cornelius's ghosts?"

"Nothing, but I like to think about that fact every so often."

"Do you now?"

I nodded. "Quit stalling and tell me your 'something else' theory."

"You're going to think I have a screw loose."

"Please, I know you have a screw loose. You have to in order to spend a perfectly good Sunday night with my children."

"I like hanging out with your kids."

"Not to mention putting up with their mother pawing you left and right, trying to kiss you all of the time."

"Yeah, there is that." He grimaced. "But that's the price I have to pay to enjoy Layne and Addy's company."

"Why I oughtta," I said in a mobster voice and mock punched him. "Come on, Doc, tell me."

"Okay." He took a deep breath, releasing it slowly. "I think Cornelius isn't a ghost whisperer."

"The whole chanting bit and hearing them talk in his walls is a hoax?"

"No, both of those things are legit. He's just not a whisperer. More like a ghost magnet."

"A magnet for ghosts?"

Doc nodded. "Think of him as the Pied Piper, only instead of rats or kids as the legend goes, Cornelius is leading around a herd of ghosts."

* * *

Monday, October 29th

The breakfast crowd at the morgue was dead.

I'd have preferred to face off with brain-hungry zombies rather than the two surly detectives waiting for me outside the same door I'd entered Saturday night for Eddie's secret meeting. Only this time, the door knob was missing. The area around where the knob had been was concave, the paint flaking off where the metal was now creased. Criminy, had someone taken a battering ram to it?

A new latch and padlock secured the broken door on the other side of the crime scene tape.

"Morning, sunshine," I said to Cooper as Detective Hawke unlocked the padlock and pushed open the door.

"Can it, Parker."

"Sounds like someone didn't eat his Wheaties this morning." I'd have to stock Doc's cupboards if Cooper and I were going to start having regular breakfast pow-wows.

I turned to Detective Hawke and his dark caterpillar eyebrows. "Where's your pen and notepad, Colombo?"

"Right here." He patted the breast of his jacket.

"Good. Pull 'em out and let's get to clicking." Some of us had a desk to jockey in between practicing lines for a television show. "Just a warning, though, before we get going. I'm in no mood for any hair comments, got that, Detective?"

"Relax, Ms. Parker. Nobody here is trying to attack you. We just have a few questions."

I raised my brows at Cooper. "I thought you got your fill of answers during yesterday's anal cavity search over toast and coffee."

"You had eggs and bacon," he said, his face stiff.

"Hold up," Hawke said, turning his back to me. "Are you socializing with one of our suspects?" he whispered to Cooper.

"I can hear you loud and clear, Detective Hawke," I said. "It's a small garage with a concrete floor, remember?"

"Would you plug your ears for a moment, Ms. Parker?"

"You'll need a warrant to make me."

Cooper glared over Hawke's shoulder at me. "Parker, you need to put the brakes on your mouth this morning."

"Fine, but I don't think you're going to enjoy trying to figure out my answers via a game of charades. I'm willing to try, though, if you two are good at guessing."

After nailing me with his trademark squint, he focused back on Hawke. "Not that it's your business but just to clarify, I'm currently renting a room from Parker's boyfriend. That is why my interrogation yesterday occurred over breakfast."

"What's wrong with your house?"

"There's a squatter living there."

"I thought your uncle was moving in with you."

"One and the same."

"But why … oh, I get it. You're keeping your distance from him because the chief took you off the murder case."

"Yes, something like that."

"That's smart. You need to keep your distance so I can solve this and move on to your next problem case."

Cooper's steely eyes flashed with something scary that made me take a step back from the two cops. "Right as usual, Detective Hawke, which is why I questioned you earlier about needing me to be here with you two this morning. If I'm not on this case, you should be interrogating Parker on your own."

Hawke shuffled his feet. "Yeah, well, it's wise to have backup with certain suspects."

"Backup? You think Parker's dangerous?"

"More like unstable."

"Uh, hello." I waved at them from five feet away. "I'm standing right here still, listening to every word."

Cooper nudged his chin in my direction. "Your suspect is

waiting, Detective."

Hawke aimed his notepad and pen my way. "Ms. Parker, explain your purpose for being here in the Mudder Brothers morgue on Saturday, October 27th."

"You're kidding. You dragged me down here this morning and that's your leading question?" I shook my head. "Jeez, Quincy just rolled over in his grave."

"Just answer the question," Cooper snapped.

"Detective Cooper," I said, "I thought you promised to play good cop with me today."

Detective Hawke turned his back on me again, lowering his voice. He brushed shoulders with Cooper, invading his personal space. "Did you talk to my suspect in advance, Coop?"

Cooper's nostrils flared. He stepped back, putting some distance between them again. "Only to order her to meet us here, as previously discussed."

"I hate to interrupt your lovers tiff," I said, walking around Hawke so I could face them both. "But how can I be a suspect when I have an alibi for Saturday night?"

"You're referring to Nat?" Hawke asked, scribbling something in his notepad.

Cooper and I both did a double take about Hawke's familiarity with Natalie.

"You mean, Ms. Beals," Cooper corrected.

"Of course, *Ms. Beals.*" Hawke shot Cooper a knowing leer.

Cooper's face froze, muscles rigid yet pulsing. For a split second, I thought he might pull an Addy and leave a big red welt on Hawke's face. Instead, he unclenched his jaw and settled for poking his partner in the chest. "You'd better not let the chief find out you're fraternizing with witnesses or you'll be off the case, too."

Warning issued, he walked over to the door leading to the crematorium furnace and pretended to inspect the jamb.

"I'm not fraternizing," he defended and then returned to his notepad, a hint of a smile curling the corner of his lips. "Not yet, anyway."

Cooper looked down at his feet for a moment, then shook his head and turned back to us. "Let's get this over with. I have work to get back to."

Cooper could hold his horses for a moment longer; I had some more foundation work to do on Detective Hawke's and my relationship.

I shoulder bumped Hawke, speaking his language physically. "You should be careful around Natalie," I baited, mentally steepling my fingers as I put into action one part of my evil plan to sidetrack the big doofus. "She has a rather seedy addiction that tends to get her into trouble around men."

"Oh, yeah?"

"Uh huh. You could end up with some telltale bruises," I winked at him, "if you get my meaning."

The bruises I was actually referring to were those around his eye after Natalie nailed him with a right jab or two for getting fresh, but judging from the way his gaze widened and jaw dropped, he took a handcuffs and whip direction with his thoughts.

Cooper cleared his throat from where he now leaned against the wall. His expression was giving me frostbite. "I thought we were here to question Parker about the events that occurred Saturday night, not gossip about Ms. Beals like a pair of junior high girls."

Hawke wiped his mouth with the back of his hand. "Right. Ms. Parker, where were we?"

"You were asking her about Eddie Mudder," Cooper bit out.

"Oh, yes, that's it." He held his pen over his notepad. "Did Eddie Mudder mention anything about someone who might be looking for him? Someone who might want to kidnap or hurt him?"

Yes, but I didn't think either detective would appreciate my bringing up the notorious albino twin who'd had a starring role as the villain in several of my previous reports. "No, he didn't mention anything about someone looking for him." I did my best to evade that question without outright lying.

Hawke wrote down my answer.

Cooper's gaze on me narrowed. I had a feeling he was trying to use x-ray vision to penetrate my skull and read my mind. I smiled at him, imagining how satisfying it would feel to smash a whipped cream pie in his face.

"Did Mr. Mudder appear nervous to be alone with you?" Hawke continued with his interrogation.

"No, I didn't notice any anxiety issues about being alone with me when we were talking." Eddie's anxiety had been all about who might see us, not about chatting with me in a dark morgue.

"Why did he insist on meeting you here instead of inside the funeral parlor?"

"He wanted to be alone." No lie there.

"Why? What was the reason for being so top secret?"

A big scary albino with all-seeing snake eyes. "Eddie wanted to talk to me in private. I believe his cousin is currently residing with him in the funeral parlor. Out here we were alone." I made a point of staring toward the door to the freezer where they kept the bodies on ice and put to work the other plan I had for distracting Detective Hawke. "Well, mostly alone."

Hawke followed my gaze. "Mostly? Was someone else in here with you?"

I tilted my chin down, looking at him through lowered lashes. "More like something," I whispered in my best spooky voice.

Hawke set his jaw. "If you're going to play that medium baloney with me again, I'm not buying."

I shrugged. "Believe as you will, skeptic, but Eddie and I had an audience Saturday night." I stared toward the door again. "Just like we do now."

Cooper shook his head, squeezing the bridge of his nose. "Christ, Parker. Don't start this shit."

Hawke frowned at me for several beats before returning to his notepad. "And what was it Eddie Mudder wanted to talk to you alone about? What was so important that he insisted on you meeting him here in the middle of the night?"

"Is midnight the middle of the night? I suppose it is now that we are heading toward winter solstice."

"Ms. Parker," Hawke clicked his pen several times, trying to frazzle me, I could tell. "Answer the question."

I stalled a few more moments, frowning in the direction of the fake ghost, and nodding like I agreed with what it said.

"Eddie was worried."

"About what?"

"My reputation."

Hawke's caterpillar brows got all squiggly. "What about your reputation?"

"Eddie knows about my ability."

"To see ghosts?"

"Yes, that one."

"You have other abilities, Parker?" Cooper butted in.

"I have many."

"Don't distract her," Detective Hawke said, holding his hand out to silence Cooper. "So, Eddie Mudder wanted to meet you in the morgue at midnight to discuss your ability to see ghosts."

Cooper cursed under his breath.

"Yes. I'm rather wary of anyone knowing about this ability of mine, and Eddie knew that, so I'd appreciate it if you kept it top secret, too."

"Maybe we should have waited to stage this meeting with Parker until midnight," the Peanut Gallery said.

"Maybe we need to perform a séance with her," Hawke jested back.

"Maybe you should," I challenged. "Unless you two big strong detectives are too scared."

Hawke snorted at me.

I resisted the urge to reach out and clamp his nose shut.

"Did you see or talk to Eddie Mudder after leaving here at …" Hawke turned back a few pages in his notepad, "approximately twelve twenty-five a.m.?"

"No. As I told Detective Cooper three times, I returned to my Aunt Zoe's house and spent the rest of the night there with my kids and Natalie."

"Does Ms. Beals often spend the night at your house, or was this a special occasion?" Hawke asked.

I frowned at Cooper. "I move to strike that question from the record."

"This isn't court, Ms. Parker," Hawke said. "You can't move to strike."

"Want to bet?" I shifted into a martial arts stance that I'd once seen in a movie. Something called "the cat" position if I remembered correctly. I leaned forward poised to strike. "What do you call this?"

"The end of the interrogation," Cooper said, pushing away from the wall. "Detective Hawke, we need to wrap this up before Parker tries to hypnotize you or something even more absurd than ghost-chatting and séances."

"One more thing." Hawke pulled a card from his pocket and held it out to me. "Have you seen this before?"

I took the card, recognizing it immediately. "Of course. It's my business card."

"Can you explain why it was left on the slab in there," he pointed at the freezer room door, "in place of where the body from the ranch was stored?"

I blinked. "It was where?"

He caught my elbow and dragged me over to the freezer door. When he opened it, a gust of cold air hit me, smelling a bit like the walk-in freezer where my mom's butcher kept the beef we'd ordered every fall.

I cringed as Hawke pointed at an empty metal shelf. "Your business card was found there, where the body was."

Cooper stepped forward, shutting the freezer door in our faces. "I think it's clear this business with her card is news to Parker."

"Or is she pretending it's news?" Hawke moved in too close, staring down at me, all scrutinizing and menacing.

"Step back, Detective, or I will bite." I gnashed my teeth for effect.

He obliged, lucky for him.

I frowned down at my business card. Why had it been in the Mudder Brothers freezer? I flipped the card over, noticing the words scrawled on the back for the first time.

WE WANT WHAT BELONGS TO US!

My breath caught. Those were the same words someone had left months ago on a note inside my purse after I'd been hauled to jail by Cooper and bailed out by Doc.

I looked up to find Cooper's steely gaze watching, assessing, trying to read me again.

"All right, Ms. Parker," Hawke said, "you're free to go for now." He held out his hand for my business card, which I was happy to return, wiping my hands on my coat as if that could wipe away the slimy feeling those words had left behind. "But don't go too far, because I have a feeling you and I are far from done when it comes to this case."

I was too discombobulated to give a smartass comeback.

Cooper came over and led me to the door, which was good since my feet seemed to have forgotten how to walk on their own.

"I'll take Parker to her truck and make sure she doesn't get any ideas about sneaking back in here on her own. You lock up."

Detective Hawke nodded, turning his back to us as he stared toward the freezer door.

I waited until we were out of earshot on the other side of a closed door to ask Cooper, "Why are you protecting me?"

"Amazingly, I believe you're innocent of this mess."

I stared openly at him. "Who are you, and what have you done with Detective Cooper?"

"Shut up, Parker."

"Seriously, why are you being nice to me?"

He smirked at me. "I owe your boyfriend for rescuing me from Uncle Willis's love shack. Consider yourself lucky to have Nyce on your side."

I considered myself lucky when it came to Doc every damned day.

"You and I need to talk more about what Eddie and you really discussed Saturday night, but not here, not now."

"Oh, boy. I can hardly wait."

He stopped next to the driver's side door. "You don't have any idea who wrote that note on the back of your business card, do you?"

I shook my head.

"Or what it is that belongs to whoever wrote it?"

I shook my head again.

"Do you think it has anything to do with how you know there was mead in those bottles in the crate?"

I shrugged, not wanting to talk about the message or the mead right now. I just wanted to go find Doc and let him help me carry this new burden.

"Fine, play your games, Parker, but if there's something more that you're not telling me about this shit," he waved his hand toward the garage, "I advise you to come talk to me." He opened my door and waited for me to climb up into the Picklemobile.

"I will," I told him and meant it, and then climbed behind the wheel.

He frowned in at me. "What I can't figure out is if whoever stole the body, the one trying to pin this all on you, is a civilian or a member of law enforcement."

Or something non-human with creepy snake eyes. "Which is worse?"

"I don't know." He stepped back so I could shut the door. "Get out of here, Parker, before I change my mind about arresting you for obstructing justice with those tricks you were playing in there with Hawke and decide to throw your ass in jail."

He didn't need to tell me twice.

I left Cooper squinting after me through a cloud of exhaust.

Chapter Fifteen

Meanwhile, back at Calamity Jane Realty ...

I parked behind Calamity Jane Realty and sat in the cab of the Picklemobile for a few moments, staring into the rearview mirror at the office's back door.

I needed to go in there and face the day like I hadn't already paid a visit to the morgue this morning. Like someone or something wasn't trying to drag me deeper into the mess out at Harvey's ranch for Lord only knew what diabolical reason.

We want what belongs to us!

What was it they wanted? Was it the freaky flesh-covered book I'd swiped from that wacky tart Lila months ago when she'd tried to hook me up with a demon in her version of speed dating/incubus mating? Or was it something else? Something like Prudence's collection of teeth? Or could it merely have been an explanation of why they had taken the faceless body back, as in the body belonged to them?

I needed to talk to Doc, but he was down in Rapid this morning meeting a friend of a client who looked to be another new opportunity. Doc was the only one who knew about the previous identical message I'd received.

I fiddled with the Picklemobile's smiley face keychain, pondering whether or not to tell Cooper about the previous message. But how would the detective react? Would he be pissed I hadn't told him about the first message? Would he get even nosier about what else I'd come across in my adventures with the albinos? Would he arrest me for withholding a key piece of evidence?

At the least, he'd be perturbed as hell for hiding stuff from him. Learning about all I'd been up to behind his back might change his mind, too, about believing in my innocence on the faceless body-napping case.

So Cooper was out as a confidant on this one, but there was someone else who knew most of the members of the Deadwood police force—Natalie. She'd either grown up with, dated, or tossed back drinks with most of the guys and gals in blue. She had the goods on several of their extracurricular activities and knew most of their spouses to boot. I'd have to call her and fill her in, but not until later. She was still down in Rapid hanging out with her cousins according to the text she'd sent last night.

I collected my purse and the three coffees I'd stopped to pick up at the Tin Cup Café. According to the quick call I'd had with Mona after leaving the morgue, Ray and Ben were already on location at an old bar in Sturgis rumored to be haunted by a slew of biker gang members killed three decades ago during the big motorcycle rally. That meant Mona and I should have a nice, quiet morning during which she could clack away on her keys as usual while I stared at my computer screen and did my best to figure out who was trying to mess up my future as a free woman.

I opened the back door, slipping inside carefully, trying not to dump coffee on my tan suede boots. I left the door open for the moment. Coffee delivery duties first, then I'd tend to the door and my coat.

Jerry's office door was open a couple of inches. I hesitated, listening to see if he was on the phone. A scuffling sound came through the crack but nothing else.

I balanced the tray of coffees on one arm and knocked twice. "Morning, Jerry," I pushed opened the door. "Here's your—"

It turned out Jerry wasn't alone after all.

Luckily for me, I'd already had a shock this morning registering around 7.5 on the Richter scale, so catching Mona and Jerry in a back-bending lip lock only caused a small bump on my seismometer.

Mona scrambled free of Jerry's arms, her cheeks complementing her dark red hair. She covered her lips and looked away from me. I resisted the urge to tell her that the horizontal pink stripes on her white sweater were now diagonal.

"Sorry to intrude." I carried the coffee tray over to Jerry's desk, keeping my focus on the coffee lids. I pulled my cup free and then shot Jerry a quick smile. "I'll let you two get back to your … uh … meeting."

Wow, and I thought donning a bathing suit in public was a squirmy proposition. I couldn't exit Jerry's office fast enough. Closing the door behind me, I hung up my coat in the hallway, shut the back door, and then clomped with extra loudness to my desk so the two love birds would know I wasn't pressing my ear to Jerry's office door.

I whistled as I started up my computer, wondering what Jane's ghost thought about her ex-husband making out with her best friend in her old office. The same office where Jane and Ray had shared a lust-filled romp a couple of nights before her death. What in the hell was in the air in there?

While my computer came to life, I shipped a text off to Natalie, telling her I needed to chat with her about Detective Hawke's latest body snatching accusation and something else that had come up this morning.

I was scrolling through the day's listing of MLS properties when Jerry's door opened.

"I'll be back this afternoon," Jerry said loud enough for my ears. "Call me if you two need anything."

The back door opened and closed, leaving me alone with Mona and one huge trumpeting elephant in the room. I avoided making eye contact with her as she joined me in the front office, letting her settle into her chair and get to clacking.

"Your stripes are crooked, hot lips," I said without looking, a smile splitting my face wide. When I peeked over, her cheeks were flushed. I wasn't sure if that was Jerry's doing or mine.

She straightened her sweater. "There's an explanation for what you saw."

"Oh, yeah?" I rolled my chair across the wooden floor and rested my elbows on her desk. "I'm all ears."

She covered her face with her hands and groaned.

I tugged on her wrists, pulling her hands down. "I promise not to tell a soul, now give me this so called explanation for having Jerry kiss you like he was heading off to sail the seven seas."

She checked the back door, and then took a sip of her coffee, her hands trembling slightly. "Jerry and I have a bit of a history."

"No shit." I waved off her look of surprise. "You two practically sizzle when you're together. I keep expecting to get burned when I sit next to you during company lunches."

She fanned herself, but the red from her cheeks crept down her neck. "I knew this was going to be a problem as soon as Jerry showed up to take over."

"What happened in the past between you two? Inquiring busybodies are dying to hear all of the sordid details."

The bells over the front door jingled. I turned, flipping into professional Realtor mode. "Welcome to Calamity Jane Realty," I stood, walking over to greet the older couple that had interrupted my quest to finally find out what the story was with Mona and Jerry. "How can we help you?"

"I believe these two are here to see me, Violet." Mona joined us, her cheeks faded back to a warm pink. "Hi, I'm Mona Hollister. You must be Mr. and Mrs. Rogers."

I returned to my desk and left Mona to work her magic on the couple, who planned to retire on a small ranch where they could raise pedigree mules. I peeked at them over my computer screen. Why mules? Why not Great Danes? I focused back on the MLS listings, shaking my head. Just like the olden days, Deadwood still lured the odd, eccentric members of society out to sow their weird and wild oats. Take Doc and his medium experiments, or me and my executioner escapades.

For the next hour, I dabbled in real estate, calling back some potential clients, researching some possible places to advertise Cooper and Jeff Wymonds' places, and practicing the lines on my cue cards for tomorrow's filming at the Galena House.

During my dabbling, Mona left to show her clients a few houses, saying she'd check back in with me, leaving me alone to mind the store. Well, alone except for Jane, who might be hovering over me for all I knew, berating me on my lack of check marks under the Sold column on her favorite white board.

A while later, my cellphone rang. I checked the screen, figuring it was Mona, but the phone number didn't match. It was local, so maybe it was someone looking to sell a house.

"Calamity Jane Realty, this is Violet Parker."

"Ms. Parker, this is Principal Walker at Deadwood Elementary School."

That made me freeze. "Yes?" Had something happened to my kids?

"We had some trouble at school today. I need you to come in to my office to discuss the events and repercussions."

Repercussions? That sounded not so good. "Uh, did Adelynn try to bring a mouse into class again after recess?" She and I had had a long talk at Aunt Zoe's kitchen table after Addy's last rescue mission. She knew better than to collect pets while at school.

"Actually, Adelynn had nothing to do with this. It's your son, Layne."

My stomach cramped in anxiety. "Is he okay?" Had someone tried to kidnap him? Someone with white hair and snake eyes?

No, wait, Principal Walker had mentioned repercussions.

"I think you need to come in to my office, and we can discuss this in person, Ms. Parker. How soon do you think you can be here?"

I glanced at the clock, then around at the empty desks. Shoot, I was supposed to hold down the fort until Mona got back.

"Can this wait an hour?" I asked.

"Not really. I'd like to begin the suspension immediately."

Suspension? From school? Layne? What the hell?

I stood, grabbing my purse. I'd have to close the office for a bit. "Okay, give me fifteen minutes, and I'll be there."

"Thank you for your immediate attention to this matter, Ms. Parker."

Like he'd given me a freaking choice. I locked the front door, turned the Open sign to Closed, and raced out to the Picklemobile. I texted Mona on the way across the parking lot, telling her I had a kid emergency and needed to lock up the office for a short time.

Ten minutes later, I was climbing the front steps of the Deadwood Elementary School building, bracing myself for whatever heinous crime my son had committed. I just prayed he hadn't tried to blow anything up during science again. Inside the front office, I was ushered straight into the principal's lair where Layne sat waiting for me.

I grimaced at his black eye. I'd had to leave before they were up and eating breakfast this morning thanks to Cooper's insistence I join him and Detective Hawke at the morgue, so I hadn't seen Layne since I'd kissed him goodnight. The red welt from Addy had still been a red welt at the time, not a full-on shiner. Plus, now that I thought about it, that had been his other eye.

"What happened, Layne?" I asked, dropping into the seat next to Layne, sitting across the desk from the very serious-faced principal. "Did you get into a fight?"

"Actually, he started a fight," Principal Walker said.

"What?" I gaped at Layne, wondering what on earth had happened to my son who used to spend his time with his nose in a book on the physiology of dinosaurs. "You started it?"

"We have several witnesses confirming that he attacked the other boy," the principal spoke for Layne again, "throwing the first punch."

"Wow." I sat back, completely and overwhelmingly flummoxed. "Why?" I asked Layne.

He pinched his lips together and turned away.

"As you know from my correspondence, Ms. Parker, this isn't the first time he's started a fight in the recess yard."

His correspondence? I stared blankly at Principal Walker and his salt-and-pepper handlebar moustache.

"You know, the notes I've sent home over the past couple of weeks that you've initialed and returned?"

I hadn't seen a single note, nor signed anything of the sort. Oh, crud, this mess with Layne was worse than just a school yard fight.

I nodded, covering for my lying kid. "Right, yes, those notes, the ones I signed and returned." I was going to lock up my son in the attic and ground him for two life sentences.

"Based on his history of starting fights, I'm going to suspend him for the rest of this week." Principal Walker leaned over his desk, his sharp gaze aimed at Layne. "I hope that when you

return to school next week, Mr. Parker, you will have learned
how to keep your hands to yourself. Here at Deadwood
Elementary, we have a no-tolerance rule when it comes to
bullying."

Layne nodded, then returned to studying his shoes.

Principal Walker focused back on me. "If this continues, I'll
be forced to have the school counselor work with him to find a
solution on whatever is spurring this bullying."

Holy horseshit! This was big. Even though I was having
trouble swallowing that Layne was a bully, I said, "Of course,"
and popped up out of my chair like a jack-in-the-box. "Can I take
him home now? Or does he need to collect his things from class
first?"

"He's ready to go." Principal Walker pointed at Layne's
backpack resting near his door. "Good luck, Ms. Parker. Let me
know if we can be of further assistance."

"I will," I lied, resisting the urge to grab Layne by the ear and
drag him out to the Picklemobile. Instead I clasped my hands
together and glanced down at my son's blond head. "You ready,
Layne?"

He avoided my gaze all of the way out to the Picklemobile.
At least his survival instincts were still working, even though his
brain seemed to be broken. I waited until we were both buckled
in with the windows rolled up before turning on him. "What is
going on, Layne Alan Parker? What in the world are you doing
starting fights at school?"

"I don't want to talk about it." He stared bullheadedly out
the window.

"Ha! You don't want to talk about this? Oh, that's rich. You
don't get a choice now that you're suspended." I started the
Picklemobile and shifted into gear. "Is this why you've been
playing sick lately?" Addy had been right with her skepticism.
How much did she know about Layne fighting at school? They
were in separate classes, but they had lunch and recess together.

He shrugged. "Maybe."

I sputtered, and then bit my lip before I started yelling and
said things I regretted later. I drove toward home in silence,
wondering what in the world would spur my normally mild-

mannered, peace-loving son into picking fights.

I must have done something wrong. Was it moving him to Deadwood when he didn't want to leave his friends down in Rapid? Was it my work and some of the odd hours I had to put in? No, even with the filming and all that went into it, I was spending way more time with my kids than I used to when I worked at the car dealership. Was it Doc? I glanced Layne's way, grimacing at the bruises around his eye. Was this how he was dealing with his unhappiness about my allowing another man into our lives?

I worried about all of those possibilities until I pulled into Aunt Zoe's drive. When Layne reached for the door handle, I caught his arm.

"Listen, I have to get back to the office, but we're not done discussing this."

His lips stayed pressed tight, his hazel eyes meeting mine for a second or two, then darting away again.

"Get inside, go straight up to your room, and find a book to read. There'll be no television for you this week, no fun stuff while you're home."

"What about trick or treating?"

Good question. "Whether you get to go or not depends on the answers you give me tonight when we discuss what's causing this aggression."

He nodded, accepting his fate. "I'm sorry, Mom. I didn't mean to embarrass you."

That surprised me, spurring tears out of the blue. I let go of his arm, turning away so he wouldn't see my watery eyes, just in case he was playing me. "Apology accepted, but you're still in big trouble."

"I know. Can I go now?"

"Yes." I waited for him to make it to the front door before climbing out of the Picklemobile and following.

Aunt Zoe was standing in the front foyer, staring up the stairs after Layne when I stepped inside. She frowned at me. "What's going on?"

Without saying a word, I walked up to her and wrapped my arms around her waist. "I need a hug."

She gave me a good squeeze. "Violet, you're scaring me. Is Layne okay?"

"Yes." I stepped back and blew out a breath of frustration. "Well, no, not really. Physically he's bruised up, but there's something worrisome going on in his head."

"He got in a fight?" she guessed.

"Yeah, and he started it."

"Oh."

"And this isn't the first time this has happened." I told her about the prior notes that Layne had hidden from me, had forged my signature on.

When I finished my sordid tale of debauchery, including his week-long suspension, she was wringing her hands right along beside me. Then I told her my theory that Layne was acting out because of Doc's entrance into our lives.

Aunt Zoe's brow creased. "I don't know, Violet. Layne isn't happy about you having a boyfriend, but I thought Doc was making headway with him. There are those books he gave to Layne on Deadwood's history, and the time he's spent hanging out with them, like during Oktoberfest."

I sighed. "Well, I hope you're right, but we'll see after I get home tonight and have a chance to talk to Layne. Addy, too. She might have an idea if there's something going on at school with him that I don't know about." A lump formed in my throat. Just a short time ago my son had told me everything going on under the sun and moon; now the tide had shifted. "Aunt Zoe, what kind of a mother doesn't know her son is so bothered by something that he's picking fights at school. God, I suck at this parenting business."

Aunt Zoe took me by the chin. "You stop it right now, Violet Lynn. You are doing the best you can with what you've been dealt. You love your kids and they know it. Now, get back to work and give yourself some time to calm down and think things through, because how you handle this with Layne will set a precedent."

I gave her a grim smile. "Okay."

She turned me toward the door, opened it, and smacked me on the butt. "Go. I'll take care of Layne for now."

I paused long enough to drop a kiss on her cheek. "I'm glad you're home, Aunt Zoe."

"Me, too."

As I walked down the steps, Reid Martin rolled by slowly on the road in his red dually pickup. He waved at me, and then looked past me and lowered his arm.

Back on the porch, Aunt Zoe stood with her hands jammed on her hips. "Keep right on going, Martin!" she hollered.

He did, his laughter echoing back to us.

Opening the driver's side door, I looked up at Aunt Zoe's pinched expression. "It looks like someone else is glad you're home, too."

"If that man thinks I'm letting him get within touching distance again, he's going to find himself stinging from a shotgun shell full of rock salt."

She slammed the door behind her.

And the soap opera continued.

I backed out of the drive and headed back to work, pondering life, children, love, and everything under the cloudy sky.

I hoped Reid didn't give up on Aunt Zoe.

I hoped Aunt Zoe was right about Layne and Doc.

I hoped I could get through to my son tonight and find out what was prompting this fighting before we had to get a damned counselor involved.

But mostly, more than all of the other hopes put together, I hoped the aggression brewing inside of Layne had nothing to do with our family history, because if it did, I was pretty sure there wasn't much a counselor could do for a kid who came from a killer like me.

* * *

The rest of the afternoon sailed by, my thoughts so preoccupied with Layne and the school mess that I didn't even bite when Ray returned from the day's filming and tried to bait me with blonde insults.

"What's wrong with you today, Blondie? You been sniffing

too much of the bleach you use on your hair?"

"Knock it off, Ray." Mona stuck up for me. I'd told her about Layne getting kicked out of school when she had returned from showing a few mule-friendly places to the Rogers couple. "Jerry would be ticked if he heard you're messing with Violet the night before she's on air and you know it."

He grumbled something about Mona showing favoritism as usual but left me alone. A short time later, he grabbed his keys and said he was going to go out to take a look at a potential property, then head home.

I didn't waste energy on celebrating his departure.

Ray wasn't gone long when my phone rang. Detective Cooper's name showed on the screen. I sent it to voicemail. Cooper tried two more times, and then he called my work phone. I sent the work call to my voicemail, too, not in the mood to arm wrestle with the detective this afternoon.

Ten minutes later, the bell over the front door jingled. I glanced up into a pair of squinty, steel-colored eyes.

"I need to talk to you, Parker."

"Sheesh. Can't you take a hint, Detective?" I leaned back, crossing my arms over my chest. "I sent you to voicemail like five times. In case my nonverbal messages weren't clear, I don't want to talk to you right now."

"Too bad." He leaned over my desk, all growly and threatening like a German shepherd at the end of his leash. "You're stepping out back with me right now."

I shook my head. "Mona, call the cops for me."

"But he's already here."

"Quit fucking around, Parker." Cooper reached for me.

I hopped out of my chair, my fists raised and ready to box him in the nose if he touched me. "Try manhandling me, Cooper, and I'll break your nose again." I danced a couple of foot moves like Sylvester Stallone in one of the Rocky movies.

The detective watched my feet for a few seconds, the anger melting from his face.

"I know a few moves," I said, mocking a full on windmill attack with both arms circling around and around.

Cooper tipped his head back and laughed, a full volume,

belly-shaking laugh.

That particular sound coming from his mouth confused me into stillness. "Are you laughing or coughing up your last victim?"

"Jesus, Parker. You're the real thing. Crazy spelled with a capital C." He started down the back hallway. "Get out here and talk to me for a minute."

"Why?" I called after him.

"I have something for you."

"I don't trust Trojans bearing gifts."

"It's not a wooden horse." He stopped at the back door and looked back at me. "Come on. I have something to discuss about your boyfriend."

What about Doc? Was he okay?

I followed Cooper. "I thought you said you had something for me."

"I lied."

There was nothing as comforting as a lying lawman. "If I'm not back in ten minutes, Mona, call the other police." I aimed a mirroring squint at the bristly detective. "The nice truth-telling cops."

Cooper held the door for me. I skirted wide of him as soon as I stepped through the doorway.

"I've had a shitty day, Cooper, and it's partly your fault, so let's get this over with."

"My fault? You're the one who likes to hang out at morgues at midnight. You should be thanking me for saving you from Hawke."

"You haven't saved me. He's still bugging me every other day."

"Well, stop looking for trouble and he won't." He glanced around the parking lot, and then focused back on me, lowering his voice. "Listen, I need your help."

I looked behind me and then back at him. "Are you talking to me?"

"Yes, I'm talking to you. Knock off the wiseass shit."

"What do you need from me?"

"I want to go out to the ranch again."

"And you want me to go with you as your Realtor?"

"No, as Nyce's helper."

"What do you mean?"

"I want to see what Nyce picks up on his ghost radar."

"Why do you need me for that?"

"Because when I talked to Nyce about it on the phone earlier, he said he won't do it unless you come along, too."

"He did?" I wondered what that was about. Doc could do his medium song and dance without me.

"Yes. He expressed concern about what he may find out there and mentioned that you two work as a team now, so if you go, he'll go."

"We're a team now? Wow, that's like a form of commitment, don't you think?"

Cooper hit me with look of disbelief. "You must be confusing me for one of your girlfriends, Parker, because I could swear you just asked me about your relationship with your boyfriend? What's next? You want me to tell you what shoes to wear on your next date?"

I bared my teeth at him. "You know, if you want me to say 'Yes' to this field trip of yours, you should be a little nicer to me."

"Fine." A muscle in his jaw twitched. "Yes," he continued in a robot voice, "that did sound like a form of commitment to me."

I snorted at him. "You really do have a heart made of rusty iron, don't you?"

"Whoever told you I have a heart?"

We stood there mired in a glare standoff for several heartbeats. Then I suddenly felt worn thin, tired of the tension coiled around me and tightening by the minute. "I'll think about it, Detective, but not because you so rudely asked me to do it. It's your uncle's ranch and I'm more worried now about his welfare after finding that body in his barn."

"I thought I asked nicely."

"The word *please* didn't once cross your lips."

He rolled his eyes.

I thought about poking them in a Three Stooges move.

"I'll let you know when I think we have a clear window so

that Nyce and you can work your little magic trick."

"If you're going to be a skeptic out of the gate, I might change my mind."

"Christ, you're a royal pain in the ass." He reverted to his robot voice. "I promise to keep an open mind about your ghostly friends."

The ghosts were definitely not my friends, especially Prudence and her hair-raising ventriloquism act. I was dreading returning to her lair with the film cameras in tow, especially with how irrational she was getting about her missing box of teeth.

Box of teeth … a bell dinged in my head. Oh, hey! Here was a golden opportunity! "Before I agree to go out to the ranch, I have one demand you need to fulfill."

"This is not a hostage situation, Parker. You don't get to have demands."

"Yes, it is. I'm holding Doc hostage. If you want us to go out there, I need you to do something for me."

"You gotta be kidding me."

"Nope."

A muscle pulsed in his jaw. "Name your price."

"I want those teeth that are tucked away in your evidence locker down at the station."

"No." He didn't even take a moment to think about it.

"Okay then," I grabbed the knob on the back door. "Fun talking to you as always, Detective. Good luck with that ghost hunting business of yours." I saluted him. "Who you gonna call and all that jazz."

"Parker!"

I didn't even flinch under his barbed glare. "No teeth, no deal, Detective."

"You have a lot of fucking nerve."

Of course I did. I was a killer. "You have no idea."

Without further ado, I left him standing there huffing and puffing, probably daydreaming about blowing my house down.

Chapter Sixteen

Tuesday, October 30th

Meanwhile, back at the Galena House …

The next morning, I rushed out of the house before the kids were awake, choking down a lemon bar as I scrambled into the Picklemobile. The camera called extra early today. Yesterday Jerry had reminded me that I needed to make sure I answered on time, dressed as his own personal Barbie doll, minus the big boobs, impossibly tiny waist, and high heels-ready feet.

As I drove to the office, last night's surprise visit from my parents replayed in my head, prompting frowns from the woman in the rearview mirror. Why did my parents have the uncanny ability to choose the worst possible moments to walk in the front door?

Take that time many, many full moons ago when I was living under my parents' roof with two young toddlers in tow. I had gone to a chamber of commerce function in Rapid and met a nice, middle-aged couple who were kind and funny from the get go. They were entrepreneurs who sold what they called "Evening Activewear" for couples and talked me into hosting a sales party for them, promising me a nice profit for my time.

Being young and stupid, I had agreed, having no idea that inside of their Evening Activewear sales trunk were odd and somewhat frightening sex outfits that came with interactive toys. Even more jaw-dropping was the live demonstration they performed right there on my parents' living room shag carpet in front of Aunt Zoe, Natalie and her current loser boyfriend, and a sweet old couple who lived down the street. To make horribly uncomfortable matters even more squirmy, my parents returned early from their movie and ice cream date with my two toddlers

right in the middle of the S&M sampler display, which included a
whip, a leather thong, one of those ball-in-mouth muffles, and a
first aid kit containing a large tube of antibiotic ointment.

To this day, I am not allowed to have any friends over at my
parents' house besides Natalie. I was hoping they'd make an
exception for Doc if the time ever came to introduce him.

The on-the-carpet sex sales show was just one example of
Mom and Dad's history of inconvenient interruptions. The time
they didn't knock before entering my dorm room in college and
caught me in the midst of getting a hands-on breast exam from a
hot guy in my Chemistry 201 class was another. Their appearance
in Aunt Zoe's drive last night as I was climbing out of the
Picklemobile after a day of beating myself up for being the
world's crappiest mother added one more instance to the ever-
growing list.

My mother did not need to know about Layne's black eye.
She'd questioned my single-parenting abilities enough over the
years without evidence of my failures, often trying to set me up
on dates with her version of the perfect potential father material
for my twins. But no amount of makeup would hide that black
and blue puppy before Aunt Zoe had supper ready for all of us.
In the end, I washed my cover-up off his face and made Layne
and Addy both swear an oath of silence about school and Doc—
neither of which I wanted to talk about in front of my parents.

Downstairs, I'd explained the black eye deal by claiming
there was a bully on the loose at school, which wasn't exactly
lying since the bully may or may not be their grandson—time
would tell. But throughout supper, while Mom had coddled and
baby-talked to my son, Dad had shot me looks edged with a
mixture of suspicion and disbelief.

I never had been good at hiding the truth from him, not back
when I swore the entrepreneurs hadn't performed any sexual
activities in his favorite recliner, or last night during dessert when
I'd told him the kids and I were getting along great up here in
Deadwood and then crammed my gullet full of Aunt Zoe's
famous lemon bars.

By the time Aunt Zoe and I waved them goodbye from the
front porch, the kids were in bed and I was practically asleep on

my feet. With a starring role in front of the camera coming again bright and early, I'd kissed Aunt Zoe goodnight and headed to bed. Sleep had come surprisingly fast. The nightmares even faster, one in particular starring my son in a bleak, rage-filled future as a serial killer. The crowd outside his jail cell chanted how his mother had driven him to it, their cries echoing long after I'd woken up drenched in sweat.

Criminy, this parenting business was going to turn me into a silver-haired, shriveled hag by age forty.

I parked behind the office, stopping in only to make sure we were still on for the Galena House. Jerry made eye contact as if I hadn't caught him and Mona in a lip lock yesterday. Mona was still inspecting her fingernail polish when the three of us were in the room together.

Ray texted me while I was powdering my nose in the office restroom: *Get your ass over here, Blondie. We don't have all day.*

I typed back: *Funny, I don't remember signing up to receive inspirational texts from the president of Dickheads Anonymous.*

Before he could reply, I shoved my phone in my purse and headed out the back door.

Twenty minutes later, I passed Rosy the Riveter on the way up the front walk of the Galena House, her camera focused on the front of the square, two-story boarding house.

She thanked me for the coffee I'd stopped to grab, promising to make me look better than Loni Anderson and Dolly Parton combined in exchange for the caffeine hit.

Dickie and Honey were huddled up in the Galena House's downstairs hallway when I crested the porch steps. As I approached, handing a coffee to Dickie, Honey stepped back and turned aside, letting out a rally of sneezes.

"Excuse me," she said, taking the hot tea I'd brought her. "Thank you for this."

I nodded, looking around. "Where's Rad?" I'd grabbed a hot tea for him, too, since he'd been so sick the last couple of days of filming.

"Back at the hotel room sleeping," Honey said, and then sneezed again. "He's too sick to film, was up coughing all night."

"He should probably get that checked out," Dickie said,

slurping down some coffee. "You better take some cough medicine, too. It sounds like you're going down next."

Honey shook her head. "I'm fine, it's just allergies. These houses and buildings are so old and full of dust."

"And ghosts," Dickie added. His gaze traveled over my dark red blazer and straight black velvet skirt, ending at my black boots. He saluted me with his coffee cup. "Nice outfit today, Violet. You'll look great on camera."

"Thanks," I said, keeping mum that it was one of the outfits Jerry had picked out and bought just for this occasion. The fewer people who knew that I had less clothes sense than a retired pro-basketball player the better.

"Anyone see Ray around?" I wanted to stay on opposite sides of the hall from him if at all possible today.

"He's upstairs in Miss Tender's apartment using the facilities."

I checked the time on my phone. Ohhhh, poor Freesia. I could set my watch by Ray and his daily trip to the litterbox.

"Violet, we should be ready to set up for your part in about fifteen minutes," Honey said, swiping at her nose with the back of her hand. "Do you need more time to practice your lines or are you ready to roll?"

"I'm ready." I'd practiced while getting dolled up this morning. I held up my phone. "I'm going to make a quick phone call out on the front porch."

She gave me a thumbs up and then focused her energy on fussing over Dickie, reminding me of my mother last night with Layne.

I passed Rosy coming in through the main door on the way, her camera balanced on her shoulder while she sipped from her coffee. "Thanks again, Violet. You da' bomb."

Some days I felt very bomb-ish, the atomic variety.

Outside on the porch, I pulled up Doc's number on my phone.

"Morning, Tiger." He sounded sleepy. It must have been a late poker night over at Reid's place. Their weekly game had been moved up a day due to Halloween.

"Are you still in bed?" I'd rather be there with him than

hanging around a haunted boarding house.

"If I say yes, will you come over and perform a wake up service in your purple boots and those matching panties with the pink heart on the front?"

"Hey, who told you about my Halloween costume?"

"You wear that and we'll never make it to the bar."

"Promises, promises." I stepped down the front porch steps, turning my face up to soak up some rays of sunlight shining through a break in the clouds. I could use more sunshine in my days and more of Doc in my nights. "So, who was your fourth for poker?"

"Willis."

"I thought he had a date." Why else would Harvey have sent me a text yesterday afternoon that asked: *Boxers, a leather thong, or commando?*

"He didn't mention anything about one."

I heard the beep of Doc's coffeemaker. Coffee was ready. It was nice to start my day without Cooper chewing on me for once, although Ray's not-so-friendly follow up texts were waiting in my phone's message box.

"How was your night?" Doc asked. "You didn't get a whim to do some early trick-or-treating at any more morgues, did you?"

"No dead bodies for me, but my parents dropped by." I wondered how Doc felt about meeting them. If he were as skittish about it as I was? If we'd reached that stage in our relationship yet? If we ever would?

"They drove up from Rapid City just to say, 'Hi'?"

"And drop in for supper."

"Did you have a good visit?"

"Not really."

"What happened? Your sister didn't tag along, did she?"

"No, but I sort of had a problem I didn't want them to know about."

I heard his pantry door creak open. "What kind of problem?"

"Layne has a black eye."

"Really? I didn't think Addy had hit him that hard."

"It wasn't Addy. I got a call from his school principal

yesterday." I gave Doc a condensed version of the story, nodding at Honey when she stepped out to give me the five minute signal.

"Did Layne tell you why he picked the fight?"

"No. He didn't want to talk about it, and with my parents there last night, I didn't make him."

There was a long pause from his end. I checked my phone screen to make sure I hadn't lost his call. Then he spoke, "How do you feel about me stopping by your aunt's place to talk to him on my way to work?"

"You want to talk to Layne?"

"Yes, man-to-man, no mother or sister or great aunt involved. Unless that makes you uncomfortable."

I was actually wondering if it would make Layne uncomfortable being that one possible reason for his aggression might be Doc's presence in our lives. "You think he'll be more willing to open up to a man?"

"Maybe. There are things that go through a boy's head that might not be something he wants his mother to know because she might not understand."

I could believe that after growing up with my own flower-child mother, but I was curious about something. "Are you speaking from experience?" Doc's mom had died when he was young, but there could have been other women in his young life. His grandmother, maybe.

"I come with the same equipment as Layne, and I've been in my fair share of brawls."

I hesitated, happy that Doc was willing to try to help with Layne, yet feeling torn about giving up some control over my kids to someone else, someone besides Aunt Zoe or my parents. I'd been playing solitaire in this parenting game for a long time. In spite of all my whining and bitching about how hard it was, part of me wasn't sure I was ready to share my children on that level.

"It's just an offer to help, Violet. Don't feel obligated to take me up on it."

I didn't, but we had to start somewhere if Doc really planned to stick around like he'd mentioned.

"It's worth a try," I said, keeping my fingers crossed that

Layne would be on good behavior and that Doc wouldn't press my boy too hard for answers. Then again, maybe Layne did need to be pressed. Maybe I was being too molly-coddling and making things worse.

God, I wished children came with an instructional video on how not to screw up their lives from the get-go.

Honey popped outside again, giving me the one minute finger.

"Doc, I gotta go."

"Okay. Call me after you finish the big romance scene where you get messy making pottery with your ghost lover's help."

I chuckled. "Good looks and you've watched a romantic movie."

"I tend to think of it as a paranormal suspense."

"Come on, *Ghost* is definitely a romance."

"Oh, hey, I meant to ask you if the rumors are true?"

"What rumors?"

"The ones about you winning the next lightweight boxing championship belt. Last night during the game, Cooper gave us a demo of your knockout boxing moves."

Damn that detective! "Cooper has a bucket mouth." Just like his uncle.

"Did you really go at him with your patented windmill swings, Tiger?" The laughter in his voice was all but tumbling out of my phone.

"Cooper's lucky I didn't knock him on his ass."

"God, I wish I could have seen that."

"You've seen me make a fool of myself in front of Cooper plenty of times before."

"I actually think you managed to impress him with it."

"Well, I do have a wicked wind up."

He outright laughed at that.

Ray strode out onto the porch. "Shut it down, Blondie. They're waiting for you."

"Time's up," I told Doc. "Let me know how it goes with Layne."

"Will do if you promise to stop by and show me some of your moves later."

"Sure. You'll be impressed."

"I always am. Break a leg, Tiger."

I hung up and shoulder bumped Ray back a step as I passed in front of him. Jerry had warned us that we needed to say nice things to each other and not fight in front of the TV people, but he hadn't mentioned whether checking the dickhead into the boards was a no-no. Wait, that was a hockey reference, not basketball. I needed to keep my sports metaphors straight.

Honey led me up the stairs to the attic where the fun and games and filming would commence today. Freesia was waiting up there on the sidelines; her smile spread further up her face at the sight of me.

"Hi, Violet." She came over. "You look smokin' hot, girl. How's show business treating you?"

"Like roadkill skunk."

That made her giggle. "Have you seen Cornelius lately?"

Boy, Freesia sure had a moose-sized crush on Abe Lincoln, Jr. If Cornelius had his head screwed on straight … no, never mind. There was no way in hell Cornelius's head was on straight. Some days I wondered if it were attached at all.

"I saw him last week," I whispered, aware that Rosy was about to give us the let's get rolling cue. "Any Realtors come by in the last few days to look around?"

She shook her head. "We both know it's a bad time to try to sell a house, especially a haunted boarding house that was the setting for multiple, bizarre murders over the years."

"Don't give up hope yet. I'm in the process of wrapping up a sale for a house with a bloodier history than this place." If the Carhart house could sell after all that had gone on under that roof, the Galena House had a sure-fire chance. I just needed to find buyers with the right mindset.

"Really?"

I nodded. "You know, I was thinking that maybe I can put an ad on the same ghost-lovers website where Cornelius first saw The Old Prospector Hotel advertised." Or was it a magazine? I'd have to ask him the next time I saw him.

"Hook another ghost groupie?"

"Something like that."

"Do you know if Cornelius is planning to go to any Halloween parties?"

Maybe her attraction to Cornelius was more like an obsession, or a fetish for men who wore stove pipe hats and long woolen coats.

"He hasn't mentioned anything to me about a party." At her forlorn expression, I felt compelled to add, "but I can certainly ask him and let you know what he says."

Her smile returned, reminding me of the sunshine poking through the scattering of dark clouds outside. "Thanks. I owe you one."

"Ready, Violet?" Honey sneezed before she could catch it, and then turned away to blow her nose. The poor woman was sinking right before our very eyes.

"Let's do it."

Two hours later, I'd gone through my lines more times than I could remember while Rosy moved around, filming from different angles each time. With Rad and his camera out of commission, Rosy needed to make it look like I was being filmed by multiple cameras so that the show kept its same look and feel on the screen.

Now it was Dickie's turn to work his medium magic on screen over and over, which truth be told made me want to giggle with the way he added periodic swooning to his smoke and mirrors show. Although after the last séance Doc, Cornelius, Freesia, and I had performed in Ms. Wolff's apartment downstairs, Dickie's claim that he was sensing a dark and menacing presence in the Galena House attic wasn't far from the bulls-eye. I wouldn't call the white haired, scythe-wielding juggernaut in Apartment 4 on the first floor "dark," but he certainly had scared the bejeezus out of me that night with the way he had come at me swinging.

In between takes, I got Honey's okay to head downstairs and return a call from a new client who'd contacted me yesterday searching for a mid-priced three bedroom house in the area. To avoid being heard on camera in the attic, I made the call on the front porch.

When I finished lining up an appointment, I headed back

inside, choosing to ignore the call and voicemail from Cooper that had come in while I was on the line. Aside from Ray's earlier occasional glares between my takes, my morning was missing its usual second cup of angst, thankfully. I had a feeling listening to Cooper's voicemail would dump a whole pitcher of worry over my head.

At the base of the stairs, I hesitated, glancing down the hall at the door to Ms. Wolff's apartment. One of the pieces of police tape had come unstuck and was lying on the floor. I tiptoed down the hall trying to be as quiet as possible and plucked up the piece of tape. Out of curiosity, I tried the doorknob. It turned easily, unlocked.

Why was the door unlocked? Cooper had been insistent about Freesia keeping this apartment a no trespassing zone. Had Freesia let the film crew in? No, Dickie's charm wasn't that persuasive. What about Ray? Had he sneaked in for a peek? Had he let Rosy in while Freesia wasn't looking?

I pushed open the door enough to stick my head inside and sniff, checking for evidence of Ray. With the way he was flea dipping in Stetson for these filming days, I should be able to tell if he'd been in the apartment. The place smelled of stale wood varnish and old plaster walls, as usual.

I started to close the door when the sound of a clock cuckooing from inside stopped me cold. My head cocked; my ears went into canine mode as I listened for the sound of movement inside. Of all of the times I'd been in Ms. Wolff's apartment since that first ghastly time with Harvey, I hadn't heard any of the clocks cuckoo. They'd only ticked and ticked and ticked.

I stood there on the threshold with my ear shoved in the crack of the open door, counting the cuckoos. When I reached thirteen and the number was still climbing, I pulled my head back and frowned at the little grandfather clock brass knocker on the outside of the door. What was going on? Was one of the clocks broken? How many times was it going to cuckoo?

Glancing around to make sure there were no surly Deadwood detectives snarling behind me, I pushed inside the apartment. I quietly closed the door behind me and leaned against it.

I stood there listening to the cuckoos, my heartbeat picking up rhythm to match my breathing. Nothing moved in the apartment, at least nothing that I could see in the kitchen to my left or in the dining room at the end of the hall. It took a quick self-pep rally to encourage my feet enough to walk down to the clock-covered walls.

When I stood in front of the wall staring at all of those freaky-ass clocks, I noticed two things. First, Cooper hadn't been lying; there were several missing from Ms. Wolff's large collection. Second, and here was the real head scratcher, none of the cuckoo mechanisms on the clocks were moving. As in none of them were showing evidence of cuckooing, yet I could still hear the clock going off loud and clear.

Was I losing my mind? Had I slipped into a parallel universe? Was that even possible? Or was the ghost of Ms. Wolff messing with me? No, according to Doc she wasn't hanging around, but the ghost of Freesia's uncle, Jake Tender, could still be here after what had occurred with Doc during that nearly deadly séance a few weeks ago.

Or maybe what I was hearing was coming from one of the clocks hanging in Ms. Wolff's bedroom. I tiptoed through the living room, avoiding even a glance at the corner where Harvey and I had found Ms. Wolff's tangled body such a short time ago.

In Ms. Wolff's bedroom, the cuckooing continued just as loud as before, the volume consistent no matter where I moved through the apartment. Also, as I'd noticed in the dining room, a few clocks were missing from the wall above the dresser and none of those remaining were showing signs of cuckooing.

What in the hell? Was I hearing things? Hallucinating? Could Freesia and the film crew hear the cuckoos up in the attic?

I looked around the room, catching sight of myself in the dresser mirror. Skirting the bed, I stood in front of the mirror, straightening my jacket, trying to see myself through the eye of the camera.

Something moved behind me.

I gasped and whirled, adrenaline roller coastering through my veins.

Nothing was there besides the open door, the bed, the other dresser, and the wall of ticking clocks.

That damned cuckooing wouldn't stop!

Turning slowly back to the mirror, I stared at my reflection again, everything blurring around the edges.

Then I saw it again. There just over my shoulder. On the wall. Something was moving.

I stepped a few inches to the left and focused on where I'd seen the movement. In the mirror's reflection, one of the clock mechanisms was circling.

I looked over my shoulder, staring at the actual clocks not their reflections, and they were as still and lifeless as the rest of the apartment props.

Back in the mirror, the cuckoo popped out again and again, the scene carved below it circling nonstop on its track.

Leaning closer to the mirror, I mapped which clock it was with my pointer finger, since several of them looked alike except for the finer details—fourth from the right, diagonally above the other dresser.

As I counted, an idea struck me. Something I'd seen from a movie where a message was left on glass, invisible until it was steamed up. I leaned even closer to the mirror and breathed on it, making a small circle of fog. Nope, nothing.

Sliding over to where Layne's photo had been stuck in the frame before, I huffed on the glass, the circle wider this time. Still nothing.

I moved to the center and did it once more. This time there was a small mark in the upper middle. I stood up on my toes and nearly touched my nose to the mirror, taking a deep breath—

BOOM!

Something slammed into the mirror, making it rattle.

I screamed and scrambled backward, my hamstrings connecting with the edge of the bed, making me fall flat on my back on the mattress.

I lay there staring at the mirror, listening to that infernal cuckooing while my breath rushed in and out.

Was that real? Had I actually heard something hit the mirror, or was it just my imagination?

When nothing else happened, I stood up, my eyes locked onto my reflection. Behind me in the mirror, the cuckoo bird still popped in and out. I took a step closer to the mirror, ever so slowly reaching my finger out again to touch it.

BOOM!

The mirror shook in its wooden frame.

I yipped and yanked my arm back.

BOOM!

It rattled again, the pounding incredibly loud, like the crack of thunder when lightning strikes too close.

BOOM!

Holy shit! There was something on the other side of the mirror trying to break through.

Was it someone with white hair, snake eyes, and a blood splattered ax? Had we somehow trapped the juggernaut on the other side the last time we'd played around in the paranormal world? Could he actually break through and come into this dimension? Had I been watching too much Twilight Zone after the kids went to bed?

BOOM!

My feet didn't wait around to figure out any answers. I raced out of the bedroom and flew across the living room, wincing as another boom resounded from the bedroom. I wasted no time getting out the front door, yanking it closed behind me.

I held onto the doorknob for several seconds, my eyes squeezed tight, waiting to see if the knob turned on its own in my hand, scared to death it would.

The sound of the cuckoo clock was muffled by the wood and the blood pounding in my ears.

The doorknob didn't twist or turn, thank God. I would have probably screamed the house down if it had. I had no desire to face off with the ax-wielding albino again now that I knew his blade could take me out of the—

"Parker!"

I screeched and leapt back away from the door.

"What in the hell are you doing?" Detective Cooper stood glaring at me from the other end of the hall, just inside the front door of the boarding house. "You know you're not supposed to go near that apartment."

I opened my mouth to tell him about what I'd seen and heard on the other side of Ms. Wolff's door, but then thought twice and squeezed my lips closed.

He stalked toward me, his face rigid. "Why is the tape on the floor?"

"I didn't do it."

I stepped back when he got close. He scooped up the loose tape. "You didn't use that master key to go inside, did you?"

"No." I hadn't needed a key at all.

He reached out and turned the doorknob. It was locked. He rattled the door while he squinted down at me, double-checking whether it would budge.

I didn't say a word. I didn't have it in me at the moment. Why was the door suddenly locked? I certainly hadn't taken the time to twist the lock during my panic-filled evacuation.

"Well, what the hell were you doing here?"

"I thought I heard something in there."

"Don't you mean someone?"

"No." I licked my lips, nervous to voice the question on my tongue.

"What did you hear?"

"A clock cuckoo."

He pressed his ear to the wood. "I don't hear anything."

"Hmmm." Crap. Why was I still hearing it?

"It's probably just your cuckoo brain making you hear things."

"Probably." I was happy to let him insult me for the moment if it meant not getting my ass chewed out for trespassing behind crime scene lines.

His gaze narrowed as he stared hard at me. I got the distinct feeling he was going all Matrix on me, trying to scan my mind for rebellious plans.

I pointed at the ceiling. "The TV folks are up there. I should get back to them."

"Come with me first," he ordered, leading the way back out the front door. "I have something for you."

With one last peek at Ms. Wolff's doorknob, I followed him.

Outside on the porch, I could no longer hear the cuckoo clock, thank God.

Cooper pulled a box from his coat pocket and held it out to me. "Here."

"What's this?" I took it warily. "Did you buy me a corsage to wear to the prom, Detective?"

"Real funny. You know, I have yet to figure out what has Nyce so infatuated with you."

"It's my secret love potion."

"More like love poison." He tapped on the box. "Quit wasting my time and open it."

I did. Inside the lid was another box, only this one had familiar Chinese markings on it. I shook the puzzle box I'd found in the attic at the Carhart house back in August. "Are the teeth still in here?"

He nodded, glancing up and down the street. "Put it away, would you?" His tone was rushed, almost nervous.

I stuffed the puzzle box back into the nondescript cardboard box he'd put it in. "You took this without getting permission?"

"I borrowed it from the evidence locker for now."

"Will you get in trouble for that?"

"That's my concern, not yours."

"I don't want to get you fired."

"Don't tell me you're worried about me, Parker."

"I don't want you stalking me because I made you lose your job, making my life even more miserable than you already do."

A hint of a grin cracked his mouth. "Since I'm still part of the Carhart case, I have access." He pointed at the box. "Now that you have the teeth, we have a deal."

I nodded slowly, still trying to piece together what I'd experienced in Ms. Wolff's apartment. Why had the clock cuckooed only in the reflection? What if the juggernaut made it through the mirror? How long would I have before he hunted me down and started swinging at me again?

"Parker." Cooper waved his hand in front of my face. "What's wrong with you this morning?"

I shook off the cold fingers of dread that had started to wrap around me. "I didn't sleep well."

"Yeah," he frowned out across Deadwood's rooftops. "Me either."

"That's because you stayed up too late getting your butt kicked at poker."

"Or something like that." He turned back to me, his eyes back to their lovely shade of piercing steel. "I'll be in touch about our field trip to the ranch."

"I'll be tingling in excitement until that moment."

"Tingle away, but you'd better keep your head down."

"You plan on running around with your guns blazing?"

"No, but Detective Hawke is." His eyelids narrowed, his gaze warning. "And you're in his sights."

Chapter Seventeen

Meanwhile, back in *Scharfrichter* Land …

I avoided Ms. Wolff's apartment and its damned infernal cuckooing the rest of the day, hanging out on the front porch while Dickie recorded a piece in front of the taped off door of what I figured would soon become the infamous Apartment 4 when the episode aired.

Rosy hailed me as I was on my way out to the Picklemobile after we were done shooting for the day.

I waited on the front walk for her to join me. She looked lopsided without her camera on her shoulder.

"You know that house up in Lead where we're going to be shooting later this week?" she asked.

"The Carhart house." Which I'd have to start calling the Britton house after Zeke and Zelda moved in next month.

"Yeah, that one." She moved closer, lowering her voice. "Your buddy Ray took Honey and me over there yesterday afternoon so I could start thinking about camera angles and lighting."

Ray was so not my "buddy," but I let that one fly for the time being. "What did you think of the house?" I braced myself for a Prudence story, wanting to seem surprised if they'd witnessed something paranormal.

"It's a beautiful house."

"I know, right?" Zelda should put a sign with those words on it over the front door.

"Anyway, we went inside and I shot some preliminary stuff, bits I could use to study back in my hotel room later."

"You're very thorough."

"Yeah, well, I don't like surprises."

Rosy was going to love Prudence then. "Me either."

"I wanted to talk to you about them."

"Why me?"

"Honey mentioned that when she was in there weeks ago, something happened to her and she blacked out, ending up in the kitchen drooling like a zombie."

Honey had been pretty freaky when I'd found her that day, her mouth catching flies, the whites of her eyes showing. "Yeah, it was pretty scary. I was worried she'd had a seizure or something." I frowned at Rosy. "She didn't do it again, did she?"

If so, I hoped Prudence hadn't mentioned my name again on film.

"No, Honey was fine, although she did seem pretty antsy while we were in there."

Rosy looked up toward the porch and waved at Honey, who'd poked her head out the front door. "Be in shortly."

A cold blast of air whipped through the front yard, making me and the pine trees behind the house shiver, nearly taking Rosy's SDSU Jackrabbits baseball cap with it. "I'm glad Honey didn't suffer another seizure. One was scary enough."

"Honey might have been seizure-free, but my camera wasn't."

"What do you mean?"

"I must have recorded twenty minutes of film moving through that house, but when I went to view it last night, all that was there was me filming the porch and walking into the front door. Then it all goes dark. No video, no sound."

"Could you have accidentally turned the camera off?"

"No, it was running. I know my camera and how to use it. Besides, I didn't say there wasn't a recording; it's just all dark with no sound. At first I thought there was something wrong with it, but when I tested it after watching the non-video last night and then again this morning, it worked fine." She tugged her hat on tighter as another wind whipped passed us. "I've had my batteries drained in a haunted church before, but nothing like this has happened until now."

"It is peculiar." Prudence was anything but normal when compared to the other ghosts I'd been around since moving to

Deadwood and meeting Doc.

"Have you had any other experiences similar to this in the Carhart house?" Rosy asked. "Like when you were taking pictures of the house before putting it up for sale."

"I actually never took pictures of it. My clients provided pictures for me to use." I purposely avoided answering the first part of the question.

"Hmmm." Rosy stuffed her hands in her jacket pockets. "This makes me nervous about filming inside of the house."

"You must be used to feeling invisible fingers brush your neck or hearing footsteps coming from empty rooms by now."

"Yep, but I've never come across anything that could mess with my camera."

"We're still not sure it was a ghost." I wanted to downplay this somehow before stepping foot inside of Prudence's lair with Rosy and her camera in tow. "The ground under that house and most of Lead for that matter is worm-holed with mine shafts and tunnels. Maybe there is some powerful magnetic source underneath the ground that affected your camera." Hell, as kooky as Wanda Carhart's family had been, I'd buy that a strong magnetic force had stirred up their brains.

"Usually magnets don't affect the camera, but I wonder if it could be affected by powerful electromagnetic pulses or radio waves. I'll have to ask Rad if he knows anything about it." She patted my shoulder. "Thanks for your help, Violet. You were great today on film." Without a backward glance, she strode back into the Galena House.

Rosy should have seen my performance when I freaked out earlier in Ms. Wolff's apartment. That was Oscar-winning stuff in there.

I made it to the Picklemobile without a hitch and cruised home to Aunt Zoe's, my gut rumbling, my mouth watering for another lemon bar or three.

The sight of Reid's red dually pickup parked along the curb across the street made me do a double take. I rolled into the drive and cut the engine, waiting for any other loud bangs besides the one that came from the Picklemobile's exhaust pipe.

All was silent on the home front.

No, wait. I craned my neck, listening. A hammering noise came from behind Aunt Zoe's house.

I detoured from the path to the front door and cut through the side gate. Elvis greeted me as I reached the back yard, clucking along after me. Knowing Elvis, she was probably bitching at me for not letting her lay eggs in my closet anymore.

"You're lucky I don't decide to wiggle my nose at you and 'poof' you into a basket of fried chicken."

"Hey, Sparky. Talking to chickens now?"

I was so distracted with Elvis that I didn't notice the flannel-shirted man on Aunt Zoe's workshop roof until I was almost standing next to his ladder and the pile of shingles on the grass beside it.

"Hi, Reid." I took in the hammer in his hand and tool belt around his waist. "Something wrong with Aunt Zoe's roof?"

"That wind we had last week blew some of the shingles loose. Figured I'd better fix the roof before the snow starts or she'll have some leaks."

"She called you?"

"No. I stopped by while she was in Denver to check the place for wind damage. You were probably at work."

I pointed my thumb at the house. "Does she know you're out here?"

"She threatened to take my ladder away if I didn't leave."

"This ladder?" The one still leaning against the side of the building?

He grinned down at me. "Yeah. I won the battle."

"How?"

"I told her that if she took my ladder, I'd call for the fire truck to come rescue me and the city would undoubtedly bill her for the mess."

I laughed. "I'm amazed she didn't threaten to shoot you down."

"She did, so I showed her this." He unbuttoned several of his shirt buttons, pulling the flannel aside.

"Is that a Kevlar vest?"

"Yep. I borrowed it from Coop."

That made me laugh again, something much needed after a

day of cuckoo clocks and Ray. "I'll let you get back to it, then."

"Do me a favor, Sparky."

"What's that?"

"When she's not looking, take those shotgun shells out of the gun she keeps pointing out the back door."

"You got it. I'll sneak you a few of her lemon bars when I can, too."

"You're an angel, Sparky."

Actually, my label was much darker than that.

I headed inside the back door. A shotgun lay across the top of the refrigerator, out of the kids' reach. That reminded me of old man Harvey's grandpappy's wire-triggered shotgun. Was it still stuffed under the back seat of his pickup, or had he stashed it somewhere else?

"Annie Oakley?" I hollered, shucking my coat. "Where are you, sharpshooter?"

Aunt Zoe strolled into the kitchen as I was hanging my purse on the back of one of the chairs. "I take it you talked to our trespasser." Her eyes practically shot sparks.

Reid was smart to wear Kevlar. "Him fixing the roof is a very sweet gesture."

She stared out the back door window at Reid. "It's a ploy. When he finishes, he's going to expect me to give him something in return."

"Maybe." I joined her at the window. "Maybe not. He sure looks handsome in that red flannel, doesn't he?"

"Red has always been a good color on him. It brings out the deep blue in his eyes and makes it hard to look away."

I glanced her way. "Like now?"

She aimed a crooked smile my way. "Knock it off, cupid. I told you I wasn't going back to that fishing hole no matter how big and shiny the fish look under the water."

"Speaking of fish." I went over to the container where she was storing the remaining lemon bars and took one.

"What do lemon bars have to do with fish?"

"They're both food," I said through a mouthful of lemony goodness. When she turned back to the window, I sneaked two more bars out and hid them in a bowl in the cupboard to take out to Reid later.

"How was work today?" Aunt Zoe asked. "Anything exciting happen over at the Galena House?"

I wiped my hands on a napkin. "As a matter of fact, it did." I grabbed a glass from the cupboard and poured myself some water.

That captured her attention. She joined me at the sink. "What?"

I finished my water and set the glass down next to the sink, and then I told her about my visit to Ms. Wolff's apartment, the cuckooing clock, and the thundering mirror. When I finished, she led me over to a chair.

"Sit there and don't move. I'll be right back." She disappeared into the dining room. I heard the stairs creak.

While I obeyed Aunt Zoe like a good little puppy, I listened for sounds of my kids. The house was unusually quiet. No fighting. No doors slamming. No TV. Where were my children?

Off and on all morning, I'd been dying to call Doc, anxious to see how his talk with Layne had gone. But I'd resisted, wanting to discuss it in person with Doc first, and then Layne, so I could try to read each when they told their side of the story. But Ray had been chomping on my heels every time I'd paused to take a breath.

Midway through the day I'd finally escaped the slave driver and called Doc, but Ray had found me before we'd made it much past how the filming was going. The big jerk had insisted I get back inside to reshoot a scene, making me hang up before I'd had a chance to tell Doc about Ms. Wolff's apartment, let alone get a feel for what had come of his talk with Layne.

I glanced out at Reid, and then back toward the dining room. The opportunity to slip him the lemon bars had arrived. I stole outside and raced over, leaving the bowl on top of the pile of shingles.

"Thanks, Sparky. You've got my money in the boxing ring, too."

"Cooper's going to pay for running his big mouth."

He laughed. "Doc's a lucky guy, but after seeing a demo of your windmill swings, he'd better watch his Ps and Qs."

"Damned straight."

I waved goodbye and hurried back inside, sliding into my chair seconds before Aunt Zoe returned with a wooden box in her hands. It was mid-sized, looking like a small foot locker. She set it on the table, eyeing me suspiciously.

"Why are your cheeks pink?"

"I had a hot flash."

"You're too young for that yet."

I changed the subject. "Where are Addy and Layne?"

"Addy is over at Kelly Wymonds' house working on a project they are doing together in school. Jeff said he'll bring her home around seven-thirty." She unlocked the box lid and flipped it open. "Layne's with Doc."

I blinked. "Come again."

"He swung by around four and picked up Layne to drop off some books due at the library. Doc told me to tell you they were going to be in the South Dakota room researching a few things about some old mining claims. He figured they'd be back in time for supper."

"You're talking about Doc Nyce, right? And my son."

"Yes, Violet. You did send Doc over this morning to have a talk with Layne, remember?"

"I didn't expect them to turn into bosom buddies."

"I don't know that I'd call it that, but I told you before, Layne can relate to Doc when it comes to books."

Speaking of books, she pulled one out of the box and blew off a thick coat of dust. Actually, it looked more like an old, leather bound scrapbook.

"What's that?"

"Your past." She carefully set the thick book down on the table in front of me. "And your future."

I didn't like the sound of that. "After the day I've had, I'd rather read a dictionary."

"Violet Lynn," her tone had that strict aunty-tone that always made me sit up straight and close my lips. "Your head has been buried in the sand long enough."

"But I like the sand. It's not as scary down there."

"Listen, baby doll," Aunt Zoe said, using a nickname I hadn't heard in a long, long time. She pulled out the chair next to me and sat down. "Whether or not you accept this role as an executioner, it is who you are inside of here," she tapped on my forehead and then my chest, "and here. Trust me, if I could change it or take your place, I would in a heartbeat. I don't like the idea of you having to go through this any more than you do."

I ran my finger along the spine of the book. "What if I don't learn and keep my head in the sand? What happens then?"

Aunt Zoe stared at me, her gaze haunted. "You'll die."

"As in sooner rather than later?"

She nodded. "Things have already been set in motion, Violet. There is no running away or hiding now. The others know you're here."

"Others?"

"It's only a matter of time before they come for you."

"Come for me? What … what does that even mean?"

"They'll come to kill you," she spelled out.

"Why? What if I haven't done anything?"

"But you already have. Like I said, they know you're here. Before, you were unrecognizable."

"What if I promise not to do anything more? Will they leave me alone then?" I wasn't even sure who we were talking about yet, but I had a bad feeling Mr. Black and his brother were two of "them."

"No. By being alive, you're a threat. They will want to remove the threat so they can continue as they have been without fear."

"What about my kids?"

"I told you before; this is passed down through the female line."

"So Addy is also a threat?"

She closed her eyes for a moment, as if gaining the strength to go on. "They will take her life, too."

My eyes filled with tears. "Oh, God."

"What I'm not certain about is Layne's future."

"You said this is only passed through the female line."

"Yes, but Layne is the twin of Addy. There have been twin executioners in our family's history. But from what I can determine based on what's in this book, all of the other twins have been two females."

"So he could be safe."

She grimaced. "Maybe, but probably not. He can reproduce, just like your father did, and create another executioner. If they want to be thorough, now that they've found you, they will wipe out your whole family."

"Oh, God," I whispered, brushing away a tear sliding down my cheek. "How can I protect my kids?"

She placed her palm on the book. "By letting me show you what you need to know, to teach you what we've learned over generations on how to survive."

"You mean like witch spells and hexes?" Maybe Detective Hawke was onto something when it came to me and flying broomsticks.

"No. We're not witches. They're an entirely different breed. We are executioners."

"Cold-blooded killers."

"More like selective killers." She took my hands, squeezing them between hers. "We take out the trash."

That made me snort-laugh. "Great tagline. Do I get to wear a cape?"

She grinned. "No cape, kiddo. It'll get in the way."

"After I read this book, I'll know what to do to protect Addy and Layne?"

She shook her head. "The book is a history lesson. Over many generations, instructions have been passed down through our female line for those of us who become a *magistra*. A teacher. Magistra are those who don't become executioners. Your great grandmother was one."

"I always thought she was some kind of witch with the way she used her rune stones all of the time."

"She was an amazing *magistra*, determined to protect the family line at all costs. She could see things in people, sniff out who was a threat and who wasn't without getting too close. I've never been able to hone my skills enough to tell a bad egg without the help of triggers."

"Triggers?"

She pointed at my necklace charm that she'd made and insisted I wear every day. "That looks like a charm, but it's really a trigger. For instance, remember how you told me the big albino coming out of the Galena House looked at your necklace and his eyes turned snake-like?"

I nodded, fingering the charm.

"He saw your necklace and it triggered a reaction in him, something non-humans cannot control."

"When you said this was a protection charm, what you meant was it will help me to determine who is a threat."

"Exactly. It won't keep you from getting killed; only you can do that. The charm is merely a warning light."

"And all of the other charm covered bracelets and trinkets you've made for me and the kids over the years? Were those triggers, too?"

"Yes. I was waiting for the day when you came to me and told me someone … or rather something … had reacted to one of them."

"Why didn't you mention any of this executioner and *magistra* family business before?"

"I had to wait for a sign. That is the way."

"So Grandma-great waited for a sign from you?"

"She didn't have to wait. Remember, she had mastered a way to see things in people, including her own family. She knew from early on that my mother and I were not executioners. She also understood that my mother was a weaker link in the family line, and that I would make a stronger *magistra*. So she focused her energy on training me instead of Mom." Aunt Zoe walked over to the kitchen sink. "Your great grandmother also knew about you."

I remembered back to a day long ago in my grandmother's attic with the sunshine pouring in through the dirty window, shining down on Grandma-great's craggy face as she cast her rune stones over and over. The clack of the stones had seemed so loud in the heavy quiet. The smell of varnish and stale dust had been thick, the warm air almost suffocating. When she'd looked up, her watery eyes had locked onto me and then narrowed as she cast the runes yet again. One particular rune stone had appeared in a negative position, *Merkstave*, just as it always had whenever I was around her.

"You smell too strongly of death, little Violet," she'd said in her scratchy voice. "You're clouding up the runes. Leave me and take your threats with you."

Her gnarled hands had shooed me away. I'd raced down the attic stairs, not stopping until fresh air surrounded me and sunlight melted away the shadows filling my head.

I looked at Aunt Zoe, who was watching me while she drank a glass of water. "I always thought Grandma-great didn't like me. She'd give me this scary glare and tell me that I traveled with hidden danger in my pockets. After she'd leave, I'd search my pockets but only find lint."

"She warned me about you." Aunt Zoe set the glass in the sink. "She'd seen the strength of a fighter sprouting in you from the start. As you grew, she told me she could sense the killer budding inside of your young heart. On her deathbed, I was instructed to watch over you, to protect you with what she'd taught me, and to wait for you to blossom into the next executioner in our family line."

A chill crawled up my spine. While I was playing hopscotch and kickball, and later making out with boys under the bleachers and scraping by with a C average in algebra, I'd had an executioner growing inside of me. Too bad there hadn't been a *Most Likely to Kill* category in the school yearbook.

"What about Dad? Does he know anything about all of this teacher and executioner stuff?"

"He knows enough to watch over you and search for signs. Since I didn't live with you, he acted as my eyes."

That was why my father always had a way of seeing through my subterfuge. He was on the lookout.

"What about Mom?"

"She's in the dark."

It was more like she was in a field of flowers. Now I understood why I'd never been able to feel as carefree about life's problems as she did. I didn't imagine that executioners danced through life much.

Aunt Zoe returned to the table, sitting down next to me

again. "The job of a *magistra* is to train the next executioner on how to seek and remove troublemakers while blending in with and protecting the rest of the population. I have been preparing for this role since I was a girl, and now the time has come to teach you what I know."

"You mean like how to fight and kill?" I'd never seen Aunt Zoe harm anything bigger than a horsefly.

"No, that strength is innate in you, the executioner. My job is to provide you with the weapons, to teach you danger signs to watch for when on the hunt, and educate you on how to detect a threat before it's upon you."

This was all too much. My brain wanted to shut down while my body lounged in a tub full of hot water and bubbles. "I don't know if I'm up to this, Aunt Zoe."

She kissed me on the forehead. "An executioner is only as good as her *magistra*. I will not let you down."

"It's not you I'm worried about. I'm just me. I don't feel like a killer in here." I covered my heart.

"Violet Lynn, you are an executioner. You will fight to protect and rid this world of malicious vermin. And if you die, you will die fighting." She left no room for "buts."

I heard the sound of the front door opening. "I'm home," Layne called.

Aunt Zoe handed me the book, and then closed the lid on the box. "Take that to your room and hide it there. Read it when the kids are not around. I've tried to transcribe most of it into English, but if you can't read my writing, I'll decipher it for you."

"You want me to read this whole book?" I barely had time to shave my legs most days, let alone read something that long.

"Yes, Violet Lynn, the whole book. You need to know from whence you came." She nudged me toward the dining room, the book clutched to my chest. "Go put it away for now. Your son is waiting for you to talk to him about what he did."

I ran into Doc on his way in the front door. "How was the library?"

"Quiet." He leaned down and gave me a soft kiss. "Is that Reid's pickup out there?"

"Yeah, he's fixing the roof on Aunt Zoe's workshop."

"Really?" His eyebrows lifted. "How's that working for your aunt?"

"Her molars are grinding."

He chuckled. "How was work?"

I grimaced. "Troubling, but let's eat supper before I tell you about it." I glanced up the stairs, lowering my voice. "How's Layne? Was he rude to you this morning?"

"Not rude." Doc shrugged off his coat. "A little distant, though, which I expected."

"Did he tell you what's up with school?"

"Yes, after a little prodding, and then he made me swear to secrecy."

"But not from me, right?"

"Especially from you."

I grimaced. At what point had my son grown up enough to stop confiding in me about his biggest secrets? "You're not going to tell me if my kid is heading down the road to being a gang banger or serial killer?"

He wrapped his arms around me, staring down at me with a straight face. "Layne's a good kid. He's smart and funny, but he's also got some problems at the moment. You need to go up and talk to him. He's ready to tell you about it now."

I went up on my toes and kissed the shallow cleft in his chin. "Okay. Will you set the table for me? I think Aunt Zoe's planning on ham sandwiches for supper."

"Sounds delicious. What's with the big old book you keep poking into my chest?"

I hesitated, not ready to go into the whole executioner extravaganza at the moment. "It's an old family album." That was basically true. "I'm taking it up to my closet and then I'm going to pay a visit to my son."

"Be gentle on the kid, Tiger. He's nuts about you."

"The poor boy."

"Yeah, that makes two of us suckers." He ran his hands down over my hips and groaned in appreciation, and then he left me to join Aunt Zoe in the kitchen.

After I hid the book high up on my closet shelf, I headed down the hall and knocked on Layne's door before entering.

He looked up from where he sat on the edge of his bed. There was a stack of books next to him, while one lay open on his lap. "Hi, Mom."

I moved the stack aside and sat down next to him. "Hey, sweetie. I think it's time for you to tell me what's going on at school."

"And then I can still go trick-or-treating?"

"That was the deal, but I want the truth, and since we both know I can read your mind," I placed my palm on his head for a moment and pretended I was pulling his thoughts from it, "I would advise against any fibbing."

"Okay." He looked down at his hands. "I punched Kyle because he was being mean."

"Being mean how?"

"He was making fun of you."

"Me?" I sat back in surprise. "What was he saying?"

"He kept calling you Spooky Parker and saying that you like to kiss dead people."

That little shit. I'd never kissed a dead person in my life. Although I had kissed Doc when Prudence was sort of possessing him, so technically, I guess one could say … no, Doc wasn't dead. I was sticking with my original story. That *stinking* little shit!

"Layne, you know kids like to make up hurtful names."

He nodded, his focus still locked on his hands.

"And you know they will sometimes lie in order to get attention because they're not getting what they need at home." When he nodded again, I put my arm around him, hugging him against me. "You can't let these boys get to you, sweetie. You're going to run into bullies throughout your life." Ray, the dickhead, was the perfect example. "You need to figure out a way to handle them with your mind; use your fists when there is no other solution. You're a very bright kid, way smarter than me, so I know you can do this."

He sniffed. "Okay."

I kissed him on the head, breathing in his wonderful scent of shampoo, books, and Layne. "If you need help fighting them with your brain, come to me, and we'll come up with some brilliant plan on how to disarm them and send them away scratching their heads in confusion at what just happened."

He wrapped his arms around my waist, snuggling into me. "I will, Mom. I'm sorry I got us in trouble with Principal Walker."

"Just try not to do it again, and don't you dare hide anything else from me that you're supposed to show me."

"I won't."

"If I catch you forging my signature on any other documents, you'll be in trouble like you've never experienced before. On top of that, I'll tell your grandfather all about it."

"Don't tell Grandpa. I don't want him mad at me."

"You keep your nose clean and I won't." I pushed him back and stared him in the eyes. "You know I love you with all of my old, fat wrinkly heart?"

He smiled a tiny bit. "Yeah."

"Good. How did things go with Doc this morning?" Inquiring minds were dying to know.

"I can't tell you."

"What? Why not?"

"He made me swear to secrecy."

What?!! Doc had said it was the other way around. Hmmmm. "Fine." I stood up. "It's time to wash up and come down to supper."

"Mom?" He stopped me when I'd reached the doorway.

"Yeah?"

"Can I go trick-or-treating?"

"Sure. Doc and I will take you and your sister out after we get home from work."

"Doc's coming, too?"

I nodded, waiting to see how that went over.

"Okay," was all he said, and then rose from his bed.

"One more thing, Layne." He joined me and we headed toward the bathroom to wash up. "Did your sister know anything about you getting into fights at school?"

He winced. "Sort of."

I washed my hands first. "And how is it she managed to keep quiet about it?" Normally Addy would be racing home to tell on her brother.

Shutting off the water, he took the towel I held out. "I gave her my allowance for the past two weeks."

Ohhhhh, I should've known she wasn't entirely innocent. The little brat was extorting hush money from her troubled brother. My smile felt like plastic. "Thanks for telling me the truth, honey. Let's go help Aunt Zoe."

Supper went well in spite of my inviting Reid to join us and Aunt Zoe's periodic glares in his direction as we ate. After the dishes were cleared, and Reid had left in one piece and free of shotgun blast holes, Doc and I sat down on the back porch steps alone in the dark.

I filled him in on what I'd experienced in Ms. Wolff's apartment, and then how Cooper had brought me the box of teeth.

"So," I shivered as a cold breeze whispered over me. "What do you think is the deal with that cuckoo clock in the mirror?"

"I don't know. I'll have to think about that." He tugged me toward him, settling me on the step below him and then wrapping me up in his arms. "I'm more concerned about who or what was banging on the mirror, trying to get out."

I rested my head back against his shoulder. "It's gotta be the juggernaut, don't you think?"

"Probably, but maybe we left something else stuck in there, too."

"Like Big Jake Tender?"

"Or the greaser who got thrown against the wall."

I sat there in the quiet night, lost in the past for a few moments. "I wonder if Cornelius might have a different theory about the mirror."

"We could ask."

I needed to find out if he was partying at the Purple Door tomorrow night for Freesia, anyway, so I might as well ask about both. That brought me to another situation I'd thought about during my long afternoon of filming. "You know how Cooper wants us to go out to the ranch and see what sights and sounds you can pick up?"

"Using my ghost radar, as he calls it?"

"Yeah, that. I think we need to take Cornelius along."

Doc thought on that one without comment.

"My reasoning," I continued, "is that if your theory about him being the Pied Piper of ghosts is true, then he might draw in many more ghosts than just Harvey's grandpa. We might get more answers than with you alone."

"His presence and all that follow him might also muddy the stream," Doc said from over my head. "Might make it hard for me to figure out the details coming from individuals."

I hadn't thought of that. "True. Maybe it's not such a good idea."

"I wouldn't say that." He ran his hands up my arms, stopping to massage my shoulders. "Let me think about it. In the meantime, you can see if he'll be hanging around town for the next few days in case we decide to pull him in and ask him for his thoughts on Ms. Wolff's mirror."

I let my head droop forward as he worked the tension out of my muscles. "Hey, Doc?"

"Yeah?"

"Do you have some kind of secret pact with my son?"

"Yes. We each shared a truth and agreed not to tell anyone else."

"Is there anything I can do to make you tell me the secrets?"

"Probably not."

"What if I ask you to tell me just one of the secrets while I'm wearing only my cherry-flavored lip gloss and purple boots?"

"Nothing else?"

"Not a stitch."

"Wow, you play a tough game."

"No, I play dirty, and I am willing to play even dirtier with you, but only if you cough up a secret."

He turned me part way around so I could look at him, and then tipped my chin up. "I love it when you play dirty, Boots, but I promised your son, and I won't crack, not even for a night of debauchery with his incredibly sexy mother."

"Fine, then I'll just have to beat it out of you." I held up my fists, Rocky Balboa style.

"You know I love it when you get rough with me." He captured my wrists and tugged me toward him, his mouth closing in on mine. "But please, Tiger, whatever you do, don't go all windmill on me. I might laugh myself to death."

"Mom?" Addy's voice was like a flyswatter smack to the face. "Where are you?"

"Over here on the steps."

She turned on the porch light, blinding me. "Hi, Doc. Mom, can Kelly go trick-or-treating with us tomorrow?"

"I don't know. I need to think about it."

"What? Why do you need to think about it?"

"Because, Adelynn Renee, you are grounded along with your brother."

"Why?" she whined.

"For extorting hush money from him."

"What does that mean?"

"It means that you need to pay him back two weeks of allowance that he gave you not to tell on him."

"That's not fair!" She stomped inside, screaming Layne's name at the top of her lungs. "You're dead meat!"

"Crap, I'd better deal with that before it ends in blows."

Doc stood and pulled me up. "I need to head home anyway. I have some homework to do."

"Oh yeah, is it math, reading, or science?"

"It's history. Harvey is coming over to fill me in on his family history at the ranch."

"You want to get to know his granddad before he climbs inside of your head?"

"Something like that." He frowned down at me. "I also need to be prepared for whatever else is waiting for us out there."

Chapter Eighteen

Wednesday, October 31st (Halloween)

Meanwhile, back at the haunted house …

I woke up in bed with the Harlem Globetrotters whistling sweet nothings in my ear.

It took several seconds of their theme song playing to realize that Jerry was trying to get ahold of me on my cellphone. I knocked over a glass of water on the nightstand reaching for my phone, which pretty much set the tone for my morning.

"Hello?" I said while reaching toward the floor for my pajama pants to sop up the watery mess.

"Sorry to wake you, Violet, but we have a team member down, and I need you to sub in for him."

Overbalancing, I ended up falling out of bed and landing in the puddle of water. "Damn it!"

"I agree. It's unfortunate, but Ben can't go on camera today. He's a sick mess."

I lay on my stomach with my camisole top soaking up water, my mind trying to make sense of Jerry's sports references through the sleep fog swirling in my head. "You want me to fill in for Ben this morning?"

"I want you to go straight to the Carhart house. Ray will meet you there with Dickie and his camera crew."

"The Carhart house?" I rolled over onto my back, the floor cool against my bare shoulders. I wasn't prepared to deal with Prudence today. "I don't know if that's a good idea."

"You cleared a whole week of filming with both Ms. Carhart and the new owners, right?"

Unfortunately, yes. "I'm referring to me. I'd planned to spend today going over my cue cards so I'd be ready by tomorrow. If I go to the Carhart house this morning, I might be a mess." Meaning I might totally freak out if Prudence messed with me, like she so loved to do.

"You'll be fine once you get into the game," Jerry spoke with authority. "You'll be slam dunking your lines before you know it. I have faith in you."

Darn it, why did he have to end with that? Now I felt like I had to do it so I wouldn't let Coach Jerry down.

"All right." I pushed myself upright, rubbing a tight muscle in my lower back. "What time do I need to be at the Carhart house and what do you want me to wear?"

An hour and a half later, I pulled into the driveway at the Carhart house with a takeout tray of coffees sitting on the seat next to me. I brushed yet another dog hair off the new, dark rose pantsuit Jerry had bought for me. Between Elvis's feathers and Red's fur, I needed to start carrying a portable vacuum with me wherever I went.

Old man Harvey pulled in behind me, catching up to me as I reached the porch steps. "Yer gonna owe me big for this, girlie! I had company this mornin', and she had some big ideas for breakfast."

"I'll take you out to breakfast another day to make up for it."

"I wasn't talkin' about food, if ya get my drift." He wiggled his bushy eyebrows at me.

"Come on! I can't handle thinking about you and sex this early in the morning."

"Well, if yer gonna insist I hold yer hand in a haunted house at the ass-crack of dawn, yer gonna have to deal with whatever I throw at ya."

When push had come to shove, I'd chickened out on coming to visit Prudence without backup. Harvey hadn't exactly cooed like a mourning dove when I'd woken him up shortly after hanging up with Jerry, but since he was my self-appointed bodyguard, I didn't give him much choice about joining me.

Ray met us on the front porch, or rather, blocked us from entering. "What in the hell is *he* doing here?"

"He's my acting coach today."

Harvey leaned back on his heels, hooking his thumbs in his

suspenders. "You missed a patch while shavin', boy."

"Where?" Ray rubbed along his jaw.

He pointed at Ray's mouth. "Right smack dab in the center there, where that godawful sneer of yers is sittin'."

Ray's face scrunched up. "Stay out of the way, today, old man. Don't even try to get your face on film."

"I'm not purtied up enough for the camera today, so don't go gettin' yer balls in a vice over lil' ol' me."

I held up the tray of drinks. "If you're done beating your chest and flinging poo, Ray, I'd like to take these inside."

He stepped aside. "You have one too many. Honey isn't here today. She's back at the hotel with Rad, too sick to get out of bed."

"That's some cold." First Rad, then Honey, and now Ben. I needed to up my vitamin C so I didn't come down with it next. "Come on, Harvey." I balanced the tray in one hand and tugged the ornery buzzard in behind me by the suspenders. I didn't want to give him the opportunity to change his mind about facing off with Prudence alongside me.

We found Dickie and Rosy in the kitchen discussing his preferred camera angles. They both fawned all over me for bringing them a caffeine hit. Dickie remembered Harvey from the day we found an old mining boot with some of the foot bones and dried flesh still in it out at the ranch. Rosy warmed instantly to the dirty bird, especially after he admired her tattoos and proceeded to tell her an unfiltered story about a "popular" prostitute in Winnemucca he'd known who had the words *Bulls Eye* written across her very rounded derrière. Luckily, Dickie had left the room by that point to take a phone call from Honey. Apparently, she was trying to run things from her hotel bed. Ray joined us in the midst of Rosy's laughing and curled his upper lip at Harvey and me in turn. I thumbed my nose at him.

"Rosy, let's get rolling," Dickie called from the living room.

Ray caught my arm as we filed out of the kitchen. "I need to talk to you."

Harvey paused on the threshold. "You might want to take care in this here house, boy." He pointed at the ceiling. "The dead lady in the attic ain't no fan of tough-talkin' assholes."

"I'm not afraid of any ghosts," he told Harvey. "Especially some old broad who likes to play parlor tricks."

I looked up, hoping the "old broad" had heard that. "He's all yours, Prudence," I told the ceiling.

"You two are real jokers." As soon as Harvey left the doorway, Ray turned on me. "Listen, Blondie," he said in a hushed voice. "Detective Hawke called me last night."

Good, it was about time Hawke learned a phone number besides mine. I was getting tired of sending his calls to voicemail every day. "So?"

"He told me Eddie Mudder is missing." When I didn't react, he added, "He also said you were there shortly before Eddie disappeared."

I kept silent. What else had Hawke mentioned? Was Ray privileged enough to know about the faceless body we'd found at Harvey's, and that it had disappeared along with Eddie?

Ray's gaze narrowed. "Why didn't you tell me Eddie was missing?"

I did a double take. "I was unaware that you and I were on more than a barely speaking level."

"I told you about Mr. Black."

"Grudgingly."

"You should have told me about Eddie."

"Why?"

"Because Mr. Black may be coming for me next."

"Violet?" Dickie called from the other room. "You're up now."

"One minute, I'm touching up my makeup," I called back. I dragged Ray to the pantry so they couldn't hear us. "You think Mr. Black is responsible for Eddie's disappearance?"

"Yes."

"Did you tell Detective Hawke that?"

"Hell, no."

"Why not?"

"I told you, even mentioning *his* name aloud puts me at risk. If the cops start throwing it around, he's going to know I'm the source." Ray frowned over at the kitchen entryway. "You didn't run your mouth to the police, did you?"

"Of course not." I didn't want Mr. Black linking anything back to me, either.

"Jesus," Ray combed his fingers through his hair, messing up the moussed look he'd been sporting. "This could go really bad fast."

"You mean for Eddie?"

"Who cares about Eddie? I don't want that big ugly bastard coming for me." He poked me in the shoulder. "You should keep your head low, too, if you know what's good for you."

I poked him back. "Poke me again and I'll bite your finger off."

"You shouldn't have killed his twin, Blondie. Now we're both fucked."

Oh, please. I was fucked for way more reasons than just killing an albino bully—if he really was dead and gone. Aunt Zoe had made my state of fucked-ness crystal clear yesterday, her warnings inspiring a red-eyed morning after a night of repeated pillow beatings followed by lots of tears, both anger and fear-filled.

"Yeah, well, good luck with that, Ray." I pushed past him. "I need to go smile for the camera."

Harvey was on his best behavior all morning as we moved through the house. Well, except in between takes when Rosy encouraged him to share more of his sordid past while she double-checked that her recording was actually capturing video and sound.

Ray on the other hand was downright surly, pulling me aside to chastise me for not delivering my spiel with enough gusto, for having a sloppy shirt collar, and for not using enough hairspray to tame my "curly mess," which kept escaping the bobby pins. I understood him being scared shitless about Mr. Black coming for him, but I didn't appreciate the butthead taking out his anxieties on me.

We were about to take a break for lunch when Dickie decided he wanted to go upstairs and do one more take. His choice of setting was the bedroom where I'd been tied up in the closet with a seam ripper my only weapon not so long ago. I had claustrophobic issues now in that room, so when Dickie told me

I could wait for them down in the living room, he didn't have to say it twice.

Harvey followed on my heels, muttering about how hungry he was while making a beeline into the kitchen. I sat down on the sofa that the Brittons had bought from Wanda along with the house.

"Been all quiet on the ghost front so far," Harvey said when he joined me, plopping down on the other end of the couch.

I heard the sound of crackling paper and looked over to find him with his hand buried in a box of Chicken in a Biskit crackers.

"What are you doing?" He must have gotten into Wanda's pantry.

"Eatin'." He shoved a few crackers in his mouth. "Wanda won't miss these. Stale as cardboard."

I leaned toward him, my hand out. "Share, please."

He scooted away, hugging the couch arm.

I slid closer. "Quit being so stingy."

"Stay back, girlie," he tossed several crackers my way. "I don't want you touchin' me none."

"You're the one with cooties, not me."

"It's not yer cooties that I'm fussin' about. I don't want that kooky ghost tappin' into here," he touched his temple. "She don't need to scramble my brains any more than she already has."

I chomped on a cracker. Harvey was right; they were stale, but my stomach didn't care. "I have a feeling Prudence won't be bugging us today."

"Why's that? You lock the ol' gal in the attic?"

"No. I left her a present under the bathroom sink."

"What sorta present?"

"Her box of teeth."

Harvey harrumphed. "A harebrained idea if ya ask me."

"Why? That's what she's been wanting ever since I took her collection of teeth out of the attic."

"What she's been wantin' is to chew the fat with you."

"You're wrong." I held out my hand for more crackers. "She'll leave us alone now, at least for today."

"That there box of teeth is like a big piece of cheese in a rat-filled house." He went to dump some crackers into my palm, but too many spilled out at once. Crackers scattered all over the carpet at our feet. "Shit-fire." Bending over, he picked up a couple of crackers, blowing each of them off and then shoving them in his mouth.

"Not cheese. They're her trophies." I got down on my knees next to him. "She just wanted them back. Now that she has them, she'll be happy." At least I hoped so, anyway.

"Bull-hockey. They're bait, girl. I'll bet my left nut on that," he mumbled through a mouthful of crackers, his beard dusted with crumbs.

"How many times do I need to tell you to keep your testicles out of the betting pool?"

He reached for another cracker. "I'm just waitin' for the spook party to kick off and your noggin' to begin spinnin' around."

"The teeth are not bait." I stuffed a couple of crackers back into the box.

Ray's feet came into view, his Tony Llama boots parking almost on top of one of the crackers.

I sighed. "Now what are you gonna bitch at me about, Ray?"

He lowered his hand in front of my face, his palm cupped like he had something in it to give to me.

"What's this?" I asked, holding my palm out under his.

He tipped his hand and a tooth fell into mine.

A human tooth.

A canine tooth with bloody root strings still attached.

"Ah!" I held my hand out like it had contracted instant leprosy, but after all of the baby teeth my kids had pulled and handed to me over the years, I refrained from flinging the bloody thing across the room.

Harvey nudged me with his knee and pointed up at Ray's face.

Wincing, I slowly looked up. The whites of Ray's eyes were showing, his jaw slack with drool leaking out one corner.

Oh, hell. I'd seen that expression before. Honey had worn it a couple of weeks ago when Prudence was running the controls. And before that when Wanda had been used as Prudence's personal ventriloquist's doll in this very living room. No matter how many times I witnessed it, though, it still gave me the heebie jeebies.

"A gift for you," Prudence's voice came from Ray's mouth, reminding me of Kathryn Hepburn the way it quavered on some of her vowels, "to express my gratitude for the return of the teeth."

I scrambled sideways, bumping into Harvey's legs. I'd have scrambled all of the way out to the Picklemobile if he hadn't clamped onto my shoulder, staying me.

"Whoa there, mustang. Keep 'er steady, don't start buckin' yet."

I got his point. As much as I wanted to throw her gift tooth across the room and scrub my palm off on the carpet until I had some serious rug burns, I closed the tooth within my fist. "Thank you for the tooth. I'll treasure it."

Prudence leaned down so that Ray's nose was almost touching mine, a thick wave of his cologne making me want to gag. A whimper escaped my throat as I pushed back harder against Harvey's legs.

"What news have you brought me, Violet?" She stared into my eyes with the whites of Ray's, not blinking once.

My brain stalled out, fear flooding the engine.

Harvey snapped my ear, making me yip in surprise more than pain. "Answer her," he whispered with a growl.

What could I possibly have to tell a long dead … then I remembered an important detail that might concern her. "Some of the timekeeper's clocks are missing."

"Yes? Go on."

"Maybe five or six of them."

She pulled back, giving me a little breathing space. "This is an unfortunate turn."

So was Ray's habit of using too much of that damned cologne. Between it and his hair mousse, he was a walking fire hazard.

"One of the clocks kept going off while I was there," I continued, "but only in the mirror. It wouldn't stop, just kept cuckooing and cuckooing. What does that mean?"

One of Ray's tweezed eyebrows lifted. "Interesting."

"That it was cuckooing?"

"That you could hear the toll of the death bell." She cocked Ray's head sideways a little too far to look normal. "I wonder."

"You wonder what?"

She leaned in close again, even closer than before, and sniffed me from my temple down to the pulse at the base of my neck.

"Steady," Harvey repeated, squeezing my shoulder.

I obeyed like a good horse, holding still, taking a deep breath to keep my trembling at bay. But if I felt Ray's tongue licking me, I was pulling a Road-Runner and leaving Harvey and Prudence sitting there in a cloud of dust.

"You have grown stronger since last I saw you." She reached toward the base of my throat.

A squeak slipped out as I tried to suck my chest inside out rather than let her touch me.

Her fingers brushed my sternum. "And this? What is this?" She lifted the necklace charm from Aunt Zoe, turning it one way and then the other. "Perhaps it is a *patronus*? A protector, if you will, from the others?"

The *others*? That was the same word Aunt Zoe had used.

"What others?" I whispered.

"Our enemy. They are numerous in the Hills."

"How do you know about the others?"

She dropped the charm. "I have slain many."

"You were a … a killer?"

Her nod was slight. "As are you." She looked back up at me, still close enough that I could read the tiny blood vessels in the whites of Ray's eyes like a road map. "I, however, was proficient, more dexterous and adept. Your line has always been lacking finesse. Brutal even."

My line? "You mean my family line?"

"But of course. You are notorious, Violet. A *Scharfrichter* from the Black Forest region. A very small world it is among our kind."

"Our kind? You mean executioners?"

Ray's forehead wrinkled at the sides near his temples. He must have had a Botox treatment recently.

"Executioner," she said, as if trying the word out on her tongue. "Such an unpleasant word for our particular occupation."

And here I'd always thought Assistant Broker was belittling. "Are there more of you?"

"I was the last of my line. That is why I remained. I was waiting for you."

Swell. A ghost with a tooth fetish hanging around just for me. Considering what I'd learned last night about my imminent death, I was having a banner week. I couldn't wait to see what surprise lurked around the next stroke of midnight.

"Why me?"

"You need me." She stretched out with Ray's index finger and touched my forehead, running his fingertip across my skin as if writing on a steamed mirror.

I heard a crunching sound over my head. A sprinkle of crumbs drifted down over my shoulder. What in the hell? Was Harvey eating during my freak-out show?!!

"The others are strong," Prudence continued amidst Harvey's cracker-fest. "You will not succeed on your own." Ray's finger moved to my cheek, still writing on my skin. "Especially considering what they have already unleashed."

What's been unleashed? Was she talking about that thing in the bottom of the Open Cut again? "What makes you so sure about that?"

"They will end your line," she whispered. A tear slipped down Ray's cheek. "As they did mine."

Her words confirmed what Aunt Zoe had said. The others wouldn't stop with me. Addy and Layne would be killed, too, just as Prudence's son and husband had been murdered right before her eyes.

"I'm so sorry, Prudence."

Ray's face south of his forehead crinkled with fury. "Save your pity." Spittle flew from his lips.

I recoiled, the back of my head connecting hard with Harvey's knee. He grunted in pain, puffing out a breath of crumbs all over my shoulder.

"You have wasted precious time, *Scharfrichter*." She shoved Ray's face into mine again, bumping my nose with his. "And you smell of death."

I reacted without thinking, slapping Ray's cheek hard.

He jerked back, his eyes closing over those hideous white orbs. When they opened, his blue irises were showing.

I reached out and slapped him again.

"Jesus Christ, Blondie!" He fell back onto the carpet, holding his cheek. "What in the hell was that for?"

"I was making sure."

Harvey snickered. "Maybe you should make sure one more time."

"Don't come near me." Ray watched me warily as he rubbed his jaw. Suddenly his face paled. "What did you do to me?"

"Nothing, I just slapped you a little."

"A little?" He opened his mouth and pointed at his lower row of teeth. "Then where in the hell is my tooth?"

I gasped and then looked down at my fisted palm. Slowly, I peeled back my fingers, flinching at the sight of the bloody tooth.

"You mean this one?" I held it out to him.

Chapter Nineteen

Meanwhile, back at the Halloween party …

Harvey had saved my bacon again. This time, it had been by acting as my alibi when it came to being accused of cold-blooded tooth murder by Ray.

I had no doubt that Harvey's good word would cost me a few meals at Bighorn Billy's.

Ray and his tooth had left shortly after my second slap, an emergency trip to the dentist in the cards for his Halloween fun. My parting comment to the crybaby about having proved the rumor to be true—eating too much Halloween candy really did make teeth fall out—had gone over like a cast iron chicken.

Dickie and Rosy followed in Ray's wake, heading out to grab some lunch for all of us, leaving Harvey and me to sit and wait for their return on the front porch. Neither of us was interested in waiting inside, happy to sniff and shiver in the crisp October air instead.

"Girl, you got some explainin' to do."

"I'm not sure where to start." I stared down at my palm where Ray's tooth had lain. If I'd never moved to Deadwood, would all of this crazy executioner business still be dormant inside of me, waiting to spark and catch fire?

"I'll give you a goose—the ol' gal inside called you a killer."

"That's because I am a killer."

"You got some bright notion about livin' up to that name Ms. Wolff called ya?"

"Not a notion. More like a family obligation."

"To kill folks?"

"Not people. At least not according to Aunt Zoe."

"Yer Aunt Zoe is whistlin' this tune, too?"

"Yeah. She gave me a family history lesson last night. Turns out I have a higher purpose in life than selling haunted real estate. Go figure." I was trying to be light and funny, but it came out too acidic.

"Keep jawin', I'm all ears."

I clasped my hands together, rested my elbows on my knees, and gave him the quick and dirty version of the talking to Aunt Zoe had given me last night, ending with the bleak future outlook.

"Girl, everywhere you turn there're barbed wire fences."

"Yep. And here I am wearing a lace dress." I shoulder bumped him. "I'm thinking you may want to find someone else's body to guard. This could go the way of the Alamo in no time." After my little chit chat with Prudence back there, any hopes I'd had for a light at the end of the tunnel had been blown to smithereens.

Harvey snorted. "You kiddin? I ain't had this much excitement since one of my old flames got wind I was sleepin' with her sister and chased me through the hills with her daddy's two six-shooters. That gal was mad enough to kick a mule barefooted, I tell ya."

"Sounds like she was trying, but you wouldn't hold still."

He grinned, his two gold teeth showing. "She's the one who took her saddle elsewhere and put me out to pasture. What was I s'posed to do when her sister stopped by to show me her new set of shiny spurs?"

In spite of the crazy mess I was in, that made me chuckle. But only for a moment. "I'm serious, Harvey. You could get hurt or worse."

He squeezed my knee. "We're all gonna die someday, girlie. I'd rather go out fightin' than pissin' down my leg." He frowned across at the tall chain-link fence that divided the edge of the Carhart property from the Open Cut. "Besides, it's like I told ya a while back, somethin's gone sour in these here hills. I've felt it buildin' for years. Since I don't plan on leavin' while I'm still breathin', I might as well do my part on gettin' rid of the vermin."

His willingness to face my unknown horrors alongside me

clogged my throat with a grapefruit-sized lump. Teary-eyed, I whispered "thanks" and leaned my head on his shoulder.

"What's Doc have to say about you standin' in the middle of a stampede?"

"I haven't told him yet."

"What're ya waitin' for? Christmas?"

"Halloween." I sat upright, hitting him with a frown. "I'm afraid he'll wise up about me."

"Wisdom has nothin' to do with why that lone wolf thinks yer the moon."

I thought about Prudence and what had happened to her husband. Whatever Doc felt for me, maybe it was my responsibility to set him free before more death bells tolled.

Harvey pushed to his feet with a grunt. "My momma always told me that barkin' at a knot won't untangle the dad-burned thing." He held out his hand to me. "Might as well toss out the truth and let 'er fester in the open air."

"Might as well." I took his hand, joining him. We both stared up at the attic window for a few moments. "You feel like sticking around for some more haunted house fun?"

"I'd rather play peek-a-boo in a bone orchard at midnight, but what the hell. Let's give the ol' gal another whirl."

"That's the spirit."

"Cross yer fingers she leaves my teeth be. I'm playin' Count Dracula tonight down at the senior center's Halloween shindig and a couple of the ladies are countin' on gettin' bit."

* * *

Prudence had left us alone for the rest of the day. All remaining canine teeth were still intact when the four of us departed in the late afternoon.

The kids were dressed in their Halloween costumes by the time I got home: Layne as Einstein, Addy as a chicken. I'd had to nix her so-called brilliant idea to dress Elvis as an egg and lead her around by a leash.

Doc showed up as we were heading out the door and walked the neighborhood with us. I didn't share anything more with him than small talk in front of the kids, wanting to enjoy one more moment of being free of the "killer" label in his eyes.

Natalie was waiting for me when we got back to Aunt Zoe's, dressed as a skeleton in a black spandex outfit that showed no skin but plenty of curves. Her face was a work of art, all decked out like a skull, her dark hair slicked back.

The kids oohed and ahhed over her costume, circling her, poking at her fake bones, and then sharing the goodies they'd snatched from Aunt Zoe's treat bowl when she trick-or-treated each of them in turn.

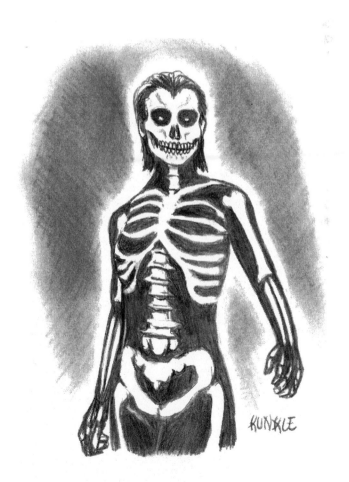

Doc went home to change, telling me he'd meet me down at the bar since Natalie was chomping at the bit to head out.

Down at the Purple Door Saloon, the party was ramping up according to Natalie. Her cousins were supposed to meet us there in half-an-hour, so I had no time to waste. I raced up to my room. Grabbing my costume and the black wig I'd borrowed from one of Aunt Zoe's old getups, I headed for the bathroom and locked myself inside. This costume was going to take some work to pull off, which meant no interruptions from my kids.

Fifteen minutes later, I stepped back to look at my handiwork. Well, it wasn't quite all I'd hoped for, but the bar's dim lights and abundance of alcohol would help.

"Vi, we need to get going," Natalie called up the stairs.

I swished to the top of the stairs, and jutted my hip to the side, blinking my long fake eyelashes with exaggeration. "Cousin Itt, is that you with your hair brushed back?"

Natalie's skeleton face grinned up at me, which sort of freaked me out after my close-up with Prudence via the whites of Ray's eyes earlier. I wasn't sure I could handle too many scary costumes tonight.

"Why Morticia Addams," Natalie said, "you look absolutely ravishing in that dress. I knew you should have exchanged those blonde curls for black locks years ago."

I started to step down the stairs, but my tight, full-length black satin dress made knee bending a challenge. I switched feet and started again. That didn't work either. Maybe I should have bought a black spandex dress instead of satin.

Natalie giggled.

"Shut it, mouth." How in the heck had Carolyn Jones pulled this off in all of those old Addams Family episodes?

I turned, holding onto the railing with both hands, and hopped down sideways.

"We should be getting this on video," Aunt Zoe said from the bottom of the stairs.

"At this rate," Natalie told her, "the party will be over before we get there."

"Nah, she's halfway down now."

"We still have the porch steps to scale."

Ten minutes later, Natalie was trying to lift my ass up into her pickup while Aunt Zoe shoved me onto the seat. Addy and Layne giggled and laughed from the porch.

Amazingly, we managed to get me in and upright without a single seam rip, and we were on our way. I blew kisses to Aunt Zoe and the kids as we backed down the drive.

"I hope Claire and Kate are there already," Natalie said.

"Why?"

"Because I'm not sure I can get your Morticia-wrapped ass out of here on my own."

"You can kiss my Morticia ass with those boney lips."

She chuckled and pulled into a parking spot a block down the street from the bar.

Just to show her up, I wiggled out of her truck cab on my own like a worm, all seams holding tight.

"Want me to call the Deadwood police?"

"Why?"

"To come down here and stop traffic long enough for you to cross the road?"

"Are you going to harass me all night?" I waddled down the sidewalk, wondering how long I was going to feel like putting up with this darn dress.

"Only until Doc gets here to take over penguin duty."

The Purple Door was pulsing with creepy, bass-filled music. A low throb of conversation filled in the breaks between songs. The lights over the bar were dimmer than usual with cobwebs strung between them. The blonde-hating bartender was dressed like a Cyclops. While I gave him my order, I imagined poking that unblinking eye in the center of his forehead with an olive pick for the sake of old grudges.

"Have fun, ladies," he said, sliding our drinks across, a rare smile flitting across his cheeks. When he wasn't scowling and snarling, he actually wasn't half bad looking, third eye and all.

"So, this is what it's like not to have the blonde stigma," I said as Natalie led me past several scantily dressed she-devils and a spot-on set of the Blues Brothers. "The bartender actually smiles at you."

"Don't let it go to your head. That smile is probably part of his costume. Last I heard he still has a chip on his shoulder when it comes to fair-haired maidens."

The antique chandeliers overhead were filled with black, white, and red bulbs, lighting up the room enough to see while enhancing Natalie's bones and other fluorescent costumes. Me? I just blended into the shadows with my black dress, which pretty much fit my mood tonight.

We made our way through a thick cloud of perfume, cologne, and beer breath filling the dance floor.

"Hey, Skeletor!" Natalie's cousin, Claire Morgan, hailed us over to a couple of tables shoved together back near the pool table turned graveyard—coffin, tombstones, half-zombies, fake fog and all.

I hadn't seen Claire in ages, and the blonde, straight-haired wig threw me off for a moment. I looked her up and down, taking in her seventies polyester plaid shirt and bell bottom jeans, her nose bandaged with steri-strips, and the football sitting on the table next to her bottle of Corona.

"How's Arizona treating you, Marsha Brady?" I asked.

"It was pure paradise until my mom showed up."

I grimaced. Claire's mother always had made me feel like a bumbling hick with the way she'd frown about my wild hair and uncoordinated outfits, constantly suggesting ways to improve my feminine appeal. Now that I thought about it, Tiffany and her always-critical eye reminded me a bit of Deborah Morgan. It was no wonder Doc's ex strummed my insecurity nerve.

"What crawled up that stupid bartender's ass tonight?" I heard a voice from the past say from behind me.

Claire blew a raspberry. "You'll have to excuse my pissy little sister tonight, Vi. She's got bartender-itis thanks to her ex-boyfriend."

I waddled around and stood face-to-face with Cindy Brady decked out in a one-piece pink polyester jumpsuit, her long blonde braids secured by bows on the ends. Jerry would probably love to get me on a billboard wearing one of those figure-hugging monstrosities. I hoped he didn't show up tonight and decide to take notes.

"Katie!" I rescued the bottle of Corona that was slipping

from her grip while she struggled to keep from spilling what looked like two cherry-filled Shirley Temples. Old man Harvey had ordered the same drink for both of my kids when we were here for lunch last week, making the kids feel big for their britches. I handed the beer to Katie's sister. "How have you been? Nat says you quit teaching."

"Well, I had for a while, but now I'm getting certified so I can substitute on the side down in Arizona."

"On the side? Are you still working at a bar?" The same bar that Natalie had said was owned by Katie's ex.

"Yeah." She smirked at me. "My life's all messed up right now. I don't know which way is up yet, so I'm just taking it one day at a time."

That was so unlike the Katie of old, who'd kept her nose to the grindstone, following the map her mother had made out for her line by line. However, being a Morgan sister, she'd still had her fair share of getting into trouble, especially when it came to her addiction to men in shackles. Although, according to Natalie, Katie's most recent ex had no black and white striped pajama-wear in his past.

"Dang, Vi," Katie gave me a quick sideways hug. "You look tight in that dress."

"She's tight in it all right." Natalie dropped into the chair across from Claire and pulled out the seat next to her, patting it for me to sit. "She's so damned tight she's gonna have trouble going to the bathroom."

I stuck out my tongue at her and lowered myself into the chair, careful not to rip my dress or spill my margarita.

"Congratulations, by the way," I said across the table to Katie. "I hear you're joining me in the parenting ranks."

She leaned forward. "Frankly, I'm scared shitless about it. How did you do it on your own with twins?"

"I wasn't alone." I nudged Natalie's arm. "Your cousin was there practically from conception."

Natalie smirked. "Had I been there at conception, I'd have chopped off Rex's dick before he'd planted those two adorable sprites inside of you, saving us the hassle of dealing with the son of a bitch ten years later."

"Yeah, but where would I be without Addy and Layne?" I'd still be an executioner with a gut-clenching task in front of me, just less vulnerable with no sweet-smelling snuggle buddies to tuck into bed each night.

Katie fished the maraschino cherry out of her Shirley Temple. "I feel so alone some days."

Claire tugged on one of Katie's braids. "You have Ronnie and me, we told you that."

"But will that be enough?" Katie looked at me for the answer.

Probably not. But I didn't want to be Morticia the Morose tonight, so I smiled. "You'll learn how to make it enough, because once that little bundle of love comes out everything else takes a back seat for a while."

"Like how long of a while?"

"I'll let you know when I get my life back."

"Holy jalapeños!" Claire pointed toward the door. "James Bond just walked into the bar."

"Jeez," Katie laughed. "He's got Daniel Craig nailed in that black suit and bow tie." She fanned herself, pretending to swoon. "Dang, now that's a chiseled face."

I didn't even bother looking over my shoulder. I knew exactly who it was and wondered what in the hell Detective Cooper was doing at a Halloween party. I thought he'd had all of the funny bones in his body replaced with razor wire. I just hoped he hadn't brought his badge-wearing ex-partner with him. After the day I'd had, I might end up knocking out a tooth or two myself if Hawke spent the evening harassing me.

Nat turned to see and whistled for our ears only. "I've said it before and will say it again, Coop cleans up real well."

"You should go for it, Skeletor." Claire took a swig of her Corona. "You could be the next Bond girl."

"No men for me." Natalie made an X sign at Cooper. "Besides, he's not into local girls."

"Except to throw them in jail." I took a sip of my margarita to offset that bitter memory.

Claire's lips flat-lined. "We know a sheriff down our way with a similar fetish. Isn't that right, trespasser?" She poked her sister in the ribs.

"Get over it." Katie poked her back, and then frowned at Natalie. "You're still avoiding men?"

"Yep." Natalie drained her bottle of beer, setting it down with a thud. "But that doesn't mean I don't enjoy watching them."

I peeked toward the bar, ducking my head as Cooper scanned the crowd. I got the feeling he was looking for someone in particular. I crossed my fingers under the table that it was the sexy skeleton beside me and not the woman who'd taken his uncle for one hell of a ghost ride earlier.

"Doc's here," Natalie said to me. "Wait until you see his costume."

Curious to see what he'd decided to dress up as, I popped my head back up in time to see Cooper flag down someone in a pin-striped suit and black moustache. "Where is he?"

"Talking to Cooper."

Just then the guy in the suit looked in my direction, his dark eyes zeroing in on me. He stuck an unlit cigar in his mouth and wriggled his eyebrows at me.

"Gomez," I said to nobody in particular. A smile started at my lips and spread clear to my heart. I pushed to my feet as he drew near.

Doc's hungry gaze ate me alive. "*Cara mia.*" He captured my hand, raising it to his lips.

"*Mon cher*," I returned in character, watching his mouth move over my skin. Little fires smoldered in its wake. I admired his costume, straightening his tie. "How'd you know?" What were the chances of him deciding to be Gomez on a whim?

"A little skeleton clued me in."

I turned to Natalie. "Bucket mouth."

Her skeleton face looked even more frightening when she laughed. "I couldn't resist seeing Morticia and Gomez together again." She stood and came closer, patting Doc's shoulder. "Looking hot, Gomez. Now do the 'Tish' thing."

He shrugged and swung me around, pulling me back against him while he held my arm out straight in front of him. "Oh, Tish. That's French," he said in a spot-on Gomez voice and proceeded to kiss his way up my black sleeve toward my shoulder.

Natalie laughed again, clapping. "Perfect! God, I love those two characters. So much heat and chemistry."

She didn't know the half of it, I thought, my insides molten from the way Doc was looking at me as he made his way closer to my mouth. I closed my eyes, letting myself sink into this moment, trying to brand every smell, every taste, every feel of it into my memory for the bleaker days ahead.

"Care to waltz, Tish?" Doc asked in my ear.

I hadn't even realized the music was still playing, my senses overloaded since the moment I'd locked gazes across the room with him. "Isn't this song a little fast?"

"We'll dance to our own beat."

"Okay, but I have to do the penguin version."

"I'll take whatever I can get." He pulled a fake hand from his pocket and held it out to Natalie. "Keep track of Thing for me, would you? This dance is only for two."

Natalie's teeth glowed along with her boney lips. "No problem, Thing and I will sit here and have a drink while we wait." She stole one of Claire's empty Corona bottles and wrapped the fake fingers around it, then clinked the neck of her bottle against it. "Come here often, stud?"

Before Doc led me to the dance floor, I introduced him to Claire and Katie. He charmed them each with some Gomez wit, his accent spot on, and then led me out to the dance floor.

"You've been practicing your lines."

"Nah. I've been a fan of the show since I was a kid." He'd barely pulled me into his arms before his lips were on mine, the moustache tickling my upper lip as his hands fanned down my sides. "I had a monster crush on Carolyn Jones."

"So you like my costume then?"

He looked down at me, his eyes full of wicked intent. "I'm going to rip it off of you later."

A quiver of excitement rippled through me, its epicenter south of my bellybutton. "Good answer." I dragged his mouth down to mine again so I could show him how much I'd missed him lately.

His muscles strained beneath the pin-striped suit by the time

I'd finished, his groan when I pulled back sounded raw, guttural. "Christ, Boots. You taste like tequila and sex all wrapped up in a tight package."

"And that's just my mouth."

"Minx." Doc ran his hands over my ribcage, his thumbs tantalizingly close to where I wanted them to be. "Natalie is waving us over."

"She has rotten timing." I pressed into him, moving my hips with purpose.

"You need to stop rubbing against me like that, Tish."

I did it again. "Does it bother, Gomez?"

The song we were supposed to be dancing to switched to something fast, loud, and throbbing. Or maybe it was me who was throbbing. I couldn't tell for sure with Doc's hands all over me.

"Violet," he leaned down and spoke in my ear. His warm breath caressed my neck, making me steam everywhere else. "I'm going to taste all of you before the night is out."

I stood there sputtering until he took mercy on me and tugged me along behind him, leading me back to the table.

Unfortunately, James Bond arrived about the same time we did. His squint tagged along behind him. As soon as Doc headed to the bar to get more drinks and introductions had been made around the table, Cooper corralled me off to the side.

"What did you do to Uncle Willis?"

"Nothing, why?" At least nothing more than usual when it came to our adventures at the Carhart house.

"He was off his feed when he came home."

"I thought you were staying at Doc's."

"I sleep there. My stuff is still at home."

"What do you mean Harvey was off his feed?" Maybe the tuna sandwich Rosy had brought him had been bad.

"He was quiet with no smartass remarks or dirty jokes."

Oh, off his feed that way. I bet it had something to do with our albino-filled future. "I don't know what's going on with your uncle," I lied.

Cooper's jaw tightened. "I don't believe you, Parker."

"Okay, Double-oh-seven, then try this on for size: Your

uncle and I had a run-in with an aggressive ghost who tore out my coworker's tooth and gave it to me as a gift."

He took a step back. "That's nuts."

"Welcome to my world."

Doc returned with another margarita, his gaze bouncing back and forth between Cooper and me.

"What'd Tish do now, old man?" he asked Cooper in his Gomez accent.

"She's telling ghost stories."

"Of course, her favorite kind." Doc handed me the drink rimmed with salt, just the way I liked it. "How'd your visit with Prudence go?"

"Not good."

He watched me lick salt off the rim, loosening his collar. "What happened?"

I glanced at Cooper, who was all ears and suspicious eyes. "What about him?"

Doc shrugged. "If we're going to do a séance in front of him, he needs to get used to this."

"All right." I took a drink first, and then dove in, starting with the teeth I'd returned. I skipped the whole bit about my being a killer and focused on Prudence's more neutral comments about the clock cuckooing a death bell toll and something having been unleashed in the hills.

"You're leaving something out," Doc said when I finished. He knew me and my tics too well.

"Nothing important," I fibbed in front of Cooper, holding my margarita glass in front of my tell-tale twitchy nose. "It isn't relevant to this."

"You told me you didn't go in Ms. Wolff's apartment," Cooper said.

"I could hear the cuckooing clock through the door," I shot back, which was the truth. His squint challenged me. I smiled in response, refusing to go head to head with him.

"Prudence really ripped out Ray's tooth?" Doc asked.

I nodded. "Lucky for me Harvey was there as my alibi, or Ray would probably have called Cooper and cried about assault."

James Bond took a drink from the shot of whiskey Doc had

brought him. "How can a ghost rip out a tooth?"

I looked to Doc for the answer, since he was way more familiar with the ectoplasmic world than me.

"I suspect that Prudence was able to control Ray enough to have him pull out his own tooth."

Frown lines creased Cooper's face from hairline to chin.

"You think she's growing stronger?" I asked. "She's never been able to control you like that."

"I fight her every time up here," Doc tapped on his temple. "Ray wouldn't have seen her coming. She swept in and took over the controls."

"Or he's just a weak-minded, poo-flinging primate."

Doc grinned. "I can see you two have been romancing each other on the job again."

Talking about Prudence and Ray's tooth reminded me that I needed to tell Doc about Mr. Black, but not in front of Cooper. As much as I couldn't stand Ray, I got the whole "don't tell the cops" wavelength. Nothing good would come of that since their badges and guns were pretty much worthless against the Mr. Blacks of the world.

"Uncle Willis witnessed this whole ghost shit?"

"Front and center, sitting right there next to me."

"It must have rattled him and he didn't want to tell me."

"That's probably it." Or maybe, like me, Harvey was wondering how much longer he was for this world.

Natalie called my name, rescuing me from Cooper's suspicions and dragging me back to the party. I lugged Doc along with me. When Cooper tried to leave, Natalie would have none of it and made him join the fun, insisting he take the seat next to her. Truth be told, the detective didn't fight her too much and actually loosened up enough with a couple of whiskey shots to entertain us with some rookie cop anecdotes.

The next hour or two passed in a blur. Between the repeating rounds of margaritas and laughs, Katie's cursing about the bartender after each trip for more non-alcoholic drinks, and Doc's teasing touches and heart-palpitating whispers, I was able to forget my life sentence as an executioner for a while.

Midway through the evening, the disc jockey decided to slow

things down a bit and played Patsy Cline's "I Fall to Pieces."

Doc leaned toward me. "Another dance, *cara mia?*"

I stood, a little light-headed after that last margarita, and waddled after him onto the dance floor. He wrapped me up in his arms, surrounding me with his scent and strength. Everything else faded into gray.

When Patsy wrapped up, Dusty Springfield's "Son of a Preacher Man" started up, seducing me along with Doc's touch as his palms crept down over my hips on the darkened dance floor. He pulled me closer, his body rigid, his hands hot through my satin dress. Apparently, I wasn't alone when it came to craving more than just a waltz in the dark.

I slipped my hand down between us, my fingernails teasing a groan from him. "Damn, Boots. That's torture."

His body's quick response made me feel impish. I touched him through his trousers again, pressing this time.

He stilled my hand, staring down at me with a fierceness that made me gulp. "It's been too long, Violet. Watching you in that dress all night has me fantasizing about dragging you into the back alley and taking you fast and hard."

I pictured that scene for a moment, considered how short life might be for me now that I was albino bait. I pulled him down to my lips and whispered in his ear, "I'm not wearing any underwear."

He jerked back, his Adam's apple bobbing. Without another word he led me off the dance floor, past the pool table graveyard, and through a windowless door that led into a shadow-filled stairwell lit by only a single flickering sconce.

Doc looked up the stairs then back at me. "Can you climb stairs in that dress?"

"If I bunny hop. I thought you said the alley."

"I changed my mind." He hauled me against him and kissed me, his mouth demanding a response.

I gave as good as I got, leaning into him as I met his tongue thrust for thrust. I gasped as his thumbs brushed over me through the satiny material, wishing he'd tear it off and touch skin on skin.

"Are you wearing a bra?" he asked, his mouth sliding along

my jaw.

"You'll have to see for yourself."

"Okay." He reached over my head and grabbed something from the top of the sconce's brass base.

"What's that?"

"A key."

Before I knew what was happening, he had picked me up and carried me up the stairs.

"What are you doing?"

"I'm going to see for myself."

At the top of the stairs, he set me down, unlocked the door, and pushed it open. "After you."

Once inside, he kicked the door closed behind us. The click of the lock echoed in the long, empty room. A coppery glow from one of the back alley street lights poured through curtain-free windows across the wood plank floors. At the other end of the room, I could see a neon Vacancy sign from a hotel just down Main Street through one of the three tall windows. The plaster walls were water-stained in spots and zig-zagged with cracks.

"What is this place?" I asked. It smelled of dust and old paint. "It has such a lovely mustiness."

"Part of the old Badlands' brothels. They separated this section off a couple of years ago when they remodeled the Purple Door. Before that, the upstairs rooms were connected so that the girls could move from one building to the next."

"Aren't the brothels supposed to be haunted?"

"Some of the sections are, but the ghost stays mainly in the other end for some reason. I have yet to sense her down this way."

"You've been up here a few times?"

He nodded. "I know the owner."

"Is he a client?"

"And a fellow Deadwood history fan."

"So that's how you knew about the key?"

"He lets me come up here whenever I want so long as I lock up when I leave." He backed me into the wall next to the door.

I raised an eyebrow. "Do you bring your waltz partners here

often, Gomez?"

"You're the first and only, Tish." Doc played with a lock of black hair from my wig. "Is this thing attached?"

"With a couple of bobby pins."

"Take it off."

"That will ruin your Morticia fantasy, won't it?"

"I stopped thinking about her the first time we danced tonight." He tugged gently at the wig. "Take it off."

I obeyed, shaking out my curls. "Anything else?"

"Kiss me."

I pointed at the moustache. "Your turn."

He peeled it off. "Better?"

"Let me see." I went up on my toes and softly placed my lips on his, playing the part of a sweet and innocent maiden. "It doesn't tickle anymore."

"Sweet Jesus, you're such a temptress." He took my face in his hands and proceeded to kiss the breath right out of me, not stopping until I was a moaning, writhing hot mess.

The fast pounding beat of the music in the bar downstairs matched the tempo of my pulse. I wanted to rub my leg up and down his, wrap them around him, but both were trapped by the damned tight dress.

"Doc," I whispered as he licked and nipped my earlobe, "touch me."

He caught my wrists, laced our fingers together, and held both hands captive against the wall on each side of my head. With his body alone, he seduced me, putting pressure in all of the right spots. I whimpered, angling my hips for more, but was thwarted by the dress and his evasive teasing.

"Were you serious about not wearing panties?" He traced my collar bone with his tongue.

"I don't kiss and tell," I said between gasps.

His mouth burned across the swells of my chest, tickling the skin rimming the neckline of my dress. I arched my back, aching for his mouth to move lower and caress the throbbing parts of my body, to kiss and bite me through the satin. Need built inside me, making me hot and ready for everything he had to offer.

I moaned again, my body longing for more of him. If only

this damned dress weren't in my way. Next year, I was going to make sure I was easily accessible to his touch.

If there was a next year.

That thought sobered me, bringing me back to a simmer. Maybe it was the margaritas loosening my tongue, or maybe it was Prudence's warning surfacing, but suddenly I needed to clear the air.

"Doc."

He must have sensed something had shifted, because his body stilled and he looked up at me. Whatever he saw on my face prompted him to release my hands. "What's wrong?"

"There's something I need to tell you."

"What?"

I looked out the window at the Vacancy sign, trying to come up with a smooth way of spilling the truth.

In the end, I just let it fly. "I'm a killer."

Chapter Twenty

Meanwhile, back in a haunted brothel …

D oc cocked his head to the side as if he weren't sure he'd heard me right. "Are you playing Morticia again?"
I wished. "No. Aunt Zoe told me the truth after I ran into the juggernaut's twin outside of Ms. Wolff's apartment, the day Layne's photo went missing."

"She told you what truth?"

I pushed away from the wall, restless with dread at how this conversation would end. "I'd been avoiding Aunt Zoe." The floor boards creaked underfoot as I walked over to the windows and looked out over Main Street. "Avoiding the truth ever since she first told me." The sidewalks were filled with people dressed from macabre to sexy, none of them worried about being hunted down and brutally murdered. "But last night she made me face it. She made me understand how this has been in my family for too many generations to count."

"Your family has been killers for generations?" Doc still stood by the door, his face rippled with shadows.

"Not all of my family, just the females. It skips generations, sometimes several."

"But it didn't skip you."

"Nope."

"Executioner," he tried it on for size. "Ms. Wolff knew."

"That and more, I suspect. Unfortunately, she's too dead to explain how."

He crossed his arms and leaned back against the wall. "Who do you kill?"

"Non-humans mostly, I guess."

"Like the Juggernaut."

I nodded, searching the crowded sidewalks below. Were they down there? Watching? Waiting for me to step outside, vulnerable in a drunken stupor?

"And the others," I added.

"What others?"

"I don't know yet." I looked over at him, trying to gauge his reaction to my news, but the shadows hid too much. "According to Aunt Zoe, I'll find out soon enough. What I did to Mr. Black's twin alerted the others that I'm here. They'll be coming for me now."

"Mr. Black?"

"The twin I didn't stab at Mudder Brothers that night."

"His name is Mr. Black?"

"Yes, but you can't tell a soul or he'll come for Ray."

"Your coworker, the jackass?"

"Yes. He's the one who told me the other one's name."

"Ray Underhill actually helped you?"

"Crazy, I know, but these are cuckoo times."

Doc nodded slowly. "Why are you telling me this now?"

"Because when Prudence confronted me today, she reaffirmed Aunt Zoe's warning about my family being a target."

"This warning was what you left out earlier when you told Cooper about what happened at the Carhart house."

I wrapped my arms around my midsection, holding in the weight of this killer business. "Harvey heard Prudence's bleak prophecy about my future. He understands the risks now. I suspect that's what had him off his feed, as Cooper put it."

"The risks to you and your kids."

"To him, too, if he and his shotgun continue to act as my so-called bodyguards." I looked down at the street, swallowing the trepidation that was making me hesitate to continue. "And to you," I added in a quiet voice.

Over a growing din leaking through the floor from the bar below, I heard the sound of clothes rustling. "You're worried about me?"

"Of course."

"Why?"

Just one word from him, and yet so many answers flooded

my head, none of them safe for my heart's sake. "Do I have to spell it out for you?"

Footfalls came toward me, floorboards creaking. "I like to hear you spell."

I turned. He'd come halfway and then stopped.

"They didn't just kill Prudence's son, the last of her line." My voice wavered. I cleared my throat. "They murdered her husband, too."

His poker face gave no reaction. Didn't he get it?

"Doc, I'm a killer from a long line of killers. An executioner lacking in finesse, according to Prudence, who shared my vocation before they slaughtered her and her family. Hanging around me could be bad for your health."

Still a hard mask—no grimace, no wince, no rejection. Hell, couldn't he give me something? I was teetering out here at the end of the plank, a dark abyss swirling below.

"Listen, Doc, if you want to walk out of here and never look back, I'll understand."

His gaze narrowed. "That was my line."

"It's a good one."

"Because it was honest. Come here, killer."

I crossed the floor, the dress making me feel like a waddling idiot.

His dark gaze held mine, but that was it, no other touching. "You and your kids are in danger."

It wasn't a question, but I nodded anyway.

"It's about time we found out what you are and what you're capable of."

I grunted. "I'd rather just be a single mom with two kids."

"Single, huh?"

"Well, I mean not necessarily single, but … of course I don't expect you to want to … you see, I've been single a long time so I just … Damn it, Doc, I'm making a big fucking mess of this."

The corners of his mouth twitched. "You sure are."

I raised my hands in exasperation. "What do you want me to say?"

"I want you to be honest."

What did he think I was doing when I started down this I'ma-killer path? "Honest about what?"

"What's really going on here."

"I thought I was."

"We're dancing again, Violet."

I might have been a little tipsy, but I knew for a fact we were currently standing still. "My feet are planted firmly on the floor."

He took my hand, lifting it to his lips. "Mine aren't, *cara mia*."

Gomez was back, minus the moustache. That was an abrupt shift from reality. "Don't you understand, Doc?" My heart began to gallop at the sight of his lips flitting across my knuckles. "This is your opportunity to walk away without getting dragged into something that could go south fast."

"I understand perfectly." He led me over to the shadow-dappled wall next to the door. "What are you wearing under that dress?"

"Doc, you could suffer the same fate as Prudence's husband."

"I know." He leaned down and captured my mouth in a slow, heartbreaking kiss. When he came up for air, he ordered, "Turn around. I want to show you something."

"How can I see it if I have my back to you?"

"Trust me. Turn."

Frowning, I did, facing the other way.

"Now put your hands on the wall."

What in the hell? "Did Cooper deputize you?"

"Do it."

I did it, wondering what was next. A pat down for weapons? The snap of a rubber glove?

I felt a tug near my ankles. Then I heard a tearing sound. "What are you doing?" I looked over my shoulder.

Doc was kneeling on the floor at my heels. "I told you I was going to rip this dress off of you."

He tore the dress seam that ran up the center in the back, ripping it clear up to my thighs.

My legs were finally free. "Thanks." I started to turn. "That was driving me—"

"Put your hands back on the wall," he said, still kneeling at my feet.

"What?"

"I'm not done. Turn around. Spread your feet apart."

My body began to tingle in anticipation. "What are you doing, Doc?

"Finding out if what you said was true."

Oh jeez, was he really going to do what I thought he was going to do? The shadows weren't deep enough to hide my flaws, leaving me too exposed for comfort. "Doc, that's not my best side."

"I beg to differ, *cara mia*." His fingers started at my ankles, his touch tender, tickling, and then they slid up to my calves, leaving a searing trail in their wake. "Close your eyes." His tone left no room for argument. "Let me show you why I'm not going anywhere tonight."

I obeyed again and leaned my forehead against the cool plaster, pushing all fears and inhibitions from my thoughts. This was Doc touching me, making me writhe and ache. I was safe with him.

His fingers traveled higher, caressing as they climbed. He lifted my dress, inch by inch. His lips singed up the inside of my leg, his tongue licking circles on the tender skin of the back of my knees. My thighs quivered in anticipation.

He bit my inner thigh just above my knee.

I moaned as a shot of lust rocketed through me. "Doc," I whimpered, needing more of him touching me. More of his mouth, his hands, his tongue, his …

"I said I was going to taste you tonight, Boots."

My dress lifted higher, cool air tickling where his tongue had left a wet trail behind. I gulped, sweat coating my skin.

He nibbled his way up the back of my thigh, and then grazed his teeth along the trembling inner flesh.

I ached deep, clear to my core, turned inside out by his fingers teasing closer and closer to where I really wanted him to touch, needed him to touch.

My dress shifted up onto my hip bones, the satin whispering around my waist.

Doc sucked a breath through his teeth. "Sweet Jesus." He slid his free hand up the back of one thigh, his fingers spread wide across my skin. "You were telling the truth." Then his touch feathered across my bare bottom, caressing and tickling each cheek before trailing down my other thigh. He came so close to where I needed him, yet so far as he teased first with his lips, then his teeth, then his tongue.

"I don't like to lie to you."

"Really?" his knuckles grazed across me, making everything inside of me tighten almost painfully.

I gasped. "Really."

"Then tell me what you *really* want me to do to you."

"Touch me."

He slid up behind me, his suit fabric rasping over my bare skin. He took one of my hands and placed it where my dress was bunched up at my waist, making me hold up the fabric. "Where?"

I rocked my hips back into him. "Everywhere."

"That will take all night," he pushed my hair aside and kissed the nape of my neck. "There's no way I can last that long, not with you moving against me like that."

"Then start here." I caught his hand and planted it south of my belly button.

His palm slid downward but paused, his fingers almost touching but holding back. "Show me, Boots."

I covered his hand with mine, guiding him to the exact spot, helping him touch me how I needed it. His woodsy scent surrounded me, making me feel tipsy with lust. Pleasure spiraled higher and higher, taking me up with it. I heard a zipper somewhere in the midst of the passion fogging my brain and moaned a "yes" as Doc's touch moved faster, circling me ever closer.

"Violet," Doc kissed the shell of my ear, and then traced it with his tongue.

I arched back into him, my breath a gasping pant.

He pulled his hand free.

I cried out. "Don't you dare stop, Doc."

He grasped my hips. "I told you I was going to take you hard and fast tonight."

"Yes!" I shifted, opening up to him, wanting that to happen as much as he did.

Without another word, he slammed into me, all of the way, driving me against the plaster.

I cried out, my fingers curling around his, everything exploding behind my eyes as waves of pleasure rocked me. He held still a moment, letting me ride out of the wake.

"That was incredible," I said when I could speak again.

"We're not done. Hands back on the wall, Boots."

Tonight, I was his to command. I moaned as he sparked another fire to life inside of me, fanning the flames with each thrust, with each heated whisper of how good I felt, how much he craved me, how much he fantasized about me. Then he reached up, cupping my breast through the satin, his fingers pinching and rubbing, and he told me exactly what he wanted from me.

My body obeyed in a flash, my self-control shattering. I cried out with release, my voice lost in a sudden cacophony of shouts and yells coming up through the floor from the bar below.

Never before had a man marked me like this, all aggression, power, and lust. Never before had I been so willing to let one. But it was Doc, and I'd been putty in his hands from the first time he'd touched me. Tonight was no different ... except something was.

Something in him.

I pushed back into him, capturing his hand that was exploring my chest. I lifted his fingers to my lips, biting the tips of several and then licking them better.

"Violet," he growled in my ear, straining against me, moving faster. "Do that again."

I did. This time I bit harder, licked longer, sucked on the last one.

He swore at the ceiling, then slammed me into the wall with his final push, holding me there as his muscles quaked all around me.

"Holy shit, Boots." His forehead rested on my shoulder, his hot breath fanning my skin where the dress dipped low.

I reached my arms up and back around his neck, kissing the underside of his jaw when he raised his head. "So what was it you wanted to show me?"

He chuckled, sliding a kiss across my lips. Then he pulled away. When my dress was back down and his fly was zipped, he turned me around to face him, his eyes dark, mesmerizing as he stared down into mine.

"I don't care that you come from a long line of killers."

"You don't?"

"No. You know why that is, *cara mia*?"

I shook my head, wondering what Gomez line would follow next. "Why, *mon cher*?"

He slid his hands up my arms, over my shoulders, cupping my face, making my heart roll onto its back and purr. "Because I love you, *querida*."

Then he leaned in and kissed me, slow and tender, hypnotizing my lips and tongue.

But not my brain, which stumbled to a dazed stop.

Had he really just said what I'd thought he said? The actual four letter "L" word set between "I" and "you"? Or after all of these months of being head over heels for him, was I now having post-sex hallucinations?

When his mouth gave me a second to come up for air, I stared up at him. "Did you just say ..." I trailed off, afraid to repeat it aloud and then have to remove my foot from my mouth if I'd misheard him. Then another possibility made my blood cool. "Are we still playing Gomez and Morticia here?"

A police siren chirped outside the window before Doc could reply. Red and blue lights flashed over the plaster walls. I suddenly realized that all was silent downstairs—no bass beat, no din of conversation, nothing. Only a periodic blast of monotone voices from a police scanner coming up through the old plate glass windows.

Doc towed me over to the front of the building, keeping us off to the side, out of view.

"Is that—" he started.

"The three musketeers," I finished. "Hey, that cop is holding Thing, isn't he?"

"I think so."

We watched as another cop opened the back door of the cruiser and waited for Claire, Katie, and Natalie to crawl inside.

He shut the door behind them, knocking on the roof once they were caged.

Doc put his arm around my shoulder, kissing my temple. "Well, Tiger, looks like you're going to have to step foot inside the Deadwood Police Station again."

"Damn it." I watched the cruiser cart them up the street toward the cop shop. "I have a feeling this isn't going to end well."

* * *

Doc and I managed to slip downstairs and into the bar without anyone seeing us come in through the back stairwell door. I waited out front, my Morticia wig in hand, while he got the low down on why the three musketeers had been hauled away.

He joined me outside a few minutes later, holding my hand as we walked to his car. "According to the Blues Brothers, it all started with Cindy Brady."

"Katie started it?" That wasn't her style. I would have put my money on Claire. Although, those pregnancy hormones could really do a number on a woman's tolerance level, especially around drunks. I knew from experience.

"In their words, Cindy got into a yelling match with Cyclops the bartender after he made some derogatory remark about her being a ditzy blonde. When he threatened to call the police on her, she threw a mug of beer in his face."

"She'd been annoyed at the bartender since Nat and I arrived. Something about her ex-boyfriend who owns a bar down in Arizona."

"While Cyclops was calling the cops, Cindy climbed up onto the bar and leapt onto the bartender's back, beating him over the head with poor innocent Thing."

"She beat him with a rubber hand?" My laughter echoed off the brick buildings.

When we reached Doc's Camaro, he held the door for me, continuing the tale. "So the bartender grabbed the beer tap nozzle and sprayed Cindy in the face with beer as he swung around trying to shake her off. Meanwhile, Marsha Brady tried to race to the rescue and slipped on the wet floor, knocking all three of them down where they wrestled around in a heap."

"You're kidding." That must have been the commotion I had noticed below when I was in the midst of having a back arching orgasm that would have knocked my socks off if I'd been wearing any. I waited for Doc to slide behind the steering wheel. "Why was Nat dragged off with them?"

He started up and backed out of the parking spot. "The Blues Brothers claim that when Marsha, Cindy, and the Cyclops were on the floor brawling in a puddle of beer, some drunk in a Where's Waldo costume yelled for Marsha and Cindy to show him their chests. At that point, the skeleton babe strode over and clocked Waldo in the chin, knocking him out cold."

Doc pulled out onto Main Street and headed toward the police station. I pictured the whole Three Stooges routine, giggling.

"Nat does have a wicked uppercut," I said as Doc took a left at the light.

"So does Thing according to Cyclops."

I burst out laughing. By the time Doc pulled into the cop shop, I'd sobered enough to head inside and rescue my friends.

Doc's grip on my arm held me in my seat. He looked me over, the parking lot lights making his face more rugged. "You might want to put the wig back on for now."

"Why? Is my hair a mess?"

"You look like a wild woman who had sex against the wall in the alley behind a bar."

"We were upstairs in a haunted brothel."

He shook his head, letting out a low whistle. "God, you were so damned hot, all soft and wet, ready and moaning." He groaned, adjusting his pants. "I have to stop thinking about you up against that wall, or we'll have to make a quick trip to my place before getting the girls out of jail."

Had he really said he loved me in Gomez speak? Did that actually happen? Or had I just been high and still stuck in fantasyland from the killer sex we'd had?

"We need to do that again," I told him. Especially the end

part where he told me, Violet Parker—not Morticia Addams—
that he was in love with me. In the meantime, I'd have to wait
and see if he said it again before getting ahead of myself and
removing the muzzle from my heart.

He twirled one of my blonde curls around his finger. "I
didn't hurt you, did I?"

I leaned over and grabbed him through his suit pants, making
him suck in a breath. He was rock solid in my palm. "You were
brutal and fierce, raging against me. Just thinking about it makes
me want to hike up my dress and climb on your lap for more."

"Christ, Boots. You paint a hell of a scene."

"Oh, yeah? Well, picture this. The next time we try that
position, I want you to bend me over your desk. I have a fantasy
about making a mess all over your spreadsheets."

He growled, grabbing me by the back of the neck and
hauling me against him. He kissed me like he wanted to eat me
alive. If we had been in his bed, I would have let him.

When he let me go, I squeezed him once more and smiled
slow and sultry. "Hold that thought, big boy. I'm gonna go find
out how to spring those jailbirds. Come inside when you get your
kinks worked out."

I slipped on the Morticia wig and climbed out. Before I made
it to the station's front steps, I twisted my dress sideways at the
waist so that the ripped seam looked like a side slit. Making sure
the girls were still tucked in my dress, I straightened my shoulders
and went in to face off with Deadwood's finest.

Cooper came through the door that led to the back offices
and jail cells a minute after the front desk clerk had called and
announced that Morticia Addams had arrived to see the three
troublemakers.

The detective looked me over, one eyebrow lifting at what he
saw. "Where's Gomez?"

"He's parking the car."

"Good. I need to talk to both of you."

"If this is about what happened at the bar …"

"It's not." He tugged on his tie, loosening it. "I got called
away by Hawke while Nyce and you were dancing. I must have
been gone not much more than a half hour when all hell broke

loose there."

"Katie's pregnant," I explained. "Her hormones are like hundreds of little Yosemite Sams with six-shooters a-blazin'. That bartender is lucky she beat him with a rubber hand instead of a whiskey bottle."

His lips twitched. "Well, to give Kate some credit, the bartender was being an asshole to her. I was up there one time when she was ordering. He called her a blonde bimbo for no reason. I think he was getting off on riling her up."

I grimaced. "Yeah, speaking on behalf of the blonde nation, that crap doesn't go over well with most of us. Nor do the stupid ass blonde jokes."

"I noticed that." He glanced behind me as the front door opened and Doc walked in. "Hey, Gomez."

"Bond, old boy. Good to see you here."

"Come on back." Cooper waved for us to follow him. "I think Natalie really did a number on her hand," he said over his shoulder. "I gave her an ice pack until they're done with the paperwork. She may need a trip to the hospital when she's done here."

"What do we need to do to get the three of them out of here?" I asked as we walked down the long linoleum hallway toward his office. I caught a glimpse of Claire minus her Marsha Brady wig sitting at one of the desks, a piece of paper in front of her, a cellphone up to her ear. Where were Katie and Natalie?

"Nothing." Cooper held his office door open for us. "I took care of it. They're just writing up their side of the story in case assault charges are filed against any of them." He shut the door behind us and leaned against it.

"So, if they're good to go, what's with the trip to the principal's office?" I asked. One of those a week was plenty.

"I want to have the séance at Uncle Willis' place on Friday night."

I looked at his calendar on his desk. "No way, that's the Day of the Dead."

"I thought that was November 1st," Cooper said.

"November 1st is the Day of the Innocents," Doc clarified. "November 2nd is the Day of the Dead."

"So? We don't celebrate that up this way."

"I know," I said, "but don't you think it's creepy to have a séance on the Day of the Dead?" I looked to Doc. "Aren't we asking for more trouble than usual? That has to be as bad an omen as having it tonight, I'd think."

"What's the big deal about tonight?" Cooper asked.

"All Hallows Eve is when the dead come back looking for bodies to possess. I think we should wait for a night when the dead are resting peacefully."

Doc grinned at me. "When we're together, *cara mia*," he said in his Gomez voice, "every day is Halloween."

I poked him in the side. "*Cállate*, smartass."

"Tish, that's …"

"Spanish," Cooper filled in dryly.

"Close enough," Doc winked at me, kissing my wrist.

"You two need to get a room."

Yes, we did, preferably not in a haunted brothel this time. But Cooper was staying at Doc's house, damn it, so we were limited to flirty glances and wall sex.

"Although your dress now has a rip that I don't remember seeing earlier," Cooper said, looking us over with that all-seeing squint. "And Gomez here seems to have misplaced his moustache."

Doc chuckled. "Maybe I should file a missing moustache report."

"Anyway, Detective," I detoured the conversation, my cheeks warm. "How about Saturday night?"

"Nope, Friday is the one night I know Hawke will be down in Rapid. He's not coming back up until Saturday afternoon. It has to be Friday. I don't want to take any chances on getting caught."

"What about next week?" I asked.

"I gave you the box of teeth, Parker. It's your turn to pay up on our deal." He crossed his arms over his chest. "Friday night is the date. My uncle will be there with us."

"Fine."

Doc squeezed my hand, giving me a reassuring smile. "We'll be there," Doc said to Cooper.

"Good." The detective reached for the doorknob, but then hesitated, hitting me with a hard stare. "When you show up, Parker, make sure you have my great grandfather's sawed-off, double-barreled shotgun with you."

"I don't have it." At least I didn't think I did, unless Harvey had stashed it in the Picklemobile without telling me.

"Then you have two days to find it. Trust me, you don't want me to talk Detective Hawke into getting a search warrant to come hunting for it. With your history, Lord only knows what else he might find."

Chapter Twenty-One

Thursday, November 1st

Meanwhile, back at the grocery store …

I think I'm allergic to cops," I told Doc on the phone early the next morning.

"All cops? Or two detectives in particular?" His voice was still scratchy from sleep.

I wished I were there under the covers next to him instead of on my way to get a protein shake for Cornelius. Jerry had beat my alarm clock to the punch again this morning, telling me the latest game plan involving Rosy the Riveter, a certain ghost whisperer, and me. Ray had been benched after yesterday's surprise visit from the tooth fairy, and now Dickie was out of the game thanks to that nasty cold bug the rest of his crew had—well, except for Rosy.

"All cops," I told Doc, "but the one sleeping in your spare bedroom gives me the hives from just a glare."

He chuckled, deep and throaty. It sounded incredibly sexy, making my body get steamy in all of the Doc-sensitive spots. Ever since his goodnight kisses last night, which had involved a lot of heated whispers about how he was going to torture me with his mouth until I delivered on that massage I'd promised him last week, my ears hadn't stopped smoking.

I killed the Picklemobile's engine in front of Piggly Wiggly, scaring the bejeezus out of several birds when the old truck backfired.

"Where are you?" Doc asked. "And why aren't you here offering me breakfast in bed?"

"I'm at the grocery store." I climbed out of the Picklemobile and started across the parking lot. "I can bring you a protein shake."

"I'm not talking about food."

Poof! There went more smoke.

His line sent me into a déjà vu spin, only there was a dirty old buzzard in the other version of this conversation. "You remind me of Harvey."

"Me fantasizing about having your body for breakfast reminds you of Willis? That just seems wrong." He yawned. "Maybe I'm still asleep and having a twisted dream."

I stepped inside the store, heading straight for the deli where they kept their cooled drinks. "Harvey was cursing at me yesterday for interfering with his morning tail."

"And for good reason. Damn it, woman, get over here and let me lick your thighs again."

Last night's tongue lashing he'd given me in the haunted brothel replayed in my head. I stood there overheating in front of the cooler full of protein drinks.

"Doc," I whispered, turning my back on the deli counter lady waiting to see if I needed help. "If you don't knock it off, I'm going to have to go over to the fresh vegetables section and redirect one of those water mister nozzles down the front of my dress."

"Which dress?"

"White with pink stripes." Another one of Jerry's outfit choices. Even though Dickie wasn't there to be on camera, Jerry wanted me to be prepared in case Rosy wanted to do some filming.

"I don't remember that one. Are you wearing panties today?"

"Are you serious?"

"When it comes to you, definitely." I heard the sound of a door shutting. "There's only one reason you would be at the store buying a protein shake this early. Is this part of the deal to get your Planet of the Apes pal to join us tomorrow night at Willis' ranch?"

"No. Jerry called this morning and told me I need to take the camera-woman over to do some filming at Cornelius's hotel. I know better than to show up at his door this early without liquid protein." I didn't want him to scare Rosy off, although I was starting to get the feeling that it would take more than a ghost or a cranky Abe Lincoln doppelganger to impress Rosy. "When I have a moment alone with Cornelius, I'll see if he's available tomorrow."

I sort of hoped he was busy. While Cooper may have spoken his piece, I was still against doing the séance on the Day of the Dead. If we couldn't get our Pied Piper lined up, then the deal was off as far as I was concerned.

"Call me when you get an answer from him." The sound of the shower kicking on came through the phone. "If he's game, I'll phone Cooper and let him know we're definitely on."

"This is a bad idea."

"You mean the séance or you joining me in the shower?"

"Both."

"What are you afraid of?"

"An axe-wielding juggernaut and you turning on the cold water again so you can get your rocks off by rubbing soap over my high beams."

A chuckle came through the line. "*Ay yi yi.*"

"*Au revoir, Gomez.* I'll call you later." I hung up before he started giving me a play-by-play of what he wanted to do with me in the shower. I doubted the store manager would appreciate finding me in the freezer while I consoled my undersexed libido with a gallon of peanut butter fudge ice cream.

On the way to Cornelius's hotel, I battled the fear tightening my guts about the ghosts I'd heard on Cornelius's recording last week. I was a dud. Those ghosts couldn't hurt me. At least I didn't think so.

Cornelius opened the door for Rosy and me on the second knock. His thigh-length, Hugh Hefner inspired scarlet silk robe, lack of pants, and crooked stovepipe hat knocked the words right out of my mouth and left my tongue jumbled on the floor next to them.

As he ushered us inside his domain, Rosy and I exchanged raised brows but kept our comments to ourselves. I in particular would like to have scrubbed my brain on one of those old fashioned washboards to remove the image of Abe Jr.'s black furry pencil legs from my memory. Seriously, the guy looked like he was wearing the bottom half of a gorilla suit.

My fear of what unseen guests were waiting in his suite seemed silly in the sun-brightened rooms. Didn't he usually keep his blinds closed? I wondered what was with the change in procedure this morning.

With my past experience with the eccentric ghost whisperer, I'd warned Rosy on the elevator ride up to his suite that Cornelius was a bit odd. Rosy took one look around his suite, pausing on the numerous monitors, expensive meters, fancy stereo equipment, and empty bottles of protein drinks and crossed her arms over her chest. "You have a K-II Meter, huh? You know they offer a lot of potential for false positives, right?"

And they were off.

For the next forty-five minutes, Cornelius led Rosy around his suite, showing off his expensive gadgets and ghost toys, including his EMF, EVP, and other acronym based doodads. I followed behind them trying to pay attention, only to get mired repeatedly in remembering the words behind each of the letters. When they moved onto paranormal terms, such as "intelligent" versus "residual" hauntings, I got sidetracked by trying to apply it to Prudence's presence in the Carhart house. Then Cornelius mentioned "matrixing," and I tumbled down a rabbit hole that started with Keanu Reeves trying to bend spoons with his mind and ended with his trapping demons in mirrors. Apparently I suffered from ADD this early in the morning.

When Rosy excused herself to use the restroom thanks to the extra-large coffee I'd purposely brought her this morning, I cornered the furry legged, paranormal groupie.

"Cornelius, I need your help tomorrow night with a séance."

"Tomorrow?" He looked at his wrist, which held no watch. "That's the Day of the Dead."

"I know. A bad night to have a séance, right?" Nothing like a leading question, but time was short. That coffee would only buy me so much time.

"A very bad night."

"That's what I thought. We should probably reschedule it, don't you think?"

"Absolutely not."

Skirrrch. "I don't understand."

He sat down on one of his bar stools. "Of course you don't, Violet. That's why you need me."

Most days, I needed him like I needed a hot poker jammed in my eye. I glossed over his reply and continued on course. "I really don't think we should do it tomorrow."

"It's in your nature to say that."

"Because I'm not a paranormal investigator?"

"Because you channel."

I scratched my head, wishing I'd grabbed an extra large coffee for myself. "Shouldn't a channeler be more willing to open up the airwaves on a day when the dead are restless?"

"No. You'll be flooded."

"Remind me why that's a problem."

"Flooding can stop your heart ... or worse."

"What's worse than stopping my heart?"

"Getting trapped inside another realm."

He had a point there. If I had to choose between being trapped in Ms. Wolff's apartment back in time with that juggernaut and his creepy ax or being plain old dead, I'd take the dirt nap option any day.

"Let me get this straight," I took the bar stool next to him. "Even though this is going to be dangerous for me, you still think we should do the séance?"

"Definitely."

"In spite of my reservations?"

"Because of them."

This conversation was beginning to actually hurt. My brain needed some reinforcements. I stole his protein drink from him and gulped down several swallows, licking the crappy vanilla-flavored liquid substitute for steak off my lips. "Explain that, Professor Enigmatic."

"Your reservations will help you maintain a safe channeling width. If you were excited to go into this, then I wouldn't want to do it, because you would undoubtedly open too wide."

Yeah, I had that problem when it came to sex with Doc.

"Yet again," Cornelius continued, "in your channeling wisdom, you recognize the potential dangers and are already preparing mentally to keep the channel narrow."

But what if I weren't even really a channeler, but rather an executioner, and doing this séance on the Day of the Dead was going to round up something much scarier than an ornery old ghost with nobody there who knew how to close the gate?

I sighed. I was sticking with my original opinion—this was a big mistake. What I couldn't figure out was why Doc wasn't more worried about it. He seemed at ease not only with taking this risk but also having a skeptic with a badge in the audience. I was beginning to suspect he'd done this before with cops somewhere along the line. He was certainly at ease with Cooper's presence.

"We'll have the séance an hour and eleven minutes after the sun sets," Cornelius decreed.

"Fine, whatever." But if things went south tomorrow night, I was going to blame Abe Jr. just because he frustrated the hell out of me most days. "Do you want me to pick you up, or would you like directions to the ranch?"

"Neither."

"Right. You want to use the transporter beam then?"

"You're spunky this morning, Violet. It must be that dress."

I suspected it had more to do with my goal to keep breathing for a little bit longer, something I feared this séance would hinder.

"The thing is," he stroked his goatee, measuring me with those cornflower blue eyes, "you may not be fit to drive afterward."

He had a good point. "I'll line up a ride for both of us then. Do I need to get any supplies?"

"Nope, I am already stocked up. Although they sent me a voodoo love doll instead of the Wanga bag I wanted, so I'll have to improvise."

The toilet flushed.

"Don't mention any of this in front of Rosy," I told him. "Or anyone else. This séance is private."

"I understand. But there is one more thing, Violet."

"What's that?"

"I don't think you should reach into the darkness tomorrow

night with your mind."

"Why's that?"

"Because of that little girl ghost of yours that keeps talking to me," he started.

"She's not mine." I wanted no association with Wilda Hessler if I could help it.

The sound of running water stopped.

"Maybe not, but she keeps mentioning your name."

"What's she saying?"

Cornelius leaned closer to me. "Roses are red, Violet is blue. Wolfgang is dead, Violet is, too."

Goosebumps covered me from toes to scalp.

Before I could croak out any kind of response, Rosy joined us again. I covered my shock with a wide smile.

Cornelius left to get some pants on so he could take us around from room to room and give Rosy a good feel of the place.

I rubbed my arms, looking around the suite, wondering if Wilda Hessler was standing next to me, her blonde ringlets trembling with rage, her dead eyes overflowing with hate. Was her brother still here? His face melting off again?

By the time Cornelius was dressed and ready to go, I was waiting out in the hall trying to figure out what Wilda meant with that stupid poem. Was it just a pissed off little girl out to scare me, or did she know something about the others that I should be more afraid of than I was?

Something to do with that clock in Ms. Wolff's apartment and its cuckooing death toll?

Something that would end my game as an executioner before I'd had a chance to get rolling?

* * *

When I pulled into Aunt Zoe's driveway I was surprised to see Jeff Wymonds' truck sitting there ... and not in a happy-to-see-him way.

After a day of touring with Rosy around Cornelius's hotel, as well as several other reportedly haunted locales in Deadwood to film extra background footage, I wasn't really in the mood for company. Especially if this particular company required my shoulder to cry on because his ex-wife was taking him back to court for full custody of his other testicle.

As I climbed out of the Picklemobile, I glanced down the street, wishing I would see Doc's Camaro or even Harvey's Ford pickup coming my way. Both should be here for supper any minute now. Unfortunately, I was on my own.

In the early evening air, I could hear the kids laughing and yelling in the back yard. Instead of facing Jeff, I detoured through the back gate, dropped my purse on the grass next to their slide, and squeezed my butt into one of the swings on their old swing set. The comforting scent of autumn with its crisp version of pine trees and dried leaves grounded me.

"Hi, Addy's mom," Kelly Wymonds said from across the yard.

I waved, the swing creaking as I rocked back and forth, watching the two girls do cartwheels across the yard. Oh, to be so carefree. I remembered those days way back when with Natalie— no bills to pay, no mouths to fill, no creepy-weird beings to kill.

The back door opened and out walked Jeff.

"Hey, Violet Parker." Dressed in a button up shirt and new-looking jeans, he headed my way. His blond hair looked freshly cut, his jaw stubble-free. He sat down on the swing next to mine, his musky cologne fresh on his skin and now fresh in my sinuses.

"I hear you're going to be a TV superstar soon." His grin was easy, his eyes teasing.

"Watch out world," I answered without enthusiasm. "Here I come."

We swung in silence, watching our girls try to do back bends and fall over giggling.

"I had a visitor stop by today," he told me, his eyes still on Kelly.

"Someone to check out the house?" The market was slow with winter coming on, but Jeff's house was set in a good location and had cleaned up well, including a brand-spanking new roof on his detached garage.

"Not the house. He was checking on you."

That grabbed my attention. "Me?"

"He said his name was Detective Hawke, but he looked more like a sloppy version of that private dick James Garner played on that old show."

"The Rockford Files." Hawke, damn it! That son of a bitch was still hounding me.

"Yeah, that's it."

"What did Detective Hawke want?" Besides my ass on a hot griddle?

"At first he was asking about my garage explosion. I figured he was sent by the insurance company, so I took him out to the garage and showed him the good job the roofers did. But then he mentioned you being my Realtor and wanted to know how I felt you were doing. I talked you up, of course, especially how good of a kisser you are."

"Oh, jeez." We'd had one lousy kiss, and I meant lousy. Jeff had treated my tonsils like they were clay pigeons.

"What?" He knocked my knee with his. "You are."

I grunted. It wasn't my actual kiss that had hoisted Jeff's flag. It was the beef-jerky I'd eaten before letting his tongue scrub the back of my teeth. Smoked beef was an aphrodisiac for the oversexed buffoon.

"Was there anything else he asked about me?"

"Yeah, it was sort of odd, too. He wanted to know if I'd ever heard you talk to ghosts." Jeff chuckled, not noticing that I was white-knuckling the swing chains. "I told him that whoever was spreading the Spooky Parker rumors and saying you chatted with ghosts was full of shit."

Splendid. So much for the work I'd done to convince Detective Hawke that I was a medium and not a witch. But I couldn't be mad at Jeff. He had no idea how much the tide had turned for me since our do-you-believe-in-ghosts conversation months ago.

"I like that dress." Jeff reached out and rubbed the skirt fabric between his fingers. "Sort of reminds me of something Beaver Cleaver's mom would wear, minus the pointy boobs."

I was too tired from being hounded by the cops to let my insecurities about my non-pointy, post-baby boobs flare up.

"You look nice tonight," I told him, redirecting attention onto him. "You got a hot date?"

"As a matter of fact, I do. Your aunt said I could bring Kelly by for the night. But if that doesn't work for you, I can cancel the slumber party."

"It's fine." I spun a little in my swing. "A slumber party? This must be some date."

"Oh, we've had sex lots of times already, so it's not like a cherry popping night or anything."

Good old Jeff. He had such a way with romantic phrases. I could only imagine his whispered, heart-stopping vernacular while "popping cherries" between the sheets.

I heard an engine rumble to a stop up front and prayed Doc would come to my rescue soon.

Aunt Zoe yelled out the back door for the girls to go inside and wash up for supper. She looked over at me on the swing.

I tried to smile, but my mouth really wasn't up to it.

Her face wrinkled with concern, but she left us alone anyway.

As soon as the back door closed, Jeff dug in his pocket and pulled out a little jewelry box. "I have something to show you," he said in a low voice, "but keep it to yourself." He lifted the lid. Two matching gold rings were jammed into the blue velvet base.

I stopped spinning. His divorce wasn't final yet. As messy as the whole break up had been with his soon-to-be ex, I'd have thought he'd want a breather before cinching another tourniquet around his nut sack.

"Are those what I think they are?" Although, I wasn't accustomed to seeing two of them in a jewelry box and usually there was a diamond involved, but maybe Jeff's new woman wasn't into sparkly rocks.

"Yep," he closed the box with a snap. "Nipple rings."

"Eww. I mean, ouch." I winced at both the thought of having a needle jammed through my nipples and at Jeff's choice for show and tell this evening. Hell, now I was probably going to check out his girlfriend's chest when I met her, looking for those rings, and undoubtedly get caught staring. That was an embarrassing moment just waiting to smack me upside the head.

"Keep your fingers crossed she's willing to try them out

tonight and get rid of the studs she has in there now."

Come on! Did he have to paint a high definition picture to go with those rings? He might as well call me after the show was over and give me the X-rated details.

"Are those like the equivalent of trading high school rings these days on the dating circuit?" Doc and I hadn't quite reached the jewelry exchange level in our relationship. We had just made it to edible soap.

"Sort of, but she knows I'm just in it for the fun stuff until this divorce is history." He held up the box. "You should try these sometime. They're supposed to really get your engine revving, make your nipples super sensitive."

Hmmm, the last time I'd talked to anybody about the sensitivity of my nipples, I'd been pregnant with twins and the man had been sticking his rubber-gloved finger in my hoo-haa. Oddly enough, this moment with Jeff felt pretty much the same, only more ham-handed.

The back door opened and Elvis ran out, clucking down the steps. Thank the chicken gods for the interruption!

Harvey followed in the hen's wake. "What're you two doing out here?" He came down the steps to join us.

Talking nipples, I thought, but knew better than to go down that red-lit alley with the old buzzard. "Just swinging until supper is ready."

Aunt Zoe had called me before I left work, telling me she was making baked chicken and rice pilaf tonight, which had me salivating on the way home.

Harvey looked down at the box in Jeff's hand. "What's in the box?"

Jeff popped it open and held it out.

Harvey whistled through his teeth. "Nipple rings, boy howdy!"

Of course Harvey would know.

The old man looked at me, then at my chest. "You gettin' your hooters pierced?"

I crossed my arms over the objects in question "No!"

"Don't go gettin' all uppity on me, girl. I don't know what sort of kinky toys Doc and you are into these days."

"They're mine." Jeff snapped the box closed. "I have a hot date tonight."

"Does she have one of those tongue studs, too?" Harvey asked.

Jeff's grin looked like someone had stuffed a boomerang between his cheeks. "Yep, with a diamond tip on one end."

Harvey blanched a little. "How's that feel?"

"Scratchy at first, but she does this trick with her tongue where she takes my—"

"Oh, my God, stop!" I stood up. "Jeff's sex life and appreciation of tongue studs is not appropriate pre-supper conversation."

The back door opened. This time Doc walked out on the porch. He leaned against the porch post in his work garb—khakis and a green button-up shirt. One of his eyebrows rose as his gaze settled on our trio. "Zoe wants to know what you three want to drink."

"Something with tequila in it." I grabbed my purse.

Jeff and Harvey followed me onto the back porch.

"I should take off," Jeff said.

"The stud-meister here has a hot date," Harvey explained. "He won't be grubbin' with us, but I'll take a glass of some of that sweet lemonade of Zoe's."

Doc gave me a once-over, hitting me with a smoldering glance before returning to Jeff. "Hot date, huh?"

Jeff pulled that blasted ring box out of his pocket again and flipped it open under Doc's nose. "I'm hoping to break these babies in tonight."

"On anyone in particular?" Doc asked.

"My woman." He closed the box and pocketed it—for good I hoped, since my kids didn't need to have a hands-on lesson about nipple rings tonight. "She's got a bunch of other piercings, too."

I was surprised no drool leaked out of that huge grin Jeff was sporting as he bragged her up.

"She sounds pokey," Doc said.

"Hokey pokey, if you ask me." Harvey hooked his thumbs in his suspenders. "Does she like to shake it all about," he asked

Jeff, wiggling his bushy eyebrows at him.

And we were back in the gutter again. "I'm going inside."

Doc caught up with me at the door, holding it for me. Inside the kitchen, he helped me shuck my coat. "Not into nipple rings, Tiger?"

I pushed up on my toes and gave him a quick kiss just because I could. "I'll pierce mine if you pierce yours."

He winced, dittoing my earlier reaction. "How'd the rest of your day go?"

I'd called him earlier after leaving the hotel to tell him we were definitely on for tomorrow, damn it.

I shrugged, heading to the sink to wash my hands. "Ray's threatening to bill me for that stupid tooth incident."

"What stupid tooth incident?" Aunt Zoe asked, sweeping in from the dining room to check on the tray of baked chicken in the oven. I'd been too whipped last night to tell her about yesterday's go around with Prudence.

While Harvey and Jeff continued their nipple discussion outside on the porch, I filled Aunt Zoe in on my enlightenment at the Carhart house, making sure to include the bit about Prudence's family line now being extinct and how ours was considered brutal by comparison.

Doc set the table, pulling out a chair for me as I talked. Harvey joined us midway through. Jeff must have left via the side gate, because he didn't follow Harvey inside.

When I finished with the part about my realizing it was Ray's tooth in my palm, Aunt Zoe had a hint of a smile. "Ray shouldn't have insulted an executioner—even a dead one. That'll teach him."

"So what do you think?" I asked her, really wishing she'd laugh about it all and tell me it was a hoax she'd somehow engineered to mess with my head. That all of this executioner talk was one big Halloween practical joke.

She came over to the table and sat next to me, taking my hands in hers. "I think you're very fortunate that Prudence waited for you to come."

Fortunate? "She scares the living daylights out of me."

Harvey snorted in agreement. "The ol' gal almost puts me off my feed."

I shot him a smirk. "You seemed perfectly able to chow down on crackers in the thick of things yesterday."

"I said almost."

Aunt Zoe squeezed my hands. "Violet, this is a good thing. It may not seem like it when she's in your face like she was yesterday, but Prudence can help you in ways I can't because I'm not an executioner. You need to talk to her more, learn from her."

"How do I do that? She's dead."

Aunt Zoe looked over at Doc, who was stirring the rice on the stove. "Sounds like you need a medium to act as your interpreter."

Doc stopped stirring. "I know one who could help."

"No," I said without hesitation.

"Violet, listen," he started, joining us at the table.

"No, I won't listen, not even for a second. I don't like her inside of your head."

"It's what I do."

"Not this time. Not with her."

"Why not?" Aunt Zoe pressed.

My answer made my face warm before I even said it, but I needed to make my feelings clear, especially with these three who were on the inside of this executioner business with me.

I pulled my hands from Aunt Zoe, clasping them together in my lap. "Because ..." I squirmed in my seat and started again. "Because I'm intimate with Doc, and I don't want to share him with her." I looked over at Doc, unable to read from his expression whether or not he thought I was being silly. "I'm afraid seeing her use you as her ventriloquist doll over and over will make it hard for me to separate you two when it comes to sex." Or even have sex with him, and I really liked getting naked with Doc, especially when he got busy with his hands.

"You don't want to bump uglies with a dead woman?" Harvey asked, his tone edged with laughter.

"Not if I can help it. In spite of how good Demi Moore made it look, I'm just not that into ghosts."

"Okay." Doc squeezed my shoulder. "We'll find another

person to act as a conduit for her."

"I think Prudence already did. Remember how I told you she wanted me to bring her the librarian?" He nodded and I continued, turning to Aunt Zoe. "Zelda Britton is an actual librarian who's into ghosts. I think Prudence might have tested her out when I was showing her the Carhart house. She recognized a replacement for Wanda, who was very easy for Prudence to control."

"Does Zelda know about this?" Aunt Zoe asked.

I shook my head. "She's very excited about living in a haunted house, though, so maybe with a little nudge, she'd be okay with my coming over to visit Prudence periodically."

"We'll give Zelda a try then," Doc said. "But we have a more critical situation to deal with tomorrow night."

"What's tomorrow night?" Aunt Zoe asked.

"They're comin' out to my ranch to gab with my grandpappy's ghost."

"Why?" Aunt Zoe frowned at Harvey.

Doc answered. "Detective Cooper wants us to have a séance."

Her eyebrows practically hit the ceiling. "Cooper does?"

"Coop's up against a wall," Harvey explained. "He's got dead bodies all around and no breadcrumbs to follow."

Aunt Zoe leaned back, shaking her head in disbelief. "I never thought I'd see the day when that boy saw anything other than black and white."

"I'm not sure he does," I grumbled.

"He will," Harvey predicted. "Mark my words."

Doc fiddled with his fork. "We need your help, Zoe."

I frowned at him. "We do?" I didn't like the thought of putting her at risk along with me. Who would take care of my kids if both of us ended up dead?

His dark eyes leveled on me. "The last few times Violet was involved in a séance, something else showed up, too. Something darker, more substantive than just ghosts."

"You mean the albino," Aunt Zoe said.

He nodded. "He's one example. I can't protect her on the other side, especially if she heads off on her own like she did in

Ms. Wolff's apartment."

"I didn't head off on my own."

"Yes, you did, Killer."

"Not on purpose."

Doc focused back on Aunt Zoe. "Is there any sort of weapon Violet can use to protect herself the next time she decides to go exploring without me?"

Aunt Zoe rubbed her forehead. "This is where it gets tricky."

"Tricky how?" I asked.

"Tricky because *you* are the weapon. Not anything that you carry necessarily, because the way to execute an 'other' varies from being to being."

Harvey grunted. "That's a helluva pickle."

"Can't we look up what our ancestors used in that book you gave to me? Get some ideas at least?"

She shook her head. "For one thing, it's not a how-to-kill book. It's more of a who-they-were and how-they-died reference. For another, what works for one executioner may not work for another."

"What?" How come this job came with rules that made no sense? I had a feeling I was going to be better at selling real estate than killing, and I sucked rotten eggs as a Realtor.

"You have to figure out what works for you."

"That makes no sense." I frowned at Doc. "Does that make any sense to you?"

His brow matched mine. "Whether it makes sense or not, it's a problem." He turned to Aunt Zoe. "She has to start from scratch?"

"Unfortunately. You see, just as we have to change and adapt to our environment as a species, the others have to change and adapt as well. Only this adaptation happens much quicker than most animal lifeforms on Earth. So, what your great great-aunt might have used to kill a being may or may not still work for you. We have to experiment to see."

"Experiment meaning I have to kill something to figure out if that method works."

"Exactly."

"I said it before," Harvey spoke up, "and I'll say it again, girl.

You keep findin' barbed wire fences."

I put my head down on the table and banged my fist a few times, making the plates and silverware rattle.

Aunt Zoe's touch was tender on my back, soothing. "Sweetie, what you're not taking into consideration is how strong you already are."

I sat up. "I can't even evict a damned chicken from my bed most days. How am I supposed to kill nasty, vile creatures?"

"They won't all be vile. Some are quite attractive."

"Great. That makes this game even more fun. How will I know if the hot looking guy coming on to me is out to kill me and not just lure me into the sack?"

"I'll let you know," Doc said with a half-grin.

I shook off my poor-me blues. "Okay, so you've given me triggers that will help me know when I'm facing off with trouble, right?"

"The triggers will alert you when you're dealing with something not entirely human. It's then up to you to figure out if the being needs to be executed or let be." When I scrubbed my hands down my face over that frustrating answer, she explained, "An executioner doesn't kill indiscriminately, Violet. You kill only those who are a danger to all others, including humans, if necessary."

"So," Doc leaned forward, resting his elbows on his knees. "If execution is necessary, Violet may or may not need a weapon to kill?"

"Correct."

"Christ," he said, blowing out a breath. "The enemy could be standing right next to her, and she might not even realize it."

"She'll know."

"How?" I asked.

"By your instincts. Different species will set you off in different ways. Some might make your ears ring; others might make you feel sick to your stomach."

Sick to my stomach … Come to think of it, Dominick Masterson had always made me feel nauseated whenever he was near, and he'd crashed through a concrete wall unscathed when he'd escaped from the basement of the Opera House. Holy crap!

"You need to tune into your mind and body more often, testing the waters as you go."

I touched Doc's thigh. "I'll have to be more careful from now on during séances."

He nodded, but I could tell from his tight expression that he wasn't thrilled about Aunt Zoe's answers.

"Maybe you should be holdin' onto good ol' Bessie when you go under tomorrow night," Harvey said.

"I don't think guns are going to help you, sweetie." Aunt Zoe pushed back her chair.

"How do you know that?"

"You tested it firsthand at Mudder Brothers that night the albino came after you, remember?" She slipped on a pair of oven mitts. "You said the bullets didn't even slow him down."

"So bullets don't work on the albinos," Doc said.

"Probably not most of the others, either." Aunt Zoe pulled the tray of chicken out of the oven and set it on the stove.

"Why not?" I wanted bullets to work, dang it. A sniper rifle would be perfect.

"I don't know for certain that this is true for all species," she said taking off the mitts, "but my guess would be that through adaptation over the centuries since the first firearms were invented, most of the others have adapted to withstand bullets somehow."

"Even silver bullets," I said, half-jokingly.

"Those are just Black Forest fairytales from the Brothers Grimm. They didn't quite get it right."

I heard Layne yell out Addy's name overhead, followed by footfalls coming down the stairs. Little girl giggles echoed into the kitchen. It was time to eat and return to our regular programming for a while.

"If I can't use guns," I whispered, "what can I use?"

She leaned down and kissed my forehead. "Sorry, kiddo, but when you kill, you're going to have to get your hands dirty. Filthy, bloody, dirty."

Chapter Twenty-Two

Friday, November 2nd (The Day of the Dead)

Meanwhile, back at Calamity Jane Realty ...

I tossed and turned for most of the night with an aching gut. Not the stomach flu type, nor the nausea that usually keeps my anxiety company, but a deep ache that wouldn't go away.

The next morning, the kids chattered around me at the breakfast table, Kelly joining in on the fun. Layne actually smiled at me when he came downstairs for the first time since before I'd told Addy and him that I was dating Doc. Maybe life was rebounding on this front, my kids finally starting to accept Doc in our daily world. I hoped so, anyway.

But Layne's smile didn't ease the pain in my gut.

I forced some toast down my throat, skipping a coffee chaser to keep from making worse what I worried might be an ulcer. After instructing Layne to work on the homework his teachers had sent home with his sister, I took Kelly and Addy to school.

When I pulled into the parking lot at work, Ben's Subaru wasn't there. He must still be sick. Crap, that was some nasty crud.

I stepped out of the Picklemobile, noticing Ray's Suburban was missing, too. That made my shoulders loosen, but the stomach ache still didn't budge, damn it.

The lack of Doc's Camaro in the lot didn't surprise me. He'd mentioned that he wanted to spend time reading up on the history of the area surrounding Harvey's ranch before tonight's séance. I thought about texting him sweet nothings to see if flirting with him would make my stomach feel happier, but if he was sleeping in or preparing mentally for tonight, I didn't want to bug him.

In the office, Jerry was talking quietly with Rosy. From the looks of it, they were checking out something on her camera that she'd recorded earlier. I slipped by without saying a peep, wanting to hide at my desk for a while and lose myself in normality while scanning through today's MLS listings.

Mona's jasmine perfume filled the front office with a sweet ambiance. Her clacking on her keyboard was the equivalent of white noise to me. After small talk with Mona about a couple she took to see a few places yesterday, I slipped into silent mode and let my mind wrap around what had become of my previously, blissfully mundane life.

An hour later, my stomach ache hadn't relented one iota. In spite of it, I'd replayed Aunt Zoe's words and warnings about this killing business until my brain was numb. They seemed less jarring now, but I was still choking on the part about killing things as part of my daily lifestyle. I didn't even dare let myself dwell about my kids in relation to all of this. Just the thought of Mr. Black coming within sight of either of them made my gut clamp down even tighter.

The sound of Jerry saying goodbye to Rosy dimly reached my conscious. I came back to earth in time to hear him say something about next week before the back door shut behind her.

"Violet," he called out a short time later. "Can you come in here for a moment?"

Oh, great. Now what new idea did he have for the next time I was in front of the camera? I walked back and stood in his doorway. "You called me?"

He didn't look up as he scribbled some notes. "I was just watching some of the films from the last couple of days."

I tried to slip on a look of interest to make him think I cared about this reality television show right now—never mind the fact that I could possibly get slain during a séance tonight. "Oh, yeah?"

"I'd like you to try to hold your shoulders back more when the camera is on you. It'll give you a more commanding presence in front of the audience and make them think you have something important to say."

Crap. If I couldn't give a commanding performance on camera, how in hell was I going to make an albino quiver on its feet? Something cracked inside my head, a rushing sound built in my ears. I kept my face frozen while pieces fell off of me on the inside.

"About that dress you wore yesterday," he started.

But that was all the further he got because the dam holding back the worry and frustration and fear and rage that came with grappling to accept my new role sprung a big old leak. Much to my horror, tears filled my eyes.

A weird mewling sound escaped through my lips. Turning away, I swiped at the tears, praying Jerry wouldn't notice.

"Are you okay, Violet?" he asked, his focus on me when I turned back to him.

"Yes, I have something in my eye." My eyes filled faster, breaching the dyke. I scrambled through my blazer pockets, trying to find a tissue, anything to sop up this leak in my main line.

He stood up. "Violet, you're crying." He sounded as shocked about it as I was.

"No, I'm not."

"Both of your eyes are leaking tears down your face."

It was nice of him to give me a definition of crying, but it wasn't helping. Actually it was making it worse. First my stomach had turned traitor on me; now my head was leaking. Criminy! I was turning into a superfund site.

"I'm okay," I told Jerry, not sure if I really was or not.

Jerry stepped closer, his hands out but not touching me, uncertain. "What should I ..."

A sob wailed out through my lips before I could seal them shut.

He jumped in surprise, his eyes wide. "Man down on the court!" he yelled out through his open doorway. "Mona! Tissues, quick!"

I heard Mona's chair slide back, the sound of her heels clicking on the wood floor.

"I told you, Jerry, I'm okay." Another mewl sounded from my chest.

Mona gasped from the threshold. "What did you do to her, Jerry?"

He pulled his hands back, clasping them together. "Nothing, I swear. I was going to tell her that she looked great yesterday in the dress we'd picked out."

The dress *he'd* picked out. I couldn't even choose a decent outfit on my own. How was I going to protect my children from certain doom?

My throat began to burn, the tears dripping onto Jerry's floor now. My gut churned, my ears burned. Jeez louise, what was wrong with me? The urge to take flight sprouted wings. I needed to get the hell out of there until I could pull myself back together.

"I gotta go," I said, mopping at the tears. Without giving Jerry a chance to respond, I ran out the door, grabbing the tissues from Mona on the way.

"Vi," she called to my back.

"Just give me a minute, Mona," I said but didn't stop. I pushed out the back door and ran out into the cool sunshine, ping-ponging between the cars in the lot in my rush to escape.

The sound of screeching brakes didn't slow me. I needed to get to the safety of the Picklemobile before I short-circuited and made an even bigger fool of myself.

I was tugging open the pickup door when someone seized my other arm.

"Violet," Doc said, stopping me. He turned me around, his frown deepening when he saw my face. "What's wrong?"

I shook my head. "Something broke."

"In your office?"

"No, in me." I swabbed away more tears, but they just kept coming. "I can't stop doing this." I pointed at my eyes.

He reached out and wiped away a fresh batch of tears that were rolling down my cheeks. "You've sprung a leak, Tiger."

"I'm a big soppy mess."

"Maybe so." He tucked me into his arms, his chin resting on the top of my head as he rubbed up and down my back. "But you're my big soppy mess."

The stupid waterworks kept pouring, smudging my mascara on his cream shirt. "I'm getting makeup on you." I sniffed, breathing in the scent of his skin. A calm filled my gut, replacing the ache that had been there before.

He kept holding me close. "What started this?"

"Jerry critiqued my acting." I rested my forehead on his chest. My laugh was short and harsh. "He was trying to be helpful, but it made me realize how incompetent I am playing the part of an executioner."

Doc pushed away enough to look down at me. His eyes searched mine for I didn't know what before he glanced away, blowing out a breath. "I'm going to cancel the séance. We can do it another night. You're not ready."

He was right. I wasn't. But would I ever be ready?

"I'll call Cooper and tell him it's not going to happen."

While I liked the sound of that, I knew we couldn't keep delaying the inevitable. Being an executioner was in my blood. It was what I was made to do. The only way this was going to get easier to handle was by facing it head on.

"No," I told him.

"No what?"

"Don't call him."

"Violet, you don't have to do this tonight."

What was it about Doc that always made me feel able to face the unknown rather than hide from it?

"I sort of do and we both know it." I dabbed my tears with the tattered remains of Mona's already soaked tissue. "I just have to figure out how to get a grip on my fears and lock them back up in the attic." I tapped my head.

"You've had a hell of a week, sweetheart." He leaned against the Picklemobile, still holding my hand. "On top of it all, you've sort of been dunked into the paranormal world without being allowed a chance to catch your breath. Don't you think it's normal to have some side effects after learning you come from a line of killers and that those you care about most are at risk?"

Like a gut ache? And nonstop tears? He had a point, but I highly doubted executioners blubbered and cried when the going got tough. "You've been through a lot of weird shit like this in your life, right?" When he half-shrugged half- nodded, I continued. "Have you ever had a sort of break down?"

"Sure," he answered quickly.

Too quickly for me. My gaze narrowed. "With tears?"

"Not tears. Mine comes out in other ways. Why do you think I go to the rec center several times a week?"

"To flex your muscles in the mirror?"

He laughed, deep and rich, bringing back the sunshine. "Not quite. I deal with my stress by working up a sweat."

"I could help you with that next time." I tried to give him a sex kitten smile, but it probably looked more like a water-logged cat, all crazy haired with sad eyes.

"That's a deal, Boots." He grasped the lapels of my blazer and pulled me closer, kissing me with soft lips. There were no sparks this time but still plenty of fire to roast my chestnuts.

I moaned in complaint when he pulled away.

"What do you think?" he asked, leaning against the Picklemobile again. "Should I call Cooper? Tell him we're going to spend the night on my couch watching the Duke ride off into the sunset instead of playing with ghosts?"

I thought about it—Doc being there with me at Harvey's place, my gut no longer hurting, my tears dried up. "We'll hang out with the Duke tomorrow night. Let's celebrate the Day of the Dead with some ghost stories."

He squinted at me, making me feel like I was on the uncomfortable end of a microscope. Cooper must be tutoring him each morning at the coffeemaker. "Okay," he crossed his arms over his chest, "but you have to promise me something first."

"What?"

"You won't leave my side tonight no matter what happens."

"Where would I go?"

"Somewhere I can't follow."

"Maybe we should have Cooper handcuff us together," I joked.

"We'll save that for tomorrow night after the Duke." His face sobered. "I'm serious, Violet. You may be a killer, but you're not indestructible."

That very thought had been gnawing at my gut all morning.

"In my experience, caution will keep you breathing."

"I like breathing."

"I like you breathing, too." His lips curved slightly, his gaze drifting south. "It makes your chest go up and down."

I stepped between his legs, wrapping my arms around his neck, and breathed against him several times.

"Vixen," he said, his hands exploring my hips.

"What time are you picking me up tonight?"

"After you eat probably. Cooper and Harvey are meeting us out there."

"I don't think I'll be able to stomach much food."

He pushed me backward and faced me toward the office. "Try anyway." He smacked my butt into gear.

"Fine, bossy," I tugged him along with me. "We have to get Cornelius, too. He doesn't know where to go."

"Expect me earlier then." He walked with me back toward Calamity Jane's. "You gonna be okay?"

Taking everything into consideration, I snorted. "No. Not until tonight is over."

He squeezed my hand. "I'll be right there with you."

"I know."

But would that be enough?

* * *

Aunt Zoe made me eat. She stuffed me full of breakfast food—scrambled eggs and bacon and red bell peppers, telling me protein and vitamins were key to keeping up my strength and stamina. If I kept eating this sort of executioner fare, I was going to end up big as a house. I could sit on my victims and squish them to death.

Doc showed up right as the kids were sitting down to eat, early as promised. Like me, he wore jeans. His red flannel shirt made his shoulders seem broader, reminding me of a lumberjack ready to go chop a cord of firewood.

I kissed my kids on their heads, trying to soak up their scent enough to get me through what was to come. I sent a silent prayer to the executioner gods that I made it home to see them again before the night was over. Aunt Zoe squeezed me tight and then checked for the third time that I still wore all of the charms she'd decorated me with earlier.

"Take care of her," she told Doc, giving him a hug and a kiss on the cheek.

"I will."

"Put this in your pocket," she ordered and handed him a glass charm. It looked similar to something she'd made for my brother to keep with him during his travels.

Doc pocketed it without question. "You ready?" he asked me.

Nope, but I nodded anyway.

"Give me one minute." He poked his head into the kitchen. I heard him tell my kids to keep an eye on Aunt Zoe tonight and make sure she ate all of her supper, brushed her teeth, and got to bed on time.

Addy giggled.

"Watch after Mom," Layne ordered back.

"Yes, sir."

"Just don't leave her alone," Addy added, her tone serious.

I frowned toward the kitchen as I slipped on my coat. Had Addy sensed something about tonight? Was she going to follow right behind me in this potentially heart-stopping line of work?

Aunt Zoe patted my arm. "Out of the mouths of babes."

"I hope it's only that."

Doc returned to open the door, ushering me out into the twilight. A breeze rattled the world around us, making things creak, rattle, and squeak. I didn't need Mother Nature adding eerie effects to the darkening world. It was chilling enough minus the spook-fest soundtrack.

I handed Doc the keys to the Picklemobile. "Let's leave your car here, safe and sound in Aunt Zoe's drive."

He didn't argue, holding the old truck's passenger door open for me.

I called Cornelius on the way, asking him if he needed help toting his equipment down from his suite. He didn't. He waited out behind The Old Prospector Hotel for us, two mid-sized cases sitting at his feet. Doc secured them in the back of the truck, while I scooted into the middle, making room for the Pied Piper and his stovepipe hat.

The drive out to Harvey's ranch was filled with Cornelius asking us what we knew about the ghost we were going to try to call forth. We took turns filling him in on what we'd learned from Harvey.

By the time Doc had pulled to a stop in Harvey's driveway, the sky was dark except for a line along the horizon. The Picklemobile's headlights swept across the house and spotlighted the old barn.

Cornelius stared through the windshield. "We'll have the séance in there," he announced.

I followed him out the passenger door. "In the barn? Why? You think the spirits will be more active in there than the house?"

"No."

Leaving the headlights on, Doc closed his door and leaned against the hood, frowning across at the old barn. I wondered if he'd picked up the scent of something foul, or if he were trying to figure out Cornelius's reasoning along with me.

"Then why do you want to have it in the barn?" Did he know about the faceless dead guy somehow? Had Detective Hawke been badgering him for information about me, too?

"I've always wanted to have a séance in an old barn."

He had to be kidding me. "What's the appeal?" I'd rather be warm and cozy tonight in Harvey's dining room with all of the lights on in the house.

"It's spookier than the house."

Exactly. I didn't need spookier. I was going to have enough trouble trying not to pee my pants tonight.

I heard the rumble of a truck coming up the road. Seconds later, the vehicle bounced toward us along the potholed driveway. Squinting in the headlights, I was pretty sure I knew who was about to join our little party.

The engine cut. The headlights clicked off. The driver's door opened and shut.

"Am I late?" Natalie asked, joining Cornelius and me on the right side of the Picklemobile.

"Just in time," I told her. "Cooper and Harvey should be

here any minute now."

"Do you know her?" Cornelius asked me.

Doc looked across the hood at me. "Did you tell her?"

"Yes and no," I answered both in turn. "Nat, you remember Cornelius Curion."

"Of course." She lightly slugged Cornelius on the arm. "Who could forget that hat?" She rounded the front of the truck, leaning on the hood next to Doc. "So, what's this clandestine meeting all about?" She pointed at Cornelius. "Did Cooper say it was okay to tell him about the *ed-day ody-bay* in the *afe-say*?" She switched to her top secret pig Latin.

Cornelius frowned at me. "Where was the body?"

I glared at Natalie. "Way to go, code talker." I turned to Cornelius. "I didn't think you understood that language."

"I don't. I told you before, I don't speak Spanish."

"Then how did you know about the dead body in the safe?"

"There was a safe involved? Like a gun safe or bigger?"

"You're saying you didn't just figure out Natalie's code words about the dead body we found out here a couple of weeks ago?"

"No. That is exciting news."

Not really. "Then how did you know about the body?"

"I didn't. Not that one anyway. I was referring to the dead body in the old cemetery you told me about on the way here."

"Cooper is going to put a bullet in your ass for letting that cat out of the bag," Natalie told me.

"Me? What are you talking about? It's your fault."

"Speaking of Cooper," Doc said. "I believe he's coming up the road now."

While we waited for Harvey's pickup to come up the drive, I asked where Claire and Katie were.

"They're on their way back to Arizona towing a moving trailer behind them."

Harvey rolled to a stop behind Natalie's truck, his country music blaring through the closed windows. Cooper was out the passenger door before his uncle shut off the engine. "Who invited Ms. Beals?"

"I did."

"This isn't a public event, Parker."

"She needed to be here."

He scoffed.

"What? She was here when we found the dead guy in the safe."

Not to mention that it was high time Natalie found out about this executioner business.

Cooper stormed up to me. "You told Curion about the damned body?"

"Not on purpose."

"Jesus Christ, Parker. Why don't you just start putting announcements in the paper?"

Cornelius leaned over to me. "This kind of negative energy is going to fog the channels."

"Cooper can't help it," I said. "He was snapping at the doctor on the way out of the womb."

"Just ignore Coop," old man Harvey said, sidling up next to me. "He's got his bloomers in a twist about someone maybe catchin' wind that we're here."

"Will you get fired?" Natalie asked.

"More like demoted even further," he told her.

"Now, Coop, I've told you before, there's nothin' wrong with writin' parkin' tickets for a livin'."

He nailed his uncle with a glare.

"Whose grandfather are we summoning tonight?" Cornelius asked.

"Mine." Harvey buttoned his canvas coat. "Grandpappy was an ornery cuss who had a real likin' for homemade hooch. He kept a still out back behind the barn. I got some bottles of it left down in my root cellar."

I'd tried Harvey's family hooch recipe before. It stripped some of the varnish from my esophagus going down and finished the job coming immediately back up.

"We're going to need some of that hooch." Cornelius grabbed his cases out of the back of the Picklemobile. "Plus something important to him. Better yet, something personal."

Harvey scratched his beard. "Well, if I remember right, besides the homemade hooch, he also liked painted ladies and guns—the bigger the better."

"Bigger guns or bigger ladies? Doc asked.

Cooper chuckled. "Probably both."

"Did he have a favorite?" Cornelius asked Harvey.

"Well, I remember a hip-heavy, strawberry blonde who went by the name … what was it … Ginger?" Harvey told him.

"We'll start with the gun."

"Grandpappy didn't go anywhere without his ol' shotgun."

"A talisman, perfect! Bring it to the barn." Cornelius led the way.

"What a great idea." Cooper crossed his arms, taking that wide-legged cop stance of his. "Uncle Willis, why don't you bring great grandfather's double-barreled, sawed-off shotgun to the barn?"

"Uh …" Harvey said, looking at me for help.

Don't look at me!

Cooper's glare landed on me. "Why is he looking at you, Parker?"

"I don't know." I hid my twitching, telltale nose.

"You could at least try to sound convincing when you lie."

I flipped Cooper off because he wasn't on duty and couldn't arrest me for anything.

"Are we really having a séance?" Natalie asked Doc.

"That's the plan."

"Why do I get the feeling this isn't the first time you guys have done this?"

"It's not," I told her. "I figured it would be easier to show you than tell you."

"Show me what? You're not going to sacrifice me to any demons or anything, right?"

"Not tonight," I said.

"Good, because I'm not wearing the right underwear to lure in any demons. With these granny panties, I'd be lucky to reel in a drunken sailor."

"We need to get moving," Cornelius called from in front of the barn doors. "Otherwise, we might not reach the ghost before midnight."

"What happens at midnight?" I asked.

"We lose the moonlight."

"And that's bad because … ?"

Cornelius looked at me like I was fresh off the turnip truck. "Why, Violet, I'm surprised you don't know."

"Know what?"

"Moonlight keeps the boogeyman away."

Chapter Twenty-Three

Meanwhile, back at the ranch …

This is stupid," I officially declared from my bale of straw throne in the middle of the old grain bin room. The same place we'd found the faceless body.

"Don't be such a spoilsport." Natalie giggled. "You look like you're doing a photoshoot for a gun magazine."

I snarled at her, even though she was right. Cornelius' bright idea for luring Harvey's grandpappy was to put all of the ghost's favorite vices in the center of the room: his shotgun, his hooch, and his preferred type of hanky panky partner. Unfortunately for me, Grandpappy had always preferred blondes, so here I sat instead of Natalie, looking like a big dodo, holding one of the bottles of homemade hooch from Harvey's root cellar and that ding dang sawed-off shotgun.

"I don't think this is going to work," I said to nobody in particular.

"Don't be a skeptic, Violet," Cornelius said from the sidelines where he was setting up one of the many meters he'd brought along. "You'll throw us off balance."

"Should I start om-ing now?" Natalie settled cross-legged on the straw-littered barn floor.

"Maybe we outta put Violet in a bikini," Harvey said from where he leaned against the big safe. "Grandpappy always had a hog-killin' time at the burlesque shows when they'd pass through Deadwood."

"I'm not wearing a bikini."

"She could just strip down to her bra and underwear," Natalie offered on my behalf.

"Keep it up, knucklehead," I hefted the old sawed-off

shotgun, pointing it in her direction, "and I'm gonna hobble your lip with some hot lead."

"Ya mean rock salt," Harvey said.

Cooper snorted at his uncle. "I still can't get over how that old shotgun magically appeared tonight. It's like a goddam miracle. Where did you say you found it again?"

Harvey mumbled something and then looked away, pretending to study the rafters.

I looked at Doc, who was standing off to the side watching us in silence. I wondered if he were ready for all of this. Neither Natalie, Cooper, nor Harvey had ever witnessed him at work. Was he feeling pre-performance butterflies like me? Or was he cool with being the center of attention?

"What do you think, Doc?" I asked. The meager light from Harvey's lantern would mask any of his usual signs that ghostly visitors had joined us.

"Think about what?" He stuffed his hands in his front pockets. "Natalie om-ing? The shotgun miraculously appearing? Or you stripping down?" He ended with a wink.

Harvey wheezed. "Oh, we know all about yer feelins when it comes to her unmentionables."

"Everything is ready." Cornelius brought us back to the business at hand, the séance. He'd switched his stove-pipe hat for his one-horned Viking hat. That must have been in one of the cases that he'd stacked on top of each other to use as a makeshift chair. He looked me over like I was one of his contraptions. "What's your state of mind, Violet?"

Chaotic, I thought, as my gaze bounced around the shadowy room.

Harvey frowned back at me while stroking his beard. "She looks like her banjo ain't tuned quite right."

Natalie peeked through her lashes at me from her corner of the loony bin, her arms resting on her knees. "Her Zen seems kinked."

Cooper had his arms crossed as he glared from his uncle to me and back again. "Do you two realize that by hiding that fucking shotgun you've contaminated a key piece of evidence? It's useless now."

My focus shifted to Doc. He nodded once, nudging his chin toward the empty corner of the room. I knew what that meant: we had wispy company in the room.

It was time to get the show rolling.

"I'm ready," I told Cornelius.

Doc came over and sat next to me on the bale of straw. "You ready, Killer?"

Hell, no! But I nodded my head, anyway.

"Take a drink from the bottle, Violet," Cornelius ordered.

I frowned at him. "This stuff will knock me on my ass."

"We need to attract Mr. Harvey's grandfather," Cornelius said. "Just one sip of his concoction."

But the ghost was already here … unless someone else was in here with us. I shot Doc a questioning look.

He took the bottle from me and pulled out the cork. Tipping it back, he swallowed with a grimace. "Jesus! That'll eat a hole clear through your stomach."

"She's got a kick," Harvey said, pride in his voice.

Doc held the bottle out to me. "Let's do this."

I took it, gagging down a big mouthful, coughing the fumes back up through my nose.

"I said a sip, Calamity Jane. Not a slug." Doc corked the bottle and looked at Cornelius. "Now what?"

"Sit on the floor next to her boots."

Doc slid down onto the floor.

"But remain in contact."

This was beginning to feel like a game of Twister.

Doc leaned against my leg.

"Should I do some more om-ing?" Natalie asked.

"Audience participation should remain at a minimum now."

Cooper groaned, clearly having trouble believing this hokum.

Doc pointed at the detective. "If Violet leaves the room, follow her, but don't stop her."

Skeptic or not, Cooper nodded once.

"I advise strongly against waking her, as well," Cornelius said. "Retrieving a channeler or medium from another plane of existence can be very dangerous … for everyone."

"Where d'ya think she's gonna amble off to?" Harvey asked.

Doc stared up at me. "Somewhere I can't follow."

"I'm not going to leave," I told him.

"I'm just taking precautions." He turned to Natalie. "If she leaves, you need to pull me out immediately."

"But didn't Cornelius just say that's dangerous?"

"I don't care."

"But how do I even do that?"

"Pinching or biting works best, I've found," I told her.

She laughed.

I didn't.

"This is the real deal, isn't it?" she said, sobering. When I nodded, her forehead wrinkled. "You have some explaining to do when this is over."

"What about me?" Harvey asked. "What's my job?"

"Your role is to speak to your grandfather," Cornelius answered. "When I start, you'll call to him, asking questions that will draw him out of the shadows."

I glanced at the corner Doc had pointed to earlier. I had a feeling the old ghost was waiting for his cue.

"What sorta questions?"

"Those to which only he will know the answer. Once he's here, you can ask other questions."

"Like who committed the murder and why," Cooper added.

Harvey harrumphed, muttering something about getting stuck with the lousy cook wagon duties.

Silence settled into the room. Something rattled up in the rafters. A piece of metal clanged somewhere outside of the barn. I could hear my heart beating, smell the straw and dust and dry-rotted wood all around me, feel the cool air trickling over my face.

Doc leaned his head back against my thigh, closing his eyes. "Stay close, Killer." He spoke so quietly that I wasn't sure if he'd actually said it or I made it up.

Cornelius began to chant his magical come hither song. He was using more guttural tones this time, reminding me of a pow-wow song I'd heard during a television special about the Lakota Sioux tribe.

Taking a deep breath, I closed my eyes, too. I tried to clear my mind, as Cornelius had taught me, by thinking about the flame of a candle.

The flame flickered, shrinking and then growing several times, mesmerizing me.

A breeze made it ripple, the tip swaying back and forth before straightening out again.

It rounded, forming a perfect teardrop of fire.

Then something blew it out.

My heart thudded in the blackness, picking up speed.

In the darkness, I heard a crunching sound, like someone eating a handful of corn nuts.

I took a step toward the noise, but a hand caught mine.

"Whoa there, Killer," said a voice that wasn't Doc's. The tone was a little higher, slightly twangy, but the use of Doc's new nickname for me kept me from pulling free. "Don't go sniffin' in the direction of that deviltry. I got somethin' to show ya."

The hand tugged me along, pulling me into a silvery world lit by moonlight. We stood in what I thought was Harvey's driveway, but his house looked different, smaller, missing the section where the master bedroom should be. I eyeballed the barn. It too was different. The neglected building was now obviously well-kept, shining brightly in the lunar lit world, freshly whitewashed.

"This ol' place used to make me as proud as a peacock with two tails." The old man standing next to me let go of my hand. He tugged a dark glass bottle from his coat pocket and yanked the cork out with his teeth. "But then," he spoke around the cork, "my addle-headed son—worthless as owl shit he was—ran it into the ground. That boy never could get it into his thick skull that liquor was fer pleasure, not breakfast."

Great Caesar's ghost! Or rather Grandpappy's ghost. Doc and Cornelius had done it. They'd managed to lure in Harvey's grandfather. It sort of boggled my mind when I tried to wrestle with the time-space conundrum. I could use a few moments to wrap my brain around it all, but I had a feeling there was no time to sit and gather wool.

Grandpappy pocketed the cork and tipped back the bottle. "Woo! That'll put some hair on yer chest." He held the bottle out to me. "Have a snort, purty lady."

I reared back. "I'm hairy enough, thanks."

He wiggled his bushy brows at me, reminding me of his grandson. "Don't be flirtin' with me now. It's been a long time since I smelled someone as sweet as honeysuckle. Hell, my horns are so big, I can't hardly get my hat on anymore."

While I pondered if that meant what I thought it did, he took another drink.

Harvey looked a little like his grandfather, from the shape of his eyes to his open barn door ears and the slope of his forehead. Grandpappy's beard was more scraggly, though. He was also taller and whip-cord thin, sort of a mixed version between his grandson and Cooper.

Shrugging, he corked the bottle. "Have it yer way, but yer gonna wish ya had some of this here bottled courage after ya hear the cross-grained shenanigans those whangdoodles have been up to."

Whangdoodles. That was the name Harvey often used for the kooky folks who lived back in Slagton, a *nearly* ghost town located not far from this very ranch. Years back a mining accident had made the ground water undrinkable. It had thinned out the population except for a few stubborn oddballs who'd dug in their claws, refusing to abide by the EPA's warnings and head for safer ground.

The crunching sound was growing louder. "Do you hear that?" I asked.

"What?"

"Never mind." It must be something to do with the séance. Harvey was probably eating crackers again while I faced off with another paranormal being.

"I buried it all out behind the chicken coop in some ol' tins."

I frowned. "You what now?"

He held up the double-barreled, sawed-off shotgun I'd had on my lap at the start of the séance, but the wire around the triggers was missing. "That young whippersnapper five-fingered it before cuttin' dirt out of the house."

"What whippersnapper?"

He cocked his head to the side, stroking his beard like his

grandson often did. "Well, from what I figure, he was fixin' to play a little hide-n-seek. But that humbug got the budge on him. After that, he was a gone sucker."

"What's a humbug?"

"Ya mean the odd fish? Oh, his heart was all played out after their little fuss back in the bone yard."

"Who? The what yard?" Criminy, I was starting to feel like we were operating on two completely different planes.

"The whippersnapper." He handed me the shotgun stock first, which I took without thinking, noticing the same rectangular tin tag Cooper had shown to Harvey riveted to the wood. "That humbug done did run against a pill, but the rock salt made it techy as a teased snake. It ain't like the others that been here before."

"You mean the rock salt in the cartridges in this shotgun?" I held it up. As in the same rock salt Cooper had said was embedded in the barn wall? Was Grandpappy trying to tell me what had happened to the dead guy?

"Yes, ma'am."

Then I honed in on one particular word. "What *others* do you mean?"

"You sure are as purty as a field of bluebonnets." His focus drifted lower. "Nice breedin' hips, too."

Right, well breeding was one of my specialties. "Do you know who the man in the safe was? And what *others* do you mean? When had they been here?"

He held his finger to his lips, shushing me, and then cocked his head to the side again. "Well, some of them there hard cases are ugly as a mud fence. Masks make 'em bearable."

What in the world was he talking about? The masks in Harvey's tool shed? Crikey, I needed a translator.

"Way back," he continued, "long 'fore we got the deed ta this place, t'others started usin' it like some sorta stage stop, droppin' 'em off at odd times."

"Dropping off what?"

He lowered his gaze to me. "The unwanted, purty lady. Although, this whippersnapper wasn't s'posed ta be here. But ol' milky eyes was on the hunt again. That humbug always did like ta play with his food 'fore usin' one of his pig stickers on it."

I couldn't follow the ghost's one-sided conversation, and the crunching was growing louder and louder, making it hard for me to hear as well as focus. I looked around, searching for the source of the sound, wishing Harvey would come strolling out of the shadows with a boxful of crackers. I found nothing but dark skies and moonlight shadows. The crunching continued, mixed with a scratching sound every so often.

"You're hearing that, right?" I said, still searching the shadows. "Surely you must hear that."

"That crazy fool tried to pull foot, but once ol' milky eyes gets yer scent, there's no shakin' him. He figured the safe would hide him well enough, but he was dead wrong."

"Who's ol' milky eyes?"

"I reckon he shouldn't have lit from the whangdoodles. They may be ravin' distracted, but they don't mess around with their prey, they just kill it. Ol' milky eyes, though, he's downright ringy, always playin' with his food first. That runner's heart gave out before ol' milky eyes even poked his head in that safe, lucky for him. Otherwise, he'd been screamin' for mercy when the humbug cut the skin off his face."

I stood there stunned for several seconds as my brain translated and filled in what blanks it could. "So, milky eyes is one and the same as the humbug? And he's the one who cut the skin off the guy's face? And the guy was dead when it happened?"

Was I getting this … *crunch, scratch, crunch, crunch*.

"Ol' milky eyes came back later to play s'more. Boy howdy, ya shoulda heard that humbug roar when it found that safe empty."

Crunch, crunch, scratch, CRUNCH.

"How can you not hear that?" I asked, glaring over at the barn. It seemed to be coming from around back, loud and clear in the moonlit night.

"I never have seen anyone escape those pig stickers, human or the others."

"What *others*?" Was he talking about Aunt Zoe's Others?

"The mead?" he asked.

I scratched my head, wondering if I'd somehow missed the segue to the topic of mead.

"Oh, ya mean in my chicken coop? They were left by the grave digger. He got into neck trouble before he could send the message back to Slagton to come fer it."

CRUNCH! CRUNCH! CRUNCH!

I winced, the noise grating on my nerves as much as the sound of my kids fighting.

That was it. I needed to find Harvey and make him stop. This conversation was confusing enough without his chewing. "I'll be right back," I told Grandpappy.

"That shotgun don't work no more."

"I need to wire the triggers back, I know. Your grandson filled me in."

He crossed his arms. "Yer all balled up. That there is some bad medicine."

Being balled up is bad medicine? I waved off his confusing babble. "I'll be right back. I need to go tell your grandson to chew with his lips closed."

I rounded the barn, searching the moonlit world, but found nothing. Leading with the shotgun, I followed the crunching sound further back, around the chicken coop and into the shadows beyond.

The crunching stopped.

Then I realized what I was doing and fear stopped my feet cold.

What in the hell was wrong with me? I'd left Doc back with Grandpappy.

"Time to go, Killer," I whispered and turned around.

But the barn was gone.

The chicken coop and tool shed were missing, too.

In their place was a graveyard, tombstones all around, some straight and regal, others slanted or broken into pieces. They stretched up a knoll and over into the trees.

My heart ratcheted up. This wasn't the Harvey family graveyard. It was bigger with many more tombstones. The trees and hills were in the wrong places. I was still in the Black Hills but not on Harvey's property.

A cold wind blew across my face, making my shivers crawl even deeper under my skin.

I heard scratching right behind me, like fingernails on wood.

What was that?

Too afraid to look, I stood there telling myself over and over again: *There's nothing there.*

CRUNCH! CRUNCH! CRUNCH!

Drawing a shaking breath of courage, I looked over my shoulder.

What I saw made that shaky breath whoosh out like I'd been gut punched.

Not ten tombstones away in a partially dug up grave squatted a creature outlined in shadows. Every muscle in my body went into lockdown. My heart even paused to assess just how screwed I was.

A distant soundtrack from my memory replayed, Harvey's voice echoing from a day months ago in Bighorn Billy's diner … *spiked teeth, claws like scythes, and a coat made up of its victims scalps.*

The description fit. I was too far away to confirm the scalps, though. From where I stood, it looked more like patches of white fur.

The White Grizzly was what Cooper had called it, mentioning something about a legend that had been passed down from the Lakota Sioux tribe. That must mean this thing had been around since before the miners and ranchers had come to the Black Hills. Was it here before the Sioux, too? Or was there more than one?

I watched in silence as it scratched at and tore into the top of a coffin, pulled out a skull and bit into it, chewing like it was an apple.

There it was, that crunching sound that had been driving me nuts since I'd closed my eyes back in the barn. I winced with each bite, the sound reverberating in my eardrums. Why was it so damned loud? Was that my clue? Was I supposed to take on this vile creature and execute it? Why couldn't it look like a Care Bear, for crissake, so that all I had to do was rip out some stuffing and dropkick the thing into the trees?

Grunting, it threw what remained of the skull to the side and tugged on a leg bone, tearing it free of a pant leg.

What had Harvey been telling me that bright summer day so long ago? Something about the sheriff's crew, which had included Cooper back then, finding a bunch of the graves dug up, coffins opened, bones chewed on? Why did it eat the bones? The marrow would be long decayed. It didn't make sense. Then again, neither did the séance, Harvey's hooch-guzzling grandfather, or me standing here in some graveyard that just appeared out of the dark.

Scratch, scratch, CRUNCH! CRUNCH!

Moving at a snail's pace, I faced it head on, taking care not to disrupt its late night need for munchies. Then I realized something—I still held the sawed-off shotgun.

Bullets won't kill it.

So what, I told the know-it-all voice in my head. Having the weapon in my hand made me feel less like peeing my pants.

Something off to the side of the graveyard caught its attention. Then I heard it, too—twigs breaking underfoot. Someone or something was coming.

The White Grizzly lowered the femur it was chewing, its head cocking slightly as it stared out across the graves. I followed its gaze but saw nothing under the moonlight: just tombstones, wrought-iron fences and gates, and dark pine trees.

When I looked back, the thing was staring right at me.

Oh. Hell.

I turned to marble, trying to camouflage myself with the other gravestones behind me.

A guttural growling rumbled from dark lips pulled back in a snarl. Dropping the femur into the grave, it rose up on its hind legs.

And up and up.

Holy fucked up freaky-ass shit!

That must be why they called it the White Grizzly and not the White Sorta Big Weasel. It was huge! I wished it really was just a bear. I took a step back, my feet already putting Operation Run-Like-Hell into effect.

It took a few lumbering steps toward me, sniffing the air in my direction. Its growl grew louder. "*Scharfrichter*," it said in a gravelly voice.

I blinked in surprise. Had it just spoken?

While I was still trying to decide if my mind was playing tricks on me, it dropped down onto all fours.

Uh oh. That couldn't be good. Was this really happening? I clutched the shotgun tighter.

It twisted its head from side to side. Its movements were slow and deliberate, a true hunter stalking its prey.

And I was the deer in its sights tonight. What in the hell was this grotesque monstrosity? More importantly, what was it doing in my distorted dream? Or had I invaded its spine-chilling world?

I lifted the double barrels, widening my stance. Bullets might not kill it, but maybe they would give it a good limp and give me a solid head start. As my jacket sleeve slid back, Aunt Zoe's charm bracelet flashed, the silver and mirrored glass reflecting the moonlight.

The creature screeched as if in pain, the sharp sound piercing my ears. I cowered back another step, half in fear, half in pain.

"What—the—fuck—is—that?" Cooper enunciated from behind me off to the left.

The sound of the detective's voice jarred me out of my concentration on the creature. My gaze whipped in his direction. Behind him were Harvey's outbuildings, the chicken coop not sixty feet away. I glanced around, realizing the tombstones had changed, many disappeared. The cemetery had shrunk. Realization struck—I was back on the ranch, standing knee high in the grass back in Harvey's family graveyard.

And Cooper was there, his gun raised.

Unfortunately, so was the White Grizzly, its guttural growling even noisier. My anxiety rose along with its volume, my heart and pulse racing in a dead heat.

"Parker, get behind me," the detective ordered, his handgun out and aimed at the White Grizzly.

"Cooper, that gun won't stop it."

"Six bullets might damned well slow it down."

That was a nice theory, but I really wasn't looking forward to testing it. The beast took a step in Cooper's direction.

With my gaze still on the White Grizzly, I spoke to the hard-headed man. "Christ, Cooper, listen to me. Put the damned gun down and let me handle this."

"Bad idea, Parker." He pulled the trigger, a gunshot exploding in the clear night air.

That mule-headed son of a bitch!

The bullet hit the creature with a thick-sounding thud. It looked down where it had taken the shot, seeming more surprised than hurt. It glared back at Cooper and let out a roar that shook me clear to my boots.

"Way to go, Johnny Ringo," I said to him, closing the distance between us with several quick strides. "Now you've managed to piss off both of us."

The White Grizzly bared its fangs at Cooper and lunged.

Everything happened so fast, my brain didn't seem to keep up.

Cooper held his gun steady, unloading five more rapid shots into the beast before it reached him. The bullets didn't seem to faze the creature at all. It moved with lightning quickness, pouncing and knocking the detective onto his back. They rolled on the ground as Cooper struggled to throw it off, grunting and cussing the whole time. The beast gained the upper hold, pinning the detective down with its weight, its sharp claws sinking into his leather coat. Cooper shouted in pain. When it raised one front leg, its claws fully extended, I saw my window of opportunity.

Flipping the shotgun around, I gripped the double barrels and went in swinging. Babe Ruth had nothing on me.

My first swing caught it along the jaw with a solid *thwack*, sending it rolling sideways from the detective. Before it could recover, I leapt over Cooper and spun round quickly to increase my momentum, bringing the stock of the shotgun down on its skull with all the strength I could muster.

Something cracked and the beast staggered several gravestones to the right, shaking its head while snarling and whimpering. Then it let out a snorting growl and stood up on its hind legs, towering.

"You okay, Cooper?" I kept my focus on the beast.

"I think so," he said from behind me. I heard the grass rustle as he got to his feet. "What in the hell is that thing?"

"That's your White Grizzly you told me about."

It hulked menacingly, roaring at me.

"Jesus, I always thought that was an old wives' tale used to keep kids from screwing around in graveyards."

The creature shook its head a couple of times.

"You really rang its bell," Cooper told me. "Did you look into those milky eyes? I saw some fucked up shit there for a minute."

Ol' milky eyes ... This beast was what Harvey's grandfather had been talking about earlier. It was what had hunted down and defaced the dead guy.

I heard a small clinking sound next to me but didn't want to take my eyes off the beast. "What're you doing?" I asked Cooper.

"Loading my gun."

"I told you that bullets don't work."

"They make me feel better."

I knew that exact line of thinking, but I couldn't resist a jab. "Next time we hang out in a graveyard together, I'll be sure to bring your binkie and favorite blanket along."

"Shut the hell up, Parker."

The beast lowered onto all fours, getting into lunging position again.

"Don't even think about it, you ugly motherfucker," I heard Cooper say, raising his firearm again.

I repositioned my hold on the shotgun, knowing what I had to do. "Cooper."

"Yeah?"

"If you shoot me by accident, I'm going to come back and haunt your ass."

Before I could chicken out, I raced at it, circling around to the side, trying to catch the hunter by surprise. It tried to adjust and lunge at me, but I was able to cut sideways and dodge out of its path, jabbing the shotgun toward its face like it was a lance. The end of the barrel connected, nailing it in one of its milky eyes.

The roar that followed was a mix of rage and pain.

The momentum from my dash and jab sent me spinning, my boot connecting with a small gravestone sticking up out of the ground. I tried to catch my balance but stumbled. The shotgun whacked into a crumbling headstone, jarring it from my grip as I staggered further and fell onto my hands and knees. My chest just missed being pierced by a rusted metal rod stuck in the ground decorated with a circle and star midway down.

The creature recovered more quickly than I did, undoubtedly fueled by the need to rip my face from my skull, too. It sprung toward me while Cooper unloaded more lead into it.

I rolled onto my side and reached for the shotgun, but the White Grizzly beat me to it, knocking it aside.

It circled me, its teeth gnashing, its remaining milky eye sizing me up. The smell of its breath reminded me of roadkill, making me gag. It shook its head again, my earlier blow still giving it grief.

A sudden coolness spread through my limbs, a euphoric feeling almost. Somehow, someway, I was going to kill this nasty son of a bitch tonight and put an end to its reign of terror.

"You wanna dance?" I heard a voice ask, and then realized it was mine. Before I knew it, I was up on one knee, poised like a runner on the starting block, ready to go head to head. "I'll teach you the Two-step."

The White Grizzly snorted at me. I could hear its breath rattling in and out, every click of its teeth, each scratch of its claws in the dirt as it circled me.

"Violet!" Doc's voice cut through my focus.

"Stay back, Doc." This bastard was mine.

I glanced off to the side for the shotgun, but it was not to be seen, hidden in the tall grass.

"Here kitty, kitty," Doc taunted from off to my left.

The White Grizzly looked his way, the low growl starting up again.

I glanced in Doc's direction, too, wondering what in the hell he was doing. Not ten feet away, he stood next to a crooked tombstone, the charm Aunt Zoe had given him dangling in the moonlight.

"Doc, are you trying to get yourself fileted?"

"Just buying you time, Killer."

With the shotgun out of reach, bludgeoning it to death was off the table. I needed something sharp, something to bury in its ugly hide.

The beast snarled at Doc, taking another step closer.

Doc was acting as bait, and if I didn't find something to kill this vile thing real quick, he might end up as a meal.

Then I remembered the rod that had almost impaled me. With a solid tug, I pulled it free. The end that had been in the ground was pointy, not as sharp as I'd like, but it would do in a pinch.

The creature leaned back on its haunches, getting ready to lunge at Doc.

Without a sound, I attacked first, moving like my boots were on fire. It dodged too late, unable to escape me as I drove down hard with the rod, trying to penetrate its wide back. Its hide was thick, withstanding the pointed metal for a split second. Doubling my efforts, I put my weight into it, shoving harder with a grunt. Finally the rod plunged through, sinking into the beast with a swift, sickening ease.

The White Grizzly roared, rolling onto its side, taking me with it while its claws swiped wildly at my face, arms, and chest, almost catching me once or twice

I rolled off of it, scrambling to my feet again.

"Violet," Natalie yelled from behind me. "Catch!"

I raised my hand without thinking as I turned her way, plucking the old shotgun from the air as it flew toward me. Just as my dad had taught me years ago when I was learning how to belt a softball into the outfield, I choked up on the barrels and tightened my grip. Striding over to where it writhed in the grass, I stood over it just as its claws reached around and tugged the metal rod free. A dark fluid coated the white fur around the wound.

It hissed at me, lunging upward with snapping teeth.

I easily dodged the attack and then planted my boots firmly on the ground. "Go back to whatever hell you came from, you nasty son of a bitch."

It bared its teeth again.

I didn't wait for further invitation and swung, catching it square in the side of the head.

The crack reverberated up through the gun barrels, making my hands sting with pins and needles. The stock splintered, a chunk of wood flying off into the darkness, making it a ragged, wooden dagger.

The White Grizzly slumped to the ground, looking up at me through its one milky eye, its breath wheezing. A whimpering sound rose from its chest, sounding human-like.

"Say goodnight, Gracie." I raised the shotgun again, this time with the double barrels pointed skyward, and buried the splintered stock into the beast's chest.

The milky eye rolled up, its jaw sagged open, a black tongue lolled out.

All was silent.

The job was done.

"Goodnight," I whispered.

Someone grabbed me by the shoulders, pulling me back and away from the dead beast. "You're bleeding," Doc said, turning me to face him. He lifted my arm. For the first time, I noticed the gashes in my coat sleeve.

Holding his rib cage, Cooper walked over to the beast, prodding it with his boot and then leaned over it when it stayed dead. Then he jumped back. "Jesus! It's moving."

Doc pushed me behind him.

"Wait," Cooper said. "Actually, I think it's melting."

"What?"

We joined him, staring down at it. He patted his pockets and then pulled out a flashlight from an inside one and shined it on the beast.

Cooper was right. It was melting like an ice cream cone on a sun drenched sidewalk, leaving a white gooey mess on the grass.

"What in the hell was that thing?" Natalie came up beside me, grabbing my arm as she stared down at it.

"The White Grizzly," Cooper muttered, scrubbing a hand down his face.

"I thought that was just an old wives' tale," she said, echoing Cooper's earlier words.

Within seconds, the notorious White Grizzly was nothing but a big puddle of goo. Then the goo began to darken, turning into a black tar like substance that bubbled once or twice before sinking down into the earth. Within minutes, nothing was left but a stain on the grass.

"Well," Natalie said, walking over and plopping down onto a gravestone. "Now I've seen just about everything. Where's that hooch of Harvey's?"

Actually we were just getting started, but now wasn't the time to drop that bomb on her after what she'd just witnessed.

I frowned up at Doc. "You could have gotten yourself killed, damn it."

He frowned back. "I told you not to leave my side."

Natalie laughed, a hard, cold, jarring laugh. "And here I

figured we'd light some candles tonight, play with a Ouija board a little, and tell a ghost story or two." She shivered, pulling her jacket tight around her. "I'll say one thing—you guys really know how to throw a kickass séance."

"Where are Cornelius and Harvey?" I looked around, worried at their absence.

"I left Cornelius in the barn," Doc said. "He was excited about something he'd caught on one of his recorders."

"Harvey is over by his chicken coop," Natalie said.

I peered in that direction, not seeing any movement in the thick shadows of the setting moon. "What's he doing there?"

"Digging for tins of money."

Chapter Twenty-Four

Saturday, November 3rd

Meanwhile, back in Deadwood …

The morning dawned. Period. Thank God.

After last night's fun and games with old milky eyes, the sight of the sun's rays coming through my bedroom window made me feel like dancing the Charleston across the floor.

I sat up, stretching my sore back muscles. Man, I needed Doc's magic hands. Turned out killing was tough on a body, especially for an aging, out of shape mother of two.

Something grunted beside me. Or was that a snore?

I looked over. There was a lump under the covers.

"Natalie?" I whispered, trying to remember last night's events after leaving Harvey's ranch. It was a blur after the adrenaline rush in the graveyard. Cooper's sore ribs, Natalie's questions, Harvey's broken shotgun, Doc's insistence on getting me back home and safe.

The lump moved. The covers lifted and fell slightly with each breath.

I reached over and grabbed the top of my comforter, pulling it down several inches. Tuffs of white hair poked out from under the covers.

What the … ? I yanked it down.

A pair of milky eyes stared up at me.

I opened my mouth to scream, but nothing came out.

Its black lips pulled back from a set of sharp, blood-stained teeth.

A creaky sound escaped from my throat.

It snarled. Then it lunged up at me, teeth snapping.

I tried to scream again, but nothing came out.

Wake up!

I snapped upright in bed and screamed for real, blinking awake. Dark clouds filled the sky outside my bedroom window. Chicken feathers floated in the air. I caught sight of tail feathers racing out my half-open door into the hallway.

Holding my chest, I groaned and flopped back onto my pillow.

"Hells bells!" Natalie said from beside me in the bed. "You just scared five years off my life, woman!"

I looked over into her wide eyes. "I warned you about sleeping with me, but you were too big a chicken shit to stay on the couch."

"Sticks and stones, baby cakes, but creepy otherworldly beasts scare the chicken shit right out of me."

"Me, too."

"There was no way I was sleeping alone last night." She rolled onto her side facing me and leaned on her elbow. "Sorry to kick Doc out of your bed."

"You didn't kick him out. If he'd stayed, he would have slept on the couch. I don't think the kids are ready to see him gracing my sheets yet."

"Now that I've been tried by fire, tell me my dear best friend whom I've known since we were little kids, what in the heck is going on with you and how come I'm just now finding out about all of this freaky crap?"

I started with the easy answer. "What's going on with me is I've recently found out that I'm an executioner."

Her eyebrows scrunched up. "I've always wondered, is the black hood mandatory per the executioner union rules or could you wear something more uplifting, like a rainbow wig, and still be up to code?"

"Those rainbow wigs always itch."

"I suppose scratching while up there in front of the angry mob would look unprofessional."

"Exactly. You know how image conscious I am these days." That was actually true now that Jerry commented on each of my outfits.

Her grin flat-lined. "An executioner? What the blazes?"

I took a deep breath and let the whole long story gush out, starting with what happened at Mudder Brothers when I stabbed the albino juggernaut in the back, continuing through my bathroom party with the deadly bitch at the Opera House, including the bit about Ms. Wolff and the trick with mirrors during the séance in her apartment and ending with Aunt Zoe's version of my family history and my current role.

"Wow." She massaged her temples, like she was having trouble fitting my story between them. "Do you know how nutty that sounds?"

"It's a sure-fire guarantee for a straightjacket."

"And a padded room." She rolled onto her back, shaking her head at the ceiling. "Damn, Vi."

"I know." Then I remembered Prudence. "Oh, I forgot to tell you about the other executioner."

Her expression was raised eyebrows and round peepers. "There's another one?"

I nodded. "She lives at the Carhart house up in Lead. Well, she doesn't really 'live' there because she's dead. Prudence can only talk to me by temporarily possessing the living and using them as microphones."

"No way." She covered her eyes with the heels of her palms. "This is all so …"

I threw back the covers. "You already said nutty."

"*Unreal.*"

"I wish." I would have loved to go back to my pre-killer life. I stood and stretched, my body one big bruised muscle. My extra-long T-shirt felt heavy on my aching shoulders. Was this what boxers felt like the morning after a few rounds in the ring? I needed to soak in a vat of Epsom salt.

"But when I think about how you moved last night …" She trailed off again.

I bent over, reaching for my toes. My lower back twanged. *Ouch!* "What do you mean?"

"You were fast."

I hadn't felt any different from normal. "Fast like when I chase down the ice cream truck?"

She snorted. "Way faster. I'm talking freaky fast and really strong."

I bent to the side, stretching my arm upward. "I was wearing deodorant, smartass."

"I'm serious, Vi. Think about it. You broke the stock of a shotgun over that thing's head. That's not normal."

I stood upright, frowning at her. "Are you forgetting my high school softball batting record?"

"Yeah, but belting homeruns was something you were good at almost two decades ago." She sat up, my smiley face pajama top buttoned crookedly up her chest. "That thing was huge, like a big bear."

I stretched the other way, wincing at the stabbing pain in my shoulder. "I remember."

"And it was pissed off."

Yeah, and anti-*Sharfrichter*. I pointed at the bandage wrap on my forearm where it had left its still-stinging mark. "I noticed."

"Hitting it with a shotgun shouldn't have knocked it for a loop like it did, especially considering it was a girl doing the swinging." She balled up her pillow and hugged it against her stomach. "You're like the bionic woman."

I cupped my hand to my ear. "Na-na-na-na-na," I said, pretending to have super-duper hearing. "You hear that? Someone's calling for us."

"That's the bionic man's sound, dipshit."

Paradoxically, my cell phone rang.

"See, I was right, you can hear into the future." Natalie grabbed my cell phone from the nightstand. "And lookee here." She held out the phone. "It's your bionic boyfriend."

Sure enough, Doc's name was on the screen. "It was Radar O'Reilly from MASH who could hear things before they happened, dork," I said, taking the phone. "The bionic woman could hear stuff from far away."

"Same difference."

I took the call. "*Bonjour*, Gomez. How'd you sleep?"

"Tell Steve Austin I want to feel the muscles on his bionic arm," Natalie said.

I mimed zipping her lips closed.

"My bed is cold and lonely without you, Tish."

"We'll have to do something about that."

"Okay."

Okay? What did that mean? Wait. I wasn't going to go down that rabbit hole. "You coming over for breakfast, or did you eat already?" I asked him a safe, easy question.

"We already ate."

"We?"

"Cooper woke me up before dawn."

"How considerate of him." I rubbed my lower back muscles. All of that shotgun swinging had really done a number on me. "Why?"

"He had something on his mind."

"Besides Smith and Wesson's newest revolver?"

He chuckled. "He wanted to go back out to the ranch."

I stopped massaging. "Why?"

"To check the nest."

"The nest? You mean that cave up on the hill behind Harvey's place? The place they found those teeth and old clothes?"

Natalie scrambled off the bed and put her ear next to mine, listening in.

"An abandoned mine, actually," Doc said, "and yes—that nest."

"Did he go out there?"

"Yes, *we* did."

"He dragged you along?" That wasn't normal police procedure for Cooper.

"I offered to go with him."

"You offered to go with a prickly detective to a spooky ranch in the dark and climb up to a creepy, weird mine after what happened there last night?"

"The sun was coming up, and we were armed. He played nice and shared his weapons."

"Don't get me started on those damned guns of his."

"He was hurting. I didn't think he should climb up there alone."

Natalie got all squinty eyed, her upper lip wrinkling.

Apparently, last night's quarrel with the mulish detective still stung.

The White Grizzly had left its mark on Cooper when it had tackled him, its weight bruising, maybe more. Natalie had wanted him to go to the ER to make sure there was no internal damage and maybe get some stitches where a couple of its claws had torn through his leather coat. He'd flat out refused, not wanting any record of the night's events on file.

"Are his ribs still hurting? Or is it something else?"

"Just the ribs. He thinks one might be fractured. Maybe two."

He needs to go to the hospital! Natalie mouthed.

I shushed her with my finger. "I told the bozo not to shoot at that thing, but he's too hard-headed to listen."

"Reminds me of someone else."

"What's that supposed to mean?"

"I told you not to leave my side."

Natalie pointed at the phone, then her nose, then me.

I reached out and flicked her nose for taking Doc's side. "Come on," I said to Doc. "Let's not do this dance again." We'd waltzed plenty last night about this deviation I'd made in the game plan. I changed the subject. "Did you find anything up at the mine?"

"The body. What was left of it, anyway."

Natalie grimaced. I concurred.

"Had the bone eater worked on it some more?" I asked, thinking of those scary teeth from my nightmare.

"That was our conclusion."

"That's horrible." I sat on the bed.

Natalie dropped down next to me, still listening in.

"Do the cops even have a clue who the victim was?"

"Cooper didn't say and I didn't ask."

"How did the body get back out to the ranch?"

"That's still up for debate." I heard a mumbling sound in the background. "Cooper wants to talk to you."

"Now?" I was a shower and a tooth brushing away from being ready to verbally spar with the detective.

"No. He wants to meet at The Old Prospector in an hour."

I'd have to call in to work, see what was going on with the
TV crew and how Jerry felt about my being late. "Why there?"

"Because Cornelius called me."

"He called you?"

"He was looking for a 'Violet Parker' and mentioned
something about the need for a protein shake."

Why hadn't the bonehead called me? Scratch that. Cornelius
wasn't much of one for making sense, especially this early in the
morning before his precious shake.

"When I explained who he'd actually called, he told me we
both needed to come over and listen to the recording of the
séance."

"Did he hear something odd?"

"Something odd at a séance with you, Killer?" Doc laughed.
"When does that ever happen?"

"Listen, wise guy, you're like two coffees ahead of me here."

"You should have spent the night with me. I'd have woken
you up with something more invigorating than caffeine."

Natalie covered her heart and pretended to swoon. I shoved
her backward on the bed.

"Promises, promises," I said to Doc. "Did Cornelius give a
clue about what's on the recording?"

"No. He mentioned that he wants to see if you have answers
the rest of us don't, and then he told me to have you bring a
protein shake with us along with some licorice—the old
fashioned kind—and hung up."

Did he mean the black licorice? Did he want it in his protein
shake? I shook those thoughts away and returned to the more
normal topic—the séance. "Why would I have these elusive
answers?"

"Because you talked to Harvey's grandfather."

"I thought Harvey talked to him."

"No, Harvey was asking the questions."

"But didn't his grandfather speak through you or Cornelius?"

"No, his grandfather was speaking through you."

"Me?"

"At least he was until you walked out of the séance."

* * *

Doc was waiting for me in the parking garage near Cornelius's hotel. I was so busy ogling him in his green flannel shirt and black jeans that I almost ran into the concrete barrier in front of me.

After I'd killed the motor, Doc came around to the driver's side door and opened it for me. "Brakes giving you trouble?" he asked with a gleam in his eyes.

"Yeah, that's it."

His focus lowered. "Nice sweater. It looks soft, makes me want to touch." He dragged his gaze back up to mine. "Where's your sidekick?"

"Nat took Addy and Layne down to my parents' place for the night." I climbed out of the Picklemobile, reaching back to collect my purse and Cornelius's precious protein drink. "She had some stuff to take care of down in Rapid." Like making sure her aunt's house was all shut up for the winter now that Claire and Katie had left.

"You're wearing jeans." Doc shut the door behind me. "And your boots."

"Jerry told me to take the day off. Dickie's too sick to film." I hoisted my purse on my shoulder. "He lost his voice, so he sent the camera crew back to the studio for a week to start editing the footage they already have. Where's Detective Crabbyass?" I started across the parking garage. "Getting his daily dose of doughnut sweetener?"

"Hold on a second, Boots." Doc caught my hand and anchored me to a stop.

I looked back. "What? Did I leave the lights on?" I didn't remember turning them on in the first place, but Doc had a way of flipping my brain on its side.

He pulled me toward him. "You have the day off, your kids are gone for the night, and you're wearing those boots?"

"Yep, yep, and yep."

Taking my purse and the protein drink from me, he set both on the Picklemobile. "Do you have any plans?"

Now that my arms were free, I wrapped them around his

waist, sliding my hands over his back pockets. "One or two."

"Like what?"

"Flirting with my boyfriend."

"Really? To what end?"

I shrugged. "Something titillating."

"I like it when you titillate." He tipped my chin up and kissed me. "Especially when you're wearing those boots."

He tasted like a tall drink of sex and smelled like long-legged, finger-licking male goodness. What was that he'd said earlier about giving me something more invigorating than caffeine? "Do you have any clients this morning?"

"Not a one all day." He kissed me again, his hands testing out the softness of my sweater as he backed me into the side of the Picklemobile. "I'm all yours, Boots."

I think he had that backwards, especially with the way he was making me steamy in this chilly garage. I pulled his mouth back down to mine and showed him as much.

His hands slid under my sweater, feathering over my skin, making my head float clear up to the next parking level.

Somewhere between Doc's magic touch and heaven, someone honked a horn, long and rude. It echoed throughout the concrete walls, scaring my libido back into its cave.

"Hey!" Cooper barked out his window. "This is a public garage." His tires screeched as he pulled into a parking spot across from us.

Doc cursed under his breath, stepping back from me as Cooper climbed out of his car. "You have rotten timing, Coop."

The detective snorted. "Seems to me I arrived in the nick of time. Parker would probably have bitten your head off as soon as you'd finished."

"Wrong again, *Coop*," I said and bared my teeth at him. "I keep these babies sharpened only for you."

"That's 'Detective Cooper' to you, Parker."

Doc held my purse out for me. I offered to carry the protein drink, but he shook his head and put his arm over my shoulder, leading me toward the hotel.

"How come everyone gets to call you 'Coop' but me?"

Cooper shot me a pinched glare. "You're special." His lip

curled during that last word.

"Lucky me."

"Nobody else manages to piss me off on a daily basis."

"Not even Detective Hawke?"

He walked a few steps before answering, "He just annoys the hell out of me."

I smiled up at Doc. "You hear that? I'm special."

"Remarkably so in those boots."

Cooper held the hotel lobby door for us, his gaze scanning Main Street.

"Natalie sends her love," I told him as I slipped past him.

He caught up with me at the elevator. "Where is Ms. Beals this morning?"

"She has a date," I teased.

I thought I heard Cooper growl as he pushed the third floor button.

Doc nudged me, his knock-it-off expression making me feel guilty.

Fine, I'd be nice to the lovesick jerk. "A date down in Rapid with her aunt's house. It needs winterizing."

The detective grunted, looking straight ahead.

"She told me to give you a message."

Cooper's squinty eyes glanced my way.

"You're supposed to stop being such a stubborn son of a bitch and go see the damned doctor." When Doc nudged me again, I said, "What? Those were her exact words."

I saw a smile flit across Cooper's face before he corralled it and locked it back up behind those steel bars he called lips.

Cornelius opened the door before we knocked.

"Did you hear us coming?" I asked as he held the door wide.

"Wilda told me you were here." He closed the door and led the way toward the dining room.

Doc caught me as I turned around to walk right back out and return to the ghost-free safety of the Picklemobile. "Don't worry about her," he said for my ears only. "I have you."

"Yeah, well don't let go." That little girl ghost made my bladder weak.

"Wouldn't think of it."

We joined Cooper and Cornelius in front of what was starting to look like something Spock had sat in front of on the Starship Enterprise.

I took the protein drink from Doc and put it on the table next to Cornelius. "There. Now tell me why I'm here bright and surly on my day off?"

"You're the missing link," Cornelius said without looking away from his monitor.

"Between Neanderthals and Homo sapiens?"

That got those cornflower blue eyes turned in my direction. "That would certainly explain something I've wondered since I first met you."

"What's that?" My perky frontal lobe didn't slope? Was it the hair?

"Enough chit chat," Cooper interrupted. "We need to get this debriefing moving."

"I should've brought two protein shakes," I told Doc.

Cornelius frowned up at Cooper. "Has anyone ever told you that your aura is very turbulent?"

I was surprised Cooper's aura was brave enough to show its face. "His aura had better watch its P's and Q's, or it will end up in jail along with his sense of humor."

"Keep it up, Parker, and I'll toss you in there, too."

Doc squeezed my shoulder before turning to Cornelius. "You mentioned on the phone something about needing some answers from Violet."

Cornelius took it from there, flicking switches and pushing buttons, playing the part of the mad scientist ... or rather the eccentric paranormal investigator. While he got his recording ready for playback, I took a seat on the chair Doc had carried over for me, keeping a lookout for the ghost of a little girl who had her own family history as a killer.

I needed to focus on something other than the idea of Wilda standing next to me plotting my demise. "Why do you think Harvey's grandfather decided to use me as his microphone?" I asked nobody in particular.

I'd pondered this question several times since hanging up with Doc earlier—in the shower after talking to Jerry, during breakfast with my oblivious kids and sharp-eyed aunt, and on the drive down to the hotel. Why me? I'd always thought I was a complete dud when it came to ghosts. Had I been wearing blinders this whole time? Was it possible for ghosts to talk through whomever they pleased? Prudence sure seemed to be able to choose puppets at will.

My gaze honed in on Doc, who was leaning against the sofa staring back at me with a wrinkled brow. Or had someone else had a hand in it? Someone who had been a medium for many moons and knew his way around ghosts? I thought back to the voice I'd heard in the dark, the one belonging to whomever had taken my hand and led me under the moon.

Whoa there, *Killer* ... I got somethin' to show ya.

It had sounded like Harvey's grandfather, but Doc was the only person who called me *Killer*. "Wait a second," I said to Doc. "You were in there?"

He nodded. "Harvey's grandfather was being very stubborn. He was staying just out of my reach."

"The stubborn gene runs strong in the Harvey bloodline," Cooper said from where he stood by the window inspecting the street below.

"You used me as bait?" I asked Doc.

"I prefer to think of you as a temptation."

"Temptation is a more appropriate term for the technique we utilized," Cornelius explained while typing on his keyboard. "I have often had to employ personal objects belonging to the recently deceased as encouragement to show themselves."

"I'm not an object." Nor was Grandpappy recently deceased.

Cooper scoffed. "That depends on your point-of-view. Uncle Willis has often told stories about Grandpappy's love of wild women, especially blondes. He probably took one look at that crazy hair of yours and was putty in your hands."

I glared at the detective. "How's that nose healing, *Coop*?"

He glared back. Peace, love, and happiness crackled between us.

"Anyway," Doc interrupted our stare-off, "I only placed you out there to tempt Grandpappy after I'd tested the waters and he appeared to be benevolent."

"How exactly can you tell good ghosts from bad?"

"I've been doing this for almost four decades. You learn to read the signs over the years."

I'd been doing it for a couple of months and couldn't even begin to wrap my brain around it. "So I can speak for ghosts even though I'm not a medium."

Doc crossed his arms over his chest. "We don't know the full range of your psychic capacity yet."

What was he saying? That I could be an executioner and something else? It was so much easier being just a struggling single mother.

"Whether you possess a psychic ability or not doesn't matter in this case," Cornelius explained. "Your boyfriend has the ability to perceive energy beyond our realm, as well as bring information from non-physical dimensions to our physical dimension, acting as a conductor if you will."

Doc shrugged, looking embarrassed by Cornelius's explanation. "I merely held the door open for you."

"Merely?" Cornelius snorted. "Mr. Nyce is being humble. The ability to read the entity and choose how to use one's skills to facilitate the communications is not for beginners. His years of training are evident."

"Really?" I stared at Doc, feeling a little star struck and a lot foolish for my summing up his abilities as the ability to "smell" ghosts. It was no wonder he'd objected to my ignorant, simple-minded definition of what he was capable of when it came to the paranormal world.

Cornelius continued, "Usually the medium acts as a Psychophoner for the extraphysical entities in the room who want to interact with those in the physical dimension."

"So you transferred this—what was the word … this Psychophoner ability to me?"

Cornelius leaned back in his chair, studying Doc. "I would theorize that he used telepathy to transmit the information from the ghost to you."

"Which was it?" I asked.

Doc winked. "Ancient Chinese secret."

"Tell me something, Nyce," Cooper said, leaving his window

perch. "This wasn't the first time you've worked with law enforcement in this capacity, was it?"

"No."

Skirrrchh. My brain did a double take. "You never told me you helped the cops before now."

"We haven't made it there yet."

"What other stuff haven't you told me?"

He rubbed his jaw. "You're going to need to be more specific. A lot has happened in thirty-nine years."

I stared at the man I'd fallen in love with, or at least the man I'd thought I loved. This incident reaffirmed how little I knew about Doc beyond the carnal level, and here I was letting him into my children's lives. Had I jumped the gun? Confused my lust for love?

No. This was Doc. He might be wrapped in mystery, but that didn't mean he wasn't true blue when it came to his actions, which were usually focused around protecting me and mine.

As if he could read the direction of my thoughts, Doc took my hand and squeezed it. "Trust me, Violet."

I searched his face, settling on his dark eyes. Nodding, I squeezed back and returned to the reason we were here. "So, Cornelius, are we ready to do whatever it is you wanted me here for?"

"Did you bring the black licorice?"

I fished it from my purse and dropped it on the table next to Cornelius's keyboard.

"What's with the licorice?" Cooper asked. During the process of leaning back against the couch next to Doc, something made Cooper wince and then hold his side for a moment. "Does it have something to do with psychic shit?"

"Some believe its medicinal benefits are parallel to ginger, especially for stomach and digestive system complaints." Cornelius held a piece out toward the detective. "You should try some. It'll help with your heartburn."

"I doubt that," Cooper interrupted. "I have a feeling Parker is here to stay."

I flipped him off, not bothering to waste my breath on a rebuttal.

Cornelius leaned forward and hit a button. A slight static played through the speakers; then they went silent except for Cornelius's humming soundtrack in the background until old man Harvey's voice came through.

"Where'd you hide all that money Daddy jawed about?" Harvey asked.

I heard myself answer, "I buried it all out behind the chicken coop in some ol' tins."

"Holy shit!" I heard Natalie say. "Was that really the ghost speaking through Vi? Or am I on one of those stupid prank shows?"

"It's the real deal, girlie," Harvey answered.

Cooper's voice came next on the recording. "We're not here about the damned money, Uncle Willis."

"You may not be," Harvey said, "but I sure am." He cleared his throat. "Why was your ol' shotgun in the safe?"

"That young whipper-snapper five-fingered it before cuttin' dirt out of the house," I answered for Grandpappy.

"Ask about the body in the safe," Cooper directed, "not the shotgun."

I heard a shuffling sound, and then Harvey's voice was louder, like he'd moved closer to the microphone. "Why was there a body in the safe?"

"Be more specific," Cooper coached his uncle. "Ask who killed him."

"Stop ridin' on my ass, Coop." Harvey grumbled something that sounded like "know-it-all greenhorn." Then he asked, "Who killed the dead man?"

"Ya mean the odd fish?" I said for Grandpappy. "Oh, his heart was all played out after their little fuss back in the bone yard."

"Pause the recording," Cooper told Cornelius. Cooper turned to Doc. "What are we missing out on there?"

"What do you mean?"

"Grandpappy says, 'their little fuss back in the bone yard.' Who is he referring to?"

Doc shook his head. "I don't know. All I picked up was what Violet was repeating."

Three pairs of eyes turned on me. My gut churned. "What?" I asked, reaching for a piece of licorice.

Cornelius stroked his pointy goatee. "Violet, were you talking to the ghost on your own in between the séance questions?"

I grimaced. "Was that a bad thing to do?"

Doc chuckled.

Cornelius looked at him. "Did you know she could act as a retrocognitor?"

"I could do what?"

"You can gather information from entities acquired after their time in the physical realm while their consciousness lived in the nonphysical world."

I frowned at Doc.

"You can talk to ghosts," he simplified.

"You mean like Prudence?"

"This is different. She uses a medium to reach you."

"Who's Prudence?" Cooper asked.

Cornelius's blue eyes widened. "You've been talking to ghosts without me?"

I ignored them both, trying to make sense of Doc's words. "Yeah, but you were acting as a medium between Grandpappy and me."

"I just held the door open, remember. You were in there on your own, apparently conversing away in the middle of Harvey's questions. That's different than your experiences with Prudence."

It sure was, starting with the fact that I was the one speaking on Grandpappy's behalf and hadn't even realized it.

Cooper waved his hand between us. "You three can play in the paranormal sand box another time, let's keep to the task at hand—the dead guy in the safe." He turned to me. "What did Grandpappy mean about 'their' fuss in the boneyard?"

I closed my eyes and tried to remember how it had gone down. "He kept talking about some 'humbug,' which I think was another name he used for ol' milky eyes." I pressed on my forehead with my palms. "He said something about the humbug getting a budge on the whippersnapper during a game of hide-and-seek. And then there was the bone yard comment."

Cooper pointed at Cornelius. "Hit play."

"Ask him who fired the gun," Cooper said.

"Who's callin' this square-dance, boy? Me or you?"

"Just do it, Uncle Willis."

"Who fired the gun?" Harvey spoke like a robot.

"The whippersnapper," my voice replied. "That humbug done did run against a pill, but the rock salt made it techy as a teased snake. It ain't like the others what been here before."

Cooper leaned in front of Cornelius and hit the Stop button again. "Did he say anything else to you after this?"

"Let me think," I scratched my head in thought. "Oh, this was the part when I'd asked what he meant about the *others*."

Doc's stare was intense. "What did he say?"

My cheeks warmed. "Nothing about the others."

"What did he say, Parker?"

Seeing the determined glint in Cooper's eyes, I sighed and pretended my hands were the most interesting thing in the room. "He said I was as pretty as a field of bluebonnets, and I had nice breeding hips, too."

"Sex and hooch still rule that man," Cooper sniffed, "even after pushing up daisies all these years."

Cornelius leaned back, inspecting my hips. "They do seem

adequately wide enough to birth children."

Doc laughed. "The old man was spot on about your looks, Tish." His focus lowered, his lips pursing in a quiet whistle. "And you know how fond I am of your hips, *querida*."

"Oh, Jesus." Cooper groaned in disgust. "Don't you two start up with that Morticia and Gomez shit again."

I reached out and hit the Play button this time.

"Why are them there masks stuffed in the tool shed?" Harvey asked on the recording. "Where did they come from?"

"You really need to work on your interrogation skills," Cooper whispered to his uncle.

"Work on this, boy."

Natalie giggled. "Now play nice, you two."

"Well," I said for Grandpappy, "some of them there hard cases are ugly as a mud fence. Masks make 'em bearable. Way back, long 'fore we got the deed ta this place, t'others started usin' it like some sorta stage stop, droppin' 'em off at odd times."

Cooper hit the Stop button. "Dropping off whom?" he asked me.

I'd asked the same thing at the time. "He told me 'the unwanted.' Then he talked about how the whippersnapper wasn't supposed to be there, but milky eyes was hunting for its food again. There was something about that thing liking to play with its food before using a 'pig-sticker' on it. And then he said there was no hiding from milky eyes, not even in the safe."

Cooper's face scrunched up in thought for a moment, and then he nodded and reached for the Play button.

"Wait!" I grabbed his wrist, remembering something else. "Did I tell you guys … I mean did Grandpappy tell you the part about the whangdoodles?"

"No." Steely eyes pierced mine. "What about them?"

I let go of him, closing my eyes again in concentration. "Grandpappy said the whippersnapper should not have left the whangdoodles. That they don't mess around with their prey, they just kill it." I lifted my chin, my eyes still closed, picturing that moment in my memory. There was something else, what was it? "Oh, there it is. He said the guy's heart gave out before milky eyes cut the skin off his face." I lifted my lashes, realizing something I'd wondered about back at the beginning of this. "That's why there wasn't blood all over the place. The guy was already dead."

"Was there anything else?" Cooper asked, his jaw grinding on what I told him.

"Yeah, Grandpappy said he'd never seen anyone escape the pig stickers, which I think is what he called milky eyes' claws."

Without comment, Cooper hit the Play button.

"Where'd them there bottles of mead come from?"

"The mead?" I asked. "Oh, ya mean in my chicken coop? They were left by the grave digger. He got into neck trouble before he could send the message back to Slagton to come fer it."

Cornelius hit the Stop button. "That's the end."

There was something about the mead business that was picking at my brain, something I was missing. The grave digger? Neck trouble?

"At this point," Cooper told me, "you stood up and abandoned the interrogation."

I didn't abandon it. I had a milky eyed beast to find. I looked at Doc. "Does that mean I came back through the door you were holding open?"

"No, you were still in the other realm. You just walked away."

I'd gone hunting was more like it. "Where did I go?"

"That's the million dollar question," he said.

"You walked around the back of the barn with the shotgun in hand," Cooper said. "I followed in close pursuit, keeping back enough to give you free rein. You didn't stop until you reached the family cemetery."

Doc and I exchanged glances, mine questioning, his answering. "It wasn't Harvey's family cemetery when she got there, though," he said.

"What do you mean?" Cornelius asked.

"Tell them, Killer."

I shook my head. "They don't know."

"They will soon enough."

I pondered that, glancing back and forth between steely gray eyes and cornflower blue. Right. It was just a matter of time now. I answered Cornelius. "Somehow, I was transferred to another cemetery, one that was much bigger."

"What are you talking about, Parker?" Cooper crossed his arms over his chest. "I was standing there watching you the whole time. You didn't go anywhere."

Cornelius leaned forward, his jaw agape. "You mean to tell me you temporarily transported mentally to yet another realm within that realm and left your body behind?"

"Uh …" My eyes darted to Doc. "Is that what I did?"

"That's what we're trying to figure out."

"What happened next?" Cornelius pressed.

"I saw something. Some kind of beast." One I assumed was known as the White Grizzly over the centuries. "I'd kept hearing the sound of it chewing on bones the whole time I was talking to Grandpappy. That was what drew me away from the séance."

"Holy horse apples," Cornelius whispered. "You were not only acting as a Clairaudient—"

"That's someone who can hear things happening in the non-physical world," Doc explained.

Cornelius continued, "But you were also remote-viewing between non-physical dimensions. Do you know how rare this ability is?"

"That's not all," Doc said. "Keep going, Killer."

"The thing I saw, well, it saw me back."

Cornelius's eyes widened even more. "Then what?"

"I raised the shotgun and something shifted." I purposely left out the part about Aunt Zoe's trigger, not wanting to drag her into this, especially in front of Cooper.

"Shifted how?" Cornelius asked.

"Dimensionally," Doc told him.

"I was back in Harvey's cemetery." I added, "and so was the beast."

"This is beyond anything I've come across," Cornelius said, absently stuffing a piece of licorice in his mouth.

"It's fucking insane is what it is," Cooper snapped, heading back over to the window.

"What did it do?"

"It attacked Cooper."

Cornelius stood up so fast his chair fell over backward. "You materialized an ectoplasmic entity? I've heard of ectoplasmic mediums, but I never really believed they existed, that this was even possible."

"This ectoplasmic crap and multiple dimension shit are for the birds," Cooper said. "That thing must have been hiding behind the tombstone the whole time. I just didn't see it until it popped up."

"Oh, really, Mr. Black and White? Then why didn't your bullets work on it?"

"Who says they didn't?" Cooper tossed back. "How else could a woman your size take down something that big? I had to have weakened it."

I shrugged, letting Cooper think what he wanted for now. This was a pretty big pill to swallow in one gulp. Hell, I was still choking it down.

I turned to Doc. "Well, now we have two different theories on last night's events. What's yours?"

He rubbed the back of his neck, a frown taking shape the longer he stared at me. "I think you come from a long line of dimension-hopping executioners with multiple psychic abilities."

"That's quite a title," I said. "You think that will fit on my business card under Assistant Broker?"

"You'd have to use a smaller font," Cornelius said.

"A dimension-hopping executioner?" Cooper shook his head. "Jesus Christ! How in the fuck do I make this fly down at the station?"

"You want to know what I think?" I asked, taking Prudence and her repeated warnings into consideration.

All three gazes turned to me.

"I think Hell's coming to Deadwood, and all that stands between it and life as we know it is a crazy-haired, somewhat psychic, single mother who doesn't know jack shit about how to stop it."

Chapter Twenty-Five

Meanwhile, back at headquarters …

Later that evening, I pulled into Aunt Zoe's drive and cut the engine. For the first time in months, there was no sputter, no backfire—only silence. What a concept.

In the rearview mirror, I watched Doc pull in behind me and climb out of his Camaro.

He walked up to my door and opened it, looking in at me with raised brows. "Well, what do you think?"

"It rides smooth and feels so sleek." I caressed the steering wheel of the used 4-wheel drive Honda Pilot he'd helped me pick out down in Rapid City. "I'm in love."

"Smooth and sleek," he rubbed his chin, a hint of a grin on his lips. "Reminds me of someone I know."

I hopped out, catching his arm after he shut the door behind me. I pulled him down for a quick peck on the cheek. "Thank you for going with me."

He tucked a curl behind my ear. "You're welcome, Boots." His eyes turned dark and smoldering. "It was the least I could do after that massage."

I chuckled, low and wicked.

After we'd left Cornelius's hotel this morning, we'd gone straight to Doc's place, where he'd spent a couple of hours distracting me from ghosts, dead men, demons, and every other creepy creature I'd come across so far. Sex, food, sex, and more food. He reminded me how good it felt to be alive.

The massage had started as payback on my part for the deal we'd made weeks ago and ended as … well, my attempt to make him my love slave for all eternity. That wasn't so much to ask, was it?

"So, my bribe worked?" I asked, smoldering back up at him.

"Is that what that was? A bribe?"

"Maybe."

"Including the grand finale, cherry lip gloss and all?"

"Where's the fun in a grand finale without cherry lip gloss?"

He groaned. "And that encore trick you did with your tongue?"

The encore trick that had really made him come undone? "All part of the package deal." I licked my lips and winked, then ruined my seductress act by sneezing. That was my third in the last hour. *Shit!*

When I shook off the sneeze, he leaned in and whispered in my ear, "You're a vixen, Violet Parker."

His hot kiss slid across my cheek, warming me clear through my toes. My body hummed, its RPMs accelerating yet again.

A movement over his shoulder drew my gaze. "We have a problem."

"Only one?" His hands framed my face, his eyes locked onto my mouth.

"Two actually."

"Both can wait." His head lowered.

A catcall rang out from the front porch. "Yee haw! This is almost as fun as one of them ol' fashioned quarter peep shows with the burlesque girls," Harvey said to Aunt Zoe.

Doc growled in his throat, pulling back right before making touchdown. "His timing is as bad as his nephew's."

I air kissed him.

"Spend the night with me?" he asked for my ears only.

"Twist my arm." With my kids down at my parents, I was free to play slumber party with him. Although, I didn't relish the thought of being under the same roof as Cooper.

"I'd rather kiss you all over."

"Or you could just do that."

"Supper's ready, you two," Aunt Zoe called. "Don't make me get the hose."

I grabbed Doc's hand and led him up the walk.

"Nice wheels," Aunt Zoe said, looking over my head.

"I'll take you for a ride later," I told her as I climbed the porch steps and then snapped Harvey's suspenders. "Thank you for letting me use the Picklemobile for so long. She's parked at Doc's place."

He grinned, his gold teeth showing. "The ol' gal isn't going to know what hit her."

"What do you mean?" Aunt Zoe asked.

"Doc's gonna fix 'er up this winter."

I looked at Doc. "I thought you were just going to drive her while you stored your Camaro."

"The Picklemobile has good bones." He reached for the doorknob. "With a tune up and some muscle, she'll be running smooth and sleek, too."

"Reid knows his way around an engine," Aunt Zoe said, then seemed to realize whose name she'd spoken and frowned about it. "If you need any help."

"Doc spent a few years working in a garage," I told her one of the few things I knew about his past, "fixing up old cars like his Camaro."

"Good to know about Reid," Doc told her, opening the front door. "I don't mind company while I'm under the hood."

"If we're done flappin' gums," Harvey said, "I'd like to dig into them pork chops before I turn into a toothpick."

Aunt Zoe led the way inside, Doc closing the door behind us. We were sitting around a serving plate of pork chops, a bowl of applesauce, and casserole dish of green beans when the doorbell rang.

"Coop's here," Harvey said, stabbing a chop.

"I'll get it." Doc left the room.

I grimaced at Harvey. "Why is *he* here?"

"I invited him." Aunt Zoe dished me up a chop before taking one.

Criminy! Who else did she invite? Darth Vader? The shark from Jaws?

"Don't go looking at me like that," she said. "Cooper called this afternoon looking for you and Doc, saying he had news about the case."

"Which one?"

"I didn't ask. I mentioned pork chops for supper; he agreed.

End of discussion."

Cooper strode into the kitchen, his steely eyes zeroing in on me. "Hawke's been trying to reach you."

Harvey kicked out one of the kitchen chairs. "Where're yer manners, boy? Set and light a spell. We can chew the fat after we fill our bellies."

Doc returned to the seat next to me, glancing in my direction and then Cooper's.

I took out my frustration about the bristly detective invading my sanctuary on my poor pork chop. Not even the blend of rosemary and thyme Harvey had used could calm me, but I stuffed my mouth full anyway.

Cooper washed his hands at the sink and then joined us, settling in between his uncle and Aunt Zoe. We dug in, forks clinking on plates the only sound for a minute or so.

"Whose Pilot is that?" Cooper spoke first, pouring himself more lemonade from the pitcher on the table.

"Mine," I told him between bites, wondering if he were just curious or making a mental note for future parking ticket opportunities. "I got it today."

"I've heard good things about those vehicles, especially when it comes to snow and ice. Low mileage?"

"Uh, yeah."

"How's it handle on curves?"

"Easy." I shot Doc a confused look. Had I somehow slipped into another dimension, one where Cooper hadn't been built as a cyborg?

"How's the cab? Plenty of head room?"

"Doc fits in it just fine." I narrowed my gaze at him. "So does my hair."

Doc cleared his throat meaningfully, sending me a raised eyebrow while sipping from his glass.

"Leather interior?" Cooper asked, not taking the bait.

I lowered my fork. "What in the hell are you doing, Cooper?"

He looked up from the piece of chop he was slicing off, his gaze bouncing around the table before returning to me. "I believe I was asking about your new vehicle."

"What's your motive?"

"I believe they call this 'making small talk' at most tables."

I guffawed. "Since when do you and I make small talk?"

"Violet," Aunt Zoe warned. "You're being impolite to my guest."

I pointed my fork at Cooper. "Your guest has a history of throwing me in jail."

Cooper rolled his eyes. "I only did that once."

"So far," I tossed my fork on the table. "Can you blame me for being suspicious of his Trojan horse rolling into my headquarters?"

"Relax, Parker. I'm not here to interrogate you tonight."

"Prove it."

He chewed on his pork chop while squinting back at me. Sitting back, he swallowed. "How?"

"Why does Hawke want to talk to me?" Before he could answer, I added, "and don't give me any of that 'police business,' bullshit."

Cooper shrugged, slicing into the last of his pork chop. "I told him our story."

"*Our* story?" Aunt Zoe turned to me. "You told him about ..." she trailed off, glancing Cooper's way with a worried brow.

"Not *that* story," I assured her. Doc and I had been careful to keep Aunt Zoe and my history out of our discussion earlier at the hotel. "The detective is talking about the one that explains how he found the missing body in the mine out at Harvey's."

Doc grunted his disapproval of Cooper's tale, a much quieter version of his reaction outside the hotel when the three of us had discussed how Cooper would break the news about finding the body to the police chief.

"How far did you puff up the truth?" Harvey dished himself a second helping of applesauce. "Eat yer beans, boy."

Cooper stabbed a bunch of green beans. "Parker led us up to the mine using her medium abilities."

"What medium abilities?" Aunt Zoe asked.

"The ones Nyce used during the séance to get Grandpappy to talk through Parker."

Aunt Zoe's focus moved to Doc. "Telepathy?"

He shrugged. "Something like that."

"How deep does this go with you, Doc?" she pressed.

"Almost four decades worth," I answered for him.

"Our story is why Hawke wants to talk to you," Cooper continued, digging into more beans. "He's skeptical."

Doc shook his head. "I still think you should have used me instead of Violet."

I crossed my arms over my chest. "You and I both know that my career can handle the psychic stigma better than yours."

"I don't give a damn about my career. You don't need this yoke on top of everything else you're carrying right now."

"Well, I give a damn about your career."

"Why?"

Because if his business tanked, he might want to move on to the next town … without me. I'd rather throw my career to the wolves. But pride held my tongue when it came to the truth. "Because you're helping a lot of people with their nest eggs, and that's more important than me selling houses."

His gaze called *bullshit*, but he didn't say anything.

"Taking the fall again, huh?" Aunt Zoe said, not looking happy about my decision, either.

Too bad. It was my choice. "Besides, Jerry's an ace at spinning this kind of stuff. If the rumors spread, I'll squeeze into some black leather getup, glue on fake eyelashes, and sport one of those Ghostbuster proton guns for another billboard photoshoot." That was one good thing Jerry had taught me since he had taken over Calamity Jane Realty—just about anything could be spun to work in my favor, even if I didn't like the way the tables turned.

"Not to mention," Cooper added, "Parker already told Hawke she was a medium. This story enforced her charade when she was talking to ghosts in front of him."

Doc looked at me like I'd sprouted horns. "When did you do that?"

I shot Cooper a glare for telling on me. "Nat and I were messing with Hawke that day Cooper dragged us out to the ranch to search the barn and outbuildings." I scratched at a drop of dried milk stuck to the edge of the table, keeping quiet about my performance in the morgue. "Did the chief buy our story,

Cooper?"

"He's hard to read, but I'm not one to tell tall tales. Now that we have the body back, there's not much else for him to do but take my account for what it is."

"So," Aunt Zoe spoke to me, "your story is that you were hired for your medium abilities to do what exactly?"

"Grease Grandpappy's jaws," Harvey interjected, even though he wasn't in on the original brainstorming.

"Get some specifics on how and when the victim died, why the body was left in the safe, and where the body was stashed after it was moved from Mudder Brothers."

"What did you concoct for how he died?" she asked.

Cooper answered. "The victim was stabbed to death by a psychotic transient who cut off his face and bit off his fingertips postmortem."

"Which was sort of true," I said.

I had a feeling none of those body parts would ever be found, either, making figuring out who the poor guy was even harder. Not for the first time, I wondered if there were someone somewhere waiting for him to return home—a wife, parents, children? I pulled back from that vortex before it could suck me in too deep. It was better to keep thinking of him as a faceless victim, literally. Was this how Cooper lived day after day? Keeping emotional investments at bay? If so, it was no wonder he rarely cracked a smile after so many years in this business.

"What did the chief say about Violet's role in this?" Doc asked. "Does he want to interrogate her directly?"

"He's leaving further interrogation to the detective in charge of the case."

Which was why Detective Hawke wanted to talk to me.

"What did you say was the motive for the killing?" Aunt Zoe asked Cooper.

"There was no motive. The transient was not mentally sound. Why else would he slice off pieces of the guy and leave him in a safe in my uncle's barn?"

Doc draped his arm over the back of my chair. "Are they going to form some kind of manhunt for the killer?"

"That depends."

"On what?" I asked.

Cooper leveled his gaze on me. "On how detailed your description of the transient is when Hawke interrogates you further."

Shitballs. I rubbed my temple, starting to realize how much I'd thrown myself to the wolves to protect Doc's career.

Doc reached under my hair, his fingers stroking my neck, calming. "We'll practice what you need to say."

"You've done this before, too?" I asked him.

"Multiple times." He looked across at Cooper. "Besides interrogating Violet, how else will Detective Hawke be pursuing what he needs to wrap up this case?"

"He plans to go to Slagton to see if anyone has information on the victim or the transient."

"Slagton?" I glanced toward old man Harvey, who was busy sneaking Oreos from Aunt Zoe's Betty Boop cookie jar. "You think they'll let him make it back out alive?"

"I hope so since I'm going with him."

"Don't be carryin' yer brains in yer coat pocket 'round them whangdoodles, boy." Harvey spoke through the cookie crumbs on his beard. "I don't want ya endin' up as buzzard bait."

"Grandpappy mentioned the victim had escaped from the whangdoodles." Cooper stirred his lemonade, his face hardening. "Someone back there has information on this guy, and I'm going to find some answers, damn it. This John Doe deserves an identity before we close this case."

"If yer headin' to Slagton with Hawke, does that mean the clown pulled ya back on the case?"

"For now. Hawke wants my help since I know the area better. He's still in charge, though." His teeth were mostly gritted during that last line.

"Did anyone ask about the shotgun?" I asked, wondering where Cooper had stashed what was left of it.

"Hawke did. I told him Grandpappy told you the transient took the shotgun with him."

We all sat there in silence for several beats, exchanging frowns and worried brows.

I sneezed again, cursing. The last thing I needed with this shit getting deep and sticky was a freaking cold. With Detective Hawke sniffing for trouble, we had to keep our stories consistent or this house of cards would fall all over the place.

"The chief is worried." Cooper broke the silence.

"About the transient?" Doc asked.

"About outsiders."

"Right." Doc tapped his fingers on the table. "They'll turn this into an even bigger clusterfuck."

I looked from Doc to Cooper. "What outsiders?"

Cooper spoke first. "The FBI and the press."

"More wasps in the outhouse," Harvey grumbled.

"More like hornets. Damn it!" I slammed my palm down on the table, making the plates bounce and rattle.

Aunt Zoe patted my arm.

"How am I supposed to take care of the family business with all of this going on?" I asked her. "I'd have better luck playing hide and seek in the middle of a dry lakebed."

"Violet Lynn," she leaned closer, lowering her voice. "We've been doing this for centuries without the general population having a clue … and so have the others."

"Doing what?" Cooper asked.

Harvey shushed him.

Aunt Zoe continued, her gaze unwavering. "Most people can't grasp what they see as reality. Take the White Grizzly. It was known as a legend, passed down from one generation to the other. Not truth, only legend."

After Natalie had left with the kids, I'd filled in Aunt Zoe about last night. She'd disappeared into the attic shortly afterward, hollering out a "Be safe!" through the attic door as I headed out the front door.

"Don't let this Detective Hawke or any of the other piss-ants coming and going distract you from your task. You're strong enough to handle this and much more."

The phone on the wall rang.

"I hope you're right," I said, standing to answer it.

"What task?" I heard Cooper ask as I lifted the receiver.

"Hello?"

"Violet?" a familiar, Lurch-like voice asked.

I whipped around, locking eyes with Doc and then Cooper. "Eddie Mudder, is that you?"

Cooper froze, his glass mid-air.

"Yeah, it's me. Are you okay?" Eddie asked.

"Me? I need to be asking you that." I hit the speaker phone button. "Where are you, Eddie? The cops are asking around about you. Your cousin is worried something happened."

"I'm fine. I panicked that night the big ghoul came to the morgue right after you left. It took the body."

"What big ghoul?" Mr. Black? Or had he seen the thing from the cemetery? "The one who knew George?"

"No, this one was different, bigger. It had wider shoulders, a white Mohawk, and a creepy lurching walk."

Wasn't that just marvelous news? There were even bigger albinos than Mr. Black and his twin. Criminy. Wait ... a white Mohawk?

"It left a note," Eddie said.

A light went on in my head. "With my business card?"

"How'd you know that? Are you psychic?"

Oh, the irony. "The cops found my card on one of the shelves in the freezer after you and the body disappeared." Detective Hawke had given me some heartburn because of that damned card, too. I glared at Cooper in Hawke's absence.

He glared back, unapologetic as usual.

"What did it say?" I asked.

"Something about wanting what belonged to them," Eddie told me.

"That was the same thing written on the back of my card." The author apparently wasn't very verbose.

"That's what I meant," he said.

I sighed, squeezing the bridge of my nose. "What did the other note it left say, Eddie?"

"It said that if I wanted to live, I should leave the hills. So I did immediately."

I thought about the body, the note, and my business card. "Eddie, don't you think maybe that note was meant for me and not you?"

"Well, I wasn't sure until I got a phone call this afternoon.

Then it all rolled into place."

"A phone call?"

"The caller mentioned that weird word again. You know, that German word."

"*Scharfrichter*?" I said.

Aunt Zoe's face wrinkled in concern.

"That's it!"

"What did the caller say, Eddie?"

"Hold on, I wrote it down." I heard shuffling sounds. "Here we are. His exact words were, 'Tell the *Scharfrichter* that Bone Crunchers hunt in pairs.' That was it."

Pairs!!? I tore my fingers through my hair.

Doc came over and kissed my temple before leaning back against the counter next to me, his shoulder touching mine.

"Did the caller give you his name?" I asked Eddie.

"No, but his accent sounded a lot like the ghoul who came looking for you with your son's picture in hand."

The End ... for now

* To read a behind-the-scenes interview with Doc Nyce, check out the following hidden page on my website.
To open the interview page, type the password: Nyce
http://www.anncharles.com/?page_id=2133

Speed Dating with Ann Charles' Characters

Instead of speed dating with me this time, I thought it would be more fun to speed date with some of my characters. (The questions came from fans on Facebook.)

Question for Cooper from Becka L.: What made you decide to be a cop?

Cooper: It's one of the few professions that allow me to carry a gun.

Question for Aunt Zoe from Melissa T.: How are you so patient?

Aunt Zoe: After all of the years I've lived, what's the rush?

Question for Harvey from Vicki H.: What has you so spooked out at your ranch?

Harvey: There's somethin' scootin' around out there, and I don't think it's them Slagton whangdoodles this time.

Question for Cooper from Elizabeth T.: What's your idea of a perfect date?

Cooper: I don't date. That usually gets confused as a form of commitment.

Question for Doc from Diane G.: What is your favorite flavor of soap?

Doc: In or out of the shower?

Question for Violet from Tara S.: When are you going to move in with Doc?

Violet: Uhhh … (She glances across the room at Doc, her cheeks reddening.) Next question, please.

Question for Cooper from Dawn B.: What's your favorite way to relax?

Violet: Cooper is part Terminator. He doesn't relax, he just reboots and starts shooting again.

Harvey: Naw, Coop relaxes every time he unloads his gun.

Aunt Zoe: I thought he played poker with his buddies to relax. That's what Reid told me.

Doc: You mean he loses to his buddies at poker to relax, Zoe.

Cooper: Are you all done answering my question? Losing is part of my strategy, Nyce. Where's my gun? I have a theory that shooting Parker in the ass is my new favorite way to relax.

About the Author

Ann Charles is an award-winning author who writes romantic mysteries that are splashed with humor and whatever else she feels like throwing into the mix. When she is not dabbling in fiction, arm-wrestling with her children, attempting to seduce her husband, or arguing with her sassy cat, she is daydreaming of lounging poolside at a fancy resort with a blended margarita in one hand and a great book in the other.

Facebook (Personal Page):
http://www.facebook.com/ann.charles.author

Facebook (Author Page):
http://www.facebook.com/pages/Ann-Charles/37302789804?ref=share

Twitter (as Ann W. Charles):
http://twitter.com/AnnWCharles

Ann Charles Website:
http://www.anncharles.com